BEYOND SURRENDER

CHAPTER 1

Late June, 1766

Horse, rider and road shimmered in the heat that gripped the wilting countryside. The sky, framing horse and rider, was not the usual English sky. It was hard and blue, without cloud or breeze. No gulls wheeled overhead. There was only sun.

Under that punishing sun, horse and rider plunged on. The stallion strained, his muscles rippling beneath a sheen of sweat. He faltered and broke gait. A quirt lashed out, and the exhausted mount again spurted forward.

I watched, my stomach tight with anger. How dare he treat a fine animal so? And how dare he come to call? Did he think I would be as easily bent to his will as that poor beast? Well, I would teach him different. He would learn not to trifle with a Brandley.

But as I stood at the window of my bedchamber, caught up

in loathing him, I felt a prickle of apprehension. Despite the suffocating heat, I shivered.

Like a child who wakes in the night—confident he lies safe in his own bed but still frightened by shapeless and unnameable fears—I tried to comfort myself with the sound of my own voice.

"The slyness of the old fox, Nan! He knows Father is in London on Tuesdays, but how does he know Aunt Matilde and Clarie are out? Does he bribe the servants to tell him when I'm alone in the house?" I snorted my contempt. "Does he truly believe I would receive *him* unchaperoned?"

Nan's response was a sleepy grunt.

"Hum? Whuzzit? Lor' lummy, no, Danni—I ain't sleeping—"

I turned, shrugging irritably. It would never do to let him affect me so. It wouldn't do to let him get under my skin. That would only give him a subtle power over me.

"I ain't sleeping," Nan repeated, pawing her way off my bed. Earlier, she'd been doing her work, smoothing fresh cambric sheets over the bed. In the heat, the drowsies had overtaken her and she'd fallen asleep on the spot.

I hadn't had the heart to rouse her. Nan was Nan—a country servant-girl and my friend from childhood. I loved her and had stopped trying to reform her long ago.

Nan's bare feet squished on oak parquet flooring as she left the bright turkey carpet to join me at the window. Her mob cap had slid to one ear, and hair the color of boiled carrots stuck out in all directions.

"Look, Nan."

She followed my gaze out over the rose garden, beyond the grounds to the high road. She squinted as she tried to focus on the shimmering scene.

"Judas!"

"Yes. It's *he*. When he arrives, Nan, you'll go down and tell him I refuse to receive him."

She thumped down into a thin-legged chair and gave me a look designed to draw pity.

"God, Danni, whyn't you ast me to speak up to the devil

hisself? Sir Gordon's pure temper—from head to hindmost! Why—why—he's like to pick me up and throw me—"

I bit back a smile. *Throw* Nan? My father often joked that she was built to be ballast in Brandley-Cartwright ships, and he vowed that someday he'd pack her off to Malta with the next load of chickens, sheep and American tobacco.

She eyed me reproachfully. "It ain't no laughing matter, Danni."

"Neither would marriage to Sir Gordon be a laughing matter."

We fell silent.

"'Course you don't want to bed down with no old he-goat," she said loyally. "Why, I be set to run a blade through 'is liver, dast he contrive to win you!"

She rumbled on in indignation. Then, finding the day too hot to support indignation, she leaned back in the protesting chair and fanned her face with her apron, sighing. "Still, there be something about him. Them silvery eyes, maybe," she trailed on. "Built like a bull, he be. Old or no, he do stir something in the women folk." She studied me. "Mebbe even in *you,* Danni."

"Nonsense. The heat addles you." The very idea rankled.

"Then why's the rosy-reds rising to y' cheek?" she demanded impudently.

I flushed. "Mind your own cheek, girl. Any more and you'll find yourself working in the stables."

She tittered, unimpressed.

I gave her my back, picked up a book and, kicking back the skirts of my loose muslin gown for coolness, settled myself on the settee.

I tried to read, but the words seemed to jump about on the page. Nan's remark had hit the bull's-eye, piercing through to uncharted territory. I hated Sir Gordon. But Nan was right—he did stir things in me, feelings I didn't like and didn't understand. I pretended to be engrossed in reading, but Nan blundered on.

"The chambermaids at Chillburn Hall, they say he be twicet the man of any *young* buck in bed. They do say he invites the lasses two at a time. They do—"

"Oh, hush!"

"When he bedded Ruby, she told me—"

I slammed the book shut. "One more word and I shall take you to the magistrate and have your tongue slit for a Gossip."

She snickered at my empty threat, but stopped chattering.

"Now, Nan. Go down and tell Sir Gordon I won't receive him."

She searched my eyes for reprieve. Finding none, she heaved herself out of the chair and grumbled her way to the door.

"Nan?"

She turned, hope lighting her plump face.

"Behave to Sir Gordon as a lady's maid should. Comb your hair. Straighten your cap. Put on your shoes." I paused. "And for heaven's sake, refer to me as Mistress Dianna."

She heaved an enormous sigh. "Oh, certain-sure, Danni," she agreed.

As she lumbered off, I smiled wryly. My orders would, no doubt, be forgot not twenty steps down the corridor. Sir Gordon, as he was wont to do, would complain to Aunt Matilde and press home his suggestion that I should be given a proper maid—French or Italian.

My irritation with him began to rise. But then, amusement came flooding in. Let Nan be Nan. Sir Gordon detested her. I smiled at the thought of Nan in her bare feet and uncombed hair adding one more irritant to Sir Gordon's afternoon.

Nan's gossip about Sir Gordon kept intruding and interfering with my attempts to read. I'd been less than honest with her. The truth was I'd wanted to hear *all* of it. Only a few months short of being eighteen, I was ready for marriage and longed to know every detail about love.

Sometimes at night, as I lay between cambric sheets waiting for sleep, I grew hot with my imaginings. My thoughts centered on Christian Cartwright. I imagined what Christian's caresses would feel like. I imagined his tender love words when he would return from his three-year venture in Malta and urge me to become his wife.

Pride forbade my asking Nan about such things, but I was on fire to experience man-woman things. I couldn't ask Nan.

She was a servant, after all. But if not Nan, then whom? Mother had died when I was six. Aunt Matilde was a spinster. She flushed scarlet and dabbed at her temples with a vinegar-soaked cloth if even horse breeding was mentioned.

If only Father were home. Had I sent down a message too insulting in tone? Sir Gordon *was* my father's friend and a prime investor in the Brandley-Cartwright Trade Company. Perhaps I should have sent down a softer excuse. A plea of head pain. Perhaps—

Nan's bare feet slapped down the corridor and she burst in, her face white.

"Judas, Danni—" She gulped. "He say—say—if you don't come down—" She snatched at air, gulping it in.

"Yes, what?"

"He—he be set to come up here!"

"Nonsense. He would not dare. It isn't done." I laughed.

But the wildness in Nan's eyes contradicted me.

"Done or no," she went on breathlessly, "he be in the fettle to do it. His horse, he dropt deader 'n a doornail of the over-hots. And Sir Gordon, he says to me he be damned if he kill a good mount to see Mistress Dianna and Mistress Dianna, she not receive him."

It was a deliberate taunt. My anger ignited, blazing up, driving cool thought from my mind. "Insufferable boldness! Who does he think he is? Is it temper he wants? Then temper he shall get!"

With my fury boiling as hot as the afternoon, I didn't stop to consider. My heels beat a furious staccato through the long upper corridor. One of Aunt Matilde's fragrant hanging pomanders, a lemon from Tangier studded with clove, loosened and fell as I brushed past. I ignored it and flew down the winding center staircase, the ring on my hand clicking sharply against the wooden larks, roses and small creatures carved in the balustrade. I rushed through the lower hall and flung open the door of the day drawing room.

"You have no right—" I raged, then stopped short.

Sir Gordon lounged in Father's leather chair, his feet casually propped up on a stool. He'd poured himself a goblet of wine and was sipping it. He looked no more concerned over the loss of his mount than if he'd just lost a few shillings at a gaming table. The corners of his mouth twitched with amusement as his eyes traveled over me in a proprietary way. With exaggerated politeness, he rose slowly.

"I—I—" In my anger and frustration, my words came out haltingly. So his display of temper had been merely a ruse. How could I have been so stupid? So. He had won this time. Next time, *I* would win. But to win, where Sir Gordon was concerned, I must depend upon my intelligence and never again let him bait my emotions.

I flashed him an angry look to cover the uneasy thought that suddenly pricked me: Did he know me so well then, that he was able to play me as a musician plays his instrument? In confusion, I dropped my eyes to my hands, then lifted my chin again and glared at him.

He bowed with great politeness, and just a hint of mockery. "Miss Brandley, how extremely good of you to receive me." I did not reply.

He inclined his head, as though I'd offered my hand in greeting, and then he resumed his usual erect, yet casual, confident posture. It was the stance of a man certain that life will deliver all he demands of it.

A riding quirt drooped from one hand. Because of his mien, one didn't count him a short man, though he was. Even in the heat, he wore his usual black waistcoat. But in deference to the temperature, his shirt was unbuttoned at the throat, exposing a mass of black hair. The color of the hair was repeated on his head, although there it was streaked with the same silver that glinted in his dark eyes.

The strange magnetism of those eyes began doing its work upon me. I looked away quickly, unwilling to let him see the surge of fear that washed through me. Out of his presence, I felt strong and confident. Nan and I often giggled as I rehearsed the remarks I planned to hurl at him, humbling and crushing him with my wit. But in the actual presence of the man, all strength seemed to ebb out of me.

Groping for some semblance of dignity, I said coldly, "Will you take tea, Sir Gordon?"

Idly, he tapped my father's cherry wood escritoire with his

quirt. "My dear Dianna, I did not ride five miles in this damnable heat merely to take tea."

I flushed. Anger throbbed in my throat.

"Then state your mission and go!"

He chuckled softly, lounged into Father's chair and picked up his wine goblet.

"How your high spirits charm me, my dear."

As he sipped wine, he eyed me over the rim of the goblet.

"But come. I grow impatient, Dianna. It has been six months since the day I told you I mean to have you as wife."

I gasped.

"That day!"

"Yes," he said lightly, *that* day."

To keep from trembling I clasped my hands.

"I marvel, sir, that you have the gall to mention that day."

He laughed softly.

"Then you marvel easily."

I looked away.

On that day, six months earlier, Sir Gordon's wife had been buried only a week. I'd paid a condolence call with Aunt Matilde and my sister Clarie. Using the ruse that I was to come into the library and select a miniature of Lady Chillburn to keep as memento, he contrived to get me alone.

He'd been not only direct then, as now, but he'd pulled me into his arms. Oh, the iron strength of this ugly old fox! He'd frightened me, kissing me hard on the mouth. That had been my first male embrace. After the initial stunned moment, I fought—fought uselessly, as he took what kisses he wanted.

Now, standing before him, I shuddered at the memory. Without thought, my hand flew to wipe at my lips. To my dismay, the gesture seemed to please him.

He laughed softly, lifted one gleaming boot to the footstool and settled comfortably into Father's chair. "My dear Dianna. On that day, you didn't cry out. One cry, and a dozen servants would have come running." He arched a brow at me. "You didn't cry out. Further, you told no one of our little encounter. Am I right?"

Sick with sudden humiliation, I whirled from him.

"I thought as much," he said. "My sweet, you enjoyed my embrace."

"No!"

Trembling with shame, I buried my face in my hands. My cheeks burned as though touched by flame. In the past months, how often had I tortured myself with that one question: Why *hadn't* I called for help? It was pride, I'd rationalized. Pride kept me from confessing so sordid an incident to Father or Aunt Matilde. And I'd only told part of it to Nan—that Sir Gordon pressed to marry me.

As I stood there, confused and trembling, I heard him move across the room until he stood behind me. I stiffened, poised like a wild animal about to bolt. My movement arrested him and he halted at once. I could hear his breathing, smell his male smells: leather, horse, shaving soap, sweat...

His leather quirt touched my cheek. I jumped, startled. It slid down my spine to my waist.

"Don't!" I didn't dare turn to look at him.

The quirt continued to rest on my waist.

"Exquisite, my dear. Dianna, when you are my wife, you will never wear muslin. You will wear silk. Only silk."

I shuddered at the thickening in his voice.

He whispered, "I will give you gowns, jewels—my love, I will give you anything—"

I shrank from him.

"Don't touch me! I care *nothing* for gowns or jewels. I care *nothing* for you."

But his quirt moved boldly, possessively up my spine, lifting my hair. I could feel a sudden puff of cool air on the nape of my neck.

"Don't—"

I sensed his lips moving to my neck and, with a shudder, I jerked away. Stumbling against a chair, I lurched for the door.

But he was too quick.

He grabbed my wrist and sent the door slamming shut. The banging echo seemed to reverberate from one end of the house to the other. Then the echo died, leaving only the loud banging of my own heart. I froze. Because Sir Gordon was of the nobility, no servant would come in without being summoned. Call them? It would only prove to Sir Gordon that I *was* a child. Stand up to him? Refuse to be intimidated?

With a boldness I didn't feel, I looked straight into his eyes, matching his anger with mine. The sting of my rejection was apparent in the tightness of his mouth.

"Let me pass."

He didn't move. But, slowly, his facial muscles began to relax. He released my wrist. His lips twitched with the faintest suggestion of amusement, and—for me—the heart-stopping terror of the moment passed. I felt weak with relief.

"Let me pass!" I demanded again.

He laughed.

"Certainly. But first, you must compensate me for my mount."

I looked at him, dumbfounded.

"You've the gall to demand money?"

He smiled.

"Not money."

With a quick motion, he hooked his quirt into the sleeve of my dress, drew it down, then bent and kissed the bared flesh of my shoulder. It was done so quickly, I was stunned.

With a cry of outrage, I fumbled at my sleeve.

He only laughed.

"Delicious, my sweet."

All rational thought flew out the window. With a shriek of fury, I snatched the quirt from his hand and smashed it across his face.

His head snapped back and he cried out in pain and surprise.

I snarled in satisfaction at the welt rising from temple to chin and struck at him again, but he grappled for the quirt, wrenched it from my hand and flung it away. I went at him with my nails.

"You would have a foretaste of our wedding night?" he taunted. "Then you *shall* have it."

I cried out in fear and lunged for the door. With animal quickness, he caught my wrists and pinned them in the small of my back.

"My God, don't—"

But my outcry was smothered by his brutal mouth. Pressing me into the door, he kissed me savagely. I tried to break free, but he yanked down on my wrists. Dizzying shafts of pain speared me from wrist to shoulder.

"You're hurting me—" I gasped, pulling my mouth free for an instant.

"Don't fight me! Else I am forced—"

Pain and terror rendered me limp. I was unable to fight more. Crying, shaking, I was forced to endure his passion.

"That's better," he murmured, kissing me long and thoroughly, kissing me as I had never imagined being kissed in my innocent dreams of Christian. His warm moist mouth teased mine, and my bones seemed to melt. To my horror, my own body turned traitor and I began to respond to him.

"No! Oh, no—" I sobbed, and yet I opened my mouth to his.

"Cry out," he whispered. "Your servants will come—"

I moaned, wanting to escape and yet bound by dark urges.

His hand slipped under my camisole. I gasped, as new pleasure sent my blood racing. "Don't! Oh, don't—"

But my mind and body were pitted against each other. Hating myself for doing it, I lifted my mouth to his once more. We tasted freely of each other.

Then, at the height of my passion, Sir Gordon suddenly loosed his grip and let me sink slowly to the floor. I looked up at him, blinking. For a moment I didn't know if I was in heaven, on earth or in hell.

He laughed softly.

"My dear Dianna, let us save *something* for the wedding night, or your father will have my hide!"

The mockery in his voice made me want to die of shame. Choking back dry sobs, I dropped my head to my hands.

Dear God, what is wrong with me? How can I behave so wantonly with a man I hate?

He casually strode across the room. I heard the clink of decanter against goblet, the trickle of wine.

"Madeira?" he said.

I wanted to retch. This thing he had done to me—to him

it was a mere exercise. My hate was so great I felt I was choking on it.

"I despise you," I whispered unsteadily. "I shall *never* marry you. Never. I would kill you first."

He burst into laughter, leaned against the escritoire and drank his wine.

"It's your charm that captivates me, my dear. How you amuse me! A lesser woman would have vowed to kill herself. You, Dianna?" He toasted me with his wine goblet. "You vow to kill *me*. I find that utterly charming."

"I hate you."

He smiled.

"I do not require that you love me. It's enough to know that I inspire in you one thing." He paused. "Lust."

There was nothing I could say, no defense I could make. He had stripped me bare, then clothed me in this humiliation.

"How I loathe you," I whispered. "And how I loathe myself."

He said nothing but watched me as a cat watches a mouse, without worry, confident the prize is his.

"I love Christian," I burst out irrationally. "I mean to be *his* wife."

"Cartwright?"

Sir Gordon laughed, as though Christian were of no consequence. "A nice boy, Cartwright. But really, Dianna. Impossible. You are too young to know your own nature. However, *I* know you. I know that once you have slept in the marriage bed, you will require more than a nice boy to keep you happy."

"Get—get out!"

I began to shake. Not with fear but with anger. To hear Christian's name bandied about on those vile lips! To hear him demeaned!

Sir Gordon ignored my fury. He smiled and bowed formally, as though we had just spent the past hour over a pleasant tea table.

"Good-day to you, Miss Brandley."

Every fiber of my being screamed for vengeance: to strike one blow, if not for myself, then for Christian. My voice ringing with hate, I said, "Your riding quirt, Sir Gordon. Do not forget your quirt."

He paused in mid-stride, his face going dark as he touched the welt I had cut into his face. It was beginning to swell. It was a mark he would see in his mirror for many days.

I gave him an icy smile.

He nodded slightly, as though acknowledging my small victory. Silver fire began to flicker in his eyes. For one unguarded moment, we faced each other as equal adversaries. The moment passed. Without hurry, he strode the length of the drawing room and retrieved his quirt. Again, he moved to the door but, as he passed me, he stopped suddenly and touched my chin with the tip of the quirt.

"By the way, my dear future wife. Do not ever repeat the mistake of striking me. For if you do—"

His voice was cold as winter. I trembled, looking up into eyes that had become frozen steel.

"For if you do, I shall be forced to punish you."

Fear jolted through me. Quickly, I averted my eyes.

The door of the drawing room opened, then closed.

Sir Gordon Chillburn was gone.

CHAPTER 2

Worried and heartsick, I pulled myself to my feet. I had won the skirmish; but would I win the war? And what of Christian? Sir Gordon's tone, when he spoke of him, had struck alarm in me. Did he know something? Was Christian ill?

I rubbed my aching wrists. Small dark bruises were beginning to mar the skin.

In a daze, I wandered out into the corridor. Through the open doors of the ballroom, I could see two servants on ladders, rubbing lumps of beeswax into the rococo woodwork that framed the tall mullioned-glass windows.

Still dazed, I lurched toward the kitchens, passing the dining and breakfast rooms, passing the music room where a maid was discordantly dusting the pianoforte and the drawing rooms where Clarie's caged birds from Malta trilled sadly.

I stumbled down the stone steps and into the kitchen. The head cook was asleep in a chair. A kitten slept in the little hammock that her gown formed between her thighs. Along the stone wall, a scullery maid lay on a bench, snoring. On one table, a raisin cake and stuffed buns waited under a cheesecloth for tea time and Aunt Matilde's return.

Quietly, I dipped water into a basin at the servants' wash table and bathed my face and rinsed my mouth. It seemed imperative to wash away the taste of Sir Gordon, the memory of his hands on my body.

Without waking the servants, I stole out and took refuge in the banquet hall, closing the heavy oak doors behind me. The immense room was empty and cool, shaded by elms that grew just beyond the garden doors.

At one end of the room there was a nook where I kept my escritoire and worked on my father's business ledgers. The nook—the room—was the place in Brandley Manor that Father and I loved best. As we worked, we could glance up and see a life-size portrait of my mother hanging in the place of honor.

My heels echoed sadly as I approached her portrait. I stopped. Arabella stood with one graceful arm curved over the back of a chair. She gazed out at me, serene and golden. Her white shoulders contrasted with a gown of forest-green velvet.

The artist had got her eyes exactly right. I remembered. Her eyes had been an arresting blue, delicate and yet deep as the bluebells which carpeted the meadows in spring.

Usually it delighted me when people said Mother and I were alike in every physical feature. But in the past year or two, it had saddened me. From the grave, Arabella Brandley controlled my life.

On her deathbed, she'd wrung a promise from the two men who loved her to distraction—my father and her cousin, the Comte d' Delveau. She made them promise to unite the two families in marriage. When I reached the age of eighteen, I was to marry the comte's son.

I had no memory of the Delveaus. They lived in Virginia and were rich, with properties in France and in the Sugar Islands of the Caribbean. I only knew that the son had been born in Brandley Manor several years before my birth.

Now, the comte lay ill and dying in Virginia. In letters he pressured my father to fulfill the vow to Arabella. He also pressured his son.

I felt a sudden pang of pity for the young man—this North Delveau. He wanted no part of me, just as I wanted no part of him. As for my father, he'd put the vow from his mind for many years. But now it chafed and scratched, like a thistle under one's shirt.

I was in a trap. My eighteenth birthday loomed. If Christian didn't return soon—

I fled from my mother's portrait and went to my work desk. Account ledgers of every size and shape were piled high. On top of the pile, there was an open letter. I picked it up, recognized the frail, spidery script and dropped it unread. So the comte had written my father again!

With a thudding heart, I sat down and reached for the Malta ledger. Here, the script was not frail or spidery. It was strong, dear and familiar. On impulse, I dipped my head to the page and kissed it.

Christian. I couldn't remember a time when I wasn't in love with him. As a little girl, I'd trailed after him constantly. I had sat for hours in heaps of barn straw, watching as he tended to his beloved Arabians and I had perched on the arm of his chair as he worked the Brandley-Cartwright ledgers. I lived for his gentle teasing.

It was Christian who first discovered I had a quick mind for business and figures and it was Christian who pressed Father to educate me and let me participate in our families' business. I grew up adoring him. From the very first, it was a foregone conclusion in my mind that I would marry him.

Reluctantly, I put the Malta ledger aside and took up the troubled Virginia account. Soon I was lost in the business of ships, furs, barrels of salted pork and hogsheads of tobacco.

The Virginia account was particularly vexing. My brain leapt to the challenge. Old Mr. Cartwright, Christian's father, suspected the Virginia manager was fleecing us and I tended to agree. But so far, I'd not been able to uncover anything specific. I bent my head to my work, determined to go over the entire account with a fine-toothed comb.

I was deep into the mystery of why three hundred silver fox skins on page twenty-five should become thirty silver fox skins on page seventy-nine and should altogether vanish from the account by page one-hundred-ten, when my father's ebullient voice boomed out.

"Dianna?"

He strode toward me, a smile lighting the craggy features of his kind face. As he passed Mother, he stopped, as usual, and gazed at her a moment. It was a habit of which he was unaware.

Father was a big shaggy bear of a man, though growing gray and slump-shouldered. He wore a new waistcoat, but it was fashioned exactly as Arabella had liked them years ago. As I watched him, the tensions of the day began to drain out of me. I jumped up and rushed into the safety of his arms.

"Ah, Dianna!"

He gave me a quick hug.

He put his large rough hands on my shoulders and kissed my cheek. His good, safe fatherly smells—tobacco, the faint scent of saddle and horse, the peppermint sweetmeats tucked in his coat pocket—enveloped me. Suddenly, the tensions of the afternoon exploded.

"Papa, I love you! I love you so very much," I said, throwing my arms around his neck and peppering his grizzled cheeks with kisses.

Both embarrassed and pleased by my show of affection, he covered his feelings with gruffness.

"Now, now, child. Sit. Behave yourself. Sit, Dianna, I want to talk to you."

But he was the one who sat, settling his bulk into a leather chair near my desk while I flew to the mantel to fetch his pipe, tobacco and flint and a glass of canary wine from the sideboard.

With me perched on the arm of his chair we talked easily, our conversation skipping from the latest cargo arrival in London to the Virginia account to the state of Clarie's health in such hot weather. But then he fell silent, smoking for a time.

"You will be eighteen in October," he said softly.

My heart began to pound.

He cleared his throat, as though what he wanted to say was sticking.

"My child, I must tell you two pieces of news. One piece

is hard for the heart to accept, one is easy. Which will you have first, child?"

A cold ripple of fear washed over me. "The hard, Father."

He grunted. "So like you, Dianna. You have courage. You have read the latest letter from the Comte d' Delveau?"

I shook my head.

"Why not?" Testiness caused his voice to rise. "It was left on your escritoire. Which servant dared remove it?"

I met his eyes. So it was come. The moment I'd long dreaded. To save myself, I would have to pit myself against Arabella, against my father's love for her.

"I didn't read it because I did not wish to. It will be like all the other letters from the comte. I have made myself clear to you over the past years, Papa. I will not marry this unknown person—this North Delveau."

He choked on his wine. He coughed, his complexion darkening.

"Your mother wished it."

"But you do not wish it," I said firmly. "Nor do I. Nor does North Delveau."

His bushy eyebrows knitted together, a sign of thunder building. "You are my daughter, and you will do as I say."

"No, Father," I said softly, stubbornly. "You raised me as a son, teaching me the Brandley-Cartwright business. Now I claim a son's right. I will choose my own mate."

He stood up. Wine sloshed to the floor. He didn't notice. The blood vessel in his temple thumped. His voice was full of controlled anger. "Fetch the letter, Dianna. Read it aloud."

"No." It was the hardest thing I'd ever had to say.

"No?" he growled in astonishment. "By God! My own daughter says me nay." His voice rumbled louder, a portent of storm. "Get the letter!"

I stood up and looked at him, poised between flight and obedience. I wavered, and our eyes met in anger and in sorrow. Shock sat upon my father's face. He was used to my willful ways, but had never entertained the notion that I might defy him. If I'd fled at once, before the look of deep hurt spread across his features, I might have succeeded. But at that look, my heart twisted.

Obediently, I fetched the letter.

"Read it," he ordered.

With a shiver of distaste I began reading aloud. *My dear friend, Ambierce,*

I salute you from a tiresome sickbed in my country house in Virginia. My lungs are weak and the barbarous colonial quacks count out my life in months. Everyone plies me with useless cures. Even North preaches Indian medicines he gathered in his sojourns among the Nations.

However, I am not ignorant of my coming fate. I want to die at peace with our beloved Arabella. Give me Dianna as daughter-in-law. If she remains unwilling, send me Clarinda.

My heart jumped. I broke off reading.

"Father, no. Clarie is only fourteen. She's thin and sickly. The voyage would kill her."

My father nodded sadly, and suddenly I knew that if he could spare me, he would.

With a heavy heart I continued reading.

North remains opposed to the match. Only because I now lie on my deathbed, does he acquiesce.

There was more in the letter, news that the letter had been brought by North Delveau himself as he was searching for skilled London physicians to take to his father. The thought that the man was in England jolted me. But at least he had had the good sense not to come directly to Brandley Manor.

I looked up at my father.

"Say you will not require this of me, Papa."

A dozen emotions played upon his face.

"It shall be, Dianna," he said sadly. "Young Delveau will call upon you tomorrow." Stumbling to the window, I rested my forehead against a pane of glass. Its coolness steadied me. I would not win if I allowed my emotions to burst forth like a mountain stream after rainfall.

When I turned to him at last, my voice was steady, my plea one of sense and logic. The businessman, Ambierce Brandley, prized sense and logic.

"I've not confessed this to you before, Papa, but I cannot honor your vow because I have made my own choice of husband. He is a man you approve and honor."

His bushy brows lifted.

"I mean to marry Christian." I flushed and went on haltingly. "I mean—he has often called me his dearest little sister—he loves me—I know—when he returns from Malta—he will declare himself—"

A bewildered expression crossed my father's face. He cleared his throat and looked down at his wineglass as though he were surprised it was still in his hand. He set it aside.

"My poor—" he began, then broke off. I froze with apprehension. "Christian is—" He tried again, his glance going to Arabella, as though for help. "Christian arrived at Cartwright Manor last night," he blurted gently, "with his wife."

CHAPTER 3

I sat there, still and unmoving, unable to comprehend all Father had told me. Christian—married into the nobility. The match arranged by Sir Gordon!

I wanted to die.

Christian— Christian—

Nan clucked over me, proposing all manner of rash actions. Christian should be punished. She would get her brothers to beat him. Delveau? She would get her brothers to waylay him and throttle him so he would never dare approach Brandley Manor.

I scarcely heard her, and when I pushed away the brandy she held to my lips, she drank it herself in one panic-stricken gulp.

As the shock began to die away, only one thought ached in me. Christian. I had to see him. At once.

I pulled out of Nan's arms, stumbled to the garden doors and out into the rose garden. As the intense heat and sun hit me, I swayed, then lurched into a run.

Threading my way among the arbors that hung heavy with

scarlet June roses, I ran over the uneven ground. Two gardeners knelt in the dirt, digging straw into the roots of one bush. They looked up, startled, as I rushed past them.

Breaking out of the rose garden, I ran through the orchards. Tree after tree bowed to the ground, heavy with summer fruit and alive with the buzzing of bees. I hurried past the long rows of carefully tended grape arbors and, panting, scrambled over a series of low stiles.

The meadow stretched before me. It was more than a mile to the Cartwrights'. I paid no attention to the sun beating on my head and shoulders, but lifted my skirts and ran on.

The rolling countryside, as far as the eye could see, shimmered in heat. No birds sang. Only bees buzzed in the buttercups and red clover. Grasshoppers rasped and chirped in the long grass, jumping from my path in alarm. Flocks of sheep scudded off slowly, like low white clouds, as I pumped toward them.

By the time I reached the low rise that led to the Cartwrights', I was out of wind. My bodice was soaked. I made myself walk slowly, but my heart left me and raced ahead to Christian.

Married. Married.

The alien word throbbed in my brain. I could scarcely comprehend it. Three years since I'd seen him, but in those three years we'd corresponded. His letters had been openly affectionate. Or had I read too much into them?

No! Hadn't his letters always begun and ended with the usual endearment: *My dearest little sister, Danni—*

Oh, God!

Was that the extent of his feeling for me? Sister?

I stumbled up the hill, running faster.

No. He loves me as a man loves a woman. He must or I shall die.

Anguish tore at me. I stumbled up the path among the elms, the old path of my childhood. I'd taken it so often in my relentless pursuit of Christian. I stopped for a moment and steadied myself against the trunk of a tree.

Sister.

If that was where Christian stood in the matter, then it was

22

my fault. I'd not been plain enough in my letters. If he'd known how much I wanted to become his wife, surely he'd not have taken another!

I cursed myself bitterly.

Oh, to have written straightforward letters! His marriage was my fault. But surely this step could be remedied? Divorce was not unheard of. If I made myself plain to Christian? If I told him that no woman could ever love him as deeply as I?

Surely he would— Surely— Or if divorce was impossible, we could run away together—to Malta—to Virginia. Oh, God—anywhere—

I rushed on, grasping at hope, and burst out of the stand of trees into the stable yard behind Cartwright Manor.

There was no noise in the yard except for the occasional restive stamp of a horse's hoof or the loud buzzing twang of a horse fly. The stables formed an ell in the yard. Two horses— magnificent Arabians I'd never seen before—stood tethered in the shade of the ell.

A figure, half-squatting, held the hoof of one Arabian. The posture of the figure showed deep concern. I knew him at once. Joy welled up. Tears of happiness swam in my eyes. I dashed them away.

"Christian—"

He stood, turning. He took a few steps out into the sunlight, then shaded his eyes with his hand and looked in my direction. How fine he looked! He was twenty-eight now, and his body had become slightly thicker and even more manly than I remembered. Tan breeches clung to his well-muscled legs, and a white shirt, open to the waist, showed a chest deeply browned by his years in the Mediterranean. His tawny hair was sun-streaked and contrasted sharply with his dark brow.

"Yes? Who—"

He frowned. Then his deep blue eyes cleared and began to sparkle. A broad smile lighted his face.

"Danni!"

He opened his arms to me in the old way. The child in me responded. Laughing in pure joy, I went flying into his arms. He caught me just as he'd always done. He twirled me round and round as I shrieked and giggled, reliving my childhood. His low rich laughter was music in my ears.

He stood me on my feet, steadying me. Then he took both my hands in his and looked down at me, puzzled and seemingly taken aback.

"But I mustn't do that anymore," he said, reddening. "Dearest little sister, you are all grown up!"

He dropped my hands, put his fists on his hips and pretended to scowl.

"Who gave you permission to grow up?"

Joy had stolen my voice. I could only shrug and shake my head. There was so much I wanted to say.

He chuckled at my discomfiture. I could only grin up at him, feeling myself in heaven.

"Let me look at you!" he demanded, frowning, though his eyes danced in delight. "Turn around. Slowly, Danni. Turn."

Laughing with joy, I met his gruff demand. Slowly, I turned, loath to pull my eyes from his face even for an instant. He appraised me with frowns, nods and unreadable grunts—just as I'd observed him appraising many an Arabian.

"Well?" I said, laughing, breathless.

He chuckled.

"You desire my approval? You have it, Dianna! I pronounce you not only grown up, but a dazzling beauty for good measure."

His low rich laughter enveloped me like some sweet embrace.

"How the young swains must buzz around Brandley Manor these days! Drones buzzing around the queen bee!"

I smiled up at him.

"You tease me, Christian. You *know* there are few young swains in a country girl's life." I paused. "But yes, one *old* swain buzzes around," I added bitterly, letting all the contempt I felt for Sir Gordon come bursting out.

Christian's smile died slowly. He gave me a quizzical look.

"Sir Gordon."

"Don't joke, Danni."

I shook my head.

His face darkened. "That's ridiculous!" he said, his tone

conveying protectiveness. "No. Of the nobility or not, he is much too old for you."

"Much too," I echoed, smiling up into the face that was dearest to me, dearest in all the world.

Christian continued to gaze at me, his look carrying bewilderment, frank admiration and—did I delude myself?—affection. He seized my hand. He tucked it into the crook of his arm, and I felt suddenly dizzy at his touch.

"Come along, Danni. I want you to meet Lady Olga. And I want Olga to meet the dearest little sister who ever lived."

I pulled back, a chill bleakness suddenly in my soul.

"Your—wife—"

He chuckled.

"Of course, silly goose. Come along. She's wonderful. You'll adore her, and she you."

I shrank back, tugging at his hand in protest, just as I used to do when I was a little girl and wanted my way with him.

He laughed.

"All grown up, but she doesn't change," he teased.

"Christian, please. Don't mock me. I *must* talk with you. Alone. Please."

He wavered.

I tugged at his hand. "Let's go out to the rock ledge on the hill, overlooking the meadow. Where we used to do lessons sometimes."

He hesitated, then chuckled indulgently.

"I've always spoiled you. Always given in to your whims. Your father used to scold me for it, and I see now that he may have been right," he said lightly. "You are a demanding young lady!"

"Please, Christian. Please."

He raised his hands in surrender.

"Very well. As usual, Danni, you are the master and I the slave."

I led the way along the path through the oaks. Christian followed, chuckling and calling out teasing remarks. We made our way to where a rock shelf jutted out from the slope of the hill, dropped down in the cool shade and gazed out at the panorama of rolling meadow and blue sky. In the heat, the fields seemed almost to dance. Far off, sheep moved over the meadow like lazy white dandelion puffs being rolled along by some slight breeze.

Christian leaned back against the rock wall. He sighed in contentment.

"I'm so glad to be home in England again."

I said nothing, praying he would simply talk on and stretch out this happy, private moment. Sitting close to him, my happiness knew no bounds. *Oh, God, make this last. Make this last forever!*

He rambled on, then broke off suddenly.

"But what is it you wish to talk of, Danni? Some girlish problem that I can help with?"

My heart began to pound. I took a deep breath.

Fearful of his answer, I said in a rush, "Why did you marry her, Christian?"

His brows shot up in surprise. He chuckled.

"I thought we were going to discuss some girlish to-do. Instead, you ply me with impertinent questions."

"Please, Christian. I *must* know. Why did you marry her?"

He tapped the tip of my nose.

"Only because I consider you to be dear as a sister will I submit to this rude and impudent inquisition," he said, laughing.

"I married Lady Olga, Danni, because I am the only Cartwright heir and it's my duty to make a good match."

He wagged a finger at me.

"Just as it's *your* duty, Danni, to make a good match. We Cartwrights and Brandleys are merchants. Rich, true, but we are common stock. It's my duty—and yours—to marry into the nobility if at all possible. Think of it! My children may become counts, barons, dukes!"

I felt a sudden swell of joy. So he hadn't married for love. So divorce was still possible.

"Then you *don't* love her."

"Love?"

Christian's voice faded. He was quiet for a long time.

"At first, Danni, I felt only admiration and respect for Lady Olga. She is some years older than I—"

"And now?" My throat tightened, waiting for his answer.

"Now?" He laughed. "Why, I do believe— Yes, now that you've turned my mind to think on it, I believe I *do* love Lady Olga."

My eyes burned with tears. I turned to him, softly resting my trembling hands on his shoulders.

"You won't divorce her?"

"Divorce?"

Both shock and amusement lodged in his blue eyes.

"Divorce! Silly goose, why should I do that?"

I could contain myself no longer. My hands tightened on his shoulders.

"Because I *love* you, Christian. My earliest memory is of loving you. I will love you forever—for as long as breath remains in my body! I hoped—all those years— I waited— Oh, Christian, I cannot live unless I am your wife. You must divorce her! My father—he will give me to North Delveau. Oh, you *must* stop him! You *must* wed me!"

I was kneeling, clinging to him, my arms around his neck.

Startled, he tried to push me away.

"Danni!"

Although he tried to peel my hands from the back of his neck I clung to him.

"I love you, Christian! I will do anything to prove it."

"Stop it, Danni! You're talking foolishness."

I pressed close. His chest was warm against my breasts.

He made a harsh sound.

"Take your hands away!"

I pressed closer, lifting my mouth to be kissed.

But he worked doggedly at untwining my hands. In desperation, I touched my lips to his. Christian did not respond, but tore roughly at my hands. I kissed him again and again— desperate, passionate kisses. I was excruciatingly aware of my breasts against his warm, broad chest. I gasped as my nipples contracted to hard nubs. Christian was aware, too.

He drew a sharp breath.

"Danni, don't—"

I sent my tongue darting into his mouth, as Sir Gordon had done to me. I felt him shudder. He groaned. He ceased tearing

27

at my hands. His own hands slid slowly down my arms. He drew me close. Hesitantly, as though fighting it, his mouth began to move willingly on mine.

"Oh, Christian," I gasped, delirious with joy.

He kissed me—sweetly, roughly, in every way imaginable. It was all that I'd ever dreamt of. Christian! My Christian in my arms. Passion coursed through me. I felt as if my body had been burnt up and its ashes were being swirled up to the very heavens. I was floating, floating into paradise.

Christian uttered endearments and harsh words—words I'd never heard before. I sent my tongue deep into his mouth. He groaned in ecstasy, then jerked his head away.

"You're a child," he said harshly, "where did you learn to kiss like a whore?"

I didn't answer, but only drew his face down.

We kissed again, and then Christian's hand moved to my breast. I could feel the tense urgency in him.

As though one body, we slowly lay back on the rock shelf. Christian pulled me under him. His handsome face, his broad shoulders suddenly blotted out the world. Holding me in his arms, he kissed my throat, my shoulders, the soft white swell of my breasts. Pleasure jolted through me. I arched my back and moaned.

Using only his strong white teeth, he tore at the ribbon lacings of my bodice. In a moment, his warm moist lips stroked the bare flesh of my breasts. I cried out in an agony of pleasure.

"Oh, my love, my darling, do to me as a man does to the woman he loves—"

I felt him stiffen. I closed my eyes, eager to receive him. But suddenly, harshly, I felt myself shoved away. I fell back against the ledge, aware, for the first time, of sharp pebbles and small cutting crevices in the rock.

Christian leaped to his feet. He stood over me, panting.

"God, this is monstrous!"

He stumbled away, clutching at his groin as a spasm seemed to take him.

"Christian—"

For several moments he did not look at me. Then he turned.

A white line of tension outlined his sun-browned face. His eyes were wild and tortured.

"My God, Danni! You're a child, and I nearly stole your virginity. I will never forgive myself!"

"Oh, no, Christian! It was I—*I*—wanting *you*."

I scrambled to my feet, and placed my palms against his throbbing chest. He shrank back as though touched by fire, swatting my hands from his body.

Stunned and hurt by the sudden change in him, I stumbled backward. Only moments before, we'd been lost in tender intimacy. And now, he was looking at me as though he hated me.

"Christian—"

"Go home, Dianna," he said in a cold, hard voice. "Damn it, go!"

He pushed past me and strode up the path that led to the manor. I tried to run after him, but caught my toe in the torn hem of my gown and fell, crying in helpless frustration.

My cries pursued him, "You love me, Christian Cartwright, you do! You *know* you do!"

Fleeing from me, his head down, his shoulders slumped, Christian flinched but did not answer. Nor did he look back.

CHAPTER 4

"Are you awake at last, Danni?"

Clarie's voice, clipped and tense, probed down into my dreams and drew me up to the threshold of consciousness.

I stirred, unwilling to leave the dream. Christian was kissing me. But then, two shadowy figures appeared. The one without a face grabbed my wrist and dragged me toward a frighteningly gloomy land. I sensed the land was Virginia and pulled away, running back to Christian. Just as I fell into his arms, Sir Gordon appeared and plunged a knife into Christian.

I awoke with a sharp cry.

"Danni, are you sick?"

I opened my eyes. It was dusk. Through the open windows of my room, I could hear the birds calling to one another as they settled into the elms for the night. Clarie stood over my bed. In the dusky light, her face was pale with worry.

Smoothing my bodice I sat up. My hands lingered where Christian's lips had been. A pang knifed through me. After this afternoon, how could I bear to lose him? How could I bring myself to obey Father and marry someone else? Virginia! It was so far away. Never to see Christian!

"Danni, you *are* ill."

"No." My whisper shook. "Truly, I'm not."

Clarie shifted onto my bed. She peered at me through eyes that threatened to fill with tears. Although Clarie was fourteen, she still had a child's body. Spells of weakness in her heart and lungs had slowed her development. As yet, she had no hips or breasts, but she had lovely soft gray eyes and hair the color of fall chestnuts. And like many who suffer early in life, she was wise beyond her years.

"Aunt Matilde has been crying all afternoon. Father says you *must* marry the young Comte d' Delveau and sail to Virginia with him."

Her eyes brimmed with tears of anger and helplessness.

"Oh, Danni. You're my only sister, and I shall never see you again!"

She threw herself into my arms with a small choking sob. I hugged her, my mind spinning. Christian—Sir Gordon—Delveau. Where would it all end?

"Shsssh, Clarie, don't cry," I implored in a shaking voice. "We mustn't let that happen. We can't—"

I stroked my sister's shining hair, murmuring assurances I did not believe. God, I was in a box! I couldn't think it through. My thoughts shot out in a dozen directions but always veered back to the same starting point: Christian. Only Christian. He was all that mattered. I had to be near him. I loved him and he loved me. Wasn't this afternoon proof? If things had gone on only moments longer, I would now be his mistress. That joyful bonding—that moment of intimacy—would be a seal and a pledge. After that, no one—not my father, not Sir Gordon, not all the vows in the world—could drive us apart. And perhaps Christian would get me with child. The thought of carrying his child gave me a pleasurable jolt. Let the world scorn! I would not care.

Clarie drew back at the tremor that coursed through me. She looked up, puzzled.

"I will *not* marry North Delveau, Clarie," I said, feeling an iron resolve begin to fill me. "I will not go to Virginia. I will stay here in England."

She stared at me.

"Danni," she began haltingly. "Oh, it's breaking Papa's heart to think of sending you away! But he can't bring himself to break his vow to Mother. Only if the young comte rejects you, will he feel the vow is no longer binding—"

Her voice hung in the air.

I smiled grimly.

"Exactly."

"Danni? Could you be thinking of—"

"Father will be in London when this—this—colonial—calls. I shall behave so unpleasantly to him that all thoughts of marriage will fly from his head."

Clarie frowned thoughtfully. She moved to the window and stared down at the darkening rose garden. Then she turned.

"No. He will see your unpleasantness as a challenge. You are too beautiful."

She sighed deeply as I moved through the darkness and placed my hand on her shoulder.

"Oh, Danni, if only, for one day, you could be as homely as—well, as *Nan*. All fat and freckled and with a tooth missing—"

Her passionate outburst ended in a long sigh.

"Like Nan..." I echoed, an idea forming and making my heart beat with hope.

"Danni!"

Fearfully, I went on.

"I think I can bully Nan into it. I'll threaten her. I'll tell her that if I must go to Virginia, she must go also. But what about Aunt Matilde?"

Clarie gasped.

"Aunt Matilde would do anything for us, Danni. She is terrified of Virginia. She says it is full of murdering Indians. She says you'll be murdered and scalped if you go." She broke off, taking a deep breath.

"Then it's settled," I said grimly.

"But when Father finds out—"

"He will thrash me," I admitted, not caring. "But by that

time, North Delveau will be sailing the Atlantic Ocean—alone." I did not add—*and I will be in Christian's arms.*

In the night, the heat wave broke, dissipating under an onslaught of wind, rain, thunder and lightning. By morning, the countryside lay clean and fresh-washed. A cool breeze blew off the meadow bringing with it the fragrance of wild honeysuckle.

The sun shone brightly, painting the wet meadows with gold. Everything that the sun touched, from the lark soaring on high to the sheep grazing in the meadow, turned golden. The whole world had received the Midas touch. It was a good omen.

I'd awakened with a sick stomach. I didn't like duping my father, but I must do it—for Christian. I would remain here in England, and in time, Christian would take me as his mistress.

As for Delveau, he deserved to be duped. Who did he think he was, coming to call on me as one might call at a stable to inspect a horse one considered buying! Did he really suppose I would have an unmannered colonial as husband? Titled or not, he was certain to be a rough boor. He had lived among Indians, had he not!

I shuddered and prepared for the day's unpleasant task.

By one o'clock, my father was gone and the puzzled household staff had been dismissed for the afternoon. Granted a holiday measure of wine, they disappeared gleefully and without question.

We took up our posts.

Nan was scared out of her wits. Close to tears, she perched precariously on the edge of the settee in the drawing room. She wore Aunt Matilde's gray silk gown. Adding to her misery were Aunt's spare corsets. Clarie, gowned in a pretty dress of daffodil dimity, sat next to Nan—ready to poke, prod or prompt as the need might be. Whenever a tear slid down Nan's cheek, Clarie dealt with her firmly.

"You know you need say nothing, Nan! Only rise, curtsy and give him your hand. Can't you do that small thing for

Danni? Do you want her to go to Virginia and be murdered by Indians?"

"Oh, miss," she bawled, "I be *that* scared!"

"We're all scared!" Clarie snapped.

"Oh, Dianna," Aunt Matilde said, opening her vinegar vial and inhaling it, "maybe we should not! Please, dear girl, reconsider. If your father finds out—what will he do to me, his own sister!"

"We *must*, Aunt," I said firmly, pouring her a glass of sherry for courage and giving one to Nan and Clarie, as well. I led Aunt Matilde to her chair, then hurried to my station in the entryway.

I wore an old frayed dress of India calico, a black apron and a mobcap over my hair. Anyone who saw me would assume I was a maid.

The heavy carved oak doors stood open to the fresh breezes. As I waited, my emotions swung wildly. I was afraid of this North Delveau, and at the same time I felt a contempt for him. Was he such a spineless young man that he would accept his father's choice of wife for him? Or did he not care? Was marriage of so little interest to him, that anyone would do as wife?

I waited. A half-hour passed on snails' feet. At last, two horses appeared in the tree-lined lane that led to Brandley Manor. The first horse blocked my view of the second. The rider on the first horse was clearly a servant. As he drew closer, I could see he wore coarse colonial clothing and a shabby hat. He was a plump young man, with a smiling face and reddish hair clubbed back in an indifferent style.

As the second rider came into view, I shrank back in the shadows of the door to examine him. For an instant, my heart stopped. I thought he was Sir Gordon. But in a moment, all resemblance to Sir Gordon began to fade. Still, the effect was to turn me into a quivering mass of nerves. I fumbled for the doorframe, steadying myself. With my heart still pounding with fright, I looked down at North Delveau.

He sat a horse in the same casually arrogant manner that Sir Gordon had. His hair and his eyes were black, like Sir Gordon's. But as he dismounted with the easy grace of a born rider, I could see he was much taller and finer-featured than Sir Gordon. His appearance was, if not handsome, oddly arresting.

With an imperious gesture that his servant did not seem to resent, he gave his reins to his man. The servant grinned, making remarks and nodding at the long marble staircase that led up to the door. Delveau gave the man a black look, and I shivered, knowing that if I had been on the receiving end of such a look, I would have cringed. Yet, the servant did not cower. He only grinned again and led the horses away.

I shrank back into the shadows as Delveau turned and stared up at the open doors. He scowled, and I could not mistake his deep irritation and discomfort at the task facing him. All was plainly written in his expressive eyes.

Suddenly, he began loping up the long marble staircase— not with an air of eagerness—but with the deliberation of a man who disposes of unpleasant chores by doing them as directly and swiftly as possible.

I dropped my eyes to the floor and curtsied.

When I stood again, he easily towered over me. I was startled by the thin white scar that cut across his temple and down his cheek, spoiling his looks but granting him, instead, an almost savage mien.

And for a fleeting moment, I felt sympathy at his obvious unhappiness. He wanted the Delveau-Brandley alliance as little as did Dianna Brandley.

But when he spoke, my sympathy vanished.

"Well, wench?" he demanded impatiently. "Will you show me in, or will you not?"

Startled by his rudeness, I flashed him an angry look, then blanched at my own behavior. I was a servant, not Dianna Brandley.

Curtsying, I tried to cover my confusion.

When I looked up at him, a curious expression went rippling over his countenance. Whether amusement, surprise or simply admiration for a pretty servant girl, I could not tell. The expression vanished as quickly as it had appeared.

"Announce North Delveau," he said in a voice that bespoke

one who was accustomed to being obeyed. "Miss Dianna Brandley and her aunt expect me."

His accent was not entirely colonial. His French father had tainted his speech, lending a curiously haughty tone to his words.

I bridled at the superiority in his voice. But, remembering my role, I choked back my annoyance and led him to the drawing room.

As I opened the drawing room door, Aunt Matilde and Clarie swayed slightly. Patches of geranium flamed in Aunt Matilde's cheeks. Clarie grabbed Nan's hand, and Nan, her face as red as her hair, flayed her face with her fan.

"Mr. Delveau, M'am."

Aunt Matilde dabbed at her lips with her vinegar-soaked cloth one last time. Then she hurried forward, hand outstretched. Her voice, when she found it, was shrill with nerves.

"Comte d' Delveau, welcome to Brandley Manor. I am Ambierce Brandley's sister, Miss Matilde Brandley."

Delveau bowed. He took her hand, brushing it politely with his lips.

"Your servant, Miss Brandley. But forgive me"—he paused, giving her a forthright smile—"I do not use the title. Should unhappy circumstances place it in my hands, I do *not* intend to accept it. In Virginia, we prize equality of all men."

I looked at him sharply. His tone held none of the imperiousness he'd used with me, yet his message was clear: *If Dianna Brandley thinks marriage to me means becoming a comtesse, then she is mistaken!*

Aunt, in her flustered state, missed his message.

"Equality of all men? What an extraordinary idea! Tell me, Com—*Mr.* Delveau, in the colonies are all women equal also? Would a scullery maid be my equal?"

Delveau's dark eyes flashed with amusement.

"I'm certain *no* one could be your equal, Miss Brandley. My father speaks of your kindness to him and to my mother during the two years they spent here."

Aunt Matilde beamed, momentarily forgetting her nervousness.

"You were born here," she said unnecessarily.

His lips twitched with humor.

"Yes."

"That was several years before Dianna was born—" She broke off, throwing me a stricken look. Remembering herself, she went on formally, "Forgive me, Mr. Delveau. May I present my nieces? My younger niece, Miss Clarinda Brandley."

Delveau moved to Clarie without hesitation and smiled at her as she curtsied. He reached for her hand. Shyly, as though surprised at being treated like a grown woman, Clarie extended her small hand. He took it solemnly, bowed and brushed his lips across it.

Clarie was enchanted.

"Everybody calls me Clarie, not Clarinda. You may, also, if you like."

She blushed furiously.

"Clarie it is—if you will call me North?"

"Oh, I will—North!"

I frowned at her in warning. She caught my glance and instantly became more formal in bearing. She flashed me a quick apologetic look.

Aunt Matilde pressed her vinegar-soaked cloth to her temple. Her voice rose to a periously high pitch.

"And may I present my niece, Miss Dianna Arabella Brandley?"

My heart leapt to my mouth. I stared at Nan and prayed. She seemed frozen to the settee as though she would hide there forever, half hidden by the tea table and tea tray before her. At last, discreetly elbowed by Clarie, Nan struggled to her feet. She stood wavering in indecision for a moment. Then, simultaneously, she extended her hand as we'd taught her and dropped into a curtsy. As she curtsied, her knee caught the tea tray. Cups, saucers and silver jingled.

"Judas!" she ejaculated.

There was an awful moment of deadly silence, then everyone talked at once. Delveau declared himself charmed to meet her, Clarie burst into questions about Indians, Aunt Matilde sputtered about his ocean crossing and I rushed forward asking permission to fetch the tea and cakes from the kitchen.

The moment was agonizingly awkward. Everyone, including Delveau, seemed to take an avid and sudden interest in the tapestries that hung upon the wall. My eyes flew to Delveau, and I could have sworn that amusement had flickered in those dark eyes for an instant.

Aunt Matilde gripped Delveau's arm firmly.

"Please sit next to me, Mr. Delveau," she said shrilly, leading him as far from Nan as possible. She indicated a chair that was perfect for our purpose. If he wanted to look at Nan, he must shift around, impolitely giving Aunt his back.

He sat down, a ghost of a smile on his lips.

When I flew back from the scullery with tea, I swooped up the tea tray from in front of Nan and deposited it on a table at Aunt Matilde's side. She sighed audibly in her relief.

Aunt Matilde's face had gone ashen. Her hand rested upon her heart as though she'd gone her limit. But while I was getting the tea, Clarie had wisely engaged Delveau in animated conversation.

She peppered him with questions.

"But how could you live with savages, North? Surely, aren't they animals? Is it difficult to learn their language? Have you ever fought them, North?"

Clarie pulled her chair closer, her eyes wide with fascination as he answered her questions with a gentle patience that surprised me.

"The scar on your face—did it come from fighting savages, North?"

Aunt Matilde leaned toward Clarie and wagged a finger in warning.

"Don't be impertinent, Clarinda."

Clarie reddened, looking away in confusion.

"I'm not offended, I assure you, Miss Brandley." He turned to Clarie and smiled at her. "The scar came from a tomahawk," he said lightly.

Clarie made a face.

"A tom—a—what?"

"Tomahawk. It resembles a short, small ax."

Clarie gasped.

"He could have killed you!"

Delveau stirred uncomfortably.

"But he didn't!" he said, making an effort at lightness.

"More tea?" Aunt announced firmly, glaring Clarie into silence.

Conversation became a ship becalmed. Aunt Matilde valiantly took the tiller, steering the talk into amenities. She recalled the Delveaus' stay at Brandley Manor. She expressed her regret at the death of North's mother. She inquired about his father's health, about the shocking state of government in the colonies and about North's voyage.

Throughout the questioning, Delveau glanced at Nan only once or twice. Clearly, he did not mean to have any part of marriage with her. As for Nan, she sat marooned on the settee, her face behind her fan. She did not dare pick up the cup of tea Clarie set before her, though she looked at it with longing. Occasionally, a tear slid down her cheek. I knew she felt dreadful about her outburst, and I wished I could comfort her.

Aunt Matilde caught my eye. I nodded. With renewed confidence and a voice that was much less shrill, she adroitly dismissed Delveau.

Setting her cup upon her saucer with a firm, final-sounding click, she said, "Mr. Delveau, it was so good of you to call!"

He picked up her signal and rose instantly. I could not mistake his slight sigh of relief.

"Not at all, Miss Brandley. It was good of *you* to receive me."

He bowed over her hand.

Clarie stood and curtsied. With hesitant shyness, she extended her hand.

"Good-bye, Clarie," he said, soberly kissing her small hand.

He bowed in Nan's direction.

"Good afternoon, Miss Brandley."

I opened the drawing room door. When he exited, I shut the door smartly behind me. I could hear a sudden flurry of muffled voices.

Briskly, I led him to the entryway and stood aside. He strode across the threshold without a word or look. Halfway down the staircase, he paused. He glanced up at me and scowled.

"Lead me to the stable, wench," he ordered. His tone of voice was again high-handed, imperious.

I bridled at the bossiness but, gritting my teeth, I obeyed. Lifting my skirts, I hurried down the staircase and led the way.

"Wench!"

I stopped, turning.

"I understand the Brandleys have an impressive rose garden. Lead me to the stable by way of the garden."

Biting my lip in irritation, I hurried back to him and set out in the opposite direction. Delveau strolled behind, as though he had all the time in the world. He moved indolently, not caring in the least that an impatient housemaid waited, twitching her skirts in irritation.

Why doesn't he hurry!

I longed to be rid of him before something happened to unveil our deception.

As he dawdled, my anxiety grew.

"Sir, if you please?" I pleaded meekly, as though I were a tired servant with a hundred tasks still before her.

He caught up to me in three long swift strides. I hurried on, relieved. As we passed the largest of the rose arbors—a lattice tunnel of crimson roses—I felt a touch at my waist.

Startled, I whirled around.

Delveau's arms closed around me in an instant. He seized me, pulled me into the rose arbor, and before I knew it, he'd tumbled me to the ground beneath him.

For an instant, I felt nothing but shock and panic. Then anger boiled up. So! He was one of those men like Sir Gordon. A helpless housemaid was a plaything to be used and discarded.

"How dare you!"

Stunned, infuriated, I slapped at his face, pushing, kicking. He reached out, captured my wrists easily and pinned them to the ground above my head. He threw one leg over my wildly kicking legs, trapping them. An amused, insolent grin lit his face.

I opened my mouth to scream, then thought better of it. Screams would only bring the servants.

"When Miss Brandley hears of this!" I choked on my rage. "What do you think you're doing!"

He grinned.

"I only want to see what you hide under that mobcap, wench."

He let go of one wrist, tugging at my cap. My curls spilled out. In that instant, with one hand free, I raked my nails across his face, drawing blood.

He winced in surprise.

I struggled to get free, but he easily recaptured my hand, and thereafter only my panicky breathing filled the silence.

"I merely wanted to see what you hid under that mobcap. And a treasure of sweet-smelling honey and gold it is. But now that you have attacked me, wench, I demand reparations." He paused, laughing. "A kiss for the scratch?"

"Don't be ridiculous!"

"Give me your lips. Come, wench."

I turned my head from him.

He went on, his low voice full of amusement.

"I make it a practice never to kiss wenches unless they are willing. I suppose I shall be required to wait—in this position—until you are willing. I have plenty of time."

With a squeal of anger, I renewed my struggle. But he only pressed his body against me the more firmly. I made a savage sound deep in my throat and then, as the full knowledge of his anatomy dawned on me, I flushed as crimson as the roses surrounding us.

He laughed knowingly.

Humiliated, I shut my eyes and strained to shrink as far from him as possible.

The minutes went by much too slowly. My humiliation and rage increased by the second. But he remained nonplussed, unembarrassed.

I began to struggle again. The more I struggled, the more tightly he gripped. I was keenly aware of his body, aware that his heart beat slowly and calmly while my own heart raced. What a devil he was! This was commonplace to him. Panic thudded in my throat.

Suppose someone discovers us?

"I'm waiting, wench," he said lightly.

With a furious whip of my neck, I turned my face to his.

"Blast you! Take the kiss and go!"

42

I closed my eyes to avoid looking into those dark laughing eyes. Shivering, I pursed my lips to endure his kiss. An involuntary tremor of excitement jolted through me. I shrugged it off.

Several moments passed and still he did not take his kiss. I waited with pursed lips, my humiliation deepening. God, I hated him! He was worse than Sir Gordon! Teasing, toying!

Then I felt warm lips brush mine as lightly as butterfly wings.

He rolled off me and stood up. I opened my eyes in disbelief.

"Is—is that all?" I stammered without thinking.

His low rich laughter filled the shadowy arbor. He cocked one eyebrow at me.

"Disappointed?"

My cheeks burned with embarrassment and fury as I scrambled to my feet.

"Damn you!" I could not help hissing. "Damn you and be gone!"

But it was I who was gone, running as fast as my feet could carry me. I plunged into the house through the servants' door, flew up the narrow servants' staircase, ran down the corridor, and into my room. Panting, I stumbled to my window.

Below, in the rose garden, North Delveau stood with his hands on his hips, his head thrown back in laughter. He was laughing aloud, as though someone had just told him a very good joke.

CHAPTER 5

For the next few days I walked on eggs.

My feelings for Delveau were wildly ambivalent, swinging from hot fury over the liberties he'd taken in the garden to cold fear that he might know who he had taunted.

Did he suspect? Had that prompted his crass behavior in the garden? And would he, relishing the punishment I was sure to get, expose me to my father? I chewed at my worries as a dog at a bone. Delveau *couldn't* know. Still . . . his behavior did not jibe with the gentlemanly way he'd treated Clarie and Aunt Matilde or with my initial impression of him, that first fleeting impression of cool intelligence. . . .

I felt as though an ax hung over my head. I prayed fervently that Delveau would put an end to my agony, either by promptly penning his declining note to my father or by exposing me.

I said nothing about what had happened in the rose garden to Clarie or Aunt Matilde or Nan. I didn't want to worry them. They had stress enough.

Nan was scared. She tiptoed about the house, meek as a

mouse, expecting, at every moment, that Delveau or my father would jump from the shadows and throttle her.

Aunt Matilde lay sick with a headache. Her conscience had stricken the moment Delveau left. She'd been in bed ever since.

Clarie was in ill temper, too. But her temper was for different reasons. She moped about, sighing and bemoaning the fact that *she* wasn't old enough to marry Delveau.

"Oh, he is so handsome, Danni. I wouldn't mind the tomahawk scar if I were married to him. He is such a gentleman . . . and he did seem to like me. Danni, do you really think he liked me?"

"He's no gentleman!" I snapped at Clarie. "And you should thank your lucky stars that you need have nothing more to do with him!"

"Well," she said, tears collecting in her long lashes, "you needn't scream at me, Danni."

We were all on tenterhooks, our nerves stretched taut. I longed to run across the meadow and into the solace of Christian's arms, but knew I could not. Aggression, on my part, would only drive him from me. I knew Christian, knew his sensitive nature. He must think it all through on his own, without my interference. But a dozen times a day, my feet started out for Cartwright Manor, and a dozen times a day, I jerked myself back.

Father remained in London on business, and whenever one of his messengers arrived at our door, I blanched in hope and in fear. But all of the messages were mundane. Hadn't Delveau written my father? Why was the man delaying? Couldn't he find some tactful way to reject me that would allow neither Delveaus nor Brandleys to lose face? Was the man a complete dolt?

And then my heart would thump with hope—perhaps Delveau *had* written. Perhaps my father felt he must break the news to me face-to-face. Yes, I exulted. Surely that was it!

As the days passed with nothing horrible happening, Clarie and I began to relax, and Aunt Matilde ventured out of her bed. Word came from my father that we were to prepare for a small dinner party honoring Christian and Lady Olga. The older Cartwrights had been invited and Sir Gordon, too. My father would return on the afternoon of the party.

It was tonic for Aunt Matilde. She threw herself into the project with zest, and a genial chaos descended upon the house. Under Aunt Matilde's firm hand, every servant was pressed into service. Even the undergardeners were brought in and put to work sweeping down the tapestries.

By five o'clock on the day of the dinner party, everything was ready. Roasted fowl and glazed saddle of mutton waited on silver trays in the kitchen. A crock of lemon sauce for the trout stood in a pail of cold spring water. Garnishes of greens and bright pickled peaches stood in bowls upon the carvery.

In the dining room, the banquet table sparkled with crisp white linens, silver wine goblets, silver and gold flatware, and the finest china. Crystal bowls of white roses and blue delphinium reposed among the silver candelabra. A wine steward, his shoes covered with felt sacks, worked at the sideboard, opening and decanting the wine. In the largest drawing room, musicians tuned their instruments, sending rills of violin music throughout the house.

Excited, I ran upstairs to bathe and dress, knowing in my heart that my preparations were for one person's eyes and his alone. I ransacked my wardrobe, uncertain of Christian's taste in gowns and full of regret that I, myself, had taken so little interest in what I wore. I had nothing new, and that was my own fault. I was impatient with dressmakers and their interminable fittings.

Nan grumbled while I pawed through the dresses in my wardrobe. Would he like me in pink? I held the pink against me and studied it in the French looking glass, swaying slightly as though dancing. No, not pink. I threw it aside and pulled out the blue. It was lutestring silk, but too plain. The salmon-colored tabby silk with satin flowers seemed suddenly too fussy, and the neckline too high. I seized several others, discarding them for faults I'd never noticed before.

"Lor' lummy, Danni," Nan complained as she put the discards away, "you ain't going to no ball! It's only a dinner!"

I turned and stared at her. A ball? That was it—my ball gown. Over Nan's vigorous protests that the gown was not

47

suitable, I made her help me get into it. I hadn't worn it for a year, and the bodice was tight. As Nan laced it from behind, the neckline crept lower and lower until it was fully as low as London ladies of fashion wore their necklines. My father called those women Hoydens.

But I looked into the glass and gave a pleased cry of surprise. The gown suited me splendidly, and in it, I looked much older. It was silk. A soft claret-wine red. The sleeves were flowing and long, caught tightly at the wrists with tiny cuffs and three garnet buttons. The underskirts and overskirt were of the same soft claret-red silk.

The effect of the gown was striking. My hair, swept up in a tumble of soft curls, served as a pale and delicate contrast to the richness of the red. With hands that shook with excitement, I fastened garnet earbobs in my ears, then stepped into red pumps.

"Well, Nan? Will Christian like it? What will he say, do you think?"

She eyed me with stern admiration. She opened her mouth, shut it with a snap, then opened it again.

"No bones about it!" she said. "Mr. Christian will say the same thing your pa and aunt will say: 'Dianna, for shame! Get up to your room and get a fichu!'"

My hopes sank. I turned to the glass and stared at my pretty cleavage. Nan was right. My father would not hesitate to say exactly that—and in front of guests if need be.

With a sigh, I let Nan tuck a white lace fichu into my neckline. The change was startling and disappointing. How could an inch of lace make such a difference? Without it, I looked like a woman of possibilities. A man would gaze and begin to wonder. Now? I looked like what I was—a young virgin. Swallowing my disappointment I hoped with all my heart that Lady Olga would prove to be an unattractive woman who wore her own necklines up to her ears.

Voices rose from the drawing room as I could hear my father's booming baritone, the timber of his voice jovial, good-natured. Another voice blended with father's, and my heart jumped. That would be Christian. He was early. No doubt he'd come early to talk business. Possibilities throbbed. I would go over ledgers with him alone. Perhaps he would agree to stroll with me in the garden. Perhaps in the privacy of one of the arbors . . .

I flew down the stairs, skipped lightly through the corridor, and with an eager smile on my face, ran into the drawing room nearly to collide with North Delveau.

"Dear heaven!" I gasped.

I froze, staring up at him in growing horror, knowing that any moment he must comprehend and explode in anger. I shut my eyes, swaying slightly, as though to ward off a coming blow. But when I looked up at him an instant later, I found myself looking into dark, amused eyes. But the amusement held traces of both triumph and anger.

"Ah, Miss Brandley," North Delveau said easily, "you are looking even more lovely than the last time we met, if that is possible."

I couldn't speak, couldn't move. He reached for my ice-cold hand, drew it toward him and bowed, brushing my hand with his lips. I jerked my hand away.

My father rambled on happily, hugging my shoulder in greeting. "Dianna, how are you my child? Is everything ready for this evening? Where is Matilde? I chanced into young Delveau in London and insisted he come. He should spend one night in the house in which he was born, don't you think?" Father said expansively, not waiting for my answer. "More wine, young man? Come, come, you must make yourself at home!"

My mind spun dizzily. So Delveau knew! Yet he hadn't exposed me. Why? I stole a look at him. His cold triumphant eyes met mine.

Just then, Clarie flew into the drawing room, a greeting for Father on her lips. She stopped short at the sight of North and stared at him, her gray eyes growing large as doves.

Aunt Matilde appeared on Clarie's heels, chatting with the head footman who trailed after her, nodding at her instructions.

"Please serve the jellies before the mutton. I know the mutton is served *before* the jellies in some houses—but I have always felt the jellies should come before—" She glanced up at North and smiled absently. "Before the—"

A look of absolute horror passed over her face.

She stared, dumbfounded, as Delveau greeted her pleasantly. Then she turned and marched from the room. I made a motion to flee, too, but North was suddenly at my side. He took my arm. His hand, hidden from sight in the sleeve of my gown, gripped my elbow so painfully that I winced.

He smiled at my father.

"When I last visited, your daughter promised me a thorough tour of your famous rose garden, sir. May we have your permission to do so now?"

My father's bushy brows lifted in surprise. He rubbed his chin, a silly, matchmaking grin spreading across his face.

"Er...certainly, young man. By all means!"

North's fingers bit roughly into my arm, making a lie of his cool easy words. Clamping my elbow in a viselike grip, he propelled me down the length of the drawing room and toward the garden doors which stood open to the terrace.

"You're hurting my arm!" I whispered, retaining the good sense to smile up at him as I said it, for appearance's sake.

"You deserve to be hurt," he said through his teeth while turning to look at me and smile for my father's sake.

At the garden doors, he turned, still painfully gripping my arm, nodded his head respectfully to my father, and then flashed a quick forgiving smile at Clarie.

With a rough but hidden push, he shoved me out onto the terrace.

"How did you find us out?" I demanded, jerking away from him.

He didn't answer.

Instead, he seized my arm again and yanked me along, propelling me over the terrace and into the rose garden. When we reached the tunnellike privacy of the largest rose arbor and entered it, he loosed his grip. His dark eyes flashed in anger.

"You forget, Miss Brandley. My father loved your mother very much. Her portrait hangs in our home."

"Oh!"

I felt stunned and incredibly foolish. And confused. If he'd known from the start...

"I knew you at once. You are almost the image of Arabella."

He folded his arms across his chest and looked at me coolly. "Almost," he repeated with emphasis. "But Arabella's portrait reveals her to have been a lady. You, Miss Brandley, are *no* lady."

I caught my breath sharply. It was a slap in the face, sudden and unexpected, deliberately cruel. I hit back.

"And you are no gentleman! My arm—"

I rubbed at the ache in my elbow where he had yanked me along, not caring he was hurting me.

He looked down at my arm as I rubbed it, and I detected a softening in his features.

"I'm sorry about your arm. I had to get you out here as quickly as possible—"

"So you could again throw me on my back and have your way?" I said coldly.

To my irritation, he laughed, his low rich laughter filling the rose arbor and putting me at a disadvantage. He sank to the marble bench, casually drawing up one leg until his gleaming boot rested on the edge of the bench. He lounged there, his arm upon his knee.

"Miss Brandley," he said, still chuckling softly, "for an unwed girl, do not your thoughts fly rather quickly to the subject of lust?"

At his taunt, I could feel the color rush to my face. Oh, he *was* cruel. So this was why he'd not exposed me at once. He meant to savor his revenge, twisting it out of me little by little. And when he was done with his insults, he would go in and reveal all to my father. . . .

I shot him a look of hate, whirled around and started to fly from the arbor. But he was on his feet at once. He grabbed my wrist and dragged me back into the arbor.

"Let me go!"

I slapped at him, but he caught my other wrist.

"Peace, Miss Brandley. Calm yourself."

"Let me go!"

"Much as you and I might enjoy wrestling upon the ground, that was not my purpose in bringing you out here."

I tried to wrench away but he took me by the shoulders and shook me.

"Listen to me!" he demanded harshly. "I want this alliance as little as you do! I will let go of you only if you promise to sit quietly and bridle your tongue! We *must* find some way to extricate both of us from this damnable vow."

I saw in his eyes that he truly meant what he said, and relief flooded through me. I sank limply onto the marble bench. Tears came unbidden. I tried to choke them back, but the tensions and emotions of the past few days had been too much. My heartbreak over Christian's marriage, my frightening passions, awakened by Sir Gordon and then stirred to the boiling point in Christian's arms. The threat of being packed off to Virginia with a husband I did not even know. The terror of the thought of never seeing Christian again.... Oh, God, I would make myself live without his kisses if I had to, but never to see him? Never to talk with him?

I covered my face with my hands and wept, not caring that Delveau watched, not caring that he probably laughed within himself at my distress.

He said nothing until I cried myself out. When I finished, he gave me his handkerchief to dry my eyes.

"Poor little Dianna," he said softly, with unexpected kindness.

I choked. His kindness rankled. Weren't he and his father's obsession for Arabella at the bottom of all my troubles?

"Spare me your pity!" I said savagely.

The scar on his face moved in anger. His mouth tightened.

"Of course," he said coldly. "In Virginia, when one comes upon a rattlesnake and takes pity upon her—not destroying her at the first opportunity—one always lives to regret it."

I glared up at him.

"I do not care two sticks what you think of me. I only care about remaining in England. I love someone. My only desire is to be near him."

"Then we understand one another, Miss Brandley."

As I watched him, his scowl suddenly softened. He looked away, but not before I caught an unguarded expression. A strange and tender yearning glowed in his dark eyes for a moment.

"I, too—" He paused, hesitating. "I, too, am committed."

I looked at him in surprise, and I felt a sudden prick of contrition. I'd been so involved in my own feelings in the past days that I'd spent not even a fraction of a moment wondering what Delveau felt. With a wrench, I realized I knew nothing of his personal life, nothing of the hopes, dreams and loves of this young Comte d' Delveau.

I studied him with new eyes. Yes. Of course there would be a woman. Such fierce, scarred handsomeness must stir a passionate response in some women. I shivered. His air of brooding intensity would draw women to him. There was, I was reluctant to admit, a deepness to the man. One could never suppose he had lived a shallow life. I could well imagine that if North Delveau were "committed"—if he loved to that extent—then he loved his woman with every ounce of his being.

A pang of envy stabbed me. Wouldn't I give the moon and stars to have Christian love *me* like that? Wouldn't I give all I owned to have Christian love me as intensely as the young Comte d' Delveau loved his own woman?

An odd new pain invaded my heart and set it to aching. I felt all the fight drain out of me.

"Is she beautiful?" I asked softly.

He stared at me, stared at me and yet did not see me. His gaze was upon someone thousands of miles away.

"Very," he said, a tenderness throbbing in his low voice. But then, instantly, he stood up and shrugged, scowling at me for invading his privacy.

"The blame for refusing the match must fall upon me," he said. "I shall tell your father that Dianna Brandley and North Delveau mix about as well as oil and water." He gave me a wry smile, but somehow I could not smile back. "I'll tell him that such an alliance could only destine each of us to a lifetime of the greatest unhappiness."

He fell silent, and his words seemed to vibrate in the air— sensible, pragmatic and yet pricking my heart with an odd pain I could not identify.

"Yes, fine," I said, staring down at my hands in my lap. "And *your* father?" I asked softly.

He winced, and suddenly I knew why he had honored the

foolish vow, even to this point. He loved his father, as I loved mine.

He looked at me.

"I will tell him the truth. That I would sooner take a rattlesnake to my bed as make a wife of Dianna Brandley."

The insult stung but I did not rail back at him. Suddenly, I'd lost all heart for battle. Besides, I knew I deserved the insult.

I rose to go, rising with quiet dignity.

"I'm sorry," he said flatly. "I needn't have said—"

I put up my hand to stop him.

"We are of the same mind, North Delveau. You do not like me, and I do not—like—you." Why were those words so difficult to utter? I went on softly, "The marriage, as you say, could only be a disaster."

He bowed. He smiled slightly.

Gently he said, "I will explain to my father that Clarie is still a child. For a man of my years to wed her would be obscene."

I inclined my head in a nod.

"I thank you for that, Mr. Delveau," I said stiffly.

Violin music began in the drawing room. Rills of sweet music floated out upon the rose-scented air. The evening was growing dusky, darkening so slowly and gently that each rose seemed to glow like a jewel. Crickets began to sing at our feet, and fireflies twinkled faintly in the grass.

The problem was solved. I would stay in England and Delveau would sail back to Virginia alone. Then why were we standing here, looking at each other so unhappily?

He was first to move.

"Will you accept my arm to go in, Miss Brandley?"

Stiffly, I took his arm.

He looked down at me, smiling slightly.

"Perhaps, for the sake of what I must tell your father after the dinner party, we should pretend to dislike one another throughout the evening?"

I looked up at him sharply. Was he making sport of me? His eyes glowed with gentle amusement, and I knew he was teasing. I sensed the teasing was his apology for earlier harsh words.

"Pretend?" I said, laughing despite myself. "I doubt that either of us will have to pretend."

"True," he admitted honestly.

He tucked my hand into the crook of his arm, and without another word we strolled toward the music, the gay laughter, the sound of corks being drawn from bottles of the special white wine that came from the Champagne country in France.

CHAPTER 6

We moved through the pale blue duskiness of the summer evening toward the drawing room which was ablaze with light.

Violin music filled the air. Voices, happy and jovial, floated out to us. Wineglasses clinked. Servants bustled about with silver trays of tidbits and goblets of bubbling white wine.

Preparing ourselves to play our parts, we paused outside in the growing darkness. Fireflies hovered over the grass, edging my gown with living diamonds.

Delveau and I quietly absorbed the scene within. Across the room, Sir Gordon—erect as a general—talked animatedly with Christian's father, old Mr. Cartwright. Mrs. Cartwright, a tiny wren of a woman, nodded brightly. Aunt Matilde swished to and fro, discreetly directing servants with a shake of her kerchief.

I scanned the room for Christian. As I caught sight of him, my fingers tightened on Delveau's arm.

Delveau gave me a quizzical look, then followed the direction of my gaze.

underway, she turned her energies to the wedding feast, sparing no effort or expense.

Delveau stayed away. Friends and neighbors honored my coming wedding with dinner parties. To each invitation, Delveau responded with a terse but polite note in the negative. He could not come. Business pressed. Regretfully, he must decline.

I was forced to swallow my pride and endure the embarrassment of attending the dinners and parties on the arm of my father rather than on the arm of my betrothed. I knew I deserved Delveau's cuts, but still . . . Did he have to be so cruel? It seemed a foreshadowing of what the marriage would be. Or was I wrong? Would there be no marriage? Would he jilt me at the altar?

My only solace in those days was Christian. Whenever I could escape the dressmakers, I ran across the meadow to Cartwright Manor. Christian was kind and solicitous, but I noticed he went to great lengths never to find himself left alone with me. His attitude both hurt and gave hope.

One wheel of the coach lurched into a pothole. Father caught my hand, steadying me. I pushed aside the bouquet of white satin ribbons that hung above the coach window, and looked out. The lane was full of coaches, landaus, chaises and horsemen—all heading toward the church. I could see our servants running along on foot, crossing the fields, taking the crow's route to church where they would be permitted to stand in the rear and watch the ceremony.

It was the custom, in our parish, for the bridegroom to ride out on horseback, escorting the bride's conveyance to the church. At the church, he would hand her out of the coach and lead her up the stone steps and into the sacred rites. But there was no sign of Delveau. My father looked crossly out the window.

By the time we jounced into the churchyard, I was distraught with worry. Would he show up at all? Our coachman drew up to the honored spot at the base of the stone steps as I clutched my flower bouquet with apprehension. I peered through the window, searching the crowd for Delveau. His tall dark figure was nowhere to be seen.

Seeing Christian, remembering the touch of his mouth on my lips, my throat, my breast, I trembled. My pulse quickened.

"Ahhhh," Delveau said softly in a mocking tone.

I ignored him. My eyes were riveted to Christian. He was chatting gaily with my father and with Clarie. A woman I'd never seen before—it had to be Lady Olga—clung to his arm as though she would never let go.

I was overjoyed at her appearance. She was fortyish and beginning to gray at the temples. A plump little dumpling of a woman, she had merry brown eyes and smiles that went everywhere. I had to admit that except for her claim on Christian, I should have liked her instantly.

But I watched her, disliking her, feeling needles of jealousy. As I studied her, Lady Olga, unaware of her own gesture, rested her free hand on her thick waist for a moment. It was a fleeting gesture, but as it began to sink into my mind, I felt the world start to slip and slide under me.

Dear God, no! She can't be with child!

I gripped Delveau's arm with both hands. For a few terrifying seconds, I was plunged into jealousy so profoundly deep and black that all rational thought was stripped away. I swayed, dizzy and in agony. At last, the initial thrust of pain passed. I felt shaken. An unbearable ache gnawed steadily into my soul. I gasped for air.

Delveau stiffened. He scowled.

"So. Like the rattler, you intend to eat from another's nest."

"What is that to you!"

He gave me a look of dislike. "True. It is nothing to me. Nevertheless, Miss Brandley, I suggest you get control of yourself and throw a cloak over your passions before we join the party."

"I am perfectly in control!"

He laughed softly. Not a warm laugh, yet one in which I detected sympathy. Surprised, I looked up and saw amusement in his eyes. He bent his head to whisper to me. As he did so, his lips brushed my hair.

"If you are perfectly in control, Miss Brandley," he whispered, "then would you—perhaps—extract your nails from my arm?"

I recoiled at once, unaware I was still hanging onto him.

Delveau pushed his coat sleeve back, then the white ruff of his shirt. He rubbed the half-moon indentations on his wrist. He winced, grinning.

"Fang marks."

"You have my apology," I said curtly and turned from him.

He chuckled but I paid no attention to him. My gaze went to Christian. Christian seemed restless, as though he were waiting for something to happen, for someone to arrive.

I smoothed my hair, then my skirts. Impulsively, I pulled the silly lace fichu from my neckline, determined I wanted to be as alluring as I could be. I wanted Christian to look at me and recall the sweetness of our embrace, to look and remember that the embrace was still to be finished.

Impatient to fly to Christian, I whirled round, searching for somewhere to throw the fichu.

"Allow *me*, Mademoiselle Rattlesnake."

He chuckled softly, snatching the fichu from my hand. I grabbed at it, but in a moment he'd tucked it inside his shirt. With a mocking smile, he rebuttoned his shirt.

"You will give it back!"

"Will I?" He chuckled. "I think not. I will keep it as a souvenir. Whenever I look at it, I will thank God for my narrow escape."

I pushed past him.

"And I will send up devout prayers of thanks when I see the tail of your horse," I snapped.

I flounced off, ignoring his low rich laughter, ignoring the arm he offered. Quickly forgetting him, I stepped through the garden doors and hurried toward Christian.

Had Christian told anyone he'd seen me since his return? His expression, when he caught sight of me, gave no clue. His face was a curious blending of delight and sadness. I made up my mind to enlist him in deception. I would begin carving a chasm between Christian and his homely little dumpling of a wife.

"Christian!" I called out gaily, for everyone to hear. "Three years! Three years since I've set eyes upon you!"

He reddened, moving toward me, then hesitating. There

59

was misery in his eyes. He looked dreadfully uncomfortable. But he bowed, accepted my outstretched hand and brushed it with his lips. He held my hand no longer than absolutely necessary.

Loudly, for everyone to hear, I scolded him playfully.

"Christian Cartwright! I am as a sister to you, and you won't even greet me with a kiss?"

Everyone, with the exception of Delveau and Sir Gordon, laughed. Christian's eyes flashed angrily. His color heightened.

I flung my arms around his neck and the others applauded. I gave him a chaste peck on each cheek and hugged him. Reluctantly, his arms received me. I could feel the stiffness in him.

Playfully, I laughed, nuzzling his cheek until his lips became entangled in my hair. We were both keenly aware that I was pressing my breasts into his chest.

"God, Danni, don't!" he whispered in my hair.

His passionate outburst exulted me. So our encounter had *not* left him unaffected. He cared! He desired me! Giddy with sudden happiness, I turned to be introduced to his wife. Full of the thrill of Christian's passionate response, I could feel only goodwill toward her. Christian was *mine*, not hers. I greeted her warmly, and Lady Olga's merry eyes smiled unconditional acceptance of me.

"My husband quite dotes on you, Dianna. Since he calls you sister, I must make you my sister, too. Our home—and our hearts—are always open to you, my dear!"

At her generous speech, I felt a twinge of guilt. And as she embraced me, I felt ashamed. She was a good and honest woman. Yet I plotted toward her unhappiness. Then I gazed up at Christian, and guilt vanished.

"Lady Olga, may I have the loan of Christian tomorrow? My riding mare seems on the verge of going lame. I'm terribly worried. I trust no one to doctor Goldie as I trust Christian."

"Of course he shall come," she said generously.

"No!" Christian said. Anger and a confusion of feelings pulled at his face. "I'm much too busy tomorrow!" Then he added more gently, "I'm sorry, Danni. What you want is impossible."

"But no, darling," Lady Olga pursued, smiling up at him. "For Dianna, you must. All else can wait."

Sir Gordon broke in. "Goldie was sound the last time *I* saw her. You're imagining lameness, Dianna!" Sir Gordon's tone was testy.

"Pardon—"

Delveau, the tallest and most commanding man in the room, strolled into the center of the controversy. "I breed racing horses in Virginia," he said easily. "Horses are my specialty. Since I'm staying the night, I'll be happy to look at Miss Brandley's"—he paused, bowing slightly to me—"mare."

I glared up at him.

"I am certain that would be too much trouble, Mr. Delveau!"

My warning was clear. He ignored it. Mischief danced in his eyes.

"And *I* am certain it would be no trouble at all, Miss Brandley!"

Christian gave Delveau a grateful smile and went to him, hand outstretched for introductions. Activity quickened all around me and my moment was lost, thanks to Delveau.

I stood there, glowering at him. He pretended not to notice. Introductions whirled around me, with North and Lady Olga the centers of attention. The musicians struck up a gay tune, a quadrille, and my father declared everyone must have one more sherry or wine before dinner was served. Off in one corner, old Mr. Cartwright gallantly handed Clarie through an old-fashioned dance. She glowed in excitement.

I moved toward Christian, but he evaded me, slipping across the room. North Delveau sauntered about, talking with everyone. As he moved past me, I hissed, "Why do you interfere!"

He grinned at me. "Oh? Do I interfere?" he whispered.

My eyes filled with sudden tears, tears of frustration. He was making sport of me. He was spoiling everything. Obviously he considered my love for Christian a whim of the moment. Did he see me then, as such a shallow person? Angrily I blinked back tears. Why should I care *what* he thinks of me! It is Christian that matters.

His grin faded, but a smile lingered.

"Forgive me. I've been amusing myself at your expense. I wanted to see to what lengths you would go."

His sympathy and candor infuriated me more than his teasing and willful interference.

"You will see!" I promised savagely.

As I moved among the guests, talking and laughing, Delveau's eyes seemed to follow me. A mocking smile played on his lips. To calm myself, I hurriedly drank a glass of wine, then reached for another.

Sir Gordon appeared at my side, his erect figure stiff with anger. A vein throbbed dangerously at his temple.

When I reached for a third glass of wine, he took it from my hand and set it on a table with an angry thump.

"You're up to something, my dear Dianna."

I shrugged, refusing to meet those obsidian eyes.

"I know the signs. Your color is too high. You toss your head about as a bold filly tosses its mane. You are carrying your chin regally high, like a queen who plans to order an execution."

"I? Up to something? How ridiculous. It is you!" I deliberately took up the wine he'd put from me and drained the glass. *"You* arranged Christian's marriage!"

His eyes narrowed to slits.

"I told you I mean to have you, Dianna. I did not say I would get you by *fair* means."

I tried to move away, but he stayed my arm. He looked at me angrily yet admiringly. He nodded in Delveau's direction.

"Why has this foolish old business of Arabella's vow come up again?" he demanded. "I thought I had been successful in influencing your father against it."

The wine was affecting me. I giggled inappropriately.

"Andre Delveau lies dying in Virginia and my—"

Sir Gordon cut me off, finishing my statement in cold fury. "And Ambierce Brandley, still calf-struck over a long-dead wife, feels compelled to fulfill that vow!"

I giggled at his unusual loss of composure. He gave me a black look. I taunted him further by swaying sensuously to the violin music.

"You're drunk, Dianna! And that neckline displays far too much of your charms!"

"Drunk or sober, Sir Gordon, I shall wear my neckline as I please. And as for marrying, I shall marry neither you nor the wretched young Comte d' Delveau." I added, "North Delveau reminds me too much of *you*, Sir Gordon."

His black brows lifted in surprise. His gaze swept from me to Delveau who stood across the room, deep in conversation with my father and Lady Olga and Christian.

Sir Gordon stared at Delveau as though seeing him for the first time. A strange expression passed over his face. The vein on his temple seemed to throb all the more. He made to set his goblet on the table, but missed, and the goblet smashed to the floor.

I gave a little cry. It was the first time I had ever seen Sir Gordon make a clumsy movement. A servant moved discreetly toward us with a cloth. Sir Gordon's hand closed on my wrist.

"Delveau be damned!" he whispered. "I want you. I mean to have you." He strode off.

A cool breeze suddenly played through the drawing room, causing all of the candles to flare up and hiss. Yet none of the blue and yellow flames could match the fire that blazed in Sir Gordon's eyes as he spoke those last words. Shivering, I reached for another glass of wine and hurried to Aunt Matilde, linking my arm in hers.

She smiled up at me, delighted with her party.

"Dianna, dear girl," she said uncertainly, "should not that gown require a fichu?"

All Brandley parties eventually settled on one topic: trade. At dinner, with Christian on my right and Delveau seated, annoyingly, directly across, the major topic of conversation was the troubled Virginia office and the possibility of heavy losses if the colonies should become restive under the king's high taxes and boycott British imports.

Ordinarily, I would have much to say on the subject. But tonight, with the sleeve of Christian's coat occasionally brushing against my arm as we dined, I fell silent with my thoughts.

Food was impossible. I picked at each course and nervously consumed too much wine.

North's opinions, as a Virginian, were much sought. Christian spoke passionately to the subject, and my father damned the king for a fool who'd set his course upon destroying honest businessmen with his outrageous taxes. The colonies were sure to retaliate, my father warned. Delveau concurred in that opinion, but Christian and his father vehemently denied it. Aunt Matilde and old Mrs. Cartwright joined forces and offered the mild opinion that a king was a king by divine right. And as such, he should not be called a fool. Lady Olga's opinions were identical to Christian's, and all through the discussion, Clarie sat wide-eyed and wondrous, enjoying her first adult party.

"What the Virginia office wants, Ambierce, is one of the owners in residence," Sir Gordon put in coolly.

I stabbed him with a look. Of course, he was suggesting Christian! My father and Mr. Cartwright were too elderly to go.

Sir Gordon's glance flickered over me. He spoke on.

"Trouble between the king and his colonies is sure to come," he put in smoothly, "but all trouble passes eventually. An owner—in residence in Virginia—could assure that the Brandley-Cartwright Company incurs no losses during the troublesome years."

He glanced meaningfully at Christian. Christian nodded, understanding.

Alarm rang through my brain. I stared at Sir Gordon, wishing I could poison him with a look and shut him up. Across the table, there was a dry chuckle. I looked quickly. Delveau hid his smile in his wineglass.

Christian leaned forward.

"We've been considering that step for some time. With an owner in residence, we could expand to Philadelphia and Savannah, capturing the fur trade from the West and realizing a greater profit margin on tobacco in the South."

My breath caught in my throat. Unthinking, I reached out and placed my fingers on his sleeve. He trembled slightly, but didn't look at me.

He went on, "Lady Olga and I sail to Virginia as soon as the *Joanna* is ready. We shall settle in Alexandria."

Speechless, I could only stare at Christian. He avoided my eyes.

A flurry of comment exploded around the table.

Stunned, I burst out with, "When did you decide?"

He looked at me, then looked away. I could see a red flush spreading up his neck.

His voice shook when he answered.

"Six days ago, Danni."

It was a sword in my heart. Six days ago we'd been locked in the sweetest embrace I had ever known. And I had good reason to believe Christian thought it sweet, too. How could we react so differently? I was willing to give up everything just to be his—whether as wife or mistress. He? He had decided to run from it.

With a shaking hand, I reached for my wineglass.

Discussion burst out around the table. Mr. Cartwright addressed his daughter-in-law.

"My dear, can the voyage be harmful to you in your—er—happy condition?"

Lady Olga flashed him a smile.

"Sir, I am as healthy as a peasant. The child isn't due until November. By then we shall be comfortably settled in Alexandria. The voyage? I shall sail with one of my maids who has midwife skills. But the need for such skills is highly unlikely."

North Delveau leaned toward her. I could tell from the warmth in his face that he liked this plucky little woman.

"Lady Olga, I too sail on the *Joanna*. I am taking two physicians to Virginia to treat my father. If you'll permit me, I should like to place them at your service during the voyage."

Lady Olga beamed.

"How good of you, sir!"

A tumult of discussion followed, with everyone talking at once. Soft melodies drifted in as the violin music began again in the drawing room.

I touched Christian's arm. His hand jerked slightly.

"How long shall you be gone?"

He stared into his wineglass. He did not want to look at me, but at last he turned. I searched his eyes. His eyes—always so blue and honest to inner feelings—told me what his mouth would not admit. He wanted me, yearned for me and yet feared me.

"Three years, Danni," he said, answering my spoken question. "I expect to be gone three, possibly four—"

"That long!"

Wine made my outcry louder than I intended. Several heads swung toward me. Christian shifted uncomfortably, and when Aunt Matilde addressed him, he turned eagerly to her, giving me his back.

I signaled a footman to fill my glass.

With the violins playing, conversation grew louder and more jovial. I took no part in it. I sat drinking my wine and feeling as though my very heart were being torn out. Three years! Possibly four!

I signaled the footman again, but Sir Gordon, conversing with old Mrs. Cartwright, intercepted my signal. He frowned the footman off. Angrily, I signaled the footman still again, but he obeyed Sir Gordon and carefully avoided my eyes. Enraged at Sir Gordon's attitude of ownership, I pushed back my chair and stood. The table seemed to be rocking. I steadied it with my hands.

All eyes swung to me. Conversations fell apart in midsentence.

"Danni," Christian whispered, "you've had too much wine." He half-rose to help me but I shrugged him off.

"Everyone!" I called out gaily. "I have an announcement to make!"

What the announcement was to be, I had—at the moment—no idea. My head whirled.

Across the table, Delveau stiffened. His elegance vanished, as though he scented danger. Looking at him, I did not doubt that he'd once lived with savages. Beneath his politeness and easy good manners there lurked a wildness. He leaned forward, gripping the edge of the table. He scowled darkly and the tomahawk scar seemed to dip toward me.

"Sit down, my dear," Sir Gordon suggested lightly, the

lightness in his voice belying the warning that glittered in his eyes. He had, I knew, counted my every glass.

"Announcement?" my father said. He chuckled, rubbing his chin in a perplexed way. "Say on, Dianna—"

"What is it, dear girl?" Aunt Matilde said, encouraging me.

I picked up my empty glass. I studied it as though the announcement might be written there in the dregs. What was it I meant to say? That I loved Christian? That I intended to be his mistress? That I would follow him anywhere in the world?

"No," I said aloud, "that can't be right."

Lady Olga said cheerily, "Dianna, you keep us in suspense."

The room seemed to be rocking. I looked up.

"I'm going to Virginia."

There was stunned silence.

I went on drunkenly.

"This evening, as we strolled in the rose garden, Mr. Delveau asked me to become his wife. I—I—have accepted!"

In the instant of silence that followed, I heard a snap. My eyes flew to Sir Gordon. He was holding the bowl of his wine goblet in one hand, the crystal stem in the other. His face was black with rage.

I dared not glance at Delveau. I was not so drunk as to be unaware of what I'd done. Would he call me a liar? Deny my claim? Insult me—and my father—by refusing me although I had just accepted him publicly? Or would breeding tell? Would he bend, thinking of his own desperately ill father and the vow the old man cherished?

I held my breath, not daring to face him.

The table exploded.

At once, there were cries of surprise and congratulations. The women fell on my neck, weeping, kissing, laughing, offering advice. Aunt Matilde wept into her kerchief, then pulled herself together and began musing aloud of all the things that must be done to put on a proper wedding.

Clarie laughed and cried. "Oh, Danni, he's so handsome! But can't you marry him and live here?" She hugged me, clinging to my arm as though if she didn't, I might step aboard the *Joanna* at any moment.

67

Lady Olga kissed me warmly, offering the use of her seamstress and sewing girls to prepare a trousseau. And old Mrs. Cartwright wept because my mother was not alive to see this day.

Across the table, Delveau was hidden from view. He was surrounded by the men who were pumping his hand, thumping him on the back and insisting he drink congratulatory libations.

Only Sir Gordon sat alone at the end of the table and stared at me, musing.

Christian, his honest heart seeing no deception, left Delveau and came bounding around the table to me. He took my hands. He kissed the palm of each, then drew my palms to his heart and gave me a brotherly kiss on the forehead.

"Why didn't you tell me, Dianna?"

I sensed his deep relief.

He laughed happily.

"Dearest Danni, you have made a wise choice. Be happy, Danni!"

He kissed my forehead again, but I reached up and drew his head down. I kissed his lips.

"I *will* be happy, Christian," I promised fiercely. *"Both* of us shall be!"

He looked at me blankly, not understanding. Then, the women swept me into the drawing room, talking nothing but wedding talk. The men remained at table as servants brought port and tobacco. I had just one fleeting glimpse of Delveau as I was swept away. If I had prepared myself to see anger and outrage, then I had not prepared myself for enough. What I saw in his face, as he looked at me, was pure hate.

Gladly, I turned and fled with the excited, chattering party of women.

The evening ended early.

Lady Olga, her pregnancy taking its toll, began to grow pale before the clock struck ten. Christian demanded the carriage at once, and the Cartwrights left for home.

The violinists ceased to play, hurrying off to the kitchen for their well-deserved late supper. Clarie was sent to bed. Aunt Matilde, hiding yawns in her kerchief, trundled off after Clarie.

With my head beginning to clear and the effects of the wine

wearing off, I hurried after Aunt Matilde. My heart pounded in fear of having to face Delveau.

As I rushed up the stairway, Sir Gordon stood in the shadows of the first landing. Ignoring him, I skipped up the stairs. But swift as a young man, he sprang forward and seized my wrist. He drew me down the stairs to the landing.

"Let go!"

His grip gave me pain.

"Hear me, Dianna Brandley, and understand. Your marriage means *nothing*. I mean to have you. If I must, I will follow you to Virginia and—"

My father emerged from the drawing room and started up the stairs. Sir Gordon smiled and bowed over my hand, as though engaged in a proper social farewell.

He exchanged amenities with my father, glanced at me meaningfully, then left. I started up the stairs, but my father stopped me.

"You must talk with your betrothed." He kissed me happily. "Think of it. *My* daughter a future comtesse."

I pulled away, pleading a headache. My heart pounded in fear. All evening, I'd seen hate spring to Delveau's face whenever his glance came my way.

My father insisted. Taking my hand, he drew me down the stairs and led me into the drawing room.

"Father, no, please," I begged in a whisper.

"He is your betrothed."

He left, shutting the door firmly. I could hear his blustery voice order servants to stay away.

Delveau was standing at the mantel. He didn't look at me. He stripped off his waistcoat and flung it in a chair, then loosed his shirt at the throat. Unsteadily, he strode to the sideboard and grabbed the brandy decanter. I could see he'd been drinking heavily. He poured several inches of brandy into a glass. He threw back his head and swallowed it without tasting.

Carelessly dangling both decanter and glass from one hand, he deliberately turned to me and stared. I shuddered as I looked into his face. It was raw with emotion.

He despised me. He made that plain without uttering a word.

He stared, his jaw clenched as though he did not trust himself to speak. Every few seconds, a muscle twitched in his cheek.

"I congratulate you, Mademoiselle Rattlesnake," he said, his voice venom.

He bowed in mockery, pitching forward and losing his balance as he did so. He regained his footing, poured more brandy into the glass and drank it down.

"I—I—"

I gestured helplessly, not knowing what to say. What could I offer in defense? The bald truth was I'd used him, tricking him shamefully.

I looked up at him. In his face there was more than disgust. There was desire for revenge. As I looked into that angry face, I knew he would make me pay. I shuddered, then steeled myself to stand up to him. Pay? Then pay I would! I would endure anything—beatings, a lifetime in hell itself—if it meant even one week, one day or even one hour in Christian's arms.

I raised my chin in defiance.

He laughed harshly.

"Like the rattler, she makes no apology."

I said nothing.

"I underestimated you, Miss Brandley. I should have uncovered your amusing little charade on the day we met. I should have flushed the viper from her nest."

His dark eyes blazed. He poured more brandy and drank it. He swayed slightly.

"When last I underestimated a she-snake, I was given this."

Still gripping the decanter, he roughly yanked up his sleeve. I winced as I saw the scar. It was large and ugly, like some huge spider.

He let his sleeve drop. He swayed. The decanter fell to the floor, smashing as he pitched forward again.

Instinctively, I moved to catch him.

"Stay back! By God, I don't trust myself *not* to kill you this night!"

He swayed, took two steps toward me, then pitched forward into my arms. I broke his fall, but the force knocked both of us to the floor.

I pulled myself up into a sitting position and looked anxiously at Delveau. He was unconscious. Straining to lift him, I managed to move his head into my lap.

I touched his face, smoothing back the thick black hair. With his head in my lap—so oddly boyish and so strangely vulnerable despite the wicked-looking scar jutting from temple to cheek—I felt humbled. I touched the scar gently, awed by the thought of what pain he'd endured. Hesitantly, I drew up his sleeve and stared long at the hideous scar there.

Pain. North Delveau had known much pain. And I plotted to inflict more.

On impulse, I bent and kissed his hot brow. He didn't stir.

"Forgive me," I whispered to his unhearing ears. "I don't want to hurt you, but I must be where Christian is. I love him!" I cried out passionately, as though love excused all.

He slept on. I held him for a while longer, stroking his hair in some fruitless attempt at apology. Then I eased his heavy head to the floor. I got up and found footmen to tend him.

CHAPTER 7

The coach jounced slowly along the rutted lane that led to the church. My unhappiness deepened with each passing minute, and my nerves were stretched thin.

"My Dianna, a bride," my father said in a husky voice. He leaned across the coach and patted my hand. I tried to smile, but smiles would not come.

The past week had been misery. I'd seen nothing of Delveau, nor heard from him. When I'd arisen on the morning following the calamitous dinner party, Delveau was already gone. He'd set the marriage date with my father and then vanished.

My black moods, my unhappiness, my anguished guilt went unnoticed at Brandley Manor. Everyone, from Aunt Matilde to the lowliest stable lad, threw himself into wedding preparations. Aunt Matilde sent for a horde of dressmakers and incurred my father's temper by ordering cart after cart of supplies: bolts of satin, tabby silk, lutestring, velvet; lace trims, seed pearls, buttons of gold and pewter, and miles of ribbon in every width, texture and color. When the trousseau was

A footman, hesitating and reluctant, moved to the door of the coach. Apologetically, he opened it. I felt a flush of both shame and anger creep up my throat and into my cheeks. My lashes were suddenly heavy with a wetness that blinded me.

I put out my hand to the footman, and then, suddenly, a strong hand closed upon mine. I blinked away the blinding tears and saw Delveau's cold and angry face. He smiled, savoring my tears. My lips quivered at his coldness. So, he hated me that much!

He handed me down and gave me his arm.

"You are cruel!" I whispered, my voice trembling.

He looked down at me, unmoved.

"Do you deserve anything else?"

We ascended the stone steps, slowly. I strove to nod and smile to all who clustered about. To my relief, Delveau nodded to them also. A chorus of admiring sounds ushered us up the steps. I could catch some of the furtive whispers, and although he did not react, I knew Delveau heard them too.

"She's beautiful!"

"The ivory of her gown matches her hair. She's lovely as a princess!"

"Who *is* he?"

"So handsome!"

"Striking couple. Don't they look perfect together!"

Out of the corner of my eye, I examined Delveau. Grudgingly, I had to admit I was not ashamed to be on his arm. Eschewing the fancy brocades and bright light colors that most bridegrooms would have chosen, Delveau was dressed simply but elegantly. He wore a well-fitting suit of rich brown. His silk shirt was cream with ruffs of lace at the throat and wrists. His buttons were plain, but of gold. Unwillingly, I conceded that his choice of garb suited him.

Although he seemed not to look at me, I sensed he was not ashamed of my appearance. My gown was the loveliest I'd ever owned. The boat neckline cradled my shoulders and bosom. The skirt fell straight in front, giving a hint of my long legs. At the sides and back, the satin was shirred and gathered. There the skirt fell in graceful ever-changing folds. A Venetian lace veil enveloped my head like a delicate cloud.

When we entered the cool, musty-smelling narthex, our steps echoed off the stone floor and stone walls. Marriage hymns flowed out softly from the pipe organ.

We stood waiting while the guests assembled inside. My hand began to tremble in the crook of Delveau's arm. He looked at me with annoyance, then scowled and stared out the open church doors, his eyes on the horizon of trees and meadows.

At last, on signal we moved to the altar. The ceremony began. With my hand on North's arm, I heard none of the rector's words, saw none of the ritual. Instead, tears pooled in my eyes, and memories—memories of my childhood dreams of wedding Christian—drummed and roared in my ears.

Each minute of the endless rite seemed to be an ocean wave, and Christian and I were helpless ships, the waves separating us and pulling us farther and farther apart.

With a shock, I realized the ceremony was over.

Delveau gripped my elbow firmly, turning me and propelling me down the aisle past the beaming congregation. There was Father, looking proud but stunned. And Aunt Matilde, her eyes red and swollen. Clarie, glowing with excitement, held Aunt Matilde's hand.

And then I was moving past Christian. He beamed up at me, love and pride in his open smile. I stopped. I stared at him, my heart in my throat. Dear God, what had I done!

Delveau jerked on my arm. He propelled me with fresh speed through the hollow, echoing narthex, down the stone steps and out into the churchyard where guests would greet and congratulate us.

In the courtyard, another reality hit me like a thunder clap. My knees grew weak. I was wed—wed!—to this man.

Fearfully, I stole a look at him. His face was grim. Sensing my eyes upon him, he swung his head to me, his jaw clenched, his mouth set in tight lines. His eyes raked me with anger, and then he swung his gaze away as though he could not bear the sight of me.

The crowd began to flow down the stone steps. I could hear merry cries from the younger men and women.

"Kiss the bride, North!" they called. "You forgot to kiss the bride!"

Our servants, jostling and gawking on the periphery of the churchyard, took up the cry.

"Kiss her, Sir!"

Delveau ignored them. He ignored me. My face began to burn with humiliation. How cruel he was! He should know servants would get tiddly on a day such as this, with wine flowing freely. Couldn't he placate them and shut them up? God, he was mean! God, how I hated him!

Angrily, I snapped, "You might kiss me for the servants' sake!"

He turned and gave me a look of dislike. Still scowling, he hesitated, then bent down and brushed my lips with a cool, perfunctory kiss.

The crowd roared its disappointment.

"Lor' lummy, Sir," a familiar voice shouted, "you kin do better 'n *that*, Sir!"

I closed my eyes in fury and embarrassment. I made a mental note to thrash Nan to within an inch of her life, if ever I got my hands on her. Nan repeated her challenge, and to my surprise, Delveau began to chuckle. His face lost its angry set, as though he were awakening to the humor of the situation. He waved his hand to Nan, then turned to me. Slowly, as though he did not yet know if he truly wanted to touch me, he drew me into his arms.

I stiffened, and my pulse began to race crazily. His dark head bent to mine, and instinctively, I closed my eyes. A tremor coursed through me. My lips trembled in fear.

Then, his warm firm mouth was gently exploring mine, settling into the kiss. To my surprise, I found myself yielding willingly, letting his mouth lead mine. He administered a kiss that set the servants whooping and cheering. It was unhurried and unself-conscious, tender and searching. The kiss of a lover who does not demand response but, rather, invites it. . . .

When he slowly pulled his lips from mine, I felt dizzy and oddly shaken. For a moment, I couldn't open my eyes. When I did, he did not release me at once, but held me, looking down at me. For an instant, his expression seemed to soften, seemed to invite trust and intimacy.

"North—I—I—"

My words faded. I had no idea of what I meant to say, what I wanted to say.

Then, suddenly, doors slammed shut in the depths of those dark eyes. He gave me a cold hard look. With a stiff-armed movement he put me away from him and turned to endure the congratulations of the crowd.

At last, the hubbub died down and we were allowed to board the bridal coach and begin our short journey back to Brandley Manor.

Delveau slouched in his seat across from me, looking tired and unhappy. His gaze went out the window. He did not bother to glance at me or talk.

We rode in this melancholy mood for a mile, the coachman proceeding at a snail's pace in his homely assumption that newlyweds would want time for embraces before joining the wedding celebration.

Finally, frustrated with Delveau's unreadable silence, I spoke.

"You would make me happy," I ventured softly, "if you would pretend not to hate me at the party."

He turned and surveyed me coldly.

"Madam, I haven't the slightest interest in making you happy."

His words lashed. After the strangely tender kiss, I had presumed he might feel something. Hurt and angered, I lifted my chin in defiance and stared out the window. I will *not* cry, I told myself, I will *not* cry. Alongside the lane, a small child with a long stick was driving a cow. The cow's copper bell clanked in rhythm with the beast's plodding steps.

We rode forward in silence, the clank of the bell slowly fading into the distance. At last, Delveau surprised me by breaking the silence himself.

"Madam, I am no jackass. I know the game you play. As for you and I, our relationship can only be one of barter and trade." He laughed scornfully. "What will you trade, Madam, for a bridegroom who pretends to adore you on this, the happiest day of our lives?"

His words jolted me. I swallowed in apprehension. What

would he ask in payment for his good behavior? A willing bride in bed? I could feel my face grow scarlet.

He laughed.

"Not *that*," he said cruelly. "I will tell you what you must trade, Madam. My father is ill and longs for Arabella's child as his daughter-in-law. You will behave as a proper and decent daughter-in-law to the Comte d' Delveau for as long as he lives! After that, I care not *what* you do."

His words were vicious, and he had delivered them with a stoney glare. I bit my lip and stared down at the floor of the coach. How I hated him! I could foresee what our relationship was to be. I would be a bought woman. I would be used to wait upon his father and nothing more. I would be a servant, not a wife.

"Is it a bargain, Madam?" he taunted.

I looked up and returned his glare.

"You are detestable!"

He laughed harshly.

"Is it a bargain, Madam?" he persisted.

Anger and hurt pride boiled in me. I choked out the humiliating words he demanded.

"A bargain, then!"

The coach jiggled to a halt in front of Brandley Manor to allow us to alight. Hovering excitedly at the doors of the manor were servants—footmen, serving girls and housemaids. Delveau leaped from the coach. He handed me down. With distaste I put my hand in his.

Then, taking me by surprise, he swiftly pulled me into his arms and kissed me passionately. I struggled against him, but he pinned my hands to his chest. He kissed me until I yielded, and then he let me go.

I looked up at him in fury—furious with him and with myself to the point of tears. My lips had betrayed me, almost beginning to answer the invitation in that kiss.

"Why did you do that!" I said.

Although his dark eyes flashed with humor, his voice was cool and controlled.

"Our bargain, Madam. *That* was for the servants who are watching. *This*," he said, lifting me easily into his arms and carrying me up the marble staircase, "is for all of your ogling guests!"

CHAPTER 8

"Isn't he strong, Danni! Wasn't it thrilling when he carried you into the house!"

Clarie hovered over the back of my chair, breathless with excitement, watching as I freshened myself at the looking glass in my room.

"It was disgusting," I said sharply. I wrenched off the Venetian lace crown and veil and flung them to the floor. "It was just one crude example of colonial manners," I added, pulling a comb through my hair.

Clarie eyed me in puzzled disappointment, watching as I arranged a wide ivory silk band in my hair and coaxed the curls to tumble over it in the latest Paris fashion.

"But—but—he's so handsome," she argued softly.

I gave a bitter laugh. "I hadn't noticed."

As we stepped out of my room we could see maids and footmen scurrying back and forth, doing last-minute chores to prepare rooms for the guests. Many of our guests, those who had traveled far and those whom my father wanted to honor, were to stay overnight in the guest wing. A few of them—those intimate with my father—were given rooms in the family wing. Christian and Lady Olga were assigned the spacious, well-appointed room next to mine. Elderly Mr. and Mrs. Cartwright were only down the hall, and, to my annoyance, Sir Gordon had been invited to take the room next to the Cartwrights.

As Clarie and I slowly descended the winding stairway, noisy merriment rose to greet us. It was a merry and congratulatory throng of finely dressed neighbors and friends of my father's. All of the drawing rooms were in use, and groups of musicians played throughout the house. Our servants, wearing their best, threaded their way through the crowd with silver trays of wineglasses.

As for Delveau, he kept his bargain scrupulously. He was solicitous to a fault, his hand everlastingly on my elbow. He accepted the congratulations of our guests with an easy grace that surprised me, and I was taken aback by their reactions to him. The men seemed to like his forthright manner, and the ladies seemed excited by his presence. I couldn't miss the nervous fluttering of each woman's fan as Delveau's dark head bent toward her in conversation.

I studied him over the rim of my wineglass. Why did the ladies seem stirred? His looks were not to *my* liking. He was not handsome; the tomahawk scar spoiled his chances at that. Then what? Did the women respond to his tall, lean figure? His dark hair and eyes? No, it was something more, something he communicated by the way he held his body, in the way he moved. It was as though something wild and savagely exciting lived just beneath the surface of his polite, civilized manners.

I shivered and pushed away the frightening thoughts that rose. With unbecoming haste, I finished my wine. I would not think about it—my wedding night.

While Delveau did not trouble himself to smile at me as we wandered among our guests, at least—thank God—he did not scowl at me. He lapsed into that strange scowl only occasionally, when he seemed lost in private and unhappy musing.

He was attentive, as one would expect of a bridegroom. To

my extreme annoyance, I noted that whenever the clocks chimed the hour, he roused himself to grant me a perfunctory kiss on cheek or brow. He did this on the hour, as though it were some task he had set for himself.

When next the clock chimed and Delveau dutifully bent toward me, I jerked away.

"You needn't overtax yourself," I snapped.

A look of surprise, then amusement lit his intelligent dark eyes.

"You are perceptive," he said. "But the bargain, Madam?"

As I glared up at him, the amusement drained from his eyes. His expression hardened. "I keep my end of the bargain," he said coldly. "I trust *you* will remember to keep yours?"

"What do you take me for!"

He laughed. It was not an engaging laugh.

"Madam, I would *not* like to say."

I swayed slightly, rocked by his heartless blow. Then I turned on my heel and strode off through the crowd. With his harsh words roaring in my ears, I set out to find Christian. I suddenly needed him desperately, needed his assuring glances of affection and admiration, needed his shelter.

As I made my way through the festive, wine-drinking throng, I observed Lady Olga climbing the long winding staircase. She looked wan and tired. No doubt she planned a short nap before the wedding banquet.

Excitedly, I intensified my efforts to find Christian. I would have him all to myself while Lady Olga retired. Anxiously, I asked guests and servants alike. At last, someone directed me to the music room, and I found him.

Christian stood in rapt discussion with three neighbors who were well-known breeders of fine horses. As I approached, I could hear their enthusiastic horse talk.

"—purchased her for one hundred guineas."

"Still, the trick is to acclimate them. England is not Africa."

"Surely if one takes great care in the first year, not allowing them to race, of course—"

I took a deep breath and hurried up to Christian. I linked my arm with his and smiled up at him. He looked at me blankly for an instant, then a pleased and surprised expression spread across his face.

I glanced away, giving each of the gentlemen what I hoped was a beguiling and innocent smile.

"Christian has promised me a stroll in the rose garden. Will you excuse him, gentlemen?"

Christian gave me a confused look. I could see he was still miles away in horse talk.

"I did, Dianna?" he said absently.

I laughed gently.

"Surely you won't deny the bride her request?" I chided.

The men laughed, and so did Christian. He smiled down at me with fondness.

"Horses can wait. Of course, I'll stroll with you, Danni."

We excused ourselves, and I led him out through the garden doors. Strolling arm-in-arm, we made our way to the privacy of the rose garden and wandered aimlessly about in it. Christian was in a lighthearted mood. Obviously, he thought my marriage had canceled my passion for him, and he seemed relieved, even delighted. He lapsed back into his old, easy ways with me, teasing, baiting me, questioning me as though I were still a little girl.

While I reveled in his attention, disappointment weighted me down like a millstone. *Christian, don't you love me? Don't you want me? Can't you see the sacrifice I've made to have you?*

But I smiled gamely, striving to match his gaiety and camaraderie. He was in the mood to talk, and I listened quietly, gratefully. He spoke of his plans for the Virginia office, laying out the detail with great enthusiasm. I listened, wanting my time with him to go on and on and on—this arm-in-arm closeness, my cheek occasionally brushing against the shoulder of his waistcoat as we walked. I asked questions and only half-listened to his excited answers. They were not the questions I wanted to ask, not the answers I longed to hear.

We entered one of the rose arbors and sat down on the marble bench. Christian was telling me about the plans for expanding to Philadelphia and Savannah. Heady with his nearness, I heard none of it. As he talked, one of his tawny, unruly locks of hair fell forward on his brow. I looked at it, aching to reach up and smooth the hair from his brow. Oh, to touch him!

I clenched my hands tightly in my lap and looked away, my heart pounding.

"Danni, it's splendid that you'll be in Virginia!" he burst out. "I count on you to examine the ledgers. I need your sharp eye and your keen sense of knowing when figures have been botched!"

I looked up at him. His eyes were clear and blue and so honest they nearly broke my heart. Did I have a chance with him? Or was he too strict with himself, too moral?

"Do count on me, Christian," I said, trying to keep my voice even and natural. "I understand North has a house in Alexandria as well as an estate in the country. I'll try to persuade North to live in town. Then I can come to the offices every day if I am needed." *And see you. Touch you. Become your mistress, if you will let me.*

"That *is* splendid, Danni."

He sighed a long, satisfied sigh. He looked at me and smiled with deep affection. My heart caught at his look, but then— suddenly—a cloud seemed to pass over those clear blue eyes, darkening them. He looked away.

"Danni," he said in a low, unhappy voice, "have you forgiven me . . . for . . . that day?"

Stunned at his question, I stared at him helplessly. Forgiven him? God help me! I clenched my fists in my lap, driving the nails deep into my palms to stop myself from moving toward him.

"Please, Danni. I must know you forgive me."

I didn't trust myself to speak.

"I—do." *No! I do not! I shall never forgive you for stopping too soon, for leaving me with this terrible hunger!*

"Thank you," he whispered and then lurched to his feet. I rose too, unsteadily. Our happy mood was gone. Even nature seemed to sense it. A cool breeze began to blow, rustling the leaves of the bushes and showering us with rose petals. Blue shadows crept across the garden.

"Let's go in," he said abruptly.

I put my hands on his chest in mute protest. He did not remove my hands, and I felt him tense. I shivered and closed my eyes, lifting my eager mouth to his. He kissed me gently, as one might kiss a child. But as he pulled away, I pressed my mouth to his, kissing him with all the longing, all the frustration, all the desperate yearning that was in me.

Firmly, he took me by the shoulders and put me away from him.

"Danni, what you want . . . it cannot be. If I had realized . . . but you were a child when I left for Malta. I did not expect . . ."

With my heart in my mouth, I finished his words.

"Did not expect to fall in love with me?"

With an abrupt movement, he wheeled away from me and strode out of the garden, an angry set to his shoulders.

Weighted with sadness, I sank to the bench and sat there, sifting through my unhappiness. It was my wedding day. It should have been the happiest day of my life, with the future beckoning like a Garden of Eden. Instead, my future seemed a dry and sere desert. I could expect only cruelty and abuse from the man I'd married. And from Christian?

By eight o'clock several of the courses had been served, and the wine flowed freely. Unobtrusively, as twilight deepened into night servants went about slowly lighting the candles. As each candle flared up, my anxiety heightened. The hour I had put from my mind was fast approaching. I felt ill. My throat was tight, and cold moisture coated the palms of my hands.

How would Delveau behave to me when the time came for our marital moment?

He was sitting beside me at the banquet table, and out of the corner of my eye, I stole a fearful glance at his profile. Would he come to my room, but in anger, leave me untouched? Or would he avenge himself on my body? Would he force his rights in a cruel and thoughtless manner? Or might some reserve of tenderness spring forth from him, as it had during the kiss at the church? For that kiss had not been what I'd expected. It had been unexpectedly passionate, but not selfish or demanding. I'd been stirred by the tenderness, the gentleness in it.

I shivered, remembering.

Delveau caught my shiver. He turned, his face noncommittal.

"Cold?" he said.

"No," I said quickly, then, "yes."

He studied me with cool eyes.

"I'll send for a shawl."

"I—yes, thank you."

Just then, the footman began lighting the chandelier. My eyes flew to it in undisguised panic. Delveau watched me, and when I looked up at him again, I thought I saw a fleeting expression of understanding and compassion in those dark eyes. But at once, his face hardened. He signaled a footman and sent for the shawl, then turned his attention to the others at the table. For the rest of the dinner, he said nothing more to me.

But the lighting of the candles and the soft darkness gathering in the windows and glass garden doors brought the bridal night to everyone's mind. As each chandelier was lit, Sir Gordon seemed to drink more heavily. He hadn't spoken to me throughout the day, but I'd felt his eyes upon me. It had given me an eerie, unprotected feeling. Now, as darkness descended, I could see fury in his eyes as he sat at the end of the table making polite conversation with Aunt Matilde.

I could hear the wedding-night jokes begin at the tables around us, and when one of our more tiddly guests stood up, swaying drunkenly, I cringed at what his toast might be.

He lifted his glass to Delveau and roared, "To a good night's sleep, Sir!"

My cheeks burned as raucous laughter rolled through the hall, followed by more genteel titters. Delveau merely chuckled, as though such things were to be expected and borne, but Christian gave the speaker a furious look. My father turned and, with a glance, bayoneted the fellow into embarrassed silence, while Sir Gordon tensed as though he might cheerfully kill him.

The dance music began at once in the ballroom, and silently I blessed Aunt Matilde. For a spinster, she understood much and was prepared to control her party with an iron hand. Evidently she had told the musicians to play loudly as soon as they received her discreet signal.

A guest appeared at my shoulder, asking if I would dance. Eagerly, I abandoned the table without a glance at Delveau. I was aware that Sir Gordon had got up, too, and followed me into the ballroom. As I took the arm of my partner, I felt Sir Gordon's silvery eyes upon me. I felt like a mouse being measured by a cat.

I threw myself into the dancing on the arms of many of my guests. I'd quite forgotten Sir Gordon's brooding stares when suddenly, as I stood sipping wine, breathless from a spirited country dance, his hand closed on my wrist. He took my wineglass and set it aside.

"I will now have my dance with the bride."

His possessiveness, his air of confidence both irritated me and made me uneasy.

"Impossible," I snapped, pulling away. "I'm tired."

He smiled. I winced as his fingers tightened on my wrist, biting into the flesh.

"I *will* have my dance."

I could see that he'd been drinking heavily. To resist him would have been to provide my guests with an ugly scene— or, at best, a ludicrous one.

Unwillingly, I complied.

He led me out onto the floor and handed me through the dance. For a man of almost fifty, he was surprisingly agile and graceful. He didn't speak a word throughout the dance, but his eyes and hands never left me.

When the dance ended, I trembled in relief. I curtsied low and Sir Gordon bowed as the last bars of music brought the piece to a close. I pulled my hand from his, eager to escape.

Suddenly, he took me by the arms and wrenched me close. Thunder-struck, I couldn't move.

"I will have you, Dianna, though you marry a dozen men!"

He released me at once, and it was over so quickly, that the other guests were still turning their faces to us, expressions of mild surprise and questioning in their countenances.

In panic, I rushed from the ballroom, shaking. There had

been silver fire in his eyes and a ruthless determination that struck terror in me.

A buffet supper, fully as elaborate as the dinner, was served after midnight. The buffet was followed by more dancing. By three o'clock, weary guests began to disperse, some summoning chaises and landaus, others retiring to their rooms for the night.

There was a loud buzzing in my ears, and my heart pounded in fear as I sensed my marital moment approaching. Standing close to Father and Christian and Lady Olga, I joined them in conversation though my mind was elsewhere.

Out of the corner of my eye, I watched nervously for Delveau's tall, casual figure. I was aware that at any instant he could appear, put his hands on my shoulders, and with only an imperceptible pressure of his fingers, direct me silently to lead him upstairs. It was his right. He was my legal husband. My heart banged in regret, *Oh, God! Christian!*

As the four of us stood talking, I searched Christian's face. Searched it for some sign that he, too, was distressed that I must spend this night in another's arms. But Christian carefully avoided meeting my eyes.

Finally, I could see Delveau approaching slowly through the dwindling crowd in the drawing room. I felt faint, locked my knees to steady myself and forced myself to smile up at my husband.

He was towering over me, nodding to my father, then addressing me.

"Madam, I've just learned of a physician in Cornwall, a man skilled in disorders of the lung, who might be persuaded to attend my father in Virginia. Since the *Joanna* sails in six days, I have little time. I must ride for Cornwall at once."

I was stunned. I heard Lady Olga's small startled gasp. I could feel the blood drain from my face, then rush up again as the enormity of his insult hit me. I could not believe such an affront! To leave me on my wedding night!

I swallowed. It was a cruel and deliberate act. If he'd wanted to spare me, he could have come to my room and slipped out without anyone knowing. But *this* way. In front of the guests!

And I knew the insult was not accidental; he was too intelligent for that.

My father grunted in surprise, then recovered himself. He covered the awful moment with loud talk.

"Well, well! Of course you must go, my boy!" he said heartily. "Your father's life depends upon it! He *must* go, must he not, Dianna?" Father eyed me uncertainly.

I nodded stiffly.

Delveau bowed back, just as stiffly.

"It pains me to leave you, Madam, on this, the most important occasion of my life."

It was a pretty speech to other ears, but to mine, it rang with irony and insincerity. I nodded again, haughtily.

"If Madam will permit me to take my leave?"

I could hear the whispers of surprise rippling through the covies of guests who'd overheard. I drew myself up proudly, my head high, and granted Delveau a dazzling smile.

"Of course!" I said, extending my hand in a proper farewell. He bowed once more, accepted my hand, then brushed his lips across it.

"Until the *Joanna*, Madam," he said, releasing my hand.

For one instant, our eyes met like swords crossing. Anger clashed against anger, challenge against challenge. Then Delveau turned on his heel and was gone.

Stunned, I stood there, my pride crumbling. I longed to run, but knew the report of such actions would get back to Delveau and he would exult in his victory.

So I steeled myself. I called for a glass of wine and spent several minutes sipping it and conversing with forced cheer. At last, I could allow myself to seek the privacy I craved. I mounted the stairs slowly and casually, as though I were not troubled.

But inside my room, I threw the bolt on my door and flung myself onto the bed. I sobbed into my pillow—sobbed wildly and for a multitude of conflicting reasons. I cried in relief because Delveau was *not* in my room, I cried because I was ashamed and angry that he was *not* there, I cried because I was no longer a girl but an unhappily married woman. But most of all, I cried because my bridegroom was not Christian.

When the torrent passed, leaving me burnt out and tormented, I roused myself, shed my restricting gown, stripped off my garments and, exhausted, dragged on a white silk night-shift, robe and slippers.

I blew out the solitary candle.

With a heavy heart, I moved to the windows and pushed open the mullioned glass. A huge moon hung in the sky, bathing the rose garden in milky light and setting the far meadows aglow. Only crickets and katydids broke the hushed stillness. Though I was awake and tortured with my thoughts, the rest of Brandley Manor slept.

The windows in the room next to mine were pushed out, also. Gradually, I became aware of low murmurs, voices blending softly—a man and a woman. Suddenly, the woman gasped and uttered a faint little cry of delight.

"Darling—"

With a start, I realized who occupied that room. Backing away from the window, I pressed my fist into my mouth to stop the hysteria that threatened. I flung myself onto the bed. I buried my face in my pillow and bit my lip until it bled.

Darling—

I clawed at the pillows, pressing them over my head, not caring if I suffocated but only trying to blot out the memory of that soft, sensual cry.

Darling— Darling—

I screamed into my pillow. It was as though the soft little cry were being carved into me with a hot knife. I leaped up, hysterical and frantic. I paced the room, twisting and tearing at the rosettes on my silk robe and could feel the uncontrollable screams building.

I had to get out!

Flying to the door, I rammed back the bolt and threw the door open. I flew through the corridor and down the servants' staircase and plunged out of the house and into the night, pursued by Lady Olga's soft cry of pleasure.

Christian! Oh, my God, Christian!

I fled through the rose garden, through the orchards, up

91

over the shadow-shrouded stiles and into the open meadow. Fireflies scattered as I ran, and hidden rocks struck my feet, cutting me and sending me stumbling. Still I could not stop. I ran far out into the moon-washed meadow, ran so far out into the milky night that behind me, my home was only a toy house set upon the horizon.

At last, my feet bleeding and my lungs tortured for lack of air, I threw myself down in the grass and lay there gasping.

Christian. Oh, Christian!

I willed myself to die, prayed to die. Jealousy was a dagger and I was impaled upon it. In agony, I rolled onto my back and lay there weeping up at the moon and stars, trying not to think, trying not to feel.

I seemed to lie there forever as the moon moved across the sky in its impersonal, uncaring path. One by one, the stars began to wink out as dawn nudged the darkness. With a heavy heart, I roused myself to return home. Morning would soon come. Already, the horizon to the east was etched with grayish pink.

Sick in spirit, I started for home.

Ahead of me, in the distance, something moved against the pink horizon. It was a man's figure. Coming toward me. In a few moments I was able to recognize that casual, confident stride, and a tremor shot through me.

Delveau! So he had changed his mind! What did he want of me? Why—? My thoughts tumbled in confusion.

But as he drew closer, I could see the figure was not Delveau, and a cry caught in my throat. It was not Delveau, but Sir Gordon! Had he followed me? Or had someone discovered my absence and sent the men out to search? His stride was so deliberate that my heart jumped in fear.

"What do you want?" I called shrilly as he approached.

He did not answer but continued to stride toward me. A new tenseness in his step set off a warning in my brain. I backed away, then broke and ran. But it was too late. He was upon me at once. His hands, his clutching demanding hands went everywhere. He was a man possessed.

I cried out, fighting him, while fear, an enormous black

throbbing fear, pulsed through me. With horror, I suddenly knew his intent.

"Don't do this to me!" I begged, fighting. But his mouth went where it willed—my throat, my mouth, my breasts. Wrenching free, I screamed and stumbled farther out into the meadow.

He caught me easily as I flailed my hands and nails against him. He pulled me to the ground under him, and I struggled uselessly as he pressed me into the grass. There was a sound like thunder in my ears, and I knew it was the pounding of my own heart. I grew dizzy with the weight of him. The taste of brandy was in his mouth as he brutally raked my mouth, then wrenched up on my shift.

"You are mine!" he said drunkenly.

I tore my mouth free, but he captured it again.

I fought him with every ounce of my strength, but at last, I lay under him, drained and unable to struggle more. My tears flowed, but they did not move him. Lying under him, limp as a plucked flower, I closed my eyes as a merciful blackness swirled into my brain. I seemed to be wandering about in some dark void, searching for someone whose name I could not remember.

Numb with shock, I felt the dull stab of his entry and the hot burning. And I remembered the name just as I fainted under him.

"North," I whimpered. "Oh, North—"

When I came to, I was lying on his cloak in the meadow. The sky was beginning to lighten, and somewhere a meadowlark gave its first tentative trill. I looked up at him as he sat beside me, and my tears began to flow.

"Don't, sweet," he implored softly. "I had to. I love you, Dianna."

"Love!" I sobbed, rolling from him and weeping.

He rolled me back to him, and his hand went between my thighs. I cried out, believing he would take me again, but instead he bent and kissed what he had ravaged. I reared up in protest, but he pushed me down, holding me. My strength was gone. Weeping, I let him pleasure me in ways I had never even dreamed of in my innocence. When the sharp unexpected jolts came, I gasped, then rolled away from him, curling up like a snail in my deep humiliation.

He said nothing more to me, but let me weep. Then he picked me up in his arms and carried me through the meadow. I was too weak and ill with shame to resist. He carried me carefully, as though he carried a treasure, and his firm steps stirred up a wake of fireflies. He stopped only once, to kiss me.

"You were meant to be mine, Dianna," he said. "Now you truly *are* mine."

I tore my mouth from his in revulsion, and I wept, tears of shame mingling with tears of anger.

He set me down at the servants' door, and I fell against it, numb with shock. I wanted to rail at him, claw him with my nails, plunge a blade into him. But I could only manage a trembling whisper.

"I swear—by this night—I shall—kill you—"

He laughed softly.

"You belong to the man who first takes you, Dianna," he said, "and I am that man."

With a broken heart and a broken spirit, I crept up the servants' stairs to my room. Inside my room, the windows stood open to the first rosy glow of dawn. A robin chirped encouragingly at the new day as I sorrowfully eased into my bed.

CHAPTER 9

I opened my eyes, then instantly shut them. I did not want to wake up—ever. I only wanted to die.

I had drawn the velvet bed curtains before falling into anguished sleep. Now I only wanted to stay in that dark cocoon and never leave it. I felt sick with shame and humiliation—so sick I felt I might retch.

Curled up like a snail, I heard Nan begin to stumble about outside the bed curtains. Silently, I willed her to go away. She did not. With a wrench, she yanked one of the bed curtains back and tied it to the post.

"Don't—" I protested weakly.

If she heard me, she did not heed. She went on tying back the curtains, then carried a tea tray to the bedside table and set it down with a small crash. She rambled about the room, tidying up. She picked up the white silk shift I'd discarded and turned it over in her hands, humming softly at the blood spots she saw on it.

"They did tell me he went straight to Cornwall," she said

cheerily, "but I says to myself, no. Not after the kiss I seen him give you at church."

"Nan—please—leave me alone."

She ignored me and charged on.

"So he decided to ride *you*, afore ridin' his horse to Cornwall, did he?" she said boldly. "Took a quick toss under the covers did he?"

"Be silent!" My voice shook.

She only grinned and gave me a knowing look.

"I guess you be feelin' good 'n' married this morning, Danni!"

I burst into tears and covered my face with my hands. I heard the swift clumping of Nan's shoes. The bed sagged as she sat on it and drew me into her arms.

"There, there, now, Danni," she cooed, "so you didn't like it the first time. There's not many girls as do. There, now. It gets better with time, it does."

I sobbed harder, burying my face against Nan's plump shoulder. She rocked me in her arms, clucking and cooing at my distress.

"Lor' lummy, Danni," she began gently, "the first time I got throwed in the hay, I wasn't but twelve. It was that mean Luddie Banks, the miller's son, what done it. 'N' he leaves me there in the stable, bleedin' and cryin'.

"I was madder 'n a wet hen! I marched home, I got Pa's horse whip and I went huntin' Luddie. Found him, too—in the White Swan, sloppin' down ale like he'd nary a care in the world. I took that whip and I cracks him clean across the face, so's up he jumps, yelling bloody murder. Out he runs—" She chuckled with relish. "The whip scar be on his face to this day!"

Nan's words were a blurry echo through my hysteria. She patted my head and went on.

"Twasn't 'til I be fifteen that I started liking it, Danni," she said, trying to encourage me.

I pulled back from her, sobbing.

"Oh, Nan, you don't understand."

She gave me a puzzled look.

"Then, tell me," she said simply.

I wiped my eyes and sank back into the pillows. Tell her? Tell anyone? It wasn't possible. I was so deeply ashamed, and when I remembered moments during the rape when my body had responded with pleasure, I was filled with self-hate. And when I thought of Sir Gordon, I shook with helpless anger. Tell *anyone?* No. I must bear it alone. Manage my revenge alone.

When I'd wept myself out, a black depression settled upon me, eating into my soul, crushing my spirit. I couldn't move. I couldn't eat. I couldn't bear to see anyone. As the days passed, I kept to my room. By day, I lay listless and uncaring on my bed. At night, I sat alone at my window and watched the moon travel slowly across the sky and disappear with the dawn's light. My mind was numbed. I didn't care if I lived or died.

Eventually, Father and Aunt Matilde overruled my objections and sent for Dr. Grange. The elderly physician was kind and careful, but when he gently asked me if the marriage had been consummated, I became hysterical and couldn't stop crying. Dr. Grange dosed me heavily with laudanum, and I cried myself into drugged sleep.

As I drifted toward unconsciousness, I could hear Dr. Grange giving Father and Aunt Matilde his diagnosis.

"Bridal hysteria. Quite common in well-bred young ladies. She will be her usual self in a week or two."

At last, the day came when I woke and felt the paralyzing numbness begin to leave. Slowly, my mind began to clear and I could begin to think about the events without collapsing into fearful weeping or fits of black rage.

A new anger, cold as steel, burned in me, and its flame, irrationally, did not focus on Sir Gordon but on Delveau. All was *his* fault. *He* had abandoned me on our wedding night. Had he not left, none of the rest would have happened.

Delveau!

All my hate and anger centered on that darkly handsome face with its thin white tomahawk scar. I hated him as I'd never dreamed myself capable of hating anyone. The hate was capable of murder. I longed to kill him.

Three days later, my frozen and vengeance-seeking heart, eased slightly by the prospect of making the crossing in Christian's company, I stood on the London dock and gazed up at my father's three-masted square rigger, the *Joanna*.

Her masts were stout and tall as trees. They were criss-crossed with a maze of ropes and crossbars. High up in her rigging, gulls perched, crying to one another and flapping their wings. The ship creaked pleasantly as she shifted in the stirred waters of her mooring. A ramp extended from ship to dock. The ramp rose and fell softly, in rhythm with the ship's gentle movement.

Nan tugged at my skirts.

"I ain't walkin' on that rolly plank, Danni! Judas, I ain't!"

"Hush, girl. Of course you will, if you are coming with me. It's the only way on to the ship."

Nan began to wail in fear, mumbling that she was not coming. I ignored her. In the past week, she'd changed her mind a dozen times a day. Yes, she was coming with me—definitely, positively. No, she was not—savages in Virginia, Judas! And all that water, when she could not swim a stroke.

Clarie, her face flushed with excitement, skipped up the ramp and was on the ship. Father followed, helping Aunt Matilde and steadying her on the softly swaying ramp.

I stood on the dock, my jaws clenched in icy determination. I would not board the *Joanna* except properly. And that being on the arm of the man who was my husband. Insult me in front of my guests on our wedding night, would he? By God, he had married me, and I would see him forced into the proper social behavior toward a wife. I was prepared to stand on the spot until hell froze over, if need be.

I scanned the long ship from stern to bow, looking for Delveau. At last I spied him, standing near the bow of the ship. He was leaning casually against the rail, his waistcoat removed and flung over one arm. He appeared to have been standing there a long while, studying the dock. So! He had been watching me all the while.

I stared up at him, making my face an expressionless blank. He looked down at me, his face similarly sullen and devoid of expression. Then, with an irritated shrug, he pulled on his waistcoat. With the long strides of a man who faces an unpleasant task, he was soon up over the ramp and down on the dock at my side.

We looked at each other with undisguised dislike.

But as I glared up at him, his expression of dislike changed into one of puzzlement and then one of controlled alarm.

"You look like the very devil," he said. "Have you been ill?"

"And what if I have been!"

I knew very well what I looked like. My eyes had dark circles under them, my healthy color had faded and I'd lost weight. With unexpected gentleness, he touched my shoulder.

"Someone should have told me."

I stabbed him with a look.

"How fortunate I am to have such a solicitous husband!"

I was satisfied to see him flinch. He removed his hand from my shoulder at once. He bowed, stiffly offering his arm. Stiffly, I took it.

He led me up the ramp, then stopped halfway.

"What of your maid?" he said coldly.

I looked back at Nan. I'd forgotten her. Delveau had the irritating effect of muddling my thoughts. Nan was wailing loudly and hanging onto the coach wheel. In vain, our coachman was trying to pry her loose and coax her up the ramp.

It was a ludicrous sight, and any other time I would have laughed. So would Delveau, I sensed. But we were both too unhappy to see the humor in it.

"I—I don't know," I said. "Could you—"

He nodded curtly. As we stepped onto the ship, he shouted for his man. The man's name, apparently, was Sandy. He was a big, robust young fellow, perhaps overly plump, but with clear happy eyes, and an endearing smile that spoke of shyness.

Delveau nodded toward Nan. Sandy grinned and loped down the ramp. Delveau and I leaned on the rail, watching to see what he would do.

First, Sandy knelt on one knee, earnestly supplicating Nan.

After a few minutes, she stopped wailing. She peered cautiously at the young man and then broke into a wide grin.

He went on talking with her, and after a time, Nan trustingly gave him her hand. But at the last moment, she flung herself from him and grabbed the coach wheel, hanging on for dear life and wailing in fright.

Sandy repeated the routine, coaxing her patiently. Again, at the last moment, Nan flung herself from him and clutched the wheel.

At last, Sandy pried Nan's hands from the wheel, hefted her up into his strong arms and carried her up the ramp. Nan kicked, sobbed and swore, but Sandy held her firmly.

I caught Delveau's soft chuckle as Sandy did not set her down but carried Nan, now a strangely submissive and clearly enchanted girl, to the stern of the ship where he set her upon a heap of coiled rope and fell down beside her, still holding her hand and talking earnestly.

I looked up at Delveau and, for an unguarded moment, I warmed to the look of amusement in his eyes. Then, instantly, we both regretted the intimacy and turned from each other.

Introductions filled the deck. There was the captain to meet and the first mate, then the two doctors who would attend the comte. The first was Dr. Tibbs, a thin, springy middle-aged man who was going bald at the crown of his head.

The second was young Dr. Osborne and his shy bride, Missy. Dr. Osborne was a heavy man and nearsighted. He wore thick spectacles that magnified his eyes and made them appear fishlike. His wife, Missy, could not have been much more than Clarie's age, and she was so painfully shy that she blushed when anyone spoke to her. I could see she would be no company to me at all on the voyage since she seemed to have no opinions of her own, but looked to her young husband to supply them.

My father introduced us to the remaining passenger, a Mrs. Amanda Creel, a widow and the sister of my father's Virginia office manager. Mrs. Creel was going to Virginia to take charge of her brother's household of six children. Her brother's wife had died. Mrs. Creel seemed overly outgoing for a middle-aged widow woman. She wore bright colors, and it was plain to me that she tinted her hair. Whereas Missy had no opinions at all, Mrs. Creel had an opinion on everything. But she voiced her thoughts so charmingly, with direct words and a low, well-modulated voice, that all of the men seemed quite taken with her. Clearly, she was a woman who liked men, and if I was reading her subtle glances correctly, the man she seemed most interested in was Delveau. To my irritation, Delveau and Mrs. Creel seemed to strike up a friendship at once.

I turned away in disgust.

"But where is Christian?" I asked my father when the introductions were done.

He cast a worried look upon the dock. The dock was in a hubbub. Barrels and crates were being loaded still. Ragged children were playing and shouting at the bottom of the ramp, knowing the seamen would toss a few coppers for good luck just before sailing. A beggar with a squeeze-box played a tune, and a little girl in tattered homespun danced, catching the coins Clarie threw into her apron.

"I'm sure Christian and Lady Olga will arrive at any moment. Their baggage was delivered to the *Joanna* yesterday. Their servants have readied the cabins."

The captain pushed his hat back on his head and asked my father anxiously, "They won't cause us to miss the tide?"

"Of course not!" my father said. But his tone was worried.

I spent an anxious hour at the rail with Father, watching for Christian. At last, a landau came barreling down the street and clattered onto the dock, scattering the children and street dancers. Christian leaped out of the landau and came bounding up the ramp. He looked terribly upset.

"It's Lady Olga," he said, his voice brittle and tense. "She has been ordered to bed. There are signs that our child may miscarry."

I stared at him, my heart beginning to thump wildly at the implications. Would I have him to myself for the voyage? Oh, it would cancel out all the pain, all the terror and anguish of the past days!

"Then she's not coming?" I said, unable to keep the joy from my voice.

Christian met my eyes steadily.

"We are not coming, Danni."

It was as if he had taken his fist and punched me in the stomach. I couldn't breathe. I reached for the rail. I hung on. Christian and my father talked excitedly, but I heard none of it. I was numb. He *had* to come. He had to!

"Christian?" I burst out, interrupting their intense discussion in mid-sentence.

Their heads swung to me, their faces puzzled.

"Christian, you *must* sail with me. I can't go to Virginia without you. I can't bear it. You must come—you must—"

He cut me off sharply.

"Danni, Lady Olga is my wife!"

"But what about me!"

Christian flushed, looking away, and my father misread all of it.

He said, "Dianna, you know the Virginia business as well as Christian. You can oversee things until Lady Olga is well enough to travel." He swung his head to Christian. "You must tell Dianna what you want her to do."

"I've brought papers." Christian reached into his waistcoat.

"Take her to the ship's dining room, then. There you will find privacy to study the papers. Mind you, hurry! The *Joanna* sails shortly."

Numb with shock, I hurried after Christian. I sat stiff and disbelieving at the ship's long narrow dining table as Christian spread the papers, talking rapidly and pointing to various columns. He shuffled papers and went on and on.... The fur accounts must be carefully checked and an inventory ordered.... Downey must rethink his shipping schedule and time the shipment of tobacco to arrive in London when prices are at their best.

I nodded mutely, comprehending none of it, comprehending only one thing...Christian was not sailing with me. At last he stopped speaking, breaking off in mid-sentence and giving me a worried, brooding look.

"Danni? Are you hearing anything of what I am telling you?"

I shook my head. The tears that had been collecting slowly

in my lashes went spilling as I shook my head. I could feel their cool trickle as they ran down my hot cheeks.

Christian made a choking sound.

"Don't, Danni. Don't behave like this. You—you will break my heart."

I looked up at him, hope beginning to pound. But he only dug into his waistcoat, drew out his handkerchief and wiped away my tears. I caught his hand in desperation and kissed it passionately.

"Christian? Sail with me?"

He wrenched his hand away. He refused to look at me, and when he answered, his voice was choked, husky.

"Don't talk nonsense."

"You love me!"

He got up so abruptly that his chair crashed to the floor. He stood with his back to me, his head down.

Just then, a whistle blew and bells rang. Departure was imminent. My heart leaped to my throat, and I jumped up just as Christian turned to me. I threw myself into his arms.

"Christian, I'm afraid."

"Don't be, dearest, the ship is safe and sturdy."

"Afraid I will never see you again!"

Our eyes met in mutual anguish for a moment. He put his hands on my shoulders as though he meant to push me away, and then, with a low, guttural growl, he jerked me to him and kissed me with savage possessiveness. His mouth was still moving on mine, angrily, passionately, when a cold and furious voice came from the open door.

"Madam, the ship sails," Delveau said. "Your family awaits your farewells."

I gasped, and Christian froze, then pushed me aside roughly. He rushed past Delveau. I, too, flew past my husband, my head bowed, my eyes on the floor, avoiding his hard face.

The farewells were strained. Everyone wept. Father extracted a promise from Delveau that he would bring me back for a visit. Delveau, thank God, acquiesced with at least a modicum of grace. But his eyes, when he looked at me, were full of fury.

Too soon, my family stood upon the dock and the *Joanna*

slid out of her mooring. I watched my family recede from me—Father supporting a wildly sobbing Aunt Matilde. My last glimpse of Christian was one I cherished long in my heart. He stood with his arms around Clarie, comforting her.

When I could see him no more, I blindly made my way to my cabin. Delveau followed me, and suddenly I sensed my situation. I was alone. My family was gone. There was only my husband, and he cared nothing for me. Hadn't his lack of caring led to my rape? Angry tears burned as I entered the cabin, sat down at my desk and picked up a ledger to calm my shaking hands.

Delveau followed me in and shut the door with a quiet deliberateness that struck fear in me. Fear? What more had I to fear! The worst had already happened to me. I gritted my teeth and opened the ledger, my back toward Delveau.

"So your lover does not sail with us," he said contemptuously, giving cold emphasis to the word "lover."

I continued to study the ledger.

"He is *not* my lover." As I said it, a sob caught in my throat. For, with all my heart, I mourned the truth of my statement.

Behind me, I heard Delveau cross the room slowly. His hands cupped my shoulders. I stiffened.

"But . . . you . . . hoped."

I stared straight ahead at the cabin wall. I said nothing. His hands tightened on my shoulders. I sensed both anger and sexual tension in his touch.

"My hopes do not concern you, Mr. Delveau," I said acidly. "As my lawful husband, you are master of my body. I cannot require you, even now, to remove your hands from my shoulders. But you are not, arťd never shall be, master of my hopes!"

He removed his hands as though my flesh burned. He strode across the small cabin and flung himself darkly into a chair.

"Look at me, Madam," he commanded.

I hesitated to obey. Then, frightened by the edge in his voice, I slowly shifted in my chair to face him. My hands shook in my lap. I was not nearly so brave as my words.

"Come here."

His tone was not to be disobeyed. Shaking, I got up, crossed the cabin and stood before him, a scared schoolchild before an all-powerful schoolmaster.

His eyes smoldered, and I was beginning to learn that when he was most angry, he spoke in cold, controlled tones.

"On the day I met you, Madam," he said, brittle ice crystals in his voice, "as you played housemaid in the rose garden, I told you I never force wenches. Neither do I force wives. When the day comes that you want me, Madam—and that day *will* arrive—you will have to come to *my* bed and ask me. For I will not ask you—ever!"

My mouth dropped open. Did he think, then, that I felt any attraction for him? My God! Who did he think I was, one of those fluttery-fan women at the wedding party? His audacity made my blood boil. My anger welled up, overpowering my fear.

I glared at him with all the coldness I could summon.

"When it snows in hell, Mr. Delveau. On *that* day I will come willingly to your bed!"

To emphasize my point, I stepped to the door that adjoined my cabin with Delveau's. I dropped the bolt lock. After I'd done so, fear rampaged through me. I was afraid to turn and look at him. Had I enraged him? Oh, God, it was not safe to do. I was in his power. He could do with me as he wished—beat me, lock me in my cabin, force me to do demeaning things . . .

Heart pounding, I stared down at my own feet, suddenly timid as a dove. He startled me by bursting into low, rich laughter, and my eyes flew to his face.

He was amused not angered, and I was bewildered by his reaction. He got up, came toward me and lifted my chin with his fingertips. I looked up into dark eyes I could not read.

"Poor little Dianna," he said, laughing. "Her downfall will be her monumental pride."

I swallowed.

"Then we are well matched," I whispered bitterly.

He looked at me.

"So we might be," he said.

To my surprise, he gently brushed my lips with his mouth.

Then he strode to the door, leaving me standing there, shaken and confused. His kiss had been warm and kind—stirring.

He opened the door, stepped into the passageway, then poked his head back into the room with a wry smile.

"Until it snows in hell, Madam?"

CHAPTER 10

By dinnertime, we were out upon open water. The sea chopped at the *Joanna*, but the captain insisted we were in no sea at all.

It was sea enough for me. Already I had bruises on my arms from unexpected pitches I'd taken while trying to find my sea legs. There was a sickly humming in the pit of my stomach, and my forehead was cold and moist. I tried to make little of my growing discomfort, but ignoring it was becoming more and more difficult.

At dinner, when a particularly heavy swell sent the *Joanna* tipping and scudding, Dr. Tibbs's color went to ash. Without a word, he leapt from his chair and left us.

Dr. Osborne, on the other hand, was only mildly disturbed by the sea and insisted that Missy felt perfectly well. I smiled to myself as Missy, sitting white-faced and tight-lipped beside him, strained to look perfectly well as the ship listed and then righted itself.

Mrs. Creel had come to dinner overdressed. While I wore a simple, high-necked dress of muslin, she wore green-and-black-striped tabby silk with a necklace of jet-black stones and long glittering earbobs to match. A scarf of black satin was woven into her red-tinted hair, and I could tell she'd rouged her lips and cheeks—though it was done subtly. She looked cheap and common, but the men did not seem to notice that.

Mrs. Creel drew every man's eye and she dominated the dinner table with her low, musical voice and her eagerness to laugh at every man's attempted witticism. When dinner ended, Delveau offered her his arm for a stroll on the deck. She accepted with an alacrity not becoming a widow woman, and I was left to stroll with the captain. Feigning weariness, I retired to my cabin.

To my annoyance, the friendship between Delveau and Mrs. Creel grew as the days wore on. He took her for his partner in whist with Dr. Tibbs and Dr. Osborne, while I sat alone with a book. Their friendship soon bloomed on a first-name basis, and one morning as I approached the dining room for breakfast, I heard them arguing lightheartedly about the merits of Madeira wine.

"But you are wrong, North," Mrs. Creel cried out prettily in her annoyingly melodious voice.

"But I'm *not* wrong, Amanda," Delveau teased. "You have your Madeiras mixed up!"

As I entered the room, stiff with anger, they fell silent. Throughout breakfast they addressed each other formally as "Mrs. Creel," "Mr. Delveau."

On the second week out, as I stood alone at the rail, only partially captivated by the strange spectacle of flying fish, Mrs. Creel approached and stood beside me.

"You are unwise, Mrs. Delveau, to let such a husband slip through your fingers," she said mildly.

I whirled around. I gave her a withering look. Hate for Delveau boiled hot in me. How dare he tell this low woman anything of our affairs!

She raised her hand in protest as she read the outrage in my face.

"Please do not misunderstand. North has said nothing. But I have eyes. I've not lived some forty years without recognizing an estranged young couple when I see one."

I turned and stared hard at the sea, disdaining to answer, then changed my mind.

"Go away," I said, my voice ice.

The woman had grit. Stubbornly, she did not move.

"Mrs. Delveau, your husband is a proud man. I don't know what trouble lies between you, but I do know that *you* must be the one to set it aright. *You* must go to him."

I stared at the sea, refusing her an answer.

She sighed.

"He is in love with you, you know. It is in his eyes whenever he glances at you."

My heart lurched. I clenched the rail.

"I do not need *your* advice."

She sighed again.

"I know. You are a Brandley, and I am far below your station. But, North Delveau is a good man. He deserves to be made happy."

I made a sound of disgust.

She paused. Her voice hardened slightly.

"If you won't make him happy, then others shall," she warned.

I stabbed her with a contemptuous look and stalked off to my cabin.

On a later night, I was startled awake by a sound near my head. I shifted up on my elbows and peered into the darkness, trying to make sense of my pitching environs.

I was on the *Joanna*, yes. This was my cabin.

The startling sound came again: soft laughter, followed by the low murmur of a masculine voice. I stared at the wall beside my head. Delveau. His cabin. A woman's muted laughter floated to me. Comprehension came as a shock. Delveau and Mrs. Creel. He was entertaining her in his cabin!

I leapt from my bunk, my sleepy fog dispelled in an instant. Judas! Was there no limit to the torment I must endure?

Although I had been admittedly treacherous in marrying him, his methods of revenge were fast evening the score. He had put me through a miserable bridal week and then abandoned me on our wedding night—and in front of guests. Then he'd made it plain to me that if I desired a husband's affection, I would have to ask for it! And now this! For surely he must realize I had ears.

I burned. I paced the small cabin in helpless frustration. At last, I tore the comforter from my bunk, wrapped it around my shoulders and flung myself into a chair for the night. It seemed hours before I could settle into any sort of sleep in a makeshift bed made even more uncomfortable by the question of what might be happening in Delveau's cabin.

Morning found my mood dark and grim. I dressed, then gritted my teeth and headed for breakfast. I was determined to deny Delveau the satisfaction of knowing I had overheard. I would behave as normally as possible.

He was alone at the table. A wary look crossed his face as I walked in. He stood and remained standing until I took my seat.

"Good morning," I said evenly, willing my tone to be polite yet indifferent.

"Good morning," he returned carefully.

His dark eyes narrowed slightly as he searched my face. But he said nothing more to me, nor I to him. When the galley boy brought my eggs and fried bread, I forced myself to eat with relish.

The captain soon joined us at table.

"Did you rest well, Mrs. Delveau? I fear you were tossed about by the squall line we crossed near dawn."

I smiled at him.

"I always sleep like the dead," I lied. "Father used to tease me, saying a dog fight could go on under my bed and I should sleep peacefully through it!"

The captain laughed, but Delveau looked at me sharply.

My little act was costing me in nerves. As I reached for my tea with a trembling hand, I unwittingly knocked over the cup. Tea flooded the cloth. To my surprise and dismay, I found myself bursting into tears.

The captain patted my hand.

"There, there now, Mrs. Delveau. It's only spilt tea I'm sure."

I flashed a look of hate at Delveau. He met my eyes without

flinching, and I detected satisfaction in his gaze. I leapt up and fled the room.

By dinnertime I had recovered myself. I vowed I would not give Delveau the pleasure of seeing me sulk in my cabin. I dressed carefully, selecting a gown of delphinium blue to emphasize the color of my eyes. The gown's low neckline was banded in deeper blue velvet. It clung to my bosom gracefully, exposing my shoulders and drawing the eye to the little valley between the swells of my breasts.

No one would look at Mrs. Creel tonight! I had Nan fix my hair carefully, coaxing curls to spill over a blue satin hair band.

But I was not prepared for the emotions that attacked from within as I seated myself across from Mrs. Creel at dinner. While I'd lectured myself that it was nothing to me if Delveau made love to every slattern he met, I could not account for the feelings of hurt and anger that set me shaking whenever Mrs. Creel spoke. I longed to reach out, grab those tinted red curls, and yank them out by the roots.

Carefully, I avoided being drawn into conversation lest my voice betray my agitated state. With my eyes on my plate, I picked at food while the others conversed. As usual, much of the men's conversation was directed to Mrs. Creel. Dr. Tibbs was asking, "Mrs. Creel, what duties will fall to you in your brother's household?"

She gave him a friendly smile, and I was annoyed to see the bald spot on Dr. Tibbs's head turn pink with pleasure.

"Oh, the *children*, Dr. Tibbs," she said with enthusiasm. "Mr. Creel and I were never blessed with children, and I do love young ones. I expect to have my time quite taken up in the rearing of them."

The captain leaped into the topic, wagging a finger at Mrs. Creel.

"I know your brother. He's a bit of a pennypincher. Mark me, he'll have you working in the Brandley-Cartwright office in your spare moments!"

She laughed prettily.

"That he may. I don't wonder if I may not be obliged to earn my keep by selling hogsheads of tobacco and barrels of pork!"

Dr. Tibbs entered the teasing. Grinning at Mrs. Creel, he turned to me.

"Mrs. Delveau, would you have any objection to Mrs. Creel earning her keep by working in your father's store?"

I eyed Mrs. Creel with distaste.

"I would have no objection at all," I replied coolly. "I'm sure Mrs. Creel has had plenty of experience in selling her wares."

There was an astonished silence round the table.

Two red spots began to burn in Mrs. Creel's rouged cheeks. Her eyes filled with tears. She made an attempt at rising with dignity.

"Excuse me," she said. "I am feeling unwell."

Delveau was the only man not looking at Mrs. Creel. He looked at me, his face darkening with outrage. He rose slowly, his furious eyes piercing me. I jumped up from the table and fled.

He caught up to me just as I was trying to slam the door of my cabin and bolt it fast. He pushed his way in and I flew across the small room and stood with my back to him, terrified of what he might do.

My neck jerked as I heard him slide the bolt in the lock. I wrapped my arms around my body to keep from shaking.

"Get out!" I tried.

Behind me, Delveau said nothing for a long time. He did not come near. At last, in a voice that was very low, very controlled, he said, "Please turn and face me, Madam."

I didn't move.

Again, the deadly voice.

"Turn, Madam. Do not force me to touch you or, by God, I fear what I might do."

His tone told me he meant every word. I whirled around to face him, eyes brimming with tears I refused to release in his detestable presence.

His face was dark, more terrifying than I'd ever seen it. The scar seemed very white in contrast. I shuddered as he took one step toward me.

"You will apologize to the lady."

His arrogant tone told me he assumed I would obey without question. Hate rose in me.

"No!"

I glared at him.

"And she is no lady!" I added.

He smiled coldly.

"At some other time I might be amused to hear your definition of the word 'lady.' You call Amanda no lady. What, then, do you call a woman who tricks one man into marriage so that she can bed another?"

The truth cut. I lashed back.

"You! You would bed down with anyone! I suppose next you will seduce Missy!"

He laughed harshly.

"You judge me by your own standards. But I do not steal what belongs to another."

His reference to Lady Olga stabbed me to the quick. I cast my eyes to the floor, willing myself not to tremble before him.

"You *will* apologize to Mrs. Creel."

"Never! Who do you think you are ordering about! I am a Brandley!"

"A Brandley? I think not. You are Dianna Delveau now. You have taken my name and, by God, I will not allow you to disgrace it. You *will* apologize."

I burst out, "Beat me if you will! Still, I will *not* apologize."

He smiled, and suddenly I knew I would be wise to fear the smile much more than the scowl.

"Oh, I will not beat you," he said. "But I am your husband, Madam, and it is within my power to make your life a living hell."

I was stunned.

As I stared up into his stiff angry face, I suddenly realized how completely I was in his power. He was my legal owner. He could put me to live where he pleased. He could see to it that I was separated from Christian forever! I would be a stranger in a strange land—totally at his mercy. The thought terrified me.

My voice dropped to a whisper.

"If you force me to apologize to this low woman, you bolt the door between us for all time."

He flinched. But then he laughed, and his laughter hurt my pride even though that laughter seemed to hold a measure of sadness.

"You have already bolted the door, Madam," he said softly.

He looked down into my eyes for a moment longer. For an instant, he seemed to waver, as though he might be merciful and spare me this humiliation. But then, he straightened his shoulders. He strode purposefully to the door, unlocked it and threw it open for me to pass through.

With a heart heavy with anguish, I dragged myself forward to make my apologies.

After that day, the rift between Delveau and myself was irreparable. My encounters with him were few. Few words passed between us.

The voyage became long and lonely, and I had to admit that I missed the excitement that had often marked our spirited exchanges. Somehow, the man stimulated my mind as no other man had done. I was never so witty as when sparring with him.

As for Mrs. Creel, I did not know if he slept with her. Judging from looks that sometimes passed between them, I guessed that he did. But at least he spared me the pain of doing it where I might hear.

I was lonely. Nan was small comfort. She was head over heels in love with Delveau's man, Sandy, and spent all of her free time with him. She spoke constantly of marriage, and it was painful for me to observe them together as they walked the deck at sunset. They were so innocently happy.

Then one day, Nan burst into my cabin. She gave a little sob.

"He's got him a *wife*, Danni!"

I looked up at her, not comprehending.

She said it again, sobbing.

Her meaning stabbed home. I jumped up and rushed to her, putting my arms around her.

"Nan, dear Nan, I'm so sorry. How cruel of Sandy not to confess to a wife at the start."

She stopped sobbing. She lifted her head and gave me a perplexed look.

"Not Sandy," she said, astonished at my response. "I mean Mr. Delveau."

I was shocked silent. I stared at her.

Nan's eyes widened in fear.

"It's true, Danni. Sandy told me. Mr. Delveau, he's got a Indian wife."

I reached for the wall to steady myself.

"Sandy lies."

"No he don't."

When she began to weep, I realized she was not making up stories. The room seemed to spin. I staggered to a chair and fell into it.

"Hush, Nan. Feel free to tell me all," I whispered, my voice cracking.

According to Sandy, Delveau had lived with the Cherokee Nation for two years. The chief had a beautiful daughter called Starlight. Delveau and the girl had fallen in love. The chief had given his daughter to Delveau in tribal marriage.

The marriage was not a legal one by white men's standards, but Delveau considered himself married. He kept it secret so as not to break the old comte's heart. Only Sandy knew where Delveau went on his long absences in Virginia. He went to be with his beloved wife.

When Nan was done, I ordered her out in a shaking voice. I had to be alone. My head was spinning. My heart felt as though some giant had taken it in his hand and crushed it. I was so distraught I couldn't sort out the feelings that ripped through me. Anger? Disgust? Yes, certainly. To have a husband who consorted with savages was not to be borne! But jealousy stabbed at me, too. He *loved* her. Loved!

My mind flew back to the night of the dinner party when Delveau and I had sat in the rose garden, talking about how to extricate ourselves from the pledge. I'd admitted my love for Christian. Delveau had admitted to loving, too.

What was it he'd said?

My mind spun round, bringing back the scene:

"I, too, am committed," he'd said.

And then I'd asked, "Is she beautiful?"

His eyes had gone tender with yearning. He'd stared at me, not seeing me, but seeing someone else who was far away.

"Very," he'd answered softly.

The memory tortured me. Delveau had been honest. I could not fault him there. But, never had I imagined the deepness of his commitment. To consider himself *married* to a savage!

I began to cry. I had tricked him into this marriage, and now I could see what I would reap. Though he might call me Dianna Delveau, he thought of another as his true wife.

I wanted to hate him. I willed myself to hate him. Bitterly, I reflected that Delveau had put Sandy up to telling Nan about the Indian woman. He would know that Nan would tell me. Of course! He was cruel enough to torment me in this way. . . .

I stayed in my cabin for several days. When I did rejoin the ship's small community, I was a silent and subdued young woman. I studied Delveau through the cold eyes of hate. The intensity of my feelings would scarcely allow me to pull my eyes from him. I knew he must be aware of my constant gaze, but I couldn't help myself.

One evening, as I left the ship's dining room, I was startled to find Delveau waiting for me in the passageway.

"Is there something you wish to say to me, Madam?" he asked coolly, his dark eyes puzzled.

Without a word, I fled from him.

A violent summer storm caught the *Joanna* just days before we were to anchor in the Azores for supplies. The storm sent the *Joanna* pitching and bucking.

I welcomed the storm and the terrible seasickness it brought me; physical suffering was a respite from mental and spiritual torture. As the *Joanna* bucked wildly, I lay in my bunk in misery. Nan could not serve me because she lay seasick herself. Dr. Tibbs and Dr. Osborne offered laudanum, but the drug only made me sleep deeply, then wake to redoubled suffering.

On the fourth day of my illness I lay in my bunk, too weak even to open my eyes as I heard the creak of my cabin door.

It would only be the galley boy, trying to encourage me with hot broth which tended to come up only minutes after I swallowed it.

"Dianna?"

The voice was low and gentle.

I struggled to open my eyes. It was Delveau. With a whimper, I rolled away from him. He sat on the edge of my bed and rested his hand on my arm.

"Dianna, let me help you."

"Go away!" I sobbed. "I am so sick I only want to die. Go tend your Indian wife!"

A sharp breath caught in his throat. His fingers tensed on my arm.

"By God. Sandy."

He leaped up and strode to the door, bellowing into the passageway.

"Sandy! Damn it, get in here!"

His servant came on the run.

"I will deal with your big mouth later," he barked. "Get a pot of boiling-hot tea. Bring my medicine pouch. Get fresh towels, bedding and a bucket of warm water. And tell that cabin boy that if he isn't in here in two minutes to clean up this cabin, I will have the pleasure of skinning him alive and throwing him to the sharks!"

Within moments, there was a frenzy of activity around me. Groaning with pain, I shut my eyes to it.

Delveau helped me to sit up and made me drink tea. It was bitter with herbs he'd put into it. I shuddered.

"No, please, no! It will only come up again."

"It won't," he said softly. "Trust me, Dianna. Drink it."

He held me and helped me to drink it. Then I sank back upon the pillow, fearfully awaiting the retching. It did not come. To my relief, the spasms in my stomach began to subside.

When the room was cleaned and everyone had gone out, Delveau sat on my bed.

"I'm going to wash you," he said.

"No!" I whimpered, too weak and ill to move.

His voice was kind:

"Don't be afraid, Dianna. I'm your husband. I won't hurt you."

I was too weak to stop his ministrations. His hands were surprisingly gentle and careful as he drew off my soiled shift. He helped me to scrub my teeth, and then began to wash me with toweling and warm water.

As his gentle hands worked down to my breasts, tears of embarrassment and helplessness trickled from beneath my lashes and ran down my cheeks.

He saw my tears and stopped at once. He wrapped me in a comforter, lifted me up easily in his strong arms and carried me to a chair. I sat there, dizzy, as he quickly stripped off the old bedding and put on fresh linens. He carried me back to my bunk and deposited me there gently. The fresh linens were heaven, and my stomach no longer hurt. Without even a glance at Delveau, I gave in to my fatigue and fell into deep sleep.

When I awoke again, Delveau was still in my cabin. He fed me more bitter tea and a small piece of toasted bread which I gobbled down like a starving man.

"Go back to sleep," he ordered.

My eyes closed instantly.

Hours later, as I lay drifting in the limbo between sleeping and waking, I imagined I felt warm lips lightly brush my cheek. I imagined a low voice murmured, "Sleep well, my love."

But when I woke, I knew I must have dreamed it. I shifted up on my elbows, looking round for Delveau. He was gone.

A strange feeling of disappointment tugged at my heart. I sank back upon my pillow, wondering at his kindness to me. But instantly, his kindness was blotted out by the images of Amanda Creel and the Indian woman. He was a devil. Tears slid down my cheeks.

When the storm passed, we put in to the Azores islands to take on fresh food and water. During our days there, Delveau disappeared on long walks over the island. He seemed careful to never walk in the direction in which I took my airing.

The bleakness of the windy volcanic island matched my mood. The island was lonely, and I was lonely. To cheer myself, I imagined how happy I would be if Christian were with me, walking at my side, exploring the island and strolling through the exotic marketplace near the ship's mooring.

Our journey continued on to Barbados, for the *Joanna* could not sail directly into the westerly winds of the season. She must tack her way up the American coast from Barbados.

About two months into our journey, Nan was sitting with me one day in my cabin. She was mending the torn hem of one of my gowns as I worked on business ledgers, trying to memorize essential figures.

Suddenly, I was aware of her eyes studying me. I looked up questioningly.

"How long since your woman's time come, Danni?"

Her question took me by surprise. I flipped the ledger closed.

"Why—I—don't recall. So much has happened that I haven't paid proper attention. The wedding, my bout with sea-sickness—"

She smiled knowingly.

"He's got you to breeding."

"What!"

The shock of her statement paralyzed me.

She grinned, her brown eyes dancing.

"I said, Mr. Delveau has got you with child."

It was as though she'd hit me upon the head with a board. Stunned, I rose and stumbled to my bunk. My mind flew back to a night I had sworn to put out of my mind forever. I clutched the coverlet as panic fingered the bottom of my heart.

Nan went on happily.

"Lor' lummy, Danni, look at the signs. Breasts swull up. Gown tight at the waist."

Fear pounded in me. I rejected Nan's theory violently.

"Nonsense! I've gained weight, yes. The sea air gives me an appetite, and I happen to have been eating like a pig! Women say they tend to miss their time during a voyage. It happens to many, and I don't want you to say another word about it!"

Nan shrugged and went back to her sewing.

The new worry made me stumble through the days in a numb state. Could Nan be right? Was it possible I carried Sir Gordon's child?

The thought revolted me, struck terror into the very heart

of my being. I could *not* be pregnant. For I felt extremely well, except for occasional small bouts of seasickness. I would surely know if I were with child!

I brushed Nan's ridiculous theory from my mind. As the days went by, I clung to all the stories I'd heard about women missing their times during arduous ocean crossings. I would get my woman's time, I was convinced, as soon as I left the ship and set foot upon solid ground in Virginia.

CHAPTER 11

"Judas! It ain't a very friendly-looking place," Nan said. We stood watching at the rail as the *Joanna* shuddered in the changing current and nosed into the Potomac River.

I acknowledged her statement with a shiver of excitement. America frightened and thrilled me. It was both the most beautiful land I'd ever seen and the most wild.

Virginia seemed nothing but endless mile upon mile of wilderness. Her shores were choked with marsh, bog and forest. The thick tangle of trees seemed to march directly to the water's edge, even leaning out over the water as though the wilderness wished to dominate there, too.

Its beauty made my heart stand still. It was late October and the foliage was glorious. I'd never beheld such color—reds so pure and bright that they made one's spirit sing, canary yellows and molten golds, purplish scarlets, bronzes and deep burnished browns. When the sun dipped to a low angle in the afternoons, it seemed as though all of America were aflame.

Where towns and settlements crouched along the shore, the wilderness had been beaten back. But even in those places, one felt that if the townsmen were careless and overslept one day, the wilderness would steal in and snatch back what once it owned.

Sandy's eyes shone in excitement as he stood with us at the rail, showing Nan his country. In his odd, turtlelike manner, he politely ducked his head at me and cleared his throat to speak. He nodded toward a small clearing on shore as the *Joanna* slid by.

"M'am, you be seein' your first Indian village." He ducked his head shyly again. "The Pamunky, M'am. There not be many of the tribe left. Dead mostly. From pestilence and tribe wars."

I watched the settlement slide by. I could see a few rough dwellings. They were hewn-tree huts and smaller contrivances covered with hides and sheets of tree bark. Brown children romped, playing with barking dogs. The children raced along the bank, laughing, racing the *Joanna*.

A few adults moved in the settlement. I was surprised to see they wore the clothing of the colonies, although some of the men wore britches of deer hide. I had expected them to look savage. But, rather, they looked impoverished and not so very different from London's poor.

The Potomac River surprised me. It was heavily traveled, and teeming with ships and boats of all kinds and tonnage: small inland vessels that carried tobacco and salted pork down from the plantations and large ocean-going ships like the *Joanna*. There were also fragile barks which Sandy called canoes. In the canoes were savages, going about their own business upon the river.

As the day wore on, the Potomac suddenly broadened from about a mile wide to twice that breadth. There, it formed a large, crescent-shaped bay. Nestled in the center of the crescent lay the town of Alexandria.

As we sailed nearer, I could see, on one end of the town, an immense wharf of warehouses. At the other end, a dock for shipbuilding. Skeletons of half a dozen ships under construction loomed above the horizon.

I was too excited to stand still. Christian should know of this fine bay! He should know of the forest of ship timber that filled Virginia! How much more cheaply we could build Brand-ley-Cartwright ships here—with a wilderness full of free lumber—than in Plymouth, where lumber was becoming scarce and costly, and ships were constructed at a slow rate of only one or two a year.

As we drew close enough to read the signs on the buildings, I was startled to find the name of Delveau in many places. Delveau Ship Builders. Delveau Tobacco. Delveau Trade Company. I was taken aback. I'd known the family was wealthy and thoroughly rooted in Virginia, but still . . .

The *Joanna* hove to and maneuvered into her slip opposite warehouses labeled for my father's company. The wharf and the town running uphill from it boiled with activity and commerce. Carriages and conveyances of all sorts clattered in all directions.

Men on horseback shouted to women in mobcaps who leaned out of the upper-story windows of merchants' shops to watch the *Joanna* dock. The women shouted back. All activity along the wharf seemed centered upon the loading and unloading of vessels. All was such a bustle that it was difficult to discern which ship was being loaded, which unloaded.

I was so caught up in the drama that I ran to the stern off the *Joanna* for a better view. I glanced down at our ramp as four men slung it into the dock with a crash.

Delveau stood near the ramp. As soon as the ramp settled into place, he was over the rail and onto the wharf without even a backward glance. I leaned forward to see his intent.

At that moment, a woman stepped out of the shadows of a building and hurried toward him. She wore a plain gown of blue callimanco and a cloak to match.

I caught my breath.

She was one of the most stunning-looking women I had ever seen. She was Indian—no mistake about that. She was very tall, regal in bearing and, I noted with a shock, unmistakably with child.

A dull pain spread through me as I saw joy quicken their steps as they hurried to meet. She was lovely. In the sunlight, her skin glowed a golden brown. Her delicate black brows arched over wide-set, slightly almond-shaped eyes. A sudden

123

breeze from the river caught her, rippling through her long, blue-black hair and stirring it as the finest silk is stirred out-of-doors.

I clenched the rail. It was she, of course. What was the name Nan told me? Starlight. Bitterly, I reflected that the name suited her.

Her smile grew more radiant by the moment as they drew close. I flinched, fearing he would embrace her, but he did not touch her. They stood looking at each other, not speaking but only feasting on the look in the other's eyes.

At last he bent toward her and they talked. When I saw her shoulders slump and a look of dismay shoot across her fine features, I knew he had told her. She closed her eyes as though to absorb the pain. As she did so, Delveau reached out and protectively placed his hand on her shoulder. She raised her face to his and gave him a fierce, proud smile.

I could bear to watch no longer.

Turning, I stumbled blindly to my cabin, and with shaking hands, poured out a glass of sherry. Then I sank to my bunk, trying to regain my composure. Why should it bother me so! Why should I care that he seemed to love her so! He was not *my* love. Christian was that. Christian would always be that.

Then why should my heart be so full of heaviness? Why should it throb to the point of bursting?

It is because she is a savage. His consorting with a savage is an insult to me as his wife. A humiliation! And he does not care!

My hurt flared into hot anger.

Heaping coals upon the fires of my anger, Delveau abandoned me to Sandy for debarkation. It was Sandy who arranged for the chaises, gigs and wagons to take me and my things, Dr. Tibbs and the Osbornes and Nan to Delveau's Alexandria house on Captain's Row. And it was Sandy, not Delveau, who told me we would spend the night before journeying on to the old comte's country estate.

I sat in the chaise, stiff with anger, as we started up Captain's Row. The street was cobbled and slanted sharply up from the wharf. Delveau's house was at the top of the street, overlooking the bay.

The house was four stories tall, with a dependency on each side. As I stepped from the chaise, I caught a glimpse of the garden, stretching back along one side of the house and widening behind it.

A servant respectfully held open the door. As I crossed the threshold, I hesitated, overwhelmed suddenly with a sense of change in the order of my affairs. At Brandley Manor, I had dominated. On the ship, Delveau and I had resisted each other's attempt to dominate. But here? This was his house, his country. . . .

As I entered his house, I sensed at once that he was master here. This was only his business house, and I'd expected crude and indifferent furnishings. But the house was much like the man. Touches of elegance surprised one, and everything was understated and in good taste. The floors were carpeted in soft rugs from the East. A delicate silk screen from China hung upon alabaster-white papered walls in the entryway. A half dozen doors stood open from the entryway, and I could see the same subdued elegance in every direction. All was polished and dusted as though the master had been in residence all along. Only from the kitchens came the low buzz of chaos as servants coped with the unexpected crisis of dinner for six, plus servants' fare.

I stood in the entryway, feeling out of place and wondering where to take myself, when Delveau appeared from the back of the house. He nodded to me, then greeted the Osbornes and Dr. Tibbs, playing the part of the gracious host. It was as if he had not—only an hour earlier—been consorting with a savage. I drew myself up, angered that he should take it all in his stride. One wife or two. What did it matter to him?

He summoned a servant to show the Osbornes and Dr. Tibbs to their lodgings in the dependency so they might rest before dinner. Then, without a word, he took my arm and led me through the house to the kitchens. He introduced me to the servants and bond-servants, falling into easy conversation with each as he did so. Had the expected birth gone well for the cook? A son? Fine, excellent. And how had the gardener managed to break his arm? He must be more careful in the future.

When he was done and the servants finished their polite

curtsies and bows, he again took my arm and led me to the entryway. He nodded at the gracefully curving stairwell.

"Your room is at the head of the stairs. Your things have been brought."

"Thank you," I said coldly.

I glared into his eyes.

His gaze fell away. He knew that I had seen her.

"Dianna, I—I should have explained—"

He paused, and to my deep chagrin, I felt my eyelashes grow wet with tears I couldn't control. He looked away.

"Dinner is at eight," he finished softly.

"May I have your permission to take a tray in my room?"

He flinched.

"As you wish."

I gave him my back. Picking up my skirts, I hurried up the staircase. Oh, God, I wanted out of this house! How could I bear it a moment longer? Mid-way up the stairs, I stopped and whirled around. He was standing below, watching me.

"I must visit my father's business offices at once. May I have your permission to order the chaise?"

He reached out and rubbed the banister for a time, without answering.

"You have no need to seek my permission. Order the servants as you wish."

His unexpected kindness brought fresh pain.

"I—I didn't know if I had the right—" I explained softly.

"You are mistress in this house."

A lump rose in my throat. I turned and hurried up the stairs. Mistress? In what ways would I be mistress here? To order the running of the house that his life might proceed smoothly, allowing him leisure to be with her? Hurt and anger throbbed in my veins.

My room was as fresh, clean and well-ordered as the floor below. Fresh flowers, late blooming roses, had been put in the room. I could see the flowers had been a hasty act; droplets of water upon the chest attested to it. No servant would think of such an act. Delveau. I felt both touched and angered anew that he'd made this small gesture, this wordless request for peace between us. At the same time, the fragrance of the roses

126

reminded me of home and I was filled with sudden despair. I felt so alone, so unloved.

I sank onto the little bench before the large French looking glass and stared at myself. I was nothing compared to her. The sea air had wilted my hair even though it had changed the color to a much paler gold. My skin bloomed in health, but I'd been careless in the sun. My fair shoulders were deeply tanned. My figure was full and must be pleasing to a man's eye, but on the whole I looked sea-worn.

The thought that I'd let my looks slip upset me. I sent for Nan at once. My father's business could wait. I did not intend to mope about, playing second fiddle to Starlight's dark beauty.

With Nan's help, I bathed and washed my hair. I selected the gown I'd been married in—in an unguarded moment on our wedding day, I'd seen Delveau eye it admiringly—and I sent it down to the fluting irons. Nan did my hair. The sun and sea air had bleached the tawniness out of it, and the color was almost the identical ivory of the satin gown. Nan arranged it in a pleasing tumble of curls, though stray tendrils, misbehaving after the dose of sea air, curled at my temples.

As a gesture to Delveau that I too wanted peace between us, I tucked a fragrant rosebud into my hair.

When I descended to dinner, the sun had set, the stars were out and candles glowed in the lower part of the house. A murmur of voices floated up from the drawing room. The click of my heels on the stairway brought Delveau at once.

His face registered surprise. He stood at the bottom of the stairs, appearing fresh from barber and tailor. He watched my descent without comment. He held out his hand. I placed mine on his and both our hands seemed to tremble for an instant. Then, smoothly, he led me toward the drawing room.

"You look lovely," he said unexpectedly, and I could tell from his tone that he meant it.

"Thank you."

He gave me a puzzled smile.

"Not at all. I liked that gown the first time I saw it."

The meaning of his words sank in slowly. My heart lurched to a stop. To me, the gown was only a gown. But was it more to him because I'd married in it? Did he assume I was offering him another wedding night?

I flushed, angry at his confident assumption, but angrier with myself. How could I have been so foolish as to wear it! I reddened and said nothing more. He chuckled softly and led me to join the Osbornes and Dr. Tibbs.

He seated me at the end of the table where a wife should sit and then took his position opposite. Dinner was formal, and I was glad our guests were in a talkative mood, for I sat quiet and subdued, inwardly castigating myself for my gaffe. I was deeply embarrassed. What must he be thinking as he conversed easily with Tibbs and Osborne about the problems of dealing in tobacco? His face gave me no clue.

Dinner proceeded. There were two excellent wines, a joint of roasted meat, fresh poached rock fish from the Potomac and pies of pumpkin and apple. Immediately after dining, Dr. Tibbs and the Osbornes retired to the dependency, averring, as they were leaving, that they welcomed a night's rest in a bed that did not pitch and rock.

As we stood in the entryway bidding them good night, Delveau's arm went around my waist in a casual, husbandly manner. I knew he was doing it because of the gown. My cheeks flamed up. I stiffened, realizing the gentleman in him would feel obliged to make some sort of gesture. Oh, God, how degrading! I had practically offered myself to him by wearing the dress.

The door closed behind Dr. Tibbs with a final sounding thump. My heart raced in the moment of silence that followed. Then Delveau dipped his head and softly brushed his lips on my bared shoulder.

"Dianna—"

I flinched, wrenching myself away. I would *not* be taken by him out of pity! Did he dare to presume I needed his attention?

I whirled at him.

"Please do not touch me!"

His head jerked back as though I had slapped him. His eyes flashed wide with hurt, then narrowed.

"As you wish, Madam."

I turned and fled from him, rushing into the drawing room. I stood alone on the splendid Oriental carpet, trying to sort out the thoughts and emotions that churned in me. I stood there motionless, like a wild animal caught in fear. Whom did I fear? Was it Delveau? Or was it myself?

I felt suddenly cold, chilled. I couldn't go to my room because I might meet him on the stairs or in the corridor above. I moved to the fireplace, grateful for the small October fire crackling there. I wrapped my arms around my body, rubbing away the goose bumps.

Above the carved marble mantel hung a portrait of a dark-eyed, high spirited young woman. She had North's eyes. Aunt Matilde had told me Charlotte Delveau was only eighteen when she married the middle-aged comte. There had been only one child of the match—North.

I eyed Charlotte with sympathy. What sort of match had it been for a young woman whose eyes looked so bold and alive with a love of living? What had it been like, this marriage to a man far her senior? I would never know. Her portrait gave no clue.

I jumped as Delveau unexpectedly entered the room. He ignored me, moving to the low table where he kept his tobacco supplies. He took what he wanted, then went past me, overlooking my presence as though I were no more than an extra chair in the room.

His indifference was a hundred times more insulting than his touch had been. I felt the sting of it awaken the shrew in me.

"Where are you going?" I demanded without thought.

He didn't bother to give me a glance.

"Out."

"To your Indian whore?"

The words escaped before I knew they were even in my mind. I gasped and would have offered some sort of apology, but he turned on me, his eyes blazing with fury.

"Not whore, but *wife!*"

I rocked at the insult. So he felt she was my equal! Or more than my equal. I gritted my teeth.

"Dirty Indian squaw, you mean!"

I cried out in fear as he flung his tobacco things to a chair and came toward me, his eyes full of anger. He seized me and shook me roughly. My head flew back. The rose I'd tucked in my hair tumbled to the rug.

"Goddamn you! She is my wife in the true sense of the word—as *you* are not!"

With a snarl of fury I broke loose from him and cracked the palm of my hand against his face. He jerked back, his eyes aflame. For a moment I feared he would hit me, but then, very slowly, the anger began to die in his eyes.

He reached out, took my shoulders in his grasp, pulled me close, and studied my unwilling eyes. His strong fingers pressed into the bare flesh of my shoulders.

"Could it be you are jealous, Dianna?" he asked softly.

I tried to pull away but could not. I started to cry.

"No!"

"Could it be you want to become my wife in the true sense of the word?"

A small wild sob came from somewhere deep within me.

"Let me go!"

He did not. He stared at me intently, and I could not hide the odd little shiver that ran through me as his eyes captured and held mine. His voice fell to a murmur.

"Your words are no, but your eyes and your body say yes. Which message shall I answer, Dianna?"

I glared up at him, tears of helplessness and frustration collecting in my lashes. How was it he always seemed to get the upper hand when we fought? How was it that I always ended up being the humiliated one?

At my tears, he made a soft sound, then slowly drew me into the warm circle of his arms. His head dipped down to mine. I shut my eyes, trembling, truly not knowing if I welcomed the kiss or dreaded it.

Then, his lips were moving softly on mine. It was a wooing kind of kiss. I would have had to be made of steel to resist. Gently, his mouth explored, coaxed, invited. My bones turned to water. I fought none of it. Oh, his mouth . . .

With an eagerness I knew I should be ashamed of, I returned

130

his kiss. He made a low sound of pleasure and drew me even closer.

Against my will, my hands stole up his coat and curled around his neck. For a long moment we seemed to melt into each other, as sea and sun melt together at the moment of sunset. I hovered on the brink of sweet surrender, but then, like a sudden sword slash, the image of the Indian woman cut between us.

Was I to demean myself by sharing my husband with a savage? I, Dianna Brandley?

I tore my mouth from his.

We stood looking at each other, breathless.

"Please, North, don't—don't—"

"You know nothing of love," he said softly. "Love is not one of your pretty gowns that you use one day and cast aside the next. You must understand me, Danni. When I love, I love forever."

He pressed my shoulders gently as though to press home his words.

"Starlight is my wife. She carries my child. I can no more stop myself from loving her than I can stop myself from beginning to care for you."

My heart lurched.

I searched his dark eyes. There was a vulnerability there which I'd never seen before. More, there was invitation. His eyes invited me into an intimacy that I sensed would go far beyond the physical.

I trembled and pulled my gaze from his.

He brushed his warm lips over my mouth.

"What shall it be, Danni? Shall I stay home this night and make you my wife?"

A sob caught in my throat. It was as though I did not know myself. My thoughts whirled in confusion. My pride collided with my yearnings.

He held me close, his fingers in my hair, holding my head to his pounding heart. Dizzy, I leaned into him, my cheek against the rough serge of his coat.

His lips were upon my forehead, then in my hair.

He whispered, "Be warned, little wife. If you invite me to your bed, you shall never be free of me."

Everything in me yearned toward assent. I longed to cry, "Yes!" But I could not give up my pride. Share him? With a savage? Dianna Brandley?

For a long time, I could not find my voice. When I found it, it was the faintest whisper.

"No."

He released me at once, and I felt as if I had been dropped off the edge of the world.

"As you wish, Danni."

He was gone from the room in an instant.

I fell into a chair and buried my face in my hands, trying frantically to sort out my thoughts. Was Delveau right? Did I know nothing of the true meaning of love?

The ache in my heart seemed to confirm it. Love was cruel. Painful. I *knew* I loved Christian—loved him with every fiber of my being. But why, then, did my knees go weak whenever Delveau came near? Why, then, did I thrill to his touch? Why did I enjoy our every confrontation, even our fighting and our wounding arguments? For even a fool could see that underneath our fighting and our harsh words, we were drawn to each other.

And God forbid, why did I like and respect him most when he got the upper hand over me?

I sat there, stunned, not knowing what to do.

As I huddled there, I heard him come bounding down the stairs. When he passed the drawing room door, I flinched at the sight of him. He was unrecognizable in deerskin breeches and shirt. With his dark hair and dark eyes, he might have passed for a savage.

Jolted, I sat there, tense, confused and heart-sore. If I didn't stop him, he would go to her.

I agonized. Delveau had told me once that I would sacrifice my own happiness on the altar of my pride. Was he right? Could I not, for once in my life, lay pride aside and humbly reach out for happiness?

I pulled myself to my feet and stumbled from the room. I made my way through the unfamiliar house and pushed open the heavy back door. I made my way through the dark, October-chilled garden and down the brick walk that must lead to the stable.

"North?" I called. "North?"

But only Sandy's voice answered me from the stable.

"He be gone, M'am. Be there somethin' I can get for you, M'am?"

With a heavy heart, I dragged myself back into the house and up to my room. Wearily, I undressed, pulled on a shift, snuffed out the candle and climbed into my cold bed.

Sleep would not come. Delveau's kisses lingered on my lips. His strong fingers seemed still to caress my shoulders. I tossed and turned, remembering. I got up. I relit the candle and paced the room. I found a book in a bureau drawer and tried to sit and read. But nothing gave me peace.

I took the candle and went out into the corridor. Aimless, I wandered its length, then back again. One door drew me each time I passed it. I knew it to be North's room. I hesitated long on the threshold, then opened the door and entered. I set the flickering candle on his nightstand and moved slowly about the room, touching his things—as though to touch his things would bring the owner back.

His waistcoat was thrown carelessly over a chair. I stroked it. Its roughness had met my cheek when he held me. On a table lay his pipes. I fingered them, remembering the fragrant aroma of his tobacco mixed with sea air. His buckskin pouch of herbs and medicines lay on the bed where he'd flung it. I sat down, running one finger along the fringe of the worn pouch. Had she made it for him, his Indian wife? She loved him, this poor woman who could have no hope of ever being recognized as his wife in North's world.

Sadness rushed in like a tide. A sadness both for Starlight and myself. What would become of us?

I lay back on his bed and pulled the comforter over me. With the pouch in my hand as talisman, I drifted into sleep.

At dawn, voices down in the stable yard yanked me awake. I jumped up, hurried to the window and looked out. The sun was just rising and North, still garbed in deerskin, was getting off his horse. He was giving orders to his stable man.

So he had stayed the night with her. . . .

Disappointment and injured pride smarted in me. He cared nothing that I had been left alone with the servants.

I turned in a panic. Quickly, I smoothed his bed and placed the pouch where I'd found it. He must never find out that I'd spent the night in his bed! I would die of shame.

I hurried to my room. In a few minutes there came a tapping at my door.

"Mistress?" a strange voice called out. "Mistress, the master requires you at breakfast, if you please, M'am. He says to tell you the coach leaves in thirty minutes, M'am."

CHAPTER 12

I dressed quickly in a travel costume of blue merino wool and donned the matching cloak.

Anxiously, I studied myself in the glass. Did I look all right? Would he think so?

For one who'd never been given to preening in front of a mirror, I suddenly found myself awash in self-doubt, hoping the mirror would alleviate my anxiety.

I was not unsatisfied by what I saw. The indigo blue made my hair glow like pale ivory. The color did its work upon my eyes as well, darkening them to the blue-violet of delphinium.

Yet, even as I searched the mirror, I felt a ripple of irritation at doing it. Why should I care what Delveau thought of my appearance! With a frown of self-disgust, I turned from the glass.

As I entered the dining room, Delveau, still dressed in buckskin, was at breakfast. He did not bother to glance at me. Hurriedly, he finished his food, rose and bounded up the stairs without a word or look.

A short time later, as I stood in the entryway while Nan

bossed Sandy about loading the trunks, Delveau reappeared. His conversion from savage to civilized gentleman jolted me. He was dressed in normal travel attire: boots, a rough serge suit of clothes and a three-tiered cloak of black wool.

I stepped back that he might pass through and out to the coaches and wagons. He started past me, then stopped suddenly. He reached out and touched my cheek with his fingertips.

I jumped at his unexpected touch, and my eyes flew to his face, questioning.

A faint, curious smile played at the corners of his mouth. His dark eyes were gentle.

I stared up at him, mystified. Then, at once, blood rushed to my face.

He knows! He knows I went to his room! How did he find out?

Mortified to the point of misery, I pulled my cloak around me and rushed past him to the coach. I felt his eyes follow me.

Dr. Tibbs, Dr. Osborne and Missy, Delveau and myself rode in the first coach. It was driven by two men who were armed with muskets. The second conveyance, a chaise, was loaded with valises and food hampers. Sandy drove. Nan, looking as though she were in seventh heaven, sat beside him. A wagon laden with trunks and crates brought up the rear.

To my immense relief, Delveau did not attempt any personal conversation during the journey. Rather, he played the genial host, entertaining the Osbornes and Dr. Tibbs with commentary on the passing countryside. He was attentive to questions and answered each, carefully, no matter how foolish the query.

"Shall we be attacked by savages, sir?"

Glancing fearfully at the muskets in the rack over our heads, Missy gripped her young husband's arm.

Delveau chuckled.

"The Indians are calm since Braddock's war with the French. I don't fear them. But I do fear the renegade—whether he is Indian, freed slave, British, French *or* American. But don't fret, Mrs. Osborne. Such attacks are rare. Usually, a musket volley will send renegades flying."

She was unconvinced. She hid her face against her husband's sleeve.

Delveau shifted in his seat and smiled down at me.

"Are *you* afraid?"

His tone was one of gentle teasing. I would have had to be blind and deaf to miss his double meaning. He was not referring to renegades.

My heart lurched. I met his eyes.

"No."

He smiled.

"Good."

To my consternation, I blushed under his gaze. I turned my head away. My pulse raced. I was completely certain, now. He *did* know I spent the night in his room. But how did he know? The puzzle tormented me. I scarcely listened as he turned his attention to Tibbs and Osborne, answering questions about Virginia wildlife, flora, crops and exports. In my mind I rehearsed each step that I'd taken from my room to his and back to mine. What clue had I left? I had smoothed the bed. I had placed his pouch where I found it. So how? My head ached from the puzzle. Then, quite suddenly, the answer came.

"The candle!" I said aloud, forgetting myself.

He looked down at me. His dark eyes lightened with amusement. He dipped his head and brushed my hair with his lips.

"But of course, the candle," he whispered into my hair. "You left the candle on my nightstand."

Flushing scarlet, I fixed my own gaze out the window.

When we stopped by a stream to rest the horses and refresh ourselves with food and wine from the hampers, Delveau did not hand me down from the coach. Instead, he startled me by putting his hands around my waist and lifting me down. Then, he clasped my hand in his and held it, as though we were an ordinary young couple on an outing. His hand was warm and strong, giving me such a feeling of well-being, such an aura of being under his protection, that I could not stop my fingers from pressing his in response.

He looked down at me, a pleased and surprised expression on his face. He smiled. Slowly, the smile widened to a grin.

"Hello, Mrs. Delveau," he said softly.

"Hello, North," I whispered, suddenly taken with shyness of him.

Our eyes met. For the first time, we looked at each other without feeling the need to throw up defenses and barricades. It was an intimate moment, a moment so deep and wide and high that it seemed the world was too small to contain it.

Dr. Tibbs interrupted it.

"Mr. Delveau? I was saying, sir, that I am greatly amazed to find a brick-paved road in the country!"

"What?"

Dr. Tibbs had to repeat the question before Delveau could pull his eyes from mine. Then, brusquely, he answered the man.

"The pike is not paved. It only seems so. The road is hard-packed because plantation owners roll hogsheads of tobacco down the road to the nearest waterway for shipment."

He turned back to me eagerly, but our moment was lost. For immediately, North was required to bellow at Missy, who was settling, with her luncheon plate, upon a half-rotted log.

"Mrs. Osborne, don't sit there! Such logs tend to house snakes."

With a cry, Missy sprang up and flew to her husband.

North and I smiled at each other and shrugged ruefully. But our hearts were singing, and the day suddenly seemed the fairest I had ever seen. Sunlight filtered through the golden foliage, and the air was sweet with the smell of fallen leaves. A breeze whispered in the trees. Hand-in-hand, we walked down to the stream and silently watched the golden carpet of fallen leaves drift by in the stream's current. I wanted him to hold my hand forever.

For most of the day we were jounced and jolted on a dirt road that became increasingly narrower and rougher. Around us, the wilderness blazed in color, and the sun seemed to set everything aflame. By mid-afternoon, I fell asleep, my head on Delveau's shoulder.

A back-wrenching rut in the road woke me. I looked up at him.

"When will we reach Delveau land?"

An amused expression passed over his face.

"You have been on it for the past three hours."

I sat up in surprise. I looked out the window. The country-side was becoming progressively more hilly and rolling. We were in foothills and I could see a string of low mountains on the horizon. They hung there like blue smoke.

North signaled the coachman to stop. He opened the door, got out and then lifted me down.

"The coaches must proceed by the road. You and I will take a shortcut."

I frowned, puzzled.

"You're not afraid?"

I laughed and gave him my hand.

The others went on. Hand-in-hand we scrambled up the foliage-choked hill. When we reached the top and I looked out beyond, I gave a little cry of surprise.

Just below us was a beautiful estate. The main house and the terraced gardens surrounding it made it appear much like a French chateau. Beyond the extensive gardens were clusters of outlying buildings—small cabins, houses, warehouses, barns, stables, coach houses, a smithy, meat curing huts. Beyond the buildings stretched plowed fields. In one vast field, cornstalks had been gathered and bound in the colonial way. In the same field, workers were harvesting orange pumpkins that glowed in the sunlight like bright jewels.

"North! Oh, North!"

"You like it?"

His voice throbbed with pride. I looked up at him and found his face boyish.

"North, I never expected anything so beautiful."

He kissed my cheek and led me down the sloping hill.

Within twenty minutes we were near the chateau. Excited servants and Negro slaves appeared everywhere, calling sub-dued greetings.

North gripped my hand tensely.

"My father—" he said, interpreting the servants' backward manner. We hurried.

A dignified, elderly woman—it had to be the head house-keeper—came down the marble staircase with stiff speed. She rushed to meet us.

"Mrs. Krause—"

"Thank God you've come, North!" she said, so lost in her worry that obviously she'd forgotten to address him formally. "The doctor is with him now. He says it can't be more than a matter of days. Perhaps hours." She gave a little sob and immediately apologized for it.

North took her shoulders.

"I'll go to him at once."

He went bounding up the steps. I hesitated, then flew after him. At the click of my heels on marble, he turned abruptly as though he'd forgotten about me. He held out his hand.

He propelled me along. There wasn't a moment to absorb the splendid French furnishings in the chateau or the soft honeyed look of walls papered in silk. We hurried up a wide, gracefully winding staircase and down a long corridor. At the end of the corridor, we plunged into an immense, dark bed-chamber. I blinked, unable to see for a moment or two. Then, the large four-poster bed came into view. Close by it, a fire burned in the grate, and brown velvet drapes were drawn tightly across each window. There was the acrid smell of medicine.

North dropped my hand, forgetting me.

He moved toward the bed. The doctor respectfully nodded and slipped out of the room. Carefully, North sat on the edge of the bed.

"Father?"

There was a stirring on the bed. A thin frail hand came up from the bedclothes.

North took his father into his arms. Their embrace was long and unashamedly emotional. There were words, words so soft that I could not catch them. They spoke in French, and the old comte petted his son's dark head with a shaking hand. They spoke on in low, intent whispers. At last, North again kissed his father's cheek and gently lowered him to the pillow.

He stood and said aloud, "Father, I've brought your daughter-in-law. Just as you wished."

The old man's eyes seemed to strain, searching the room for me. Hesitantly, I stepped forward. His watery blue eyes lit with joy.

"Arabella! Sweet Arabella!"

Stunned, I clutched at my throat and backed away. But North drew me forward, encouraging me with a look.

"Not Arabella, Father. Her daughter, Dianna."

The old comte raised up feebly. He stared at me, then sank back upon his pillow.

"Forgive me, my child," he whispered, his manner courtly even in illness. "It is the fever. It makes me delirious at times. But of course you are Dianna."

He lay back, panting from the effort of speaking. His eyes shone with happiness as he looked back and forth, from me to North and back again. If I had wondered why an independent man like North had tamely accepted the marriage, I now had my answer. The son loved the father as deeply as the father loved the son.

In a courtly manner, the comte gestured toward the chair beside his bed. He took a deep breath that seemed to cost him in pain.

"You are lovely, my child. As lovely as Arabella. Will you do me the honor of sitting for a few minutes?"

His smile, even in the pain of illness, was gentle and kind. In answer, I bent to him and kissed his hot brow.

"Arabella's daughter!"

Satisfaction vibrated in his weak voice.

I sat, taking his hand in mine. North sat on the bed and held his father's other hand. The comte seemed to nod off. Just as I was certain he was gone in sleep, I felt weak pressure on my fingers as he stirred.

He drew a painful breath.

"Dianna, will you forgive a dying man if he asks a question which he has no right to ask?"

"Ask what you will."

My voice quavered. I was deeply touched by his feebleness and by the love bond I saw between father and son.

He closed his eyes for a moment.

"Tell me, daughter, are my prayers answered? Are you with child? Will there be a Delveau heir?"

The words were very simple, an old man's dying wish to see his family live on. But he could not have stunned me more if he'd drawn a dagger and thrust it into me.

141

All that I had pushed from my conscious mind over the past months came rushing to the fore. No woman's time in July or August or September. This was October. Dear God, I was a full three months pregnant and into the fourth! How could I have so stubbornly resisted seeing the signs?

I sat there paralyzed, my body turning to ice. I felt the blood drain from my face. My eyes flew to North. His wry smile apologized for his father's indiscretion. But I could not smile back. Dazed and in shock, I stood up, still staring at North.

"I—I—am with child," I whispered in disbelief.

I tore my gaze from North and stumbled from the room, nearly colliding with the housekeeper.

"Please, my room—"

I followed her blindly, not seeing, not hearing her efforts at polite conversation, not even aware of where she led me. At last I stood alone in a large, beautifully appointed bedchamber. A fire blazed in the fireplace, seeming to hiss at me, seeming to know.

With child by Sir Gordon!

The old comte's poignant question had unwittingly opened my Pandora's box and loosed demons assailed me. My mind whirled. What could I do? How could I save myself? Oh, Father... Aunt Matilde... Help me...

Wildly, helplessly, I paced the room, compulsively touching each thing in it as though the inanimate could give me aid—the marble of the fireplace, the porcelain clock ticking softly on the mantel, the silk moire wallpaper, the bed with its canopy and coverlets of white silk, the rose-velvet bed curtains, the looking glass standing in its gilt frame, the chairs covered in white silk, deep rose velvet, shell pink.

Above the mantel hung a portrait of North's mother. Not gay and gypsyish as the portrait in Alexandria, but serious, almost brooding. I sensed her sympathy and knew, at once, that this had been her room.

"Oh, God," I begged her, "what shall I do?"

I began to sob, hysterical sobs. And somehow, I knew I sobbed not only for myself but for North. I sobbed for the sweet memory of this day, for the lost innocence of walking hand-in-hand through the golden wilderness, for the loss of all that had been beginning between us.

Wracked with sobs, I nearly missed hearing the tap on the door. It was North. I sensed it. Panic thudded through me. I fled from the knock. I rushed to the balcony doors and pulled them open. But what good would it do? Where could I go? I shut the doors and leaned against them. Through the glass, I could see the day dying. The sun was sinking behind the blue hills, taking with it all the flamboyant colors, leaving behind a wilderness as stark and bleak as my own soul. A wind was rising, flinging dry leaves against the window panes.

Behind me, the door opened, then closed. His booted footfalls sounded on the floor boards, then disappeared in the soft carpet. I cringed in fear, knowing what I must tell him. The clock on the mantel ticked loudly in cadence with the tripping of my heart. I flinched as a log fell in the fire with a thump, sending up a flurry of sparks that reflected in the balcony doors.

He came up behind me, sliding his arms around me and resting his cheek on the top of my head. I leaned into him, closing my eyes. I would have this moment, this moment at least.

"Thank you for that kind lie, Dianna. He dies happy."

A sob broke from me.

North turned me to him. He took my face in his hands. He gazed at me, puzzled.

"What is it, sweet?"

I shook my head, unable to speak.

His fervent kiss parted my lips, leaving no question of what the next minutes would bring. He unfastened the silk frog on my cloak, and with a rustle, the cloak slithered to my feet. I shivered as he drew me into his warm, strong arms and my tears began to flow. Oh God, how could I confess it now?

He misread my tears as bridal fear.

"Don't cry and tremble so, my love. I will be gentle."

He picked me up in his arms and carried me toward the bed. The silk coverlets danced in iridescent light as the fire's reflection played upon the fabric.

Shaking, I put my arms around his neck and searched his

dark eyes. They shone with passion, but with joy, too. I'd never seen him look like this.

"Oh, North—"

I pressed my trembling lips to his, and his arms tightened around me, safe and sure, as if he would never let me go. And then I knew—knew beyond question—that I must tell him at once. If I waited until after he would hate me the rest of his life.

I tore my mouth from his. His breath, healthy and male, lingered on my lips.

"Dear God, North, it's true. I *am* with child."

He continued to hold me as though he could not comprehend. Then a muscle twitched violently in his cheek. He set me down and my feet hit the floor with a jar.

"What are you saying?"

I shook my head helplessly, my eyes pleading. I backed away as a storm gathered in his face, darkening his skin and contorting his features. And then full comprehension came.

"You goddamn whore!"

I cried out, twisted and lunged for the door, but he caught me by the wrist and dragged me back to the middle of the room. I sobbed, hysterical and in pain from his grip.

"So you make me a cuckold for Cartwright?"

I looked up at him, stunned. Only then did my whirling mind understand that, of course, he would assume Christian!

I shook my head desperately.

"No! No! Not Christian! Believe me—I was raped—"

His palm smashed against my face. The room spun.

"Lies!"

I went reeling into the bedpost, striking my head on the hard wood. He grabbed me.

"I'll teach you to whore!"

"North—my God—please—"

But he was consumed with rage. Clutching at the neckline of my gown, he tore the gown from my body with wrenches so forceful that I was driven to my knees. I bowed my head, ill with fear at the violence as he tore at my fragile underthings, stripping me bare. He jerked me to my feet.

"By God, you will whore for *me*!"

144

He dragged me to the bed and flung me upon it. The bed quaked wildly as my body hit. Dizzy with fear, I covered my face with my hands, cowering as he stripped himself naked. Helpless, I whimpered like a beaten dog.

He was upon me at once. The bed quaked violently as his weight pressed me deep into the featherbed, and panic surged anew. I struggled, but he was too strong for me.

"Don't—" I begged. "Not like this—not in hate!"

"Whore!" he growled.

He seized a fistful of my hair and used it to wrench my mouth up to his. I groaned as my scalp seemed to tear. He raked my mouth with hard, brutal kisses, and then his hand moved down, roughly forcing my thighs apart.

"Oh, God, North, I beg you—"

"Kiss me!" he commanded.

Stunned and unable to struggle more, I yielded, going limp with shock and fear as he pleasured himself. Tears of help-lessness—and hopelessness—coursed down my cheeks. As he commanded, I put my arms around his neck and kissed him—kissed him passionately and without reservation. There was the taste of salt in our mouths, as my tears mingled in the kisses. In surrender, I gave my body to him. I ceased to own it. My body followed his, obeying his movements and adding a crescendo to each of his strokes. He gasped in sharp pleasure, and my own frightened gasps echoed his.

He gripped me tightly. He arched, and a long throbbing spasm took him. When he was done, he rolled away from me, breathless and glassy-eyed. For a moment he stared at me in disbelieving shock. And I knew the violence was done, but the sorrow would remain. He whispered my name despairingly and then passed immediately into sleep. I lay there, subdued, my cheeks wet with fresh flowing tears. I wanted to shake him awake, to rail at him. But I could not. Hadn't I goaded and driven the man into his moment of madness?

Quietly, I turned my head on the pillow and watched him sleep. I couldn't hate him. He had abused me, yes, my loins ached and my cheek, too, where he'd struck me. But hadn't I abused him, twisting his life so that I might have Christian? I deserved what I'd got.

145

In the firelight, his blue-black hair seemed to glow. Gently, taking care not to wake him, I smoothed the tousled hair from his brow. The tomahawk scar gleamed white and silky. Softly, I touched it.

He groaned in deep troubled sleep.

There was a loose comforter on the bed. I drew it up, covering us. I lay beside him, and the tension began to drain away, bringing awareness of physical pain. My head hurt. Where it had struck the bedpost, a small lump throbbed. And my cheek was puffing up. I could almost feel the bruise forming.

I lay back on the pillows, staring up at the reflected firelight dancing on the silk canopy overhead. Sleep seemed impossible, even as I drifted into fatigued slumber.

When I woke, the fire was dead in the fireplace. Moonlight streamed through the glass balcony doors, painting half the room in white light but leaving the bed in darkness.

I could not see North in the darkness, but I knew that he lay beside me. I knew, too, that he was awake. His careful breathing told me so. I felt a fresh surge of fear. I pretended to sleep, but my act did not fool him.

"Did I hurt you?"

The bedclothes rustled slightly, as though he tensed, fearing my answer.

I lied to spare him.

"No."

He raised up on one elbow.

"You are certain?"

"You didn't hurt me, North." I paused. "Rather it was I who hurt you."

He winced at my words, then lay back in the darkness. He sighed. It was a sigh of pained relief.

"I have never done such—such a—"

He did not finish. He crossed his arms behind his head and lay staring at the moonlight that poured in at the window. He said nothing for a very long time, nor did I.

At last, he broke the silence.

"What am I to do with you, Dianna?"

"Do?"

I stopped breathing. Dear God, I had not thought! Do? Do? Yes, of course he would do something! Did I truly expect him to live on with me as though nothing had happened? Even in the unlikely happenstance that his slight caring for me might someday ripen into love, his pride would demand he *do* something.

Do? What would he do? My mind tumbled in panic. Would he divorce me and bring shame to my family? Oh, I couldn't bear to see them hurt!

Do? What would he do? My mind leapt to the child growing in me. Might he not punish me through the baby? Take it away after birth and give it to some wet nurse to raise? Or deny it his name, consigning it to a label of bastard? My heart thumped with compassion for the unborn mite. Panic awakened maternal instincts that I had not known were in me.

I sat up, straining to make out his face in the darkness.

"I beg of you—don't punish the baby. He is innocent. Hate me, not him."

"*Hate* you?" He pulled himself upright. "My God!"

He touched my face. The touch of his fingers on my bruised cheek was unexpected, and I winced in sudden pain. He pulled back, then reached out again and smoothed my disheveled hair from my face. He stared at me.

"What have I done to you?" he demanded harshly.

My hand flew to hide my cheek.

He lunged off the bed, pulled on his trousers and fumbled at a side table for flint and candle. There was a scratching sound and suddenly light flickered in the room. I turned my head away, afraid for him to see. But he brought the candle near. He brushed back my hair, then slowly turned my chin to him.

"God."

He made a sound as though he were ill. Thumping the candle holder down on a table, he turned from me and began to pull on the rest of his clothes.

"But it's all right, North," I sobbed. He dressed hurriedly. I pulled the comforter around my shoulders and stumbled off the bed. I flung myself at his knees, sobbing. He pushed me away.

"But it's all right, North, it's all right—"

He jerked as though I had run him through with a sword. He laughed. It was a cold, bitter laugh.

"All right?" he mocked. "Nothing has been *all right* since the moment I met you! You have changed me into a man I do not even recognize, a cur who would beat and force a woman! You have turned my life upside-down. You have made me a cuckold for the sake of your lover, and you have so upset the woman I call wife, that I fear for the life of the child she carries!

"Then you tell me you intend to whelp a bastard in my house and give it *my* name! By God, woman! *All right?*" He laughed. "Nothing will ever be all right again!"

He pushed me away and strode to the door.

I was terrified at his tirade, terrified for myself and the baby.

"But what will you do with me!"

He turned, and as I watched, his face hardened.

"Do?"

He laughed bitterly.

"I told you what I would do on the day we wed. I have kept my part of the bargain. *You* will keep yours. You will behave as a proper daughter-in-law to my father for as long as he lives! After that, I care not what you do. Whelp your bastard. Give it my name. I care not! I will not be using the name for another woman. By God, I've lost the stomach for marriage."

He drew a deep breath.

"When my father dies," he said, his voice shaking with passion, "this sham of a union is at an end."

His words drew deep sobs from me. I sank to the carpet as though slaughtered. He wrenched the door open and was gone.

CHAPTER 13

"Judas! What's he done to you!"

Nan dropped the breakfast tray to the table with a startled crash. She stared at me as I pressed a cool wet cloth to my bruise.

I avoided her eyes.

"No one has done anything to me," I said, in what I hoped seemed a matter-of-fact tone.

"I stumbled in the dark during the night, that's all. The room was strange to me. I fell."

I went on bathing my bruise.

She approached me slowly, her eyes big and frightened. She dropped to her knees. Gently, she drew the cloth away. Her eyes widened. Her mouth quivered.

"*He* done it," she said, "God, Danni, t'were only your father here, he'd take the horse whip to 'im, he would."

I took the cloth back and hid my bruise.

"Nonsense! You imagine things. I did this to myself."

She knelt there, an incredulous look on her face.

"No," she said softly. "I know a hand to a face when I see

it. Pa, whenever he got too much ale, he used to lay on us girls w' his belt and sometimes w' his fist."

I looked at her. She would never believe I fell. In her loyalty to me she would spread all sorts of rumors about North. A hard thought came to me—let her! North deserved it. Let him live with the consequences of his passion! But my softer self would not let me behave so. *You drove North to it. You are as much responsible as he.*

"Nan, if I tell you the truth, will you promise to tell no one?"

She nodded solemnly.

I cast about for something to tell her, something she would believe.

"Mr. Delveau suffers from nightmares. He fought in terrible and bloody Indian wars. Often he dreams the savages are upon him. He dreamed so last night and accidentally struck me."

I watched her mull it over—her instinct was to reject it—then the slow reluctant acceptance of the incredible story. After all this was Virginia. Strange things were to be expected of Americans.

She sighed, shaking her head.

"Well, then, Danni. We must get you a cudgel to stow beneath the bed. If he dreams again, you must up 'n' bash him. And no bones about it!"

I smiled at her outlandish solution to a problem that didn't even exist, but the smile ended in an ache of sadness. No cudgel would be needed. North would come to my bed no more, nor I to his.

I ate my breakfast in thoughtful silence. But when Nan found a shred of my chemise that I must have missed while burning the other torn remnants, she stormed again.

"Judas! If he hurt you—"

I knew I must calm her fears once and for all.

"Nan, would he harm the mother of his child?" I asked her lightly. As I watched her thunderstruck expression, I was appalled at myself. How easily the lies accumulated, one on top of another until my very life seemed a house of lies.

A slow grin spread over her face. She came to me and gave me a stout hug.

"Lor' lummy, Danni, I told you, didn't I? On the ship, I says and you says, oh no. Lor' lummy! We're to have a baby!"

With Nan placated and bubbling about the baby, I turned my thoughts to the others in the house. The bruise on my cheek was a bad one, and there was nothing to do about it except keep to my room until it healed. I would plead travel fatigue as an excuse for not coming down. My pregnancy could be used as well.

During the next few days, I could feel the gloom that pervaded Twin Oaks. Nan brought me all the news several times a day, and none of it was good. The old comte's life hung in the balance, teetering between this world and the next. Dr. Tibbs and Dr. Osborne labored over him night and day, but his fever still raged dangerously high. North, Nan reported, almost never left his father's side. My husband looked a sight, she said, with a black beard sprouting on his unshaven face and wild, bloodshot eyes sunk in pale hollows. As Nan described North's wretchedness, I ached for him.

Confined to Charlotte Delveau's rooms and to the airings on the small private balcony, I paced restlessly. I browsed through the few books in her glass and gilt bookcase. Her journals were there as well, beautifully bound in fine Moroccan leather stamped with gold. Obviously, she meant them to be read. Idly, I flipped through the journals. One day, perhaps, I would read them. But not now. I was too full of my own sad thoughts to do justice to her pretty descriptions of parties and gowns and travels.

I started several letters to my family, but put them down unfinished. My pen could not seem to find the tone I wanted to convey—a tone of all being well with me. Those letters would have to wait. I refused to worry my family by a careless word of unhappiness or by a tone of melancholy that might permeate the lines.

When my bruise began to fade, I went for walks in the woods that lay beyond the gardens. I could leave the house without anyone seeing; my balcony steps led down into the gardens.

It was a relief to escape to the hushed quiet of the woods.

The October beauty was a healing balm for my soul. The sun was a dazzling golden orb in the clear blue sky, and the air filled with the fragrance of autumn leaves. The crunch of the leaves underfoot made a childishly comforting sound as I followed the meandering creek bank in the woods. I felt less lonely as small creatures stirred around me—the bold chipmunks, the squirrels, the croaking frogs, the brindle-colored wild rabbits that froze as I passed. Occasionally I saw a deer.

Red and gold leaves fell steadily, day by day, sometimes dropping into my lap as I sat on the clay creek bank thinking quietly.

One afternoon as I sat there brooding about what might become of me and my child, I was startled by the loud clumping of horse hooves. Heart in mouth, I sprang up just as a chestnut gelding, rambunctious and snorting, came crashing along the creek bank. I flew out of its path, and the rider reined the horse to a halt with a loud oath.

It was Delveau. I froze, not knowing what to do, where to run. I hadn't seen him since that terrible night, and I wasn't prepared to. Fear coursed through me as I stared up at him, heart pounding.

He was scarcely recognizable. His jaw was covered with unkempt black grizzle, the spirit gone from his eyes. Life flashed back in him as he saw me. His eyes glinted with alarm, then with anger. He wheeled the skittish gelding in a tight circle as he scowled down at me.

"What the hell!" he thundered. "What are *you* doing out here?"

I backed away, panic welling up.

"Come back here!" he demanded.

Fear and deep hurt and injured pride galvanized me. I couldn't let him see the bruise, I couldn't! I turned and plunged into the brush. Trapped between Delveau and the creek, I abandoned common sense. I splashed into the shallow creek, crossing it, my skirts dragging in the water and cold wetness seeping into my boots and stockings. I reached the opposite side and plunged on into the wilderness like a fool who cannot think beyond the moment.

Run! Run!

"Goddamn it!"

I heard him abandon his horse and come stomping through the underbrush, cursing me as he crossed the creek. I flew on in fear, swatting aside low branches and bushes that impeded me. When my skirt caught on a thorn bush, I wrenched at it, trying to pull myself free, sobbing in fear and anger. Unable to free myself, I dashed away the telltale tears just as Delveau caught up to me.

"Goddamn it!" he repeated.

He looked down at my skirt and wrenched it loose. The skirt ripped and he swore again. Without another word he grabbed my wrist and dragged me back the way we had come. The creek seemed doubly cold, and now my petticoats were wet to my knees.

"Get on the horse," he ordered.

I shook my head, trembling.

"I—no—please, North. I—want to walk."

He gave me a furious look.

"Will you get it through your head that this is *not* England, Madam? There are wild animals here—timber cats, wolves, snakes!"

I swallowed. How mean he was being. There wasn't the slightest sign of contrition, not the slightest sign that he regretted raping me, hitting me . . . I bit my lip, a hurt stubbornness rising.

"I fear no wild animal," I whispered.

"By God, then fear the Indians!" he shouted. "This is Cherokee country. While we are at peace with them for the present, I cannot guarantee what might happen if a Cherokee buck chanced upon you. You could be killed! Or, at best, ill used."

"Ill used!" I cried, all my hurt and anger exploding. "Then I have nothing more to fear Mr. Delveau. Already, in my short time in Virginia, I have been beaten and raped!"

His face went white. I could see my words had been as effective as a thrust lance, and immediately I could have bitten off my tongue. He was in anguish over his father. And for me to add to his grief as though I harbored no feelings for him at all? I was appalled at myself.

153

Helplessly, I lifted the palms of my hands to him in mute apology.

"Oh, North! I didn't—"

But he wheeled his horse around, got on, viciously laid the lash to the animal's flank and disappeared in a thunder of hooves.

As the sound of the hooves faded and altogether disappeared, I stumbled down the path in his wake. I was disgusted with myself, and suddenly I was afraid, too. Afraid of the wilderness that had seemed so benign and comforting until North revealed its dangers. I began to run, my wet skirts slapping coldly against my legs, curling around my ankles, tripping me.

Suddenly, to my immense relief, the sound of the chestnut's hooves returned and grew louder as Delveau came galloping. He reined the gelding to a halt.

"Come here. Give me your hands."

Quickly as a scared child, I obeyed. Immediately, I was sitting side-saddle, safe between his thighs with his arms around me, holding me firmly to the saddle. I didn't dare look at him, but his breath in my hair and on my temple made me long to touch him, to beg for a truce.

North said nothing more, nor did I. But his breathing seemed harsh and labored. Our closeness disturbed him as much as it disturbed me. As we rode on, the chestnut walking now, a sudden gust of wind whipped my hair into his face.

"Damn!" he swore, letting go of me to clear his face of it. He swiped at my hair as though the feel of it were repellent to him. His hostility made my heart sink. Oh, God, I thought, he loathes the very touch of me.

Angrily, he stuffed my long loose hair down between his chest and my back, that it might not blow up and annoy him again. His stiff, ungiving arm went around my waist in grudging support, and we plodded on in sad silence but for the creak of the leather saddle and the steady clop of the chestnut's hooves.

Overhead, a swarm of blackbirds soared. They were circling and calling, preparing to abandon Virginia and the coming winter for softer, warmer climes. How I longed to go with them! I knew I could not long survive North's coldness. I needed warmth and affection, such as I'd always received from my family and from Christian. But North—would he ever forgive me, warm to me?

When we reached the grounds, North urged his horse along the brick path to the stairway beneath my balcony. I was relieved he did not take me to a main door. My bruise was not completely gone, and I didn't want the servants to see. North seemed to sense this, and I was surprised at his sensitivity. For, surely his thoughts must be upon his father and not upon me.

He reined the chestnut to a stop and helped me slide down. But as he did so, I cried out in sudden pain.

"My hair!"

It had got twisted in the buttons of his coat. He knew the situation almost before I shrieked and came sliding to the ground with an oath of annoyance. As the horse pawed nervously beside us, our fingers fumbled to unwind hair from button. North drew a sharp angry breath as our fingers touched. I looked up at him, and for an instant, our eyes met. I was crushed by the despair I saw in him. Was the despair totally for his father? Or was some of it for us? Did he feel anything but hate for me? Suddenly, I had to know.

"North?" I began softly. "Could we—"

"Get your hands out of the way!"

Biting my lip to keep from weeping, I let my hands fall to my sides. I stood there, defeated, my eyes cast down. Breathing heavily, he untwisted the last strands of my hair and was free of me.

"You are a damned nuisance," he said as he remounted his horse.

I blinked back tears. Swiftly, I flew up the flagged stone steps and let myself into the comforting solace of Charlotte's room.

Two nights later, in the middle of the night, I awoke to urgent knocking on my bedroom door.

"Dianna? Dianna?"

Someone was calling my name. I sat up in bed, trying to make sense of my surroundings as my heart thudded. My room,

155

yes—no. Charlotte's room...the bed...the white canopy overhead...moonlight streaming in the balcony doors....

"Dianna!"

I recognized North's urgent voice. I jumped up from bed, pulling on a robe. The comte! Had something happened to him?

I hurried to the door and wrenched it open. North was standing in the corridor, his dark features illuminated in the light of the candle he carried, his grizzled face alive with excitement. His black eyes flashed.

"He asks to see you. Hurry!"

I stood there, not understanding. North seized my hand and pulled me along the corridor. I had not even a moment to plead for my slippers, and the floor boards were ice beneath my bare feet. We rushed down the corridor, crossed into a second wing and came, at last, to the comte's room.

Dr. Tibbs and Dr. Osborne were at the fire, wearily drinking a hot rum punch. They were fully as unkempt as North, but they smiled broadly as I entered.

"He's going to live!" young Dr. Osborne crowed proudly, rubbing his red eyes. "It's the steam treatment that turned the day, Mrs. Delveau. Of that I am certain. Steam and the use of fresh air in the sickroom."

"Pshaw, Osborne!" Dr. Tibbs said wearily, drawing a red poker from the fire and thrusting it into a pewter tankard of rum punch. The pungent smell of the heating rum curled into the air.

I was aghast at the comte's appearance. Thin before, he'd lost a shocking amount of weight. So thin and frail, he seemed lost among the pillows and bedclothes. But his sleep was deep, peaceful. I pulled back, not wanting to disturb him, but North stiffly put his arm around my waist and drew me up to the bed.

"Father," he said softly. "You asked for Dianna. She's here."

I was suddenly struck with shyness. How must I look for the old gentleman? My robe was a shapeless one, such as a child might wear. My hair, uncombed and sleep-tangled. Self-consciously I raked my fingers through it.

For a long time the comte did not stir. Then, slowly, his

eyelids struggled to open. The candlelight was too much for him, and his eyes teared over. He blinked with the effort to clear them.

"Dianna?" the old gentleman whispered.

"Here, sir."

His peacock-blue eyes found me again. He smiled weakly.

"My child...I wanted you to know...to know..." His words drifted away and his eyes closed once more. I thought he had fallen asleep when he again opened his eyes and whispered fiercely, "I shall live to see my grandchild!"

A tremor ran through me. North's arm stiffened around my waist. Struck dumb by the old man's words, I could only stare at him. But my thoughts flew to North. What a cruel mix of anguish and joy he must be feeling. What an unhappy trap was closing round him. I struggled to compose myself and bent down to the old gentleman.

"Sir, I earnestly pray you *will* live to see your grandchild. I pray you will live long enough to see him grow to manhood."

He laughed weakly.

"A boy? I had hoped a girl. I have already named her "

"Oh?" I said, surprised that his wits should be so sharp after so much illness. What indomitable spirit he had!

He smiled, drawing breath painfully.

"Her name is to be Charlotte Arabella."

I was at a loss for a reply. I stared down at him, suddenly realizing he was too much of a man to be coddled or placated, even in illness.

I smiled at him.

"Charlotte Arabella, sir? A strange name for a grandson And it shall certainly be a grandson. My instincts tell me so."

He laughed weakly, panting for breath. I put my fingers to his lips, signaling that he was not to tire himself with more talk.

But he insisted. Drawing a painful breath, he went on in a whisper. "I like you, Dianna. You do not condescend to humor me by telling me what I want to hear. Ah, well"—he sighed long and contentedly—"a male it must be. You and North are young. There will be more babies. Girl babies."

North's fingers flinched on my waist. He caught his breath sharply. I swallowed.

"We will name the second Charlotte Arabella," I promised, making an effort at lightness. "But only if *you* will go back to sleep this instant."

He smiled. His eyelids grew heavy. Soon he was in deep calm sleep. North released his breath in a rush. He took his hand from my waist. In the flickering candlelight, his face was raw with tiredness and emotion. I pulled my eyes away. I couldn't bear to see him like this.

"Come," he said, "I'll see you back to your room."

"You needn't."

Before I could protest any further, he'd seized my hand and was leading me out of the room into the dark corridor. He paused, scowling down at me.

"Your hand is ice," he said in annoyance.

His eyes swept to my bare feet.

Angrily he said, "Do you want to catch your death?"

Without asking my permission, he scooped me up in his arms. We'd forgotten the candle, and the only light was moonlight spilling in at the far end of the hall as he carried me in his strong arms.

"You must wear slippers," he scolded tiredly. "You could become ill."

My heart leapt with hope. So he *did* care. Beneath the coldness and contempt, were there softer, more tender feelings for me? I rested my head against his shoulder. He carried me slowly, almost as though he enjoyed the touch of my cheek against his neck.

"If you become ill," he said pointedly, "you endanger the child."

All hope washed from my heart at these words. A sadness welled up, the sadness finding solace in bitter anger. How stupid I was to hope! He cared nothing for me. It was the child, the child whose coming had given an old man the will to live.

"I can walk," I said with an angry sob. "Put me down."

I struggled against him, but he ignored my protests and strode on, tightening his grip around my waist and my legs. At my door, we moved into inky blackness. He set me down but did not immediately move away. His hand lingered on my waist. It was a strange, tense moment, one in which neither of us seemed capable of pulling away from the other. At last, his hand fumbled up to my face. The gentle gesture brought quick hot tears to my eyes. The touch was his apology. I knew it. I turned to him swiftly and, as I did so, my lips brushed his hand.

He drew back.

"It's cold in the corridor," he said softly. "Go to bed, Dianna."

And then I was left standing alone in the inky blackness of Twin Oaks.

I saw nothing of North for several days. His room was next to mine, but I heard no movements there. I could only conclude he had left Twin Oaks. To my chagrin, I realized I could not even inquire of him of the servants. They would raise their eyebrows. A wife was expected to know her husband's whereabouts. It grated on me that he didn't grant me even these outer trappings of being his wife. It was one more attempt to humiliate me, to make me pay.

The comte continued to improve and grow stronger, although I knew it would be weeks before he could hope to leave his bedchamber. Two days following our strange, middle-of-the-night interview, I went to see him, sitting by his bed until he woke from sleep. When his eyes lit upon me, his face became suffused with joy, and I was more than glad I had come.

"What a pleasure to wake to such loveliness, my dear," he whispered. "If it won't bore you, will you sit with me occasionally? It will do me more good than Tibbs's wretched tonics. But if it would bore you—"

I laughed softly.

"What woman is bored when she is being admired?"

He smiled. His peacock-blue eyes sparkled slightly.

"I like you, Dianna," he said. "You have Arabella's heart and beauty. But you also possess a good measure of my Charlotte's effervescence and wit."

I wagged a finger at him.

"And you, Comte, possess the heart and wit of a roué who would, by his pretty words, charm young women into his bed-chamber!"

My words delighted him. He chuckled. With a contented smile, he drifted into sleep.

I could not help but warm to my father-in-law. He was courtly and gentle and he seemed so ready to love and accept me into his family.

As the days went by, I made it a habit to do my reading and the writing of my letters in his bedchamber where we might converse for a few minutes whenever he awoke. Gradually, my things began to accumulate in his room: books, quills, paper, ink, even lounging slippers and shawls. I frequented his room as often as I frequented my own.

His eyes never failed to light up when he spied me, and his attention and admiration were balm for my soul. For certainly I got no attention or admiration from his son. As for myself, I felt a new sense of worth in cheering an old gentleman into health. I loved making him laugh. Our camaraderie grew quickly, promising to ripen into a warm and loyal relationship.

One morning as I tiptoed from the sleeping comte's room, I found Mrs. Krause, the head housekeeper, fidgeting in the corridor. She came straight to the point.

"Mrs. Delveau," she said uncomfortably, "I've not done my duty to you. I've not given you a tour of the house. Per'aps now, M'am?" she asked hopefully, her face red with her own sense of embarrassment at overlooking me.

"Now would be fine, Mrs. Krause," I said. "And please do not fret, thinking you've neglected me. Your energies and your thoughts in these past days have been where they should be— on the comte and his needs."

She gave me a grateful smile.

"Thank you for understanding. We—I—didn't know— what you might be like, M'am. Whether you might be as you are, or like the comtesse—" She bit her tongue and gave me a horrified look. "Oh, we *loved* Mistress Charlotte," she said quickly. "*Everyone* loved her. But she was restless and easily bored. She'd never have sat one hour in a sick room—"

I realized she was complimenting me and cut her short gently, suggesting we start the tour.

The house was two stories, with attic apartments in the third floor dormers for the maids. The second floor, both wings and the connecting main part of the house, were filled with bedchambers and sitting rooms. All were elegantly furnished in the finest fashion. There was silk paper upon the walls and damask, velvet and silk upholstery on the chairs and settees. Each room had its Turkish carpet.

Mrs. Krause said proudly, "When the comtesse was alive, not a week went by that guests didn't use these chambers. The comtesse was that fond of parties, she was!"

If the upper floor was elegant, the lower was a hundred times more so. A wide graceful stairway swooped down to the immense mirrored foyer below. The main drawing rooms were papered with honey-colored silk. The ceilings were white, embellished with gold gilt scrollwork. Crystal chandeliers of a thousand baggettes hung from the ceilings, and all of the woodwork was intricately carved and gilded.

The floors were burnished. The sweet smell of the beeswax used on the furniture filled the lower floor with a delicate fragrance. Furnishings throughout were lavish, ornate and mainly French. Mrs. Krause proudly related the history of each piece I admired. It seemed that everything had been selected by Charlotte Delveau on her travels to France, Spain and England. All was in the finest taste. When a room verged upon becoming too ornate, Charlotte had saved it with deft, wise touches—an old antique sideboard of olive wood from Cadiz or a rugged trunk of the finest Moroccan leather.

We passed through the elegant dining room and into the immense pantry with its floor-to-ceiling cupboards of fine china and silver. Snatching up shawls that hung in the pantry, we made our way out to the kitchen house.

The kitchen was a massive room with a stone floor and huge fireplaces and ovens built into the brick walls. Two enormous oak chopping tables dominated the room. At the tables stood three impish Negro girls of no more than eleven or twelve. As they giggled, they indolently peeled red apples and sliced them into a wooden bowl.

A mountainous black woman, gowned in India calico, flew into the kitchen from a far door.

"You lazy chits!" she bellowed at the girls. "You hurry, you! When the master want his dinner, then he want his dinner. You be good and sorry if dinner not ready!"

I laughed as the girls giggled and chopped only slightly faster. Apparently the woman didn't scare them one wit. The woman turned around, spied us, and her eyes widened in surprise.

"You darlin'!" she bellowed, grinning and hurrying to me. She gave me such a hug that I was almost lifted off my feet. "Miz North!" she said. "Ain't you pretty!"

I couldn't help but laugh.

She patted me on the stomach with an intuition that was startling. "Now, you tell Aunt Sally," she demanded. "This little one. When's he coming?"

"Aunt Sally!" Mrs. Krause said.

"It's all right, Mrs. Krause," I said, chuckling. "April, Aunt Sally."

She nodded her approval.

"Oh, ain't Mr. North proud!" she said. "Makin' your belly come up so soon!"

I blanched. The smile froze on my face.

"Aunt Sally, really!" Mrs. Krause scolded.

The black woman gave her a sulky look.

"Don't you Aunt Sally *me*. Mr. North's a man. And I guess a man knows what to do with what God give 'im!"

In the stifling heat of the kitchen, I could feel a tremor of coldness go through me. Mrs. Krause hurriedly guided me out to continue the tour.

"Really, M'am, Aunt Sally is impossible," Mrs. Krause apologized. "But the comte and Mr. North, they do dote on her. She's a freed slave, you know. The comtesse freed her. She works here by choice."

We toured the other dependencies with much less of a furor. The servants and slaves I met were shy and close-mouthed. I had to ask questions to get them to speak to me. When we finished touring the spring house, the laundry, the food storage rooms and the small office where Mrs. Krause kept accounts, our tour of the near buildings was done. About three hundred feet beyond the last building there stood a large cottage.

"That, Mrs. Krause?"

"Mr. North's office. When the comtesse was alive, she didn't like business being carried on in the house. She said it spoilt her parties and gave the house a dreary air." She paused, frowning. "So, the comte had the cottage built for an office."

"But it's quite large!" I said.

"Large?" she said, sniffing. "Well, I should think so. Mr. North has a lot to manage—two tobacco plantations, a sawmill on the Potomac, the ship building in Alexandria and the trade office there." She went on. "Then there's the sugar plantation in the West Indies and the comte's family estate in France. But of course, you know all that, M'am."

I did my best to hide my surprise.

"Yes, yes, of course," I lied.

I decided to wander through the cottage office. Mrs. Krause left me, hurrying back to her work.

As I pushed the door open, I could see it was furnished for business, not for comfort. Large oak tables dominated the room. Ledgers lay open upon the tables. Quills, paper and ink stood ready. The floor was bare planking, but it was waxed to a honeyed patina. Shelves and bookcases had been built into every wall, and it seemed that each of the businesses had its own case, neatly labeled. The office was as orderly as I would have kept it, and that surprised me. I hadn't known North would be so businesslike, so meticulous. Evidently, there was much I did *not* know about him.

I wandered into the adjoining rooms, studying the charts and maps on the walls, fingering the small desks where stewards must certainly come to account and report. There was an alcove in one darkened room. The alcove held a couch. I blinked. Someone was lying upon the couch, apparently sleeping. My breath caught sharply. Dear heaven, it was Delveau.

I froze, afraid to take another step, afraid of waking him. So this was where he'd taken himself. I watched him sleep, my pulse quickening. He *was* handsome, and I couldn't deny that he stirred me. He was clad in snug fawn-colored breeches and fine polished riding boots. He wore no shirt, and he lay upon his back with one arm flung up over his eyes. His strong well-muscled chest rose and fell as he breathed deeply. I had the insane urge to touch him, and instantly scolded myself for having such thoughts.

Hardly daring to breathe, I turned and tiptoed away, taking care not to let any floorboard squeak. I glanced over my shoulder at him, but he'd not moved. Then, as I reached the door of the room, his low rich voice captured me like a thrown net.

"No need to flee, little rabbit. I won't hurt you. I'm not dreaming at the moment. No 'savages' invade my nightmares."

I whirled around, reddening. So. The story I'd made up to satisfy Nan had gone from Nan to Sandy and from Sandy to North.

He swung his long legs off the couch and sat up, yawning and stretching. He gave me an indifferent look.

"My God, Dianna, but you have a facility for telling lies," he said in a bored and weary voice. "You take to lying like a fish takes to water."

I choked at the cutting words. How could he react so! I had only told the story to save *him* embarrassment.

My lips quivered at the unfairness. Angry tears rose.

"Would you have wanted me to tell the truth?"

"No!"

Abruptly, he lunged to his feet. He strode to a side table, took a brandy decanter and poured a bit into a thick-bottomed crystal glass. He sipped, then set it down with a thump, unfinished. He scowled at me, then looked away.

"You must know that I will never forgive myself for . . . hurting you," he said angrily.

His eyes filled with sadness, and my heart gave a tug. Irrationally, I found myself wanting to offer him comfort. My mind swam in confusion. Why did he stir such ambivalent emotions in me? In one moment I hated him enough to see him dead; in the next I was melting.

I steeled myself to resist him, but my softer self whispered, "Nor will I ever forgive myself for hurting you, North. To marry you . . . it was unspeakably wicked. The act of a selfish child."

His face was clean-shaven again, and I could see the small

muscle twitch in his cheek as though my apology had touched a nerve. He fumbled for his brandy glass, picked it up and drained it, then turned and stared at me.

Afraid to meet his intense gaze, I looked down at my feet. My heart beat wildly. Perhaps if I could tell him the truth? Tell him what Sir Gordon had done? If I could make him listen? Oh, I *had* to make him believe me.

"North?"

I looked up at him with scared eyes.

"North, I didn't lie to you about Christian. I've not been with him. The baby— It was rape. I—I—"

His harsh laughter cut me off. I was shocked at the crudity of it, shocked at the sudden hardness that molded his face. He hated me. I could see that now.

He flung himself upon the couch, leaning back against the wall and laughing in bitter amusement.

"Let me guess what you will tell me, Dianna: A passing tinker took you in a haystack! No? A highwayman climbed in through your bedchamber window." He laughed sarcastically. "No, you are too clever for that. You will select someone you know, someone who is far away in England. You will place the blame on him. No, Dianna. I am not such a fool as that."

His words lashed far more savagely than could any blow. I staggered back, turned and stumbled from the room, my eyes filling with tears. He was a devil. A beast! And if I, Dianna Brandley, ever harbored another tender feeling on his behalf, ever told another lie to save him, then I was insane and fit only for a madhouse!

Hot tears blinded me as I ran for the cottage door, and without seeing where I ran, I crashed into a chair. The chair banged to the floor and I fell over it, weeping in frustration.

As I picked myself up, North's strong arms went around me, helping. His face was taut with alarm and dismay.

"Danni? Are you all right?"

I choked back a sob and fought his help.

"Don't touch me! Please, just leave me alone."

But he drew me into his arms and held me close to his pounding heart, rocking me in his arms as one might soothe an unhappy child. A sob caught in my throat as he caressed me. Oh, God—his touch!

His lips were in my hair. He murmured words of comfort, and as he did so, I ceased my struggling and yielded. I couldn't stop myself from clinging to him, and he, in turn, held me so close that our bodies seemed to share the same heartbeat.

Clinging to each other, we did not trust ourselves to speak. There were no words. There was nothing more to be said. Our words could only wound, and not heal. Somehow, we both sensed that although we stood so near, we were yet as far from each other as the Earth from the nearest star.

I sighed. It was a deep trembling sigh, dredged forth from the very depths of my viscera. At the unhappy testimony of it, North released me and I turned from him and stumbled despairingly to the door. Had I ever been more desolate in my life? I doubted it.

As I lifted the door latch, his voice came softly.

"It would please me if you would dine with me tonight."

I looked back at him, hope rising.

He went on. "The servants gossip that we do not share a bed, Dianna. I cannot have them carrying gossip to my father that we do not even dine together."

My hand froze to the door latch, all hope crashing. The man was too much! Did he suppose my heart was made of granite, impervious to cracking under the onslaught of his changeable warmth and coldness?

I could not bear it. I *would* not. I knew I must save myself or be lost. Resist him or find my pride shattered and he striding victorious on the shards and shambles of it. I had to steel myself against this man. Harden myself to him and allow him no further opportunity to hurt me.

I whirled around.

"It would please you to dine with me, would it? Well, it would *not* please me. I should choke on every mouthful, just sitting at a table with you."

His head jerked back as though I had struck him. A red flush—was it embarrassment?—spread up his neck. When angered, he had a menacing way of lowering his head to look at one. He did so now, and I fought the impulse to flee in fear.

"Then, choke you will," he said. "For tonight, you *will* dine with me."

I looked away, shaking. Oh, his cruelty! Had I been a man— but I could only clench my fists and make a show of courage. I threw back my head and laughed. It was not a pretty laugh.

"I care not what stories the servants carry to your father!"

I knew I had struck a nerve. His eyes flashed with fury, but his voice became only colder, more controlled.

"May I remind you of our bargain? My *name* for your bastard, in exchange for your dutiful behavior as daughter-in-law? You will do *nothing* to upset my father, or I will make your life insufferable."

I shook with fear and anger. How I hated him! I glared at him, my mind grasping and clutching at weapons I might use against him.

"Would your father be upset to learn that his son beds a savage? And that she will soon present him with a half-breed?"

My heartless threat made the blood drain from his face. I flinched, wishing I could take back the words. I had gone too far, too far!

Hoarsely, he said, "By God, you *are* a rattlesnake."

With a furious, jerking movement he grabbed the brandy decanter and strode from me to a back room.

Shaking with anger, I snatched a ledger from one of the oak tables and hurled it after him. The ledger crashed into the doorjamb above his head, then fell to the floor without doing the work my fury intended.

I backed away, frightened as Delveau turned to me. His face was hard and grim, his mouth set in stiff, determined lines. He eyed me with distaste.

"We dine at eight, Madam," he said quietly.

CHAPTER 14

As the dinner hour approached, I sat despondent at the dressing table while Nan did my hair. I reflected on my encounter with Delveau and felt deeply ashamed for threatening him about the Indian woman. Even as I made the threat, I'd known I could never hurt the comte no matter how much I might hate his son.

Hate.

Bitterly, I reflected on the irony of my situation. Only two persons in the world stirred hate in me, and yet, one of them was my own husband and the other, the devil whose child I carried.

Delveau and Sir Gordon. I sighed in disgust. Two of a kind. So very different and yet so very much alike. Both exerted a strange power over me. Both played me as easily as a musician plays his instrument. When I was in the presence of either of them, I felt at sea and unsure of myself, as if they, not I, controlled my destiny.

I sighed heavily. Nan looked up.

"You don't like it done this way, Danni?"

I stared at her reflection in the mirror.

169

"What?"

"It's the latest Paris style, with the curls going tumble over a silk band."

I blinked dumbly.

"Lor' lummy, Danni, what's the matter?"

Her face was soft with sympathy. Weighed down, I yearned to pour out my heart to someone. But confide in Nan? It wasn't possible. I sighed. If only Christian would sail for Virginia. Christian would be everything to me—my friend, my confidant, my lover. . . .

Nan peered hard at me, her brown eyes widening in anxiety.

"Nothing's wrong with the baby?"

I patted her hand.

"No, no, the baby's fine."

I glanced at the clock. Eight. A shiver of apprehension ran up my spine. Delveau had said eight o'clock. I didn't doubt that if I failed to appear, he'd come up to my room and *drag* me down to dinner.

I stood. Nervously, I checked my image in the glass. Earlier, when Nan asked what gown I wished to wear, I'd replied indifferently. Now, I regretted my lack of interest. She'd chosen a gown of pale pink silk with long flowing sleeves and a low neckline. The delicate silk of the skirt followed my figure, outlining the small curve of my belly and making gentle pronouncement of coming motherhood. Nan had done my hair in soft curls, pale wisps and tendrils framing my face.

I sighed in dismay.

How could I hope to face Delveau as an equal while looking like this? The girl in the mirror looked too fragile to stand up to a sick cat!

Oh, well, I sighed. Perhaps Nan had chosen wisely after all. I was too heartsick to fight. I'd had enough of battle for one day. The starch was gone out of me. Let Delveau carp and rail. He'd find that on this one night, I had no spirit for railing back.

Gulping a deep breath of air for courage, I hurried along the corridor and descended the ornate winding stairway. The click of my heels brought Delveau to the foyer below. So he'd been waiting! Watching the clock like a schoolmaster! Damn him!

He leaned carelessly against the banister below, watching me. His pose was casual, but his clenched jaw told a different story. I could see he'd prepared himself as carefully for the dinner as Nan had prepared me. To my irritation, he looked disturbingly handsome. He wore a well-fitting dark waistcoat and breeches to match. His ruffled white shirt contradicted his air of ruggedness and yet—at the same time—suited him.

The set of his jaw told me he had inured himself to a grim evening. But as I descended, my silk skirts whispering, his expression wavered, softening. He smiled warily, and I warmed to the admiration in his eye. But then, his careful gaze moved to the unmistakable curve of my stomach, and he stiffened. His dark eyes flashed up at me accusingly, and I was stunned by the raw hurt I saw. Quickly he looked away.

I felt a stab of empathy. How must it be for a man to look upon his wife and see, in her swelling body, proof of another man's pleasure? North's fleeting expression of pain so moved me that I resolved to be gentle this evening, no matter how cutting his behavior might be.

By the time I reached the bottom step, he'd reined in his emotions. His face was that of an indifferent, detached gentleman who finds himself under polite obligation to dine with someone he dislikes.

"Good evening," he said coolly, offering his arm in required politeness.

"Good evening."

My hand quivered as I took his arm. My silk skirts rustled as he led me through the unique foyer. Charlotte had cleverly decorated her foyer with narrow, floor-to-ceiling mirrors, gilt ones, recessed among carved wooden panels. Our images jumped out at us, and I was struck by how well we looked together. Delveau, so dark and handsome, towered a head above me. Myself? I seemed a delicate pink and gold contrast to his dark rugged looks. I knew Delveau spied the reflections too, for I heard him catch his breath sharply.

A formal dinner was laid for two at one end of the long

dining table. The room shimmered in both candlelight and firelight. Delveau seated me, then took his place.

He signaled the serving man with a glance, and wine was poured. Dinner began. We found it difficult to look at one another and even more difficult to converse. There was simply nothing to say. The dismal dinner hour crept by. A clock ticked dolefully, and Delveau glanced at it often as though willing its hands to move faster. Clearly, he was as uncomfortable as myself. But there was a dogged set to his shoulders that warned me he meant to ride out the evening he had ordered, come hell or high water.

Only amenities passed between us.

Would I like more wine?

No, thank you.

Would I care for another serving of sauce on the poached trout?

No, thank you.

The food, though I found myself without appetite, was excellent. If Aunt Sally ran such a kitchen of offerings, it was no wonder the comte and North treasured her.

Delveau seemed completely at ease in all of this elegance and opulence, which surprised me. I'd seen him completely at ease enjoying rough food with the crew in the seamen's galley aboard ship, and I could only imagine he was equally at home in the rigorous, primitive life of an Indian village. Truly, he was a man of many faces. I wondered how many of those faces I would ever see.

When the last course was served and finished, Delveau broke the strained silence. Would I take coffee in the drawing room while he took brandy and a cigar? Startled by the unexpected invitation, I said yes and then instantly regretted it.

In the drawing room, I settled upon a green damask settee. Delveau, with brandy and cigar, stood at the mantel, staring into the fire. His back was to me, as though he'd forgotten my existence.

When my coffee was served, I sipped it as quickly as I could, then rose to leave. North did not turn around, although surely he heard the rustle of my skirts. As I crossed the drawing room to the door, a black depression settled upon me, weighting my steps. The blackness was suddenly so heavy that I longed to weep. This situation was not to be borne! Indeed, no one could long endure it. I must get away, I must escape....

At the door, I made a decision and whirled around. My words cracked the silence like rifle shots.

"North, I want to go to Alexandria and attend to my father's business. May I have your permission to go?"

"You have it!" he snapped, as though nothing would please him more than to be rid of me.

My heart sank at his response.

"I would stay a month or more, if I may? If your father can spare me?"

He scowled into the fire and said nothing. At last, he shrugged.

"Yes. It is best."

I stared at his profile, silently willing him to turn and grant me at least one kind parting look. But he did not.

"North?" I said softly.

"What now!"

I winced at his snappishness. How he must loathe me. I swallowed.

"May I— May I stay in your house in Alexandria?"

He turned, the scowl deepening in his face. He slung his cigar into the fire, then slowly strolled toward me.

My heart pounded fiercely.

When he stood before me, he reached out and gently touched my shoulder for a moment, and I quivered. Oh, that his slightest touch should move me so! It wasn't fair!

I glared up at him and he removed his hand. He gave me an unhappy smile.

"Dianna, you are my wife," he said sadly. "My home is your home. Do not distress me with this constant asking of permission."

His words brought quick tears to my eyes. I averted my face so he couldn't see how he'd moved me.

Wife.

For the first time, he had called me *wife.*

I swallowed, struggling to retain my composure.

I whispered, "Then I shall leave tomorrow, if I gain your father's consent. I shall take Nan with me."

As I spoke, one of my curls untwisted, coming undone and falling against my shoulder. Without thinking, North gently lifted the curl and drew it back where it belonged. It was a tender, husbandly gesture, and somehow it filled me with overwhelming grief.

"Take Sandy with you, also," he said softly. "The lad will be no use to me, lovesick and moping about in Nan's absence."

I swallowed hard.

"Thank you, North."

My gaze met his unhappy, brooding eyes.

He inclined his head in a bow.

"Not at all, Dianna."

A rush of emotion swept through me. It was a sudden storm, shaking me to the core. I was painfully aware that I longed for him to take me in his arms, to hold me, comfort me, to beg me not to go.

I studied his unhappy face. How could I be so torn? How could I hate him one moment and the next moment, yearn for his mouth on mine?

I whirled from him in confusion. Choking back a sob, I fled from the room. I felt his dark brooding eyes upon me, watching me go.

The November sky hung heavy and gray as I prepared to leave Twin Oaks. The coach waited, icy beads of rain drumming upon it, its six horses pawing the ground and shaking their traces, heads bowed against the wind. On top of the coach, two drivers huddled, swathed in canvas cloaks and broad-brimmed hats.

All was ready and yet I lingered on the portico, reluctant to leave without bidding North good-bye. But he was nowhere in sight. My heart ached dully. Surely he would see me off, would he not? Surely he would not let me go without some small sign of good will?

As the minutes ticked by, my hope died. I started eagerly at every step and scanned the grounds for his tall familiar figure. But the only person darting across the grounds from a white cottage beyond, was Dr. Tibbs. He reached the coach quickly, slung his valise up under the tarpaulin, then vaulted up the few stairs to greet me.

"I'm to accompany you, Mrs. Delveau," he said, grinning cheerfully and doffing his hat to run his hand over his head.

Puzzled, I frowned.

He grinned again.

"Your husband is concerned about your condition, Mrs. Delveau!" he explained.

Taken aback, I blushed.

"He is being foolish," I murmured. "I am only beginning my fifth month, Dr. Tibbs."

He chuckled, and wiped his spectacles dry with a pocket kerchief.

"He's not foolish, Mrs. Delveau. He is merely a young husband much in love with his wife!"

I felt my face redden. I turned from him, my thoughts confused, my pulse racing. Could Tibbs be right? Did North feel any affection for me? Or was his concern for the child his father would call grandson?

My eyes cast about, searching for North. Sandy and Nan huddled in a corner of the porch, holding hands, lost in lovers' talk.

"Sandy! Where is your master?" I called.

His head receded into his collar, turtlelike.

"He— He— he be gone, M'am."

Dr. Tibbs put in, "Ah, I believe he went hunting, Mrs. Delveau. And a sorry day for it! When Mr. Delveau stopped at my cottage this morning, he was wearing hunting gear—buckskin."

His words stabbed. How foolish I'd been to hope!

"Of course, I had forgotten he intended to hunt," I mumbled in my distress.

So North had not even waited for me to quit Twin Oaks before running to the woman he preferred! I clutched my cloak around me and hurried out to the coach. Servants brought heated bricks, and Sandy arranged them under our feet, then tucked us in with lap robes.

At last, the coach lunged forward and we were off. Closing

175

my eyes, I feigned sleep to escape the lighthearted conversation that peppered the journey as Dr. Tibbs, Sandy and Nan began to talk. I shut out the voices and struggled with my own painful thoughts. It tormented me that North should be with his Indian woman. Starlight! God, how the name suited her! Even large with child, she possessed a serene beauty, graceful and gentle. In all fairness, I had no right to hate her. She'd done me no wrong. Indeed, it was *I* who'd wronged her. My heart softened to the Indian woman as I remembered the sudden despairing slump of her fine shoulders as North had told her of me at the dock. She loved him.

I brushed away my tears. If North had gone to be with Starlight as she delivered his child, then he went where decency bade him go. Could I respect him if he'd abandoned her? I knew I could not. But fresh tears welled up as I recalled certain words. *When I love, I love forever!* I had to face facts. My husband was a man of integrity. He would never stop loving Starlight. He would never abandon a child he fathered. But in a sudden flash of illumination, I knew, too, that he would consider *our* marriage vows binding. He would never divorce me, abandon me.

I sighed deeply, a strange new sense of humility creeping into my pride and beginning to eat away the edges of it. My thoughts flew to North. What sort of hell must he be enduring in all this? Surely he must feel trapped? Caught like an animal in a snare, the snare growing ever tighter. How must he feel, wed to a wife he cannot trust, wed to an English girl who does not love him?

Not love him? My conscience contradicted me. *You are falling in love with him, Danni. Admit it!*

No! It is Christian I love!

But the honest voice deep within taunted, *If that is so, then why do you care that North does not love you?*

My first piece of business in Alexandria was to send for Jim Downey, my father's Virginia manager. Sending for him grated on me sorely, for it brought back memories of Downey's sister, Amanda Creel.

But my hostility toward Downey vanished the moment the

somber little man stepped into my study. For he was not at all like his sister, but seemed serious and dull as dishwater. He parted with smiles only sparingly, as though they cost him a shilling each.

I could sense Jim Downey was not happy to report to a woman, but he bore his duty with reasonable grace and respectfully answered my questions in careful detail. As the interview progressed, he seemed less and less bothered by my sex. He spoke to me as he might have spoken to my father or to Christian, and I was impressed by his lack of pretense and by the zealous interest he took in his job.

I tested his honesty and avarice by telling him we were thinking of expanding an office to the frontier, to the forks of the Ohio, placing its management under himself. Any manager who hoped to skim personal profits would be delighted with such an arrangement. In the wilderness, there would be a laxness and an absence of control over inventory. A clever manager could bilk a company of several hundred pounds a year.

To his credit, Jim Downey adamantly opposed the expansion. And when I informed him I would be spending the next few weeks examining his books, he did not bat an eye but asked which accounts I wished to see first.

While I'd not found anything amiss in the tobacco accounts, I was suspicious of the fur accounts. Figures had a way of changing unexpectedly throughout.

Watching him carefully for reaction, I said, "Mr. Downey, I will start with the fur accounts."

"Very good, Mrs. Delveau," he returned without pause. "Since my time is heavily taken with tobacco, I have entrusted the fur accounts to my chief clerk, Mr. Lasher. I shall instruct Mr. Lasher to expect your visit."

So, I thought, it's not Downey skimming, but this clerk, Lasher.

I poured Mr. Downey another cup of tea. He nodded gravely as I handed it to him. He attempted a social smile, but smiles, obviously, were not his forte.

"Mr. Downey! I prefer you say nothing to Mr. Lasher. I much prefer to find the books as they are today."

His eyes widened, then slowly narrowed as he drank in my message. He set cup and saucer on the table with a thud.

"As you say, Mrs. Delveau!"

I could see he was dreadfully upset. Obviously, he had trusted Lasher implicitly. His face reddened, then grew very pale.

With surprising dignity, he delivered a brave speech.

"If you find anything amiss in Mr. Lasher's books, you will, of course, require my resignation as well. I take full responsibility for all that happens in the Virginia office. But I want your father to know, Mrs. Delveau, that I have taken great pride in serving Brandley-Cartwright. If anything is missing, I will see to it that your father is repaid. To the last penny." He rose to leave. I put my hand on his sleeve to stay him.

"Mr. Downey, my father and Mr. Cartwright are most grateful for your loyal, faithful service. They will not hear of your leaving! In fact, they have instructed me to tell you your yearly salary is henceforth raised by fifty pounds."

For a moment, I thought he might accidentally smile. But he only turned pink with pleasure and bowed to me gravely.

"That is welcome news, indeed, Mrs. Delveau."

I followed him out to the entryway.

"Oh, Mr. Downey—"

He turned and bowed gravely once more.

"Is your—sister—well settled in your household?"

I had forced myself to ask the question. I was determined to rid myself of petty jealousy where North was concerned.

Mr. Downey gave me a sour half-smile.

"Until last evening, Mrs. Delveau, Amanda seemed most settled. However, last evening a Dr. Tibbs came calling, and today my sister seems in a dither—quite addled." He grimaced and went on. "I fear I found coffee grindings in my breakfast porridge this morning."

He bowed again and bade me good-day.

As the door closed behind him, I stared in astonishment. Mrs. Creel and Dr. Tibbs? I could hardly wait to tell Nan.

On the third afternoon of my stay in Alexandria, as I sat poring over papers in preparation for my confrontation with

Mr. Lasher, I heard the merry trills of female laughter in the entryway. I opened the door of my study just as Harold, the head houseman, tapped on my door.

At once, an apple-cheeked little woman with shining white hair swept past Harold and gathered me up in her plump arms.

"So *you* are North's wife! God bless you, my child! Why, you are even more beautiful than people say! Welcome to Virginia, Dianna!"

Kissing me heartily, she hugged the breath from me. I was astounded. Was this the way Americans behaved?

Laughing at my surprise, she said, "I am Agatha Fairfield, my dear. These are my daughters: Abigail, Caroline, young Agatha, Prudence, Jenny, Sally and Susan." She laughed. "I have no sons, so of course, your North is my son!"

No sooner had my bones been crushed by each of the Fairfields in turn, including twelve-year-old Susan, than another wave of visitors rolled in. It was a Dr. Kreik, his wife and two daughters. Behind the Kreiks came a tall, striking-looking man with russet hair and laughing eyes, who pronounced himself North's better at cards and at raising racehorses: Colonel Washington. Colonel Washington introduced his young stepson whom he had in tow.

With Colonel Washington's arrival, the drawing room exploded in conviviality. I could see at once that this big handsome man must charge the atmosphere with excitement and merriment wherever he went. Everyone was drawn to him, and it was not five minutes before young Susan was seated on the arm of Colonel Washington's chair, demanding tales of Indian scalpings. I smiled at Colonel Washington's adroitness. With ease, he turned the subject to teasing Susan about some newly acquired puppy she owned.

Slipping into the entryway, I quickly smoothed my hair and dress in the hall mirror. Who *were* these people? And how was it they seemed to be such good friends of North? Somehow, I'd never pictured him in social situations. I fussed at my hair. Had I known company was to arrive, I'd have gowned myself suitably and allowed Nan to do more than just pull a comb through my curls.

I hurried toward the kitchen to fetch Harold, hoping tea

might be made and whatever sweetmeats and tidbits that were available might be served to my guests. Hurrying, I nearly crashed into Harold as he wheeled out a large tea cart. I looked at it, astonished. There was a lovely tea arranged on the cart: a large gingerbread with a bowl of lemon sauce beside it, tarts of apple and pumpkin, a large silver tray of rolls filled with minced chicken.

I was overwhelmed.

The man looked up at me, wondering at my surprise.

"This is Virginia, M'am. Virginians, they dote on dropping in, M'am. Mr. Delveau is *always* prepared."

The drawing room bubbled with conversation and laughter. While everyone conversed with me in a most friendly manner, it was clear that Colonel Washington, with his magnetic personality, was the hub of interest. He had an eye for the ladies, and they for him. The young woman claiming the lion's share of his attention was one of the older Fairfield daughters, Abigail. She was a ravishing young woman, tall and green-eyed, with shining chestnut hair.

As I gazed at her, she sensed my eyes upon her, and swung her glance to me, tossing her long, red hair as she moved. The laughter died in her eyes as she looked at me, and her bottom lip pouted outward. She gave me a look so icy that I started. Then she turned back to Colonel Washington.

I was dumbfounded. Why should Abigail Fairfield dislike me so? She didn't even know me!

As I sat there, perplexed and pouring tea, twelve-year-old Susan Fairfield plunked down on the settee beside me. She smiled mischievously and whispered in my ear.

"Don't let Abby bother you, Mrs. Delveau. She hoped for North, you know!"

Startled at her comment, I set the tea pot down with a clunk. The precocious little girl reached for an apple tart and sank her teeth into it blissfully.

"She hoped without hope," Susan said airily, trying to be grown-up. "Abby always bragged that North favored her, but of course, he didn't." She leaned toward me, conspiratorially. "He used to call her Abby-Tabby."

"Tabby?" I whispered, taken aback by the child's candor.

"For Tabby Cat!" she said with satisfaction, throwing her sister an unfriendly look.

I opened my mouth to stop the little minx, but she went on imperiously.

"Tabby's angry that you got North. She'll try to scratch. But you must simply put her in her place, Dianna." She sighed. "After all, a woman must fight for her man."

I laughed.

"You are naughty, Susan."

"I know. I snoop, too. I read diaries and things—"

"You do?"

I looked at her in astonishment, then burst into laughter. Her eyes met mine, and our friendship was sealed in an instant.

"Susan, you *are* wicked."

She nodded happily.

Just then, a controlled angry voice cut across the room.

"Susan! I'm certain you're boring Mrs. Delveau! Come sit with me, sweet," Abigail Fairfield ordered.

Under her breath Susan muttered, "Sweet? At home Abby calls me Brat." Aloud, she threw her sister a saucy answer: "I'm not *boring* her. I'm *entertaining* her."

A furious look came into Abigail's eyes, but then she turned and gave Colonel Washington a dazzling smile.

"Susan, you must stop," I said seriously.

Another Fairfield daughter moved toward us through the crowd. There was worry in her gentle eyes. Caroline Fairfield would have been pretty except for the smallpox scars on her face. Even the wax and heavy powder she wore failed to hide them. She gave me a shy smile, then threw an imploring look at Susan. Obviously, Caroline Fairfield was the peacemaker of the clan.

"Be good, Susan, and go talk to the Kreik girls," she suggested softly.

Susan groaned but got up to leave, and I could see she respected Caroline as she did *not* respect Abby. But as she moved, she placed her small hand on my shoulder.

"Dianna, I want you to know that if you should ever die, I'll marry North and take care of him for you!"

I was touched by her honest affection for North.

"Why, thank you, Susan!"

"My dear!" Caroline gasped. "You must not say such things!"

Susan shrugged.

"But Caroline, North is my favorite person in all the world!" She gave me a pleading look. "Oh, Dianna, last Christmas before the comte became so ill, all of us went to Twin Oaks. What fun we had! North took us sledding every day!" She turned to her sister. "Don't you remember, Caroline?"

Caroline laughed softly.

"Indeed, it was fun. But, Susan, you mustn't say such shocking things."

Susan pouted for a moment.

"But North *is* fun," she insisted. "He tells the funniest jokes! And don't you remember the dancing, Caroline? And the mistletoe? He kissed *all* of us under the mistletoe!"

Caroline reddened. A look of misery passed over her gentle, pox-scarred face, and I suddenly knew that Abigail was not the only Fairfield a little bit in love with my husband. I gazed at Susan in wonder. I was loath to let her go. I was fascinated by her tales of North. I knew nothing of this side of his nature. Indeed, did I know him at all? If he was, by nature, sociable and entertainment-loving, then what had I done to him? Had *I* made him into the grim unhappy person he now seemed to be?

Tea hour ended. The visitors left in a bustle and a flurry, with other houses to call upon. I found myself with many invitations to dine and a special invitation to a country weekend at Colonel Washington's estate, Mount Vernon. Since the Fairfields were invited too, it was arranged that I would ride out to Mount Vernon with them.

My interview with Mr. Downey's clerk, Lasher, took place on a windswept, sleeting afternoon. I'd chosen the day deliberately. In such weather most persons would cling to the coziness of home or ale house, rather than pursue business. I expected to have the Brandley-Cartwright offices quite to myself.

Over Nan's arguments, I set out. Sandy drove me, though

unwillingly. The day seemed ten times windier and colder on the waterfront. Gusts of wind came sweeping around the warehouses, whipping my skirts and dampening them with rain and spray from the choppy river.

Not only did I find no trade being conducted at Brandley-Cartwright, but I found no one on duty except a cat and a snoring office lad asleep on a pallet behind the counter. I wandered about and found the office marked Joseph Lasher. I went in, snagged a faggot from the fire and lit an oil lamp. I lifted Mr. Lasher's ledgers down to the long table that served as his desk.

I spread the ledgers before me, and soon the chill day with its whining, shrieking wind disappeared from my consciousness. I was lost in the business of furs: fox, wolf, beaver, muskrat, mink, ermine, bear, raccoon. I must have been engrossed for an hour or more, taking careful notes in my own ledger, when a voice cracked out behind me.

"What the hell do you think you're doing! Who are you!"

I jumped at the voice, but did not turn around or even look up.

In a deliberately cold manner I said, "Mr. Lasher, I am Mrs. Delveau. Ambierce Brandley's daughter. And I am reviewing your extraordinarily careless books."

He drew a quick breath, then expelled it slowly. His feet shuffled nervously. Hurriedly, he moved around the table to stand before me. He was a heavy-set man of about thirty-five, balding and with tobacco-stained teeth. He rubbed his hands anxiously as he stared at me from pale eyes.

Then he laughed nervously.

"No need, Mrs. Delveau! No need to trouble yourself at all!" He gave a forced laugh. "Mr. Downey is quite satisfied with my work!"

I shot him a look of disgust.

"Mr. Downey has not studied your ledgers, but *I* have." I paused. "Your bookkeeping leaves much to be desired, Mr. Lasher."

He took a deep breath, held it, then let it out in a rush.

"I'm sure you'll find nothing seriously amiss, Mrs. Delveau." He laughed again. "A few small errors are bound to occur now and then, but"—he gave me a deprecating smile and shrugged—"in a company so large as Brandley-Cartwright, a few minor errors are to be expected."

"Expected, Mr. Lasher? I hardly think so."

His eyes narrowed as he took my measure. For an instant, I saw hate flash in those pale eyes, but then he smiled broadly.

"I'm sure I will welcome any suggestions you or your father or Mr. Cartwright might have for improving my bookkeeping, M'am." He shrugged and smiled, as though to set me at ease.

"Will you, Mr. Lasher? Fine. We begin tomorrow by inventorying the stock in the warehouse against this current ledger of yours. We will do it together."

He choked at the suggestion, then pretended to cough.

"An excellent idea, Mrs. Delveau. But may I suggest we postpone the inventory until spring? The warehouse is cold. In winter, it is certainly no place for a lady!"

I eyed him with distaste. He was a fast thinker. Obviously, the inventory was the *last* thing he welcomed having checked.

"Thank you for warning me, Mr. Lasher," I said politely. "I shall dress accordingly. I suggest you do the same. In the meantime," I paused, getting up, "I shall take this current ledger home with me to study."

His brow jumped in alarm. He made an involuntary movement toward the ledger I held, then checked himself and drew back.

So! He'd meant to sit up the night, doctoring the figures to agree with the inventory! I grasped the ledger firmly, and Mr. Lasher looked at it as a child stares at a sweetmeat that someone else is about to eat. But then, to my surprise, he recovered himself.

"By all means, take the ledger, Mrs. Delveau!"

I was puzzled by his sudden complaisance. I wondered at it as I shrugged into my cloak. Lasher was lost in thought, oblivious even to the niceties of helping a lady with her cloak. As I stalked from his office, it suddenly occurred to me what he meant to do. He had a duplicate ledger somewhere. He would alter the inventory to agree with the ledger. If I didn't miss my guess, a wagon would rumble up to the Brandley-

Cartwright warehouse sometime in the night and be loaded with furs Lasher was holding back for his own profiteering.

I smiled to myself. Did he really think I was so innocent and naive?

"Oh, Mr. Lasher," I called over my shoulder. "If you've no objection, I mean to send my menservants to spend the night in the warehouse. I understand there are thieves about! And stolen furs bring a good price just now, with winter setting in."

His head jerked up, and now he made no attempt to jolly me or to grovel. The look of hate in his eyes was unmistakable. His mouth twisted violently, as though he were biting back curses.

"Until tomorrow morning, then, Mr. Lasher."

I sensed his sneer, rather than heard it.

"Until we meet again, Mrs. Delveau!" he said in a strong and unexpectedly chilling voice that sent a shiver through me.

The next morning, I learned Joseph Lasher had disappeared without a word to anyone. There was no clue to where he had gone, and I regretted that he should escape punishment for all he had stolen in the past. But still, I rejoiced that our company was rid so easily of a dishonest man.

I thought the chapter closed, but I could not get him out of my mind. His last words stuck in my brain like arrows. They were not the words of a beaten man, but the words of a man who believed *an eye for an eye, a tooth for a tooth*. Remembering the aggression in those pale, cold eyes, I could not help but wonder how he planned to get even. And *when*.

CHAPTER 15

The day of my trip to Mount Vernon with the Fairfields dawned fair and bright. Fires were allowed to go out in the hearths in the Alexandria house, and all windows and doors were thrown open to the summerlike sunshine and balmy breezes. What strange country Virginia was! As soon as one became certain that winter had arrived with a vengeance, winter vanished and summer was back again.

The Fairfields' coach jounced along a road that followed the meandering Potomac River. Mr. Fairfield fell asleep almost immediately, his head bobbing on his chest in the pained manner of a gentleman who is bored with women's talk. Of the Fairfield daughters, only Abby and Caroline accompanied us, the younger ones being left at home.

As she'd done when I'd dined at the Fairfields', Abby talked incessantly about North, making me uneasy. Her comments seemed designed to prick and wound me.

"Has North told you how much he admires a tiny waist?" Abby asked as the coach jiggled on. "Lord. I've never known a man so admiring of a slender waist!"

I could feel myself tense, despite my determination not to let Abby bother me. North loved tiny waists? My waist was normally slender, but never—at any time—had it been as pinched and small as Abby's. And now? My pregnancy was not obvious to a man's eye, but a woman couldn't miss detecting the thickened waist. Of course Abby knew. As we rode along, I reflected sadly that slimness would not be one of my attributes in the coming months and I wondered if North would find me disgusting and ugly.

Abby rattled on about North's taste in female figures, his admiration for dark-eyed ladies, his fondness for red hair. My spirits ebbed lower and lower. Caroline, in her usual kind and gentle way, tried to fend off Abby's barbs for me.

"Dianna, isn't this splendid weather?" she cried. "It won't last long. So you must enjoy it while it is here. We call it 'Indian Summer.'"

Discussion veered to the weather. Agatha Fairfield gave a long account of Indian Summers she'd experienced in her forty years in Virginia. Even Mr. Fairfield roused himself to put in a boyhood anecdote about the weather before returning to his nap. But soon, Abby steered conversation back to her own ends. She began by raking over recent marriages of her friends.

"Lord," she said, "I can't abide an arranged marriage! When I marry, it will be a love match. A man doesn't properly appreciate his wife unless he marries for love. If he doesn't marry for love, then there is certain to be a mistress on the side!"

She flashed her dazzling but cruel smile.

"What do *you* think, Dianna?" she asked sweetly.

I knew she alluded to North and myself. The vow to Arabella must have been common knowledge among the comte's acquaintances in Alexandria. Caroline stared at the floor of the coach, embarrassed by Abby.

I opened my mouth to make some tart response, but found I couldn't. An enormous lump was rising in my throat. Even Abby couldn't know just how "arranged" our marriage was and how bitter it had become. Quickly, I looked out the window, blinking back tears.

Abby persisted.

"Dianna, I would so treasure your opinion of arranged marriages."

I glared at her, and Caroline interrupted gently.

"Abby, dear, I know *you* will make a splendid marriage. There's no girl in Alexandria with more callers!"

Abby smiled, and Caroline went on adroitly.

"Did you know that the handsome Major Hamilton will be a guest at Mount Vernon this weekend? He seemed so taken with you at church last Sunday!"

Abby leaned forward, a pleased expression on her face. She'd forgotten me.

"Did he really?"

Caroline smiled.

"Oh, yes, dear! I shouldn't be surprised if he speaks to Father!"

Mount Vernon plantation spread before us—all rolling lawns and fields and gardens, the buildings set well back from the main mansion so as not to spoil the perfect symmetry of the country setting. Far below the mansion, the river Potomac flowed deep and wide. Across the river, some of the trees still wore the gold and scarlet of autumn, but most of the trees were bare of leaves. The air was warm and soft, sweet as honey. Indian Summer, the Fairfields called it. As we descended from the coach, I could hear katydids and beetles singing long and piercingly in the shrubs and well-kept lawns. Silvery strands of spider webbing wafted through the air, sailing upon delicate breezes.

Slaves ran forth to greet and serve us. Mrs. Washington, a tiny vivacious woman, greeted me with such hospitality that I was glad I had come even though it meant a coach ride with Abby.

Mrs. Washington's bouncy little daughter, Patsy, skipped up the narrow staircase, leading us to our rooms above. To my surprise and annoyance, Abigail Fairfield followed me into my room. I ignored her and sank into the chair before the looking glass to smooth my hair. Abby preened in the glass above my head.

"Do you want something?" I asked coolly, still stinging from her remarks in the coach.

She granted me one of her dazzling, treacherous smiles. She stooped to gaze closer into the glass as she fussed with one shining strand of chestnut hair that would not behave. "I merely want to warn you, Dianna," she cooed. "People can be terrible gossips on country weekends."

I looked at her coldly, without comment, wondering what she might be driving at.

"Oh, yes, indeed, Dianna! You may hear one or two tiny rumors that may upset you. But I would pay them no attention. You know how tongues *will* wag."

"And just what will they wag about?"

"Oh, this and that."

She shrugged her shoulders, posturing from side to side and patting her slim waist as she admired her reflection in the mirror.

"To be specific, Dianna, there are rumors—North has—an Indian woman."

Eagerly, she studied my reaction in the glass.

It was an unexpected blow. I clutched the edge of the dressing table, feeling dizzy. I didn't know that others knew.

I took a deep breath to steady myself.

"I pay no attention to rumors."

The dazzling "Abby" smile flashed again.

"Why, neither do I! You are quite right to ignore rumors, Dianna. Why, when our maid, Sarah, brought gossip that you and North do not even share the same bed, why, I said to Sarah, 'Sarah! That is a foolish, wicked piece of gossip! You are *not* to repeat it.'"

I could feel my eyelashes grow thick with angry tears. I swallowed hard, but the lump in my throat would not go down. Abby did not miss noting that the barb had hit home. She scrutinized me in the glass, her chin lifting in victory.

My voice trembled.

"I cannot see how our sleeping arrangements could be of any interest to you, Abby."

She smiled archly, opening her mouth to say more, when a furious voice cut across the room.

"Nor can I!"

I jumped.

"North!" Abby cried out.

He was leaning casually against the door frame, his arms folded across his chest as though he'd been taking in the scene for some minutes. Only his deep scowl gave lie to his casual air, and that scowl, with Abby as its recipient, filled me with pure joy.

How well he looked! And how handsome! My eyes swept over him, taking him in—the elegant cut of his velvet country jacket, the ruffled shirt, snug-fitting fawn breeches and gleaming leather boots hugging muscular legs.

Our eyes met, and I thought I detected sympathy behind his frown. He strode to my side without hesitation, bent over and brushed my lips with a light kiss. Just as any husband might do. The sting of Abby's words vanished, and I looked up at him in surprise and gratitude, impulsively putting my hand in his. He gave me a small smile, his angry eyes holding mine with an intensity that puzzled.

"A good trip, chérie?" he asked, fondling my cheek.

Chérie? Dear?

For a moment, I sat dumbfounded. We had parted with such ill grace. And now? I looked up at him, perplexed. His eyes began to light with mischief, and at last I realized he meant to put Abby in her place.

My tongue faltered.

"A fine trip—*dear*. Abby was—most helpful. And, most entertaining."

His low rich chuckle told me my response had been exactly right.

"I'm sure she was, my love," he said, lifting my hand to his lips and kissing it lightly. A tremor passed through me at his touch.

Still holding my hand, he turned to Abby and gave the young woman a look that made her go pale. She backed away, stammering, "I was only trying to help, North. People do gossip about you, and I wanted Dianna to be forewarned."

North scowled even more deeply, and I was pleased to see Abby quail at his displeasure. He bowed to her. "Thank you,

Abby. Dianna and I are *most* grateful for your concern. Now, if you will excuse us, I want to greet my wife properly."

Puzzled, I studied his face. He looked down at me, his eyes dancing with humor. Then, to my amazement, he pulled me to my feet and drew me to his body as though I were some willing tavern wench.

I felt the sudden, galvanizing shock of our bodies pressing close, and there was only an instant to glimpse his face, and then my eyes slid shut of their own accord. He was going to kiss me in front of Abby—and not politely!

I shivered in unladylike anticipation and lifted my mouth to his with an eagerness I couldn't disguise. I heard Abby gasp, and then his hard, warm mouth was moving upon mine, gently at first, then with demanding passion. With shameful abandon, I reached up, slid my arms around his neck and returned his kiss fully.

Abby snorted in disgust, but I paid her no mind. Oh, the delight of being safe and warm in his arms! The world went spinning away. Everything—Mount Vernon, Abby, the Washingtons, even all of Virginia—whirled into oblivion. There was only North—North, who stirred my blood beyond all decency and reason.

Catching my breath, I gasped, "I'm so glad you came! I didn't know you were coming!"

"Little rabbit," he murmured, and there was genuine fondness in his voice.

I closed my eyes and lifted my mouth to be kissed more. His arms tightened around me, pulling me so close that I could not escape sudden and intimate knowledge of his body. I shivered at the thrill of it, and his hand moved into my hair, tangling in it, as though he meant to entangle himself in my life.

I made a little sound of pleasure, and then we were kissing again and the room seemed to spin and turn black. When at last our lips parted, it was with a reluctance on both our parts. We stood breathless in each other's arms. Light-headed and dizzy, I rested my cheek against his velvet jacket. I reveled in the comforting thud of his heart. Slowly, he began to stroke my hair.

Neither of us spoke. Then, after a long time, he said, "She's gone."

I came back to earth with a jarring thump. I began to tremble with shame and hurt. Had I made a fool of myself, responding to him in passion while *he* had only meant to teach Abby a lesson? I tried to wrench away, but he held me.

"You can stop. We've lost our audience!" I said angrily. "You only kissed me to spite her!"

He smiled down at me. His eyes lit with teasing.

"You think that's true?"

"Yes!"

I pulled away, but did not succeed. He gathered me in his arms and gave me a hard, passionate kiss.

I pushed at him.

"Don't! Don't play with me, North! Don't be cruel!"

He ignored me and kissed the thin skin of my neck where my pulse raced wildly. I tried to break away.

"And would you flee, little rabbit?" he said, chuckling softly and pressing his body into mine.

Humiliation coursed through me. He was toying. Playing with my feelings. Experimenting with me. It was intolerable that he should ride roughshod over the heart I was trying to offer.

I reared back.

"And would you rape me again!"

There was a long and terrible silence. He stiffened. He pushed me away, and I was filled with remorse. Oh, to retrieve those cruel, uncalled-for words!

"North! I didn't mean—"

His eyes narrowed.

"It is rare, Dianna, that I mistake a rattlesnake for a rabbit."

He turned on his heel and was gone at once. I sank down at the dressing table and buried my hot face in my hands. God, what was wrong with me! I *wanted* him. Yet my pride was forever throwing up barriers. Would I never surrender? Would I never yield?

Oh, North!

I knew I had hurt him deeply. I knew that the gentleman—and the gentle man—in him looked back on that night of violence with more abhorrence than I did. So why had I thrown it up to him? And his kisses, even with Abby watching, had been real and genuine. They'd carried in them apologies that he could not put into words. They had carried an unmistakable invitation—an invitation to become his wife.

I, in my foolish pride, had flung the apologies and invitation back in his face. What must he think? What must he be feeling?

Desperate to make amends, I repaired my face and hair, then hurried down to find him, determined to beg his forgiveness on my kness, if need be.

He was out on the veranda, alone, leaning against one of the white pillars. His shoulders slouched in defeat and unhappiness. He scowled as he caught the rustle of my skirts, then looked away. He went on smoking his pipe, gazing out at the panorama of water and trees.

The day was soft, gentle and fair, and I longed to make my relationship with North as perfect as the day. But the task seemed impossible.

I hesitated, studying his grim profile, but at last found courage to approach him. Touching his arm, I whispered, "I should not have said that. I'm sorry. Truly, I am."

He turned his head and gave me a cold stare. He laughed harshly.

"You're sorry? How convenient for you, Dianna. You plunge the knife in, and, when it pleases you to draw it out, you simply say you are sorry! How convenient, Madam."

I deserved it. I bit my lip.

North abruptly lunged forward and strode off the veranda, his long legs carrying him from me with a rapid finality that stirred fear. Impulsively, I lifted my skirts and rushed after him.

"Please, North," I begged as I half-ran, half-walked along at his side, "I *am* sorry. Truly."

Irritated at my running along, slipping and stumbling over the uneven brick walkway in my flimsy party shoes, he finally halted. He swore in exasperation, and I tried not to flinch at his unexpected and earthy curses.

Then he demanded, "Damn it, what do you want!"

Fear pounded in my throat.

"Your forgiveness?"

His eyes narrowed.

"You have it," he snapped. "Now, go and leave me in peace, damn it!"

He strode on down the brick path.

I hesitated an instant, then flew after him.

"North?"

"Goddamn it!"

He stopped and gave me a look meant to kill. With a fierce motion, he jammed his pipe into his mouth, clamping down on the stem so violently that it cracked and broke off. The bowl of the pipe pitched to the walkway. With an oath, he flung the stem too, and ground both under the heel of his boot.

I shuddered, knowing Dianna Brandley was being ground under that boot, too. Did he hate me so much, then?

He looked at me suddenly, his face tight with annoyance.

"For God's sake, Dianna, don't insult me by looking so frightened! I'll do you no more violence. I'll not touch you again. You have my word."

I swallowed, not knowing what to say, not knowing how to heal this awful breach between us.

"I'm so ashamed, North... saying what I did. Even as I said it, I knew you would not hurt me. I trust you."

I gestured helplessly, mutely begging him to accept my apology and truly forgive.

He stared at me for a long time, his face slowly softening. He sighed disgustedly.

"I'm damned if I know what to make of you, Dianna," he said softly, as though he were thinking aloud. "Or for that matter, what to do with you."

I looked away quickly. His face was too unhappy to bear.

The rolling lawns of Mount Vernon began to be dotted with bright silks and satins—the gowns of ladies emerging from the mansion for strolls with their gentlemen.

North frowned. He nodded toward the couple moving in our direction. I followed his gaze and saw Abby Fairfield coming on the arm of a plump young man in a scarlet military coat.

Our response was automatic. North and I moved down the brick walk, escaping the approaching couple. Hesitantly, half-fearful he would shrug me off, I took his arm. He did not seem to mind.

The stable was apparently his destination. As we strolled along through the fragrant fall air, I studied him out of the corner of my eye. What a strange man he was! North felt my gaze upon him. He looked down at me with a frown and a wary smile.

"Sometimes, I think I expect too much of you, Dianna. I forget you are so young."

"I'm not young. I was eighteen three weeks ago."

He stopped abruptly and studied me for a moment, but then we strolled on, nodding to other couples we met along the walkway.

Just outside the stables, he halted and touched my face, looking down at me as though he were trying to see into the recesses of my very mind and soul.

"Eighteen only last month?" he said softly. "Your natal day must have been a lonesome occasion in a foreign land with no one to celebrate it."

My eyes filled with quick tears at his understanding.

"Yes," I said, not daring to utter one more word because of the homesickness welling in me. I blinked back the tears and moved my chin from his hand. I *had* been lonely on my birthday. Desperately so. Even Nan, wrapped up with Sandy, had let the day pass without remembering.

North sighed.

"I forget you are so young. I forget you are hardly a grown woman."

I warmed to his sympathy, but at the same time felt the prick of being called a child.

"I *am* a grown woman, North," I said with soft stubbornness.

He studied me. Then, to my distress he burst into amused laughter and draped his arm loosely around my shoulder as though we were comrades.

"Well, then, come along, my fully grown little rabbit. Let's examine the new foals."

The stable was hushed and quiet except for the soft nickering of mares. I breathed in the clean smell of fresh straw and the good odor of healthy, well-cared-for stock. As North led me toward a loosely boarded pen in the rear of the stable, flecks of straw jumped up and clung to my skirt, and I was assailed with a longing for home. Was my horse Goldie in good health? Were my father's stable lads exercising her regularly? Would I ever in my life ride her again?

North helped me step up onto one of the pen's boards so I could see into the pen. He steadied me with his arm around my waist. In the lovely, muted sunlight spilling into the stable from the doors behind us, North's face seemed suddenly young and vulnerable. It was with difficulty that I pulled my gaze from him and looked at the animals in the stall.

The mare had twinned. Nickering softly, she seemed dumbfounded by what she had done. She made constant small noises of surprise, whuffing first at one foal, then the other. She would no sooner settle to licking one when the other would totter across the pen, claiming her attention, and she would move to lick him.

I laughed softly in delight.

"North, they're magnificent!"

He glanced at me and smiled warmly, his eyes shining with the excitement that every horse breeder feels when he views exceptional stock.

The foals, like their dam, were beautiful and unusually marked. A dove gray, they were dappled with a darker blue-gray. They carried their heads in the aristocratic manner of thoroughbreds, and their hocks were the shapely, delicate-looking hocks of swift racers.

"Don't you wish you owned them?" I whispered.

He grinned at me.

"I *shall* own them."

I smiled at him.

"Surely not? Surely Colonel Washington will never sell such a pair?"

He laughed.

"You're correct. He will never sell them. I shall have to win them at cards."

I gasped, though my startled intake was equally for the increased pressure of his hand on my waist as he helped me to stand on the board more comfortably.

"And do Virginians always wager so extravagantly?"

"Always," he said solemnly, though his eyes lit with amusement. He nodded at the mare. "I'm afraid I lost *her* to a bowl of rum punch and a gaming table."

I stared at the lovely mare, then at North.

"You once owned her?"

"And I will have her back." He grimaced. "Dianna, I may lose a few battles, but I always win the war."

His meaning was not lost on me. I smiled to myself as I carefully twisted around and put my hands on his shoulders to be lifted down. Our eyes were on the same level, and looking at each other in this way affected us both in an odd, strange way. I felt shyness, and I knew he did, too. And I felt to be his equal. He gave me a small, odd look of respect as though he felt our equality in that moment, too.

I looked at him evenly. "Like you, I may lose a few battles. But the war? Never."

He laughed softly.

"Then perhaps we are well matched?"

My heart raced at his words. I held my breath as he lifted me down. He held me in his arms a few moments longer than necessary, and I grew dizzy, thinking he might kiss me. But he didn't. Instead, he spoiled things with an unexpected frown.

"Let's join the others," he growled.

The afternoon passed pleasantly out-of-doors on the rolling lawn above the Potomac. There were bowls of punch on the veranda, and a splendid outdoor meal served from trencher tables scattered about the lawns. North was swept from me by a bevy of ladies who seemed to know him well, and I found myself enduring the compliments and silly prattle of several young men. The over-dressed fops seemed pale, uninteresting and insipid compared with my own husband, and I felt a stab of jealousy when North's dark head dipped toward the lady on his arm as he leaned down to catch her whispered comment or to laugh at a witticism. My partner for barbecue was Colonel Washington, himself. He was attentive and charming, and I was surprised to see that his attention to me drew anxious glances from North. Could he care enough to be a bit jealous,

I wondered? It seemed improbable, but still, my heart beat faster.

Later in the afternoon, I was obliged to stroll with a pompous, boring young lieutenant who constantly quoted poetry. When Caroline Fairfield wandered by, I dispatched the young man to the punch table and made my escape. I linked arms with the startled Caroline.

"Rescue me, dear!"

She glanced toward the young lieutenant, then laughed and blushed.

"Would that I had your problem."

We strolled the lawns, arm in arm, talking easily as old friends. I looked at Caroline, studying her. People said she was not pretty. But to me she was pretty. Her gentleness and generosity of spirit made her seem so.

"I have come to a sort of peace with myself, Dianna," she was saying. "I no longer expect young men to pay attention to me. So I am not hurt when they behave as I expect." She gave me a smile that was free of self-pity. "But I *do* want to marry. There is an older man, a widower past forty, who seems to like me when we meet in church. I've not encouraged him, though. I suppose I'm insuring myself against disappointment. In the event he does not propose marriage."

"And you? Do you like him?"

She blushed.

"I do. He is a man of integrity, I think. He is kind, careful with his money and he was very considerate of his late wife. And I love his children. They are darlings!"

She sighed, and we strolled on.

"But Abby would consider him a poor catch. He is of modest means, and his teeth are not of the best."

We stopped on a high bank and watched a canoe pass by, drifting on the river's current. Two boys, one of them black and the other obviously his young master, were fishing, laughing and shouting excitedly as several loose fish flopped about in the bottom of the canoe.

I squeezed Caroline's arm.

"If you like him, then Abby's opinion is of no account. Why don't you encourage him?"

An expression of the deepest misery passed over her features. She lifted her face to the slight breeze that had begun to blow off the river. She closed her eyes.

"I'm afraid that if I marry him, one day he may awake, take a good hard look at this poor face and regret taking me as a wife. I couldn't stand that, Dianna. It would be a hundred times worse than living out my life without husband and children."

"Is he really such a shallow person as that?"

Her eyes flew open.

Indignantly, she said, "He is a fine man! Please don't call him shallow!"

I smiled, took her arm and we strolled on.

"Oh!" she said as we moved along. "I see. Either I believe in him or I do not, isn't that so? If I believe him to be a good and kind man, then I must behave as though he is. I am being disloyal by expecting the worst."

There was a sense of wonder and excitement in her voice. She laughed happily, and I wondered if I might not soon have the pleasure of attending a Fairfield wedding.

We passed a pleasant half hour in sisterly talk as we strolled the grounds. We also talked for a few minutes with our host and hostess. When Caroline and I parted, she took my hand and pressed it earnestly.

"Dianna, dear, please be careful. You've caught the eye of the Stallion of the Potomac."

"Stallion of—"

She colored violently.

"It's what Father and the other men call Colonel Washington. Hasn't North told you? Colonel Washington has an eye for the ladies."

It was several moments before I comprehended what she was telling me, and then I reddened too.

"Could that be why North took time from his business concerns to be *here* this weekend?"

Caroline laughed lightly.

"Of course, dear! No man who wants to hold his wife's affections can afford to leave her long in the company of our irresistibly charming Colonel Washington!"

I fell silent, drinking it all in. Could I have misjudged North? Did he really care? Or did he merely mistrust me?

I gave Caroline a troubled look, and she, assuming I was thinking of the Washingtons, went on about them.

"It wasn't a love match, you know. Colonel Washington's Mount Vernon was in sad repair before his marriage, requiring thousands of pounds to bring it round. And Martha was a very rich young widow. . . ."

I sighed.

"I'm disappointed, Caroline. I thought the two of them not only well-suited, but in love."

She laughed gently and brushed the breeze-stirred hair from her eyes.

"They *are* in love. It is only that Colonel Washington is not yet aware of how much he loves his wife. You hear how fondly he calls her 'Patsy' and not Martha! He will discover he loves her some day. But in the meantime, he behaves as he has always behaved as a bachelor." She blushed, giggling. "The Stallion of the Potomac."

In the evening, after a sumptuous meal, many of the guests went home, leaving the houseguests to their own entertainments. Each sought his or her own pleasure. A group of women gathered in a circle and drew bits of cut-work or needlepoint from their work bags. Abby and several others gathered at the pianoforte. Groups of men played cards or clustered about the toddy bowl, planning spring horse races in Williamsburg or talking of the fierce game cocks to be had from the Sugar Islands.

One group of men, which included North and Colonel Washington, retired to the fireside with mugs of rum punch to talk tobacco and politics.

I spied the pompous young lieutenant heading toward me, a poem burning in his eyes, and I made my escape at once. To elude him, I captured a chair in the shadows, behind North, and soon was absorbed in the interesting and exciting discussion. With a pang, I realized how deeply I missed sitting in on discussions like these with Father and old Mr. Cartwright and Christian.

Forgetting myself, I excitedly threw out a question.

"But why does Virginia concentrate on tobacco to the exclusion of all else? Surely there is a great fortune to be made in grains and indigo?"

All heads swung round to me, and I caught North's surprised, but not unpleased, look as he discovered I sat near. One portly gentleman burst into wheezing laughter.

"Upon my soul, Mrs. Delveau! You are a flower in a garden full of weeds! And most welcome, too. But surely you don't want to bother your pretty head with talk of crops, stiff-necked governors and trouble on the frontier?"

All of the gentlemen except North broke into polite laughter. Embarrassed, I rose to leave. But North reached over the back of the settee and took my hand.

"Gentlemen, my wife is most unusual," he said without a trace of sarcasm. "A business ledger is to Dianna what a scrap of needlework is to any other woman. She has long been involved in the Brandley-Cartwright company's business and probably knows more about colonial trade than *you* do."

He gave me a level, respectful look.

"Please stay, Dianna," he said.

Flushing at all the unwanted attention and yet overjoyed with North's fair assessment of my abilities, I hurried around the settee and seated myself next to him. He draped his arm over the settee, his velvet coat sleeve brushing my shoulders. Sensing my discomfort at being the center of attention, he adroitly drew attention from me by flinging out a provocative question.

"I ask you, gentlemen," he said with a chuckle, "are we under obligation to sell our tobacco to Mother England? Or shall we toss the old girl on her ear and seek markets where we might realize much greater profit?"

He could not have created a better diversion. Loud, frenzied discussion followed, and quickly each man made his colors known. There were some who advocated obedience to the crown and many, like Colonel Washington and North, who held shockingly radical positions.

The hubbub went on in great heat, with tempers flaring. A young major of His Majesty's forces, a distant kin of Mrs.

Washington, burst out furiously, "Gentlemen! Your attitude is incendiary! It could only mean war in the end! And divided loyalties! It would mean brother fighting against brother!"

Colonel Washington lazily unfolded his long legs. He got up, strolled to the fire, snagged a faggot from the embers and lit his pipe.

When he finished with his deliberate fiddling, he turned, knowing all eyes were on him.

"Still," he said quietly, his heavy lids drooping, "I have observed that even brothers do sometimes fight."

The portly gentleman who'd addressed me earlier spoke up, wheezing as he spoke, his color rising.

"I think we are all agreed that war is the poorest of solutions. It would mean devastation of all that we have built up in these colonies. It would mean plunging our frontier settlers into a precarious position, fending off not only our English brothers but the savages who wait for any sign of weakness."

Another hot voice jumped in.

"And what of the Ohio Land Company? Many of us here are stockholders—you, Washington. You, Delveau. The company has settled border men and their families along the frontier and promised them protection. What will become of them? You know what happened to settler families in '55, when the French loosed their 'hairdressers'!"

Colonel Washington filled his cup from a bowl of toddy on the sideboard. He turned to North with a frown.

"You've lived among the Nations. How do you see the Indian situation in the event of war?"

North leaned forward, his face lined with concern.

"The Cherokee are moral people. I would welcome them as allies. But the Cherokee will side with the British and fight against us. They see the king—the 'Great White Father Across Great Pond'—as all-powerful. The Cherokee will take up the tomahawk and attempt to slaughter our settlers on the frontier.

"The Powhaten and Pamunky will be no problem. They are of no account, decimated by smallpox and internal Indian wars. But the Shawnee will smell the blood of battle and revel in it. They will slaughter indiscriminately—our people *and* the British. When the Shawnee run out of whites to kill, they will fall upon other weaker Indian Nations."

His voice shook with passion. He got up abruptly and went to the toddy bowl.

"By God," he said, "if I had my way, I would march the Virginia militia into Shawnee country tomorrow. I would wipe them out—every Shawnee man, woman and child."

The young major choked in indignation. He stood up and thrust out his chin at North.

"You speak like a barbarian, sir!"

"I do not!" North corrected him sharply. He strode to me, and I flinched as he picked up a lock of my hair in his hand, held it toward the major, then let it fall to my shoulder.

"This is my wife," he said to the man. "Before I would let her fall into the hands of the Shawnee . . . I would . . . take her life myself. And consider it an act of true affection."

I gasped, as did some of the men. His eyes met mine, and I knew beyond any doubt that he meant what he said. I shivered, and his face softened. He patted my cheek, as though to comfort me.

"You joke, sir!" the major continued pompously. "If you are *not* joking, then, sir, you *are* a barbarian."

I caught my breath, expecting North to lose his temper. But he only laughed harshly and sat down next to me, his smile grim as he looked at the young man.

"On the contrary," he said. "It is the British who daily prove themselves barbarians, Major. Last month, a renegade party of Osage raided the Maryland frontier, killing and scalping a border family there. A party of border men pursued the murderers, caught them and killed all but one. The one, they tortured until he revealed that an agent of the crown paid them to raid. *Ten pounds sterling for the scalp of each colonial—man, woman or child!*"

The room rumbled in anger.

North laughed bitterly.

"You see, Major, to have our frontiers constantly in flames is to the advantage of the crown. What His Majesty's agents are doing in Maryland, they will soon be doing in most of the colonies. The king means to maintain control by keeping us between the devil and the deep blue sea!"

North's impassioned speech left me as stunned as it left the major. I cried out, "My government could never be so cruel! It cannot be so!"

A low rumble of sad laughter filled the room, then died away into silence. North got up, refilled his cup, then toasted one and all in the room with a single gesture.

"My wife, gentlemen, forgets she is a Virginian now," he said wryly, lifting his cup toward me. He frowned at me, and I fell silent, ruminating on his words.

Colonel Washington got up, stretched his long arms and yawned. "Gentlemen, I propose we curtail our talk to tobacco this night. Refill your cups, by all means! We'll sup with our charming ladies at midnight and then, perchance—after the ladies retire—a game of cards, gentlemen?"

Once more, the room rumbled with good-natured talk and relieved merriment. No one, it seemed, was eager to dwell on what might be happening at this very moment out on the defenseless frontier.

North brought me a glass of wine.

"Cheer up, little rabbit," he whispered, a teasing smile on his face. "I won't hold it against you that you've the bad luck to be born British."

I stared up at him, half-irritated, half-amused.

"Thank you, North," I said crisply. "And I won't hold it against you that you've the bad luck to be born a barbarian."

He burst into easy laughter, then sat down beside me and promptly forgot me as he jumped into a heated discussion of tobacco prices.

The room grew stuffy with most of the men smoking, and the wine added to my sleepiness. Voices droned on in monotone. I was not at all aware of falling asleep, my head against North's shoulder, until I felt him shake me gently.

"You're going to bed, Dianna."

He helped me up. Groggy with weariness—the day had been full and my pregnancy drained my energy—I let him lead me through the company and up the narrow stairway. He carried a candle, and I could see the little slave girl who was assigned to wait on me, fast asleep on a pallet at my door. North made a motion to wake her, but I put my hand on his arm. It didn't seem fair to wake a sleeping child. North gave me the candle, then stooped and pulled the child's blanket up over her shoulders. She snuggled in with a contented groan.

Inside the room, he placed another log on the fire, then came to me, turned me around and, as though I were a sleepy child, began unlacing the back of my gown. I was too tired to protest. When he finished, he took a towel and lifted the kettle from the hob near the fire, pouring steaming water into the porcelain bowl on the washstand.

"Sleep well," he said, heading for the door. "I'll be back later, after cards."

I blinked. I was suddenly wide awake, as though I'd gulped a mouthful of prickling brandy.

"What do you mean?" I said, unable to keep fear out of my voice.

He sighed irritably.

"Everyone assumes we sleep in the same room. Would you have me spend the night in the stable and feed Abby's rumors?"

"No!" I said quickly, clutching the bodice of my loosened gown to my bosom. "But where will you sleep?"

He sighed again. Impatiently.

"The bed will do."

"But . . . where will *I* sleep?"

He shrugged in growing irritation.

"The bed is large enough for two."

I turned away, hurt and angry. How offhand he was with me! Did he mean simply to get into bed with me and, as Nan would put it, make no bones about it?

Stung by his casual, indifferent air, I stalked to the window and stared out upon the plantation below. It lay bathed in moonlight. The river Potomac slid by, a silver liquid highway in the moon's bright light. A feathery cloud puffed across the full moon just as North strode up behind me. I could detect anger and impatience in the sound of his boots on the floorboards.

He stood behind me.

206

"I forced you once, Dianna," he whispered fiercely. "If you think I would repeat that act, then you do me an injustice!"

He gave a bitter, harsh laugh.

"You are not, by God, irresistible!"

I slumped at the tongue-lashing and he went on without pity.

"I mean to sleep comfortably in a bed tonight. If *you* chose to sleep sitting up in a chair, then do it! Your choice does not interest me."

He was gone at once, the door closing with a thump that matched the forlorn thump of my heart. Blinking back tears, I slowly washed, brushed out my hair and got ready for sleep. Nan had packed a warm granny's gown for nightdress. As I looked at my image in the glass I didn't know whether to laugh or cry. Resistible? Definitely. I looked like a ten-year-old child.

Taking a comforter, I settled into the chair by the fire, but it was impossible to get comfortable no matter how hard I tried. Even the baby protested. He stirred deep within me, as though scolding at my choice of a night's resting place.

An hour dragged by, then another. Cramped, aching all over, I finally flung off the comforter and stumbled into bed. Sleep came at once.

I awoke to the sound of splashing. Raising up on one elbow, I blinked sleepily. Behind the screen, someone was washing at the washstand.

The room was bright with firelight. More logs had been placed on the fire, and they were blazing and crackling. In a moment, North stepped from behind the screen and into the firelight. He was naked except for toweling wrapped around his loins. With another towel, he was vigorously rubbing his dark hair dry in front of the fire.

At the unexpected sight of him, his body hard and muscular and frighteningly male, I felt my heart leap and begin to race.

I sat up in alarm.

"What time is it?" I whispered.

"Almost four," he answered without bothering to glance at me.

My throat tightened. I pushed back the bedclothes and got up.

"I feel well rested," I said nervously. "I think I shall dress and go downstairs. I'll read by candlelight until daybreak."

He turned, still toweling himself dry.

"You'll do no such thing. Go back to bed and go to sleep."

Ignoring his words, I began to gather up my clothes. I would dress behind the screen.

He crossed the room quickly, seized my upper arm in a grip of steel and led me back to the bed. "Get into that bed," he directed. "Go back to sleep."

His tone told me he was not to be argued with, but I went on stubbornly.

"I'm not tired."

He gave a snort of a laugh.

"The hell you aren't!" he said. "Now, get into that bed." He gave me a little push, as one might push a disobedient child. "In your condition, you need your rest."

His final words twisted through me, making it clear that it was the child who mattered, not me. It was the child who kept the old comte alive.

My lips quivered. Trembling under the insult, I jerked back the bedclothes and flung myself into bed, hugging the edge of it and turning my back to where he would presume to sleep. I squeezed my eyes shut. Angrily, I strangled my pillow.

"That's better," he said flatly.

I heard him move around the bed, caught the soft plop of his toweling falling to the floor. Then the bed sagged and jiggled under his weight as he got in.

I gritted my teeth. Did he care so little for my sensibilities that he would sleep naked? I wanted to rail at him, hurt him as he had hurt me.

"A gentleman would wear a nightshirt!" I hissed.

He gave a tired chuckle.

"So might I, little rabbit, if I had one with me." He yawned and settled in, his back to me as mine was to his.

As I lay there, my heart pounding, I could hear his breathing even off, growing slow and deep. There was the faintest trace of a snore.

So! Getting into bed with me did not stir or disturb him in the least! He was as calm and unperturbed as if he'd found

208

himself spending the night in a crowded inn and was required to share the bed with fellow travelers.

Well, thank God for that! I told myself, punching the pillow and settling down to sleep. Yet, tears unexplainably came rolling down my cheeks. I dashed them away with my fingers and searched under my pillow for my kerchief to stifle sniffles that seemed to be building, despite my efforts to fight them back. Soon, I had a full-scale battle on my hands. Fearful of waking North, I buried my face in my pillow and let the tears flow.

Suddenly, North's tired and irritated whisper cut through the air.

"I cannot sleep, Dianna, if you are going to bawl your head off all night."

I swallowed, choking back the sob that threatened. What a heartless beast he was! Struggling to control my voice, I whispered coldly, "You are mistaken. I am *not* crying."

He rolled over in bed with a furious lunge.

"By God, I am sick of your lying!" he whispered. "For once, speak the truth! You *are* crying, and I *will* know why. Tell me!"

I buried my face in my pillow and let the sobs come freely.

"Did I hurt you when I took your arm?" he demanded in a fierce whisper.

"No!"

"Are you afraid of me?"

"No! No!"

"Then tell me why you are crying," he demanded ferociously, "and for the first time since I have met you, make it the truth!"

His demand generated a fresh flood. I felt beaten down, crushed, stepped upon. I didn't know *why* I was crying. Or did I? A dozen answers—all of them sham—flew through my brain. I rejected them. I had to. The truth was not in them. The truth, I knew, lay hidden in how I'd felt when I'd seen North step from behind the screen at the washstand and into the firelight. The truth lay in the wild thumping of my heart as I'd beheld his strong male body.

With a last sob, I swallowed my pride.

"I'm crying because . . . because . . . I want you."

The silence that followed my words was as loud as thunder. Only a log dropping in the fire disturbed it. I heard the abrupt whoosh and hiss of sparks flying up.

For a long time, North made no response, and I lay there, clutching my pillow as waves of shame surged through me. My confession was the ultimate humiliation. My pride was gone. I was without defenses.

At last he spoke, his voice husky, quaking.

"And you think I don't want you?" he whispered. "My God!"

He touched my shoulder with a hand that trembled. Then his hand moved to my face. He smoothed back the hair that was damp from my tears. He moved close, putting his arm around me and resting his cheek lightly on mine. His touch was not sexual, but comforting.

"Shall I tell you when I first wanted you?" he whispered, chuckling softly at some memory.

One last sob tore out of me. But it was a sob of joy.

"Yes," I whispered, reaching up and curling my hand into his.

"That first day at Brandley Manor," he murmured. "I came tearing up those white marble stairs, furious at the prospect of being forced to honor my father's vow. I was determined to make Dianna Brandley hate me. But then, a most unusual housemaid came to the door. She had a sweet, scared face and eyes the color of my favorite waters in the Caribbean—bright blue, shining, clear. I knew she was Dianna Brandley, and I was intrigued and amused. I played the duped fool that I might study her. When I left Brandley Manor that day, I was a man divided. My loins ached with wanting her while my brain congratulated me for escaping such a clever woman!"

He kissed my cheek softly.

"Do you want to know what I told Sandy that day?"

I wiped away my tears, laughing. I turned to him and whispered, "Yes!"

He kissed my lips lightly, as a father might kiss his child.

"I told Sandy that being murdered and scalped on the Virginia frontier was a thousand times preferable to marriage with Dianna Brandley."

I laughed, but there was pain in the laughter. For I sensed his deep reservations. He was far from trusting me. A sudden and wounding revelation came rushing in: North was a congruent man. In him, body, mind and spirit were one. He did not compartmentalize himself as most men did, taking sexual pleasure with one woman but maintaining a trustful husband-wife relationship with still another. North's body might yearn for me, but his mind and spirit were appalled.

I raised up on my elbow and looked into his dark, troubled eyes.

"What is to become of me, North? What will you do?"

He gazed back at me, his eyes solemn.

"I don't know."

With a little cry, I collapsed against his shoulder. He held me close. Fumblingly, he stroked my head.

I yearned for him to take me, and I knew that he yearned, too. His muscles were tense, his breathing labored and harsh. Hesitantly, I reached out and softly touched his hard belly.

He drew a sharp breath and flung my hand away.

"You carry another's child!" he said angrily. "I don't want you like this."

Crushed, I turned from him. But he cursed softly, then he drew me back into his arms and cradled me, murmuring words of comfort and telling me to go to sleep.

Exhaustion, on both our parts, finally did what our wills could not. Together we drifted toward sleep. In that golden moment that comes just before sleep, the baby jolted me with a tiny kick.

North felt the movement. He lifted his head, and our eyes met in shared sadness.

"This marriage will not be without its measure of agony, little rabbit," he said softly. "Neither for you because of Starlight, nor for me because of Cartwright."

I opened my mouth to protest tiredly that the baby was not Christian's, but then shut it in despair. North would not believe me. Why should he? I had given him no basis for trust.

"Danni," he whispered haltingly, "Starlight has given me—twin sons—"

My eyes filled with tears. I rested my cheek on his shoulder, too heart-sore for words. He was soon asleep, taking me and my tears with him.

CHAPTER 16

"I think, Dianna, that I shall seek a new backgammon opponent. You are too easy to beat these days," the comte complained with a twinkle in his eye as he gammoned me, then swept the pieces from the board and totaled the score.

"Three shillings you owe me, daughter!"

His piercing eyes searched my face.

"Are you tired, my dear?"

His eyebrows lifted in sudden alarm.

"You're not ill, Dianna!"

Moving gracelessly because of my pregnancy, I adjusted his slipping lap robe and patted his hand.

"Certainly not ill, Papa Andre. Tired, perhaps. Your grandson keeps me awake nights, drumming his little feet."

The comte smiled. "But of course. *All* Delveau babies are lively in the womb."

Delveau babies . . .

My eyes fell to my hands. God protect him from the truth! I'd grown fond of Papa Andre. He was innately gentle, a courtly man. I'd found those same traits in his son. But there, all resemblance between father and son ceased. The comte was a thin short slip of a man with peacock blue eyes. Who would take him for the sire of his tall and handsome son? Yet he had been my sustenance during North's absence. Since that morning at Mount Vernon when he had announced his plans to leave for Williamsburg and the Caribbean to look into the rumors of insurrection on his sugar plantations.

Andre wagged a scolding finger at me.

"You are only a month from your ordeal. If North were here he would make you rest. You *must* give up your household responsibilities and take your rest."

"Indeed she must, sir."

Mrs. Krause sailed into the drawing room carrying a fresh pot of tea and the comte's evening tonic.

"Are you aware, sir, that Mrs. Delveau sat up last night with the lad who was hurt in that hunting accident?"

She and the comte frowned at each other, then at me.

I sighed. Was the mistress of Twin Oaks under such scrutiny that she could do nothing unobserved?

I eased into the only chair I'd found comfortable of late and arranged pillows behind my aching back. It was daily becoming more difficult to find a restful position. And this evening, there was a peculiar twinge to the usual ache.

"Young Henry was spitting blood," I explained. "He breathed easier, seeing me there."

Mrs. Krause pressed me to take a cup of tea, then said, "But the comte and I will breathe easier seeing you resting properly—in your bed!"

"Indeed!" Papa Andre added.

I laughed tiredly and sipped the tea.

My back twinged again. This time, sharply. It made me uneasy, and suddenly I *did* feel as worn and tired as Mrs. Krause said me to be. I closed my eyes and lay my head back. How surprised Aunt Matilde would be to know that on a plantation, the hardest working slave is its mistress.

There was no end to things that needed doing. The servant and slave cabins had to be inspected and ordered winterized. There was clothing and bootmaking to organize. There was the supervising of the spinning, weaving, sewing and knitting.

Then the meat-house preparations with careful preserving of slaughtered pork and beef for winter.

And the entertaining! Virginia hospitality never ceased to amaze me. Here, one was expected to take in all passing strangers on a moment's notice. And some of them stayed for weeks if the weather grew bad.

I started. The twinge again. I began to feel apprehensive. Dr. Tibbs was in Alexandria, replenishing his supply of medicines, and, no doubt, courting Amanda Creel.

Uneasy, I opened my eyes at once, sat up and looked about for Mrs. Krause. She was pouring out tonic for Papa Andre.

"Mrs. Krause, the key basket is on the sideboard." I laughed tiredly. "I abdicate."

She gave me a satisfied smile.

"If I may be so bold as to say so, M'am, it is high time! You *must* rest, Mrs. Delveau."

The comte was helped to his bedchamber by manservants. Wearily, I followed after him, wanting an early bed. Life had been terribly full and busy in these past months. Busy, and yet lonely. I missed North. His absence gave me many empty hours to reexamine our relationship, to reflect upon my own selfishness.

I felt deeply ashamed of forcing North into marriage, and when I'd returned to Twin Oaks from Alexandria, I'd arrived determined to do a proper job of being mistress.

The days had passed in relentless work. But there was festivity as well. The Christmas holidays were gay, despite the fact that the comte and I missed North dreadfully. The Fairfields came to us. Thankfully, they came without Abby, who'd married her British officer and gone to live in Williamsburg where he had duty at the governor's palace. Susan Fairfield, with her gamin spirits, cheered me, and so did Caroline, who excitedly talked over plans for her January wedding.

There'd been a packet of letters from home. Most of the news was good. Clarie was given a birthday ball to celebrate being fifteen, and Father was eager to establish his own shipbuilding operation in Alexandria. He urged me to proceed. But I'd been jolted at news that Sir Gordon planned a visit to the colonies. Oh, that he should fall overboard!

And as for Christian, the letters named him the proud new father of a baby girl. My heart leapt at the news that Christian meant to sail for Alexandria as soon as the baby and Lady Olga were able. But Lady Olga was not recovering from the birth as rapidly as everyone hoped. Aunt Matilde said she feared for her.

Then, in January at Twin Oaks, there was the problem of Nan's marriage. It threw the whole plantation into an uproar. Nan stoutly refused to marry Sandy and leave Twin Oaks before my baby's birth. Sandy had been furious. Playing second fiddle to an unborn babe!

Before North had left for the Caribbean, he had given Sandy permission to wed and had to told me where the signed deed for the 100-acre tobacco farm near Williamsburg would be. He wanted that to be his wedding gift to Sandy for his faithful service.

Sandy, in his anger at Nan's stalling, had packed up his saddlebags and gone riding off to the Philadelphia road, declaring he would wed the first wench who took his fancy. Nan went into hysterics. She spent her days crying and stumbling about—so much so, that the comte remarked drily, "Dianna, will you kindly send your girl to her room? It's tea time and I should like to enjoy my tea without someone weeping into the biscuits."

But in a few days, Sandy returned, hat—and heart—in hand. The couple enjoyed a tearful reconciliation. They compromised. They would post banns at once, then marry and live in Nan's attic room until after my baby's birth. Then they would leave and begin farming on the tobacco farm North gave them.

Slowly, I climbed the grand staircase. My legs felt heavy as lead. The ache seemed to be moving downward. I wished North were home. I would fear nothing if he were home. Oh, so much had happened in his absence! That memorable encounter with Starlight...

It happened in late November. One of the sons of a free bondsman, a boy of fifteen, had been out chopping firewood in the forest. He wandered into a nest of rattlesnakes that were not yet into hibernation. He'd been struck three times. His companions cut and drained the wounds at once, but by the time the boy was carried home, his fever was high and his body swelled with the poison.

I sat by the boy's distraught mother as Dr. Tibbs did his best. But the boy's heart was racing, and all of us sensed that the rapidly pounding heart must soon stop altogether.

Sandy, who'd helped carry the boy in, touched my sleeve hesitantly.

"M'am? Snakebite this bad—uh, M'am—only the savages kin cure it. North would send for—er—"

I stared up at him, not comprehending his meaning. Sandy's eyes skittered away in embarrassment. Red color mottled his neck.

Slowly, I understood what he was suggesting, and my own heart stopped. He meant to go for Starlight!

I stared at the floor, my heart thudding in fear and jealousy. How could I bear to have her at Twin Oaks? But the boy's fever was increasing, despite Tibbs. His poor body was taut with pain, despite doses of laudanum.

For several moments, I couldn't answer Sandy. When I did manage to answer, my voice shook.

"Please. Fetch her at once."

"Thank you, M'am."

Starlight arrived on horseback. She was accompanied by a girl who looked to be her sister. Each of them had a fur cocoon strapped to their backs. In each cocoon was a pink-cheeked, bright-eyed baby with fierce black hair. A dull ache spread through me at the sight of them. North's babies.

I was taken aback to see how well she was dressed. Her cloak was a fine one of hunter-green serge, lined with silver fox. I swallowed hard, realizing who had given her the beautiful cloak. I blinked as tears threatened. Of course, North would provide fine things for her. He loved her, just as he must love the two imps who peered curiously from their snug cocoons.

The girl took charge of the babies. With only the slightest glance in my direction, Starlight hurried to the sick boy. Her air of serenity and calm brought instant hope to everyone in the cabin. The boy's mother stopped weeping and looked up, light returning to her eyes. Dr. Tibbs stood by, alert, eager to study native medicine.

Moving with grace and dignity, she set to work. She placed knife blades among the hot ashes in the fireplace. She brewed an herb drink and coaxed it into the boy. When he lapsed into unconsciousness, she began to work on him.

As she picked up the knife, I had to look away. But then curiosity at her skills drew my eyes back. She cut the wounds, then staunched the blood with red hot blades. The smell, the sight of the wounds made me light-headed.

When each wound was opened and drained anew, she mixed herbs with grease and smeared the balm over the wounds. She laid odd-shaped leaves over the wounds, then bound them lightly with strips of cloth. Every half hour or so, she changed the dressing, casting into the fire the old leaves that were mucky with the poison being drawn out.

I visited the cabin often that day. Starlight worked on, calm and confident, only taking time to retreat to a chair in a corner to suckle her babies when they cried for food.

By evening, the boy's fever was down, and an air of celebration permeated the cabin. The boy's mother was weeping again, but this time, from relief.

"Dash it, Mrs. Delveau!" Tibbs said. "Today has been worth two years of practicing medicine in Dorsetshire!" Excitedly, he examined the leaves Starlight had used and sniffed her balm, analyzing it.

While everyone clustered around the boy as he opened his eyes and began to talk, I went to Starlight, who sat nursing one of her sons, smiling down at the baby, giving him her total attention.

She looked up, startled, as she caught the swish of my skirts. Her eyes were dark and clear, expressing neither hostility nor subservience. As our eyes met, I could see she considered us equals, and I suddenly knew North must have given her assurance that she ranked first in his heart. That she always would.

"Thank you," I whispered. My voice shook.

"You are welcome," she replied softly, startling me with her command of English.

I opened my mouth to say more, but found I could not. With quick hot tears blinding me, I hurried out. She was beautiful. North loved her. How could I ever learn to bear it?

I paused on the stairway, clutching the banister. Was it the memory of that encounter that seemed to suck all my breath away as I climbed the stairs? Or was I ill? The staircase seemed a mountain tonight. Why? Had I unknowingly strained my back? Perhaps a hot tub would help, I thought, comforting myself.

With Nan's help, I emerged from the bath feeling much better. Nan draped me in toweling and took my arm to steady me as I stepped from the brass tub. Suddenly, from between my legs came a gush of water.

I gasped.

I looked at Nan. Her face drained of color.

"God, Danni. The baby!"

"It can't be. It's too early."

I began to shake. Not from cold but from fear. My baby. It was four weeks too early.

Nan froze, unable to move.

"Ready the bed, Nan," I directed unsteadily.

My hands shook as I dried myself and pulled on a flannel nightdress. Nan flew about the room, layering the bed with confinement linen. She helped me into bed, then ran for Mrs. Krause.

I lay there alone and frightened, alternately sweating and shaking with cold. I was alone except for Charlotte Delveau, who looked down from the mantle. She eyed me with sympathy, I thought, and I fixed my eyes on her for courage. The reflected firelight danced upon her dark beauty.

When my teeth began to chatter in childish fear, I clenched my jaw and stared at Charlotte's portrait. In the past weeks, I'd grown to know her through the journals she'd left behind in this room. She was gay, capricious and a bit selfish, but also a woman of deep feelings and passions. Were she here at this moment, I hadn't any doubt but that she would take my hand and stay with me through the coming ordeal.

I stared at Charlotte for courage. Her journal entries of her stay at Brandley Manor, years before I was born, had been amusing if not complimentary about my home and family.

I have been dragged away from the Paris season to the ends of the earth! Brandley Manor is all cows and sheep and country manners. Matilde dresses like a bank clerk's wife, and there are no parties or balls. Andre and Ambierce hang over Arabella's sick bed and everyone quite ignores me. I shall have to make my own entertainment.

There were long pages of complaints about my home, and then, mention of parties and balls at Chillburn Hall.

Overnight party at Sir Gordon's. Quite gay. I went by myself. Andre and Ambierce still gloomy over Arabella's illness.

To tea with Madeline and Gordon Chillburn. A ball—in my honor!—at Madeline and Gordon's. To the spa at Bath with Madeline and Gordon. Riding with Gordon. Madeline ill with head pain. A picnic with Gordon. Roman ruins to explore. Madeline still ill.

And then, suddenly, her journal entries stopped for almost two years. Then the next entry had been about North.

North is one year old today. He walked to me this morning, dragging with him a most unwilling cat.

Charlotte...My teeth began to chatter again. Charlotte's face seemed to spin a little and then change into the face of Dr. Tibbs....Dr. Tibbs....It wouldn't do to dwell on him....Women had babies without doctors....I would, too. Surely Nan and Mrs. Krause and I would manage....

But more than Dr. Tibbs, I yearned for North. Oh, to have him hold me in his strong arms, if only for a moment, before the birth ordeal began....North...A hundred of Dr. Tibbs for only North...North...

The twinge again. This time, insistent, squeezing all breath away. When it passed, I wiped perspiration from my forehead.

Where *was* Nan? Where *was* Mrs. Krause?

I looked at the clock. I was surprised to see that only five minutes had elapsed since Nan left. My panic was playing tricks on me. I scolded myself. You are *not* a child, but a *woman*. Women endure this.

At last, Nan returned with a fretful Mrs. Krause, Aunt Sally, and a squint-eyed bondswoman who was skilled in midwifery.

Nan held my hand as the bondswoman probed at me.

She frowned throughout her examination.

"It's to be breech," she announced crossly, as though I'd done something wrong.

Aunt Sally and Mrs. Krause drew sharp breaths.

"I don't understand," I said anxiously.

"Feet first, M'am. Eight-month baby, M'am. Ain't turned proper yet for birthing."

I couldn't speak for a few moments as a sharp twinge twisted through my back, then died away, leaving me drenched with perspiration. Aunt Sally cooed and dabbed at my brow with a cloth.

"My baby—he'll be all right?"

The midwife avoided my eyes.

"My baby—he'll live?"

"I ain't tended but two breech, M'am, and—"

She fell silent.

"Yes? And?"

She was reluctant to speak.

"In one of 'em, M'am—the babe come dead, M'am. Cord wrapped around its neck, it was, M'am."

Nan cried out in protest and squeezed my hand.

"The other?" I clutched Nan's hand as another contraction twisted through me.

The woman squinted. She stared at my pillow, avoiding my face.

"Dead, M'am. Mother, too, M'am."

I turned my head away and dissolved into tears of helplessness.

"Judas! You dumb bitch! Telling Danni a thing like that!"

Nan gathered me into her arms and held me close.

"Shssh, Danni, don't cry. It's to be all right!"

I sobbed on her shoulder.

"Oh, Nan—get rid of her."

Still pressing me fiercely to her bosom, Nan dismissed the bondswoman with language I'd never heard her use before. To my surprise, Mrs. Krause completed the tongue lashing.

Aunt Sally leaned close, wiping my brow.

"Miz North, I birthed me ten babies. You think Aunt Sally's going to let somethin' bad befall Mr. North's wife?"

I clutched at her hand.

"I want my baby, Aunt Sally!"

She smiled.

"'Course you do! And we're set to work like the devil— an' pray like angels—to get us that babe!"

During the next two hours, the pains increased, then mysteriously lessened, then stopped altogether. Nan and I, in our ignorance, rejoiced. But Mrs. Krause and Aunt Sally eyed one another in alarm.

I saw the look they shared, and a tremor of fear rippled through me. I pressed my hands against my stomach. I could feel no movement. The little feet that had for weeks been giving me such a merciless drubbing were still as death.

I stared at the bleak faces around me.

"It can't be!"

They looked away.

"Aunt Sally? Mrs. Krause?"

Mrs. Krause seemed to crumble for a moment. Then she drew herself up and straightened her shoulders. She gave me a direct look.

"Here now! What are we doing!" she said tartly. "Of course your baby will live. He must!"

Briskly she took charge.

"Aunt Sally, we'll need hot soup! She must keep up her strength. Nan! Have you sent Sandy for the Indian woman as I directed?"

I looked at Nan in surprise. She ducked my glance and nodded to Mrs. Krause.

"Fine! If she can cure snakebite, she can certainly get us one little baby! Nan, get the cradle from the nursery. Clean it and line it with soft blankets. Then get the infant clothing the women have been working on."

Everyone jumped to activity under Mrs. Krause's military-like leadership, and even I plucked up courage and felt a surge of new hope.

Mrs. Krause turned to me.

"Mrs. Delveau, you must do *your* part. You must concentrate on going into labor again!"

Her command was so sincere and so ridiculous that all of us laughed. Even she smiled in embarrassment, and the fearful tension in the room abated.

Within the hour, I was again panting, riding the contractions that twisted through me. Nan stayed at my side, giving me her hand to grip and then mopping away my perspiration when each pain passed.

As the pain grew worse, I seemed to slip into a hazy, numbing void. I couldn't see clearly, and everyone seemed to swim around me. Voices echoed from great distances. Some of the voices I recognized, vaguely, as belonging to myself. I must have cried out for North and even possibly for Christian, because Mrs. Krause's head floated near. Her voice echoed down from far away.

"Your husband is in the Caribbean, dear. You remember? And of course, you're a Christian! Don't worry . . . worry . . ."

An eternity of pain swallowed me, and then there was another head looming over me. Dark skin, dark hair and a serene expression. She held a cup to my mouth, and someone else was lifting me to drink from it.

Starlight's voice came from far, far away. I blinked, trying to hear.

"Drink! Make baby come fast. Much pain—but baby live. Please drink!"

I nodded dizzily. I choked at the bitter taste and tried to wrench away. Starlight's floating face remained serene and calm.

"My baby—" I gasped.

I gulped the acrid liquid, and immediately, I felt myself being lifted from bed and made to walk. I was vaguely aware of Nan under one arm, Aunt Sally under the other. My feet stumbled and went out from under me. I cried out at being dragged from my bed.

Mrs. Krause's voice came to me from far away.

"Take a step, dear. She says you must walk—to make the baby come faster. Step, dear—come—for the baby's sake . . .
For the baby's sake . . .

223

The phrase kept spinning in my brain. Yes, for the baby's sake . . .

Suddenly, through the thick veil of fog that enveloped me, I felt new crashing pain. Pain that stabbed down, seeming to throw me to the floor.

Nan cried out. Voices whirled everywhere. The pain was a hot lance, piercing through me. I heard someone scream in agony, and wondered, vaguely, if it could be me. There was a tearing, a searing pain and then darkness rushed toward me. I flung myself into the darkness, and then I was falling—falling and twisting through miles of empty, noiseless darkness.

When I came to, I was in bed. But I was in agony. My body jerked uncontrollably in spasms of excruciating pain. I was vaguely aware that I was rolling my head from side to side, and I couldn't stop doing it.

Nan's voice called to me from miles away.

"Danni? It's a boy! And he's fine! Oh, God, he be fine!"

I tried to pull myself up to the rim of consciousness. I opened my eyes. Nan's white face hovered over mine.

She smiled a trembling smile.

"Your pain—it's from herbs she used. Only a few more hours and it'll wear off. Can you take it, Danni?" She wiped away a tear that suddenly rolled down her cheek. "Lor' lummy, I can't *stand* to see you like this."

I opened my mouth to speak, but only gibberish came out. I tried to sit up but found I couldn't even move. I felt my eyes roll in panic. Mrs. Krause brought a well-wrapped bundle near, but my eyes couldn't focus.

Then I was vaguely aware of Starlight standing near. She was wearing her green cloak, the fox fur framing her face. I tried to wrench my eyes open. I wanted to thank her, but my words were incoherent gibberish. I felt a soft touch on my forehead.

"Sleep. Fire arrows soon stop. Sleep."

A merciful blackness blotted out everything and everyone. When I came to again, I was still in agony, still unable to move. I was aware of a loud, demanding voice echoing through Twin Oaks. A door slammed. Boots stomped across the floor.

"What have you done to her! Why does she roll her head like that! Goddamn it! Where's Tibbs!"

Despite my pain, joy flooded over me. North? North? Was it only a dream?

I tried to open my eyes, but found I hadn't the strength to do so. Tears of frustration slid down my cheeks.

He touched my face and found the tears.

"Goddamn it, she's in pain! Do something!"

There was a flurry of soft voices, all talking at once.

"She'll be right as rain by tomorrow, sir—"

"She's had a difficult time, Mr. Delveau—"

"Mr. North, don't you go gettin' yourself or her in a hizzy-fit. She going to be fine!"

"Come see the baby, sir. He's your very image, sir—"

North ignored them all. I felt him sit on my bed and take my shoulders in his hands.

"Danni! Danni!" He shook me roughly. "Goddamn it, can you hear me? I love you!"

There was an angry buzz of female voices.

"Sir, don't do that!"

"Oh, sir, don't touch her!"

"Mr. North, I do declare!"

But he ignored them and continued to shake me into consciousness. At last I managed to get my eyes open, and he stopped shaking me. His face whirled, receding, then coming near.

"Chérie," he said softly, still holding my shoulders.

I looked up at him, fierce sweet joy flooding through me. North! His eyes were bright with tears. How odd, I thought vaguely. North is crying. Why does he cry? What is happening? Is the comte ill?

Despite the pain, despite the spasms that still tore through my body, I felt suddenly safe. North... What was it I meant to tell him?... That I loved him... that I'd missed him so... and I had to make him listen to the truth... the baby... it's not Christian's... never Christian's... hold me, North... The baby is not Christian's....

I struggled to speak.

He sensed my efforts and slipped his arm under me, placing

225

his ear near my lips. I wanted to say so much, but I had no control. Only odd words spilled out, here and there.

"Baby . . . hold me . . . Christian . . ."

And then the black tunnel swam toward me again. I felt North stiffen at my words. His voice came from far far away.

"I—I'm here, Dianna," he said sadly. "I'll hold you. Sleep."

When I woke, the day was well advanced. Sunshine filled the room. Everyone was sleeping where they'd dropped.

North slept in a chair beside my bed. He was leaning forward, half-sprawled on my bed, and he was breathing as though deeply fatigued. Sunshine crept across the coverlet, inching toward his blue-black hair. I had only to reach out, to touch him.

Mrs. Krause was asleep, sitting upright in a chair near the fire, her mouth agape, her chin bobbing on her bosom. Aunt Sally was gone. Nan snored on the settee, one arm dangling down into the cradle beside her. And from the cradle, I caught the first sounds of my son. He seemed to be sucking on his fist.

I felt tired and sore, but contented. My baby, alive and well. North home and beside me. A future before us all. And capping that contentedness was the memory of what North had said to me last night.

Danni! Goddamn it, can you hear me? I love you!

I stirred uneasily. Had he truly said it? Or had I dreamed it?

I reached out and stroked North's hair. The sunshine had crept into it now. It glowed blue-black in the bright light.

At my touch, he woke with a start. Alarm filled his face.

"Danni?"

"I'm fine."

I smiled.

"But what about you, love? You look"—I paused, then dipped back for something he'd once said to me— "like the very devil."

He smiled, remembering. But then, a sadness seemed to steal over his face. The sadness held a tinge of anger. I wondered at it. I touched his unshaven cheek, my fingers moving awkwardly.

"I'm so glad you're back. I missed you terribly," I whispered. "I—I love you, North."

He jerked away from my touch.

"Don't say what you do not mean!" he whispered.

It was an unexpected slap. My lips trembled as I stared at him, unable to comprehend. What was wrong? Didn't he say he loved me last night? Had I imagined it? Had I so longed for those words that my own drugged brain had served them up to me?

"Don't say anything about us," he added more gently.

He looked around. The others were stirring. He smiled, but the smile's cool friendliness was designed to keep me at arm's length. I felt despair begin to fill me.

He changed the subject.

"What will you have, Dianna? Food? A wash-up?"

I bit my quivering lip.

So we were to be nothing more to each other than polite strangers, strangers who lived under the same roof, shared the same name, but did not share the only important thing: love.

I felt my lashes grow wet. I blinked back the tears. I looked up at him. Our eyes met, and I sensed he was on the verge of saying something tender, but he clenched his jaw and looked away.

He stood abruptly. Just then, the baby gave a tiny squawk. North flushed, swinging his head toward the cradle.

I reached out and seized his hand. I drew it to my lips.

I whispered, "Don't hate him, North! I beg of you! He's done nothing wrong."

He jerked his hand away.

"What do you take me for? A monster?"

Our whispers had grown louder and louder. Mrs. Krause snorted, waking. Nan stirred. She hauled herself up sleepily, then grinned as she heard the baby's hungry cry. She picked him up and cradled him in her plump arms.

"Lor' lummy, ain't you a nice little gent! You be wantin' your mother, but first you must greet your sire."

227

Before I could stop her, Nan lumbered up to North and plunked the baby into his unwilling arms.

She bubbled, "Oh, sir! He's your very image!"

"Nan! Hush!" I begged.

North scowled at the baby. With a careful but angry movement, he held the baby out to Nan and with a terse nod, directed that she take him.

"Oh, there now, sir, you kin hold 'im. You won't drop 'im, sir, don't worry!"

"Take him, damn it!"

Nan was aghast. She took the baby at once.

North strode to the door without a backward look and my very life seemed to crash to the floor and shatter.

"North," I cried out, "will you come back later?"

He hesitated, his hand on the door.

"I have business to attend to. Then I am off to Philadelphia in a day or two."

My heart sank at the coldness in his voice.

"Please, North, will I see you before you leave?"

He nodded curtly, but the nod was noncommittal. He left.

Nan's eyes flashed fire as she tenderly put my loudly crying son into my arms.

"Judas! Just let my Sandy behave like that when we get a baby, and I'll shoot him! No bones about it, I'll shoot him!"

With a sad heart, I turned my attention to my son. I comforted myself with the knowledge that North was, above all else, a gentleman. He would never leave Twin Oaks without a courteous farewell for his wife.

But, two days later, he did just that.

CHAPTER 17

The April evening was soft and balmy. A breeze carried the fragrance of lilacs into the nursery as I tucked Jonathan into his cradle and knelt there to watch him fall asleep. He smacked his rosy lips in contentment as he settled into his baby dreams. His tiny head, as I caressed it, was warm and moist from the exertion of feeding.

I left him with Delia, his nurse. I hurried to my room. As I dressed for dinner, my fingers trembled with excitement. *North was home.* He would be dining with Andre and me tonight, and that made the evening a special occasion.

I'd seen little of him in the six weeks since Jonathan's birth. He was always gone on business—to Alexandria, to Philadelphia and Williamsburg, and even to Fort Pitt on the forks of the Ohio. And then there were the unexplained absences that came near to breaking my heart. For I knew he went to Starlight.

Oh, why did I have to care so! Was it selfishness? Or did I truly love him? If I loved him, then how was it possible to love *two* men! I'd loved Christian all my life. I was wed to

Christian in mind and spirit just as surely as I was wed to North in the legal sense.

As my new maid arranged my hair, I thought back on the night of Jonathan's birth. Had North really confessed he loved me, or had I imagined it? And had my own declaration of love for him been the truth, or was it only an emotional reaction to my suffering?

Obviously, North thought it was the latter. He shunned me. Even when he was home, he avoided making use of his room next to mine. Instead, he worked late in his cottage office and slept there.

His deliberate avoidance hurt. Hurt all the more because when we did meet, North behaved in a cordial and polite manner, inquiring after my health, coolly asking after the baby. But he was aloof. I couldn't penetrate his shield. It was clear he meant to keep me at arm's length.

And yet, I observed tiny unguarded moments when I could see he wanted to touch me as much as I wanted to touch him. There was the abrupt way his head jerked up when I entered a room. Or, the sudden spasm in his fingers when good manners required that he lend me his hand, seating me for dinner.

And yet . . . and yet . . . the avoidance.

Breathless with excitement, I hurried down the corridor. I felt I looked pretty. My figure was restored. My breasts were firm and full, a womanly look to them as they fulfilled their purpose.

I was wearing the delicate pink gown I knew North admired. My hair was caught up in a fetching tumble of soft curls, woven with pink silk ribbons. My eyes were clear and eager, and the color of them seemed to have taken on a violet hue since Jonathan's birth.

I found North and Andre in the small drawing room. They were drinking Madeira, talking companionably. Andre was tucked into his chair, his frail legs on a stool and a wool lap robe over his knees despite the balmy spring air. North sat close, and Andre draped his hand over his son's arm, tapping it lightly in emphasis as he spoke.

I hesitated in the doorway, reluctant to interrupt the father-son intimacy. But as I stood there, North sensed my presence.

He swung his head round, then arose at once and politely moved toward me.

My silk skirts whispered as I hurried forward and gave him my hand in greeting and a shy, eager smile.

"Welcome home, husband."

Three simple words, well rehearsed.

He flinched, then studied me without expression.

"You are looking well, Dianna."

I searched his guarded eyes.

"I am well, thank you." On impulse, I offered in a soft, shaking voice, "Completely well, North."

He drew back at that, and my heart sank. Abruptly, he turned to the mantel and busied himself with pipe and tobacco. But as I watched, it seemed his fingers trembled slightly.

Across the room, Andre clawed at his lap robe, struggled to rise and greet me.

"Papa Andre, don't you dare get up!" I hurried to him, took his thin hand in mine and kissed his cheek. "Dr. Tibbs says you must conserve your strength."

"Bother! For what shall I conserve it? No, my dear, you do me a disservice when you refuse to let me spend my strength on a beautiful woman."

I laughed softly.

"Very well, sir. Then I insist that *you* see me in to dinner."

He smiled broadly, his peacock-blue eyes bright with the pleasure of having his family gathered about him. He shifted in his chair to address North.

"You must give her a baby every year. It becomes her! Is she not an enchantress? I ask you, son, have you ever seen her looking more lovely?"

I quailed at the awfulness of the moment. He could not have said anything worse.

"Please, Papa Andre," I whispered, "you embarrass me."

North came forward slowly. His eyes were solemn, tinged with anger. A muscle worked violently in his jaw. But then, slowly, the coldness began to thaw in his face, and a tight, wry smile played on his lips. I sensed his change in attitude, and with a stab, I knew the change was not on my behalf. He'd made up his mind not to spoil his father's evening with aloof-ness.

The hurt must have shown on my face. Crushed, I dropped my eyes to my hands, and to my surprise, his hand touched my shoulder. I looked up.

"My father is quite right, Dianna," he said softly. "You are incredibly beautiful tonight."

And it was my turn to move away in confusion.

North set himself to his task. At dinner, he was at his best— convivial, gay, joking. He and his father served as natural catalysts for each other's wit, sparking themselves into comical repartee and then lapsing into comfortable conversation that ran the gamut from the sugar plantation to Aunt Sally's new red petticoat, which North had brought her from Philadelphia. It was as though both North and Andre sensed time was short. To watch their pleasure in each other brought joy to my heart, but a pang too. I missed my own father.

In the drawing room after dinner, the three of us sat com-panionably, talking and laughing easily. North's smiles in my direction seemed genuine though still guarded.

Possibilities raced through my mind, sending my pulse skip-ping . . .

Andre speared me with his blue eyes.

"Now, daughter, we shall have Jonathan down."

My heart took an enormous beat, then stopped.

When Andre and I dined alone, it was our custom to have the baby down for a few minutes of play. Andre would take Jonathan onto his lap and dangle his gold watch as the baby's bright eyes earnestly followed the gleam. I knew I was a poor mother, waking a sleeping infant. But for Andre, I always did it. Papa Andre was failing. His blue lips and icy hands bore testimony to that.

My eyes flew to North. His face was stiff with displeasure, the coldness returning.

"Not tonight, Papa Andre," I said quickly. "Tonight you have North."

"Tush! I want North *and* Jonathan."

He shifted in his chair and directed his shining gaze upon North.

"Son? Have you seen the baby since your return?"

North lunged to his feet and strode to the mantel.

"No."

Andre grinned.

"There you have it, Dianna. Send for Delia and the baby."

I flashed a mute apology to North.

He gave me a look of disgust and turned away.

When Delia brought the baby down, Andre made matters even worse.

"Give the baby to his father, first," he directed.

North flinched as the wiggling bundle was deposited in his arms. For a moment, I ceased to breathe. I was afraid he might accidentally drop him. But he recovered himself and rearranged the baby in his arms. He looked down at him with dislike.

Jonathan cooed loudly, feeling secure in such strong arms. But my eyes were only for North. I watched fearfully, trying to read his expression. Did he hate the baby for usurping his name without any right to it?

North frowned, and for a long time, his expression did not change. Jonathan gurgled and cooed up at him. At last, North shrugged slightly and his face softened.

Relief surged through me. So he held nothing against Jonathan! If he held a grievance against his birth—and I knew he did—it was against me, not against a helpless infant.

Delia retrieved the baby and settled him on Andre's lap. North, visibly relieved, moved to the far end of the drawing room for more port.

I picked up my glass and followed him to the sideboard. Our fingers brushed as he poured port into my glass. I stayed his hand.

"Thank you for not hating Jonathan."

He gave me an unhappy look.

"I am no monster, Dianna."

"I shall always be grateful—"

His eyes flashed in sudden anger.

"I don't want your gratitude."

"But, North, I—"

"I want nothing from you!"

My head snapped back as though he'd struck me, and I steadied myself against the sideboard. Across the room, Andre and Delia fussed loudly over the baby. My glass shook in my hand. With effort, I set it down without spilling.

I turned and slipped out the garden doors, fleeing down the hedge path, fighting tears. I had hoped for so much! But now this!

A half-moon spread buttery light over the garden, changing the mauve of the lilacs to pearl gray. I shivered, folding my arms protectively around my body as I heard North's step on the brick path behind me. I could not turn and look at him.

"That was cruel of me, Dianna. I'm sorry."

Unable to speak, I could only look up at the moon and shake my head in sorrow.

He was quiet for a long time. The moon rose slowly.

"Little rabbit, we seem to have a penchant for wounding one another."

I said nothing. I felt he might touch me, comfort me by putting his hand on my shoulder, but he did not.

Lost in our separate miseries, we stood watching the moon rise. Somewhere deep inside me, a sigh began. I couldn't stop it. It dragged itself forth, dragging with it the full weight of all the pain I'd suffered since marrying North.

"Don't, chérie," he said. "Don't cry."

Two hot tears spilled over.

Chérie. Dearest. Oh, he *was* cruel, twisting my heart this way and that! What did he want? Or not want?

I whirled to face him.

My voice shook with hurt pride.

"What do you want of me, North? Shall I come crawling on hands and knees, begging forgiveness for something I have *not* done? Do you want—"

"Stop it, Dianna."

"A divorce? Separation? Do you want me to go back to England? Do you want—"

He stepped forward in warning.

"Stop!"

"Then, what do you want!"

234

I stood panting, breathless from my tirade.

North said nothing more. His face was hidden in the shadow of a tall lilac. Around us, the buttery light continued to spread over the garden as the moon climbed steadily. From the house I could hear the faint echo of Andre's loving laughter as he played with the baby.

"What do you want of me! I demand to know!"

Suddenly, he reached out and seized my wrist in a grip that seemed to crush every bone. He pulled me to him. I cried out as his mouth, hot, hard as steel, pressed against mine. It was a cruel kiss, brutal and searing. It was less a kiss than a branding. It was as though he meant to stamp the mark of his ownership upon me.

"What do I want? I want what Cartwright owns! Your love!" I cried out in anguish.

"Oh, North, don't you know I long to own what Starlight owns of you?"

He choked. With a rough movement he flung me away.

"You stupid little—surely you know? Goddamn it, Dianna!"

He wheeled around and stomped out of the garden toward his office.

I felt weak. My knees gave way. I stumbled to a marble bench and sank down beside it. I rested my hot face against the cool marble, my heart thudding wildly.

North loved me!

I *hadn't* imagined those words the night of Jonathan's birth. And my own declaration of love had been true, too. I knew it now, knew it more certainly than I'd ever known anything. I loved him!

The thought rocked me. A hundred conflicting thoughts spun dizzily through my brain. North—only North! Not Christian.

With a wrench, I suddenly saw it all in a clear and startling light. Christian was the impossible dream of a young girl lost in fantasies about love. But North was *real*. His love was real, and I was no longer a girl but a woman. And it was North who had changed me from girl to woman!

With a sense of wonder, I drifted shakily toward the drawing room. I waited outside, until my heart slowed, and then composed myself and went in. I made vague excuses for North's disappearance. When Andre tired of playing with the baby, I carried the baby upstairs and fed him. Then I gave him to Delia. I laced up my gown and swiftly freshened my face and my hair.

North was bent over his ledgers as I pushed open the door of his office and slipped in. He glanced up in irritation, gave me a black look and returned to his work.

Haltingly, I moved into the room and stood there, shaking hands clasped behind my back. I was trembling like a schoolchild before a demanding schoolmaster. And, like a schoolmaster, North pointedly ignored me and went on with his work.

I steeled myself to wait.

I'd guessed I would find him in a temper. He was a proud man, and that fierce pride had just suffered injury. In the garden, he'd sacrificed pride to honesty. Could I do less?

I waited.

The minutes dragged by. The oil lamp on his table flared erratically. With every scratch of his pen, tall shadows jumped on the wall behind him. He looked up only once more, giving me a scowl designed to send me fleeing. But I stood my ground, wondering how to approach him. What could I say? How could I penetrate his armor? How could I tell him what was in my heart?

I waited silently, beginning to feel the utter calm that singleness of purpose can bring. Inwardly, I almost smiled. The old Dianna Brandley—Dianna, the spoiled child—could not have waited two minutes without flying into a temper. Dianna Delveau had waited twenty already.

When North finally sensed I could not be driven off by being ignored and humiliated, he looked up. He threw down his pen.

"Well?"

I opened my mouth to speak, but no words came. I looked at him helplessly, my heart knocking against my ribs. Unable to say a word, I moved toward him and, like a penitent, sank to my knees, resting my hand and my head on his thigh. His muscles jerked under my touch.

I took a deep, trembling breath. The words, unplanned and unrehearsed, spilled out slowly and from my heart.

"North, you were right when you said . . . Christian owns my love. He does. He has owned it since I was eight years old. I have loved him with . . . all . . . all the intensity and passion that fills a loving child's heart. Christian will always own that love."

I took a long, painful breath and raised my head, trembling under his cold dark gaze.

"But I am a woman, not a child. And now I love as a woman loves. My woman's love belongs to you. It is yours to do with as you please. . . . You can accept and cherish it, or you can scorn it and cast it away. It matters not. It is yours. . . . It belongs to you . . . forever."

I dropped my head and kissed his thigh softly, then rested my cheek on his leg.

North was silent. I could not even hear his breathing. He hadn't moved a muscle as I spoke.

I closed my eyes.

"I want to be your wife, North. If that means swallowing my pride and removing my objections to Starlight, then I—" I paused, swallowing hard. "I do so, even though it breaks my heart to think of you going to—" I couldn't finish. My voice cracked. An enormous lump filled my throat.

North's hand suddenly touched my hair. Not stroking it, but hovering near my head, as though in indecision.

I looked up at him through eyes that were pooling.

"I will be your wife. I will try to obey you in all things. If you want me to go now, only tell me so and I will obey. But I will not leave you unless *you* tell me to go out that door."

For a long time, he said nothing. When he did speak, his voice was unrecognizable—cracked, husky.

"Go out that door, Dianna," he said slowly, "and you . . . break . . . *my* heart . . ."

We were in each other's arms in an instant. We swayed, stumbling as the earth lurched and a table came up against us. North caught me, and then he was holding me. Holding me so tightly that all doubt vanished.

His breath was hot on my forehead.

"I want you," he said urgently. "Now!"

"Oh, North—love—"

For a moment our mouths fumbled, seeking, seeking. And then we were kissing—wild, urgent kisses that spoke of how desperately we had longed for each other over the long lost year of our marriage. He kissed me until the world went black and I slumped against him, dizzy and hardly knowing where I was—only knowing that I was home...home...home in this man's arms.

With a whisper of passion, he picked me up in his arms, strode swiftly to the back room and kicked the door shut. In the darkness, he lowered me to the couch and pushed aside my skirts. I gasped as his hand moved to my thigh. He interpreted my gasp as fear and drew back.

"Danni?" he asked in a tortured whisper and suddenly I knew how tormented he'd been by the memory of the night he'd raped me.

"Oh, my love," I whispered, reaching for him, covering his hand with kisses.

"Danni," he said. "God, how I need you!"

We came together as though our bodies had been created for each other. A glorious feeling of oneness, golden and incredibly tender. Each of us sought to give, and in the giving, received a thousandfold. I arched against him, gasping at the sweet sharp climax, and when I fell back in his arms, limp and panting, he took his moment.

When it was done, he lowered himself to my side and pulled me close. I curled up in his arms, content and shivering in the wonder of it all. The sham marriage was over. The real one was beginning. I was his, he was mine. Husband and wife. North...my husband...truly.

We lay holding each other for a long time, our hearts too full for talk. He stroked my head lovingly.

"Get the lamp, Danni," he whispered at last. "I want to look at you..."

Dizzy with love, I got up and did as he asked.

When I returned with the lamp, shadows jumped up the wall behind the couch. North had undressed. He was reclining on the couch, leaning on one elbow, a blanket pulled up to his waist. His furred chest gleamed in the lamp light, and his black hair was in wild disarray. He looked almost savage, and I shivered.

I set the lamp on the table with a nervous clatter, then turned, suddenly shy, overwhelmed by him.

He sensed my feelings, and smiled gently. He held out his hand.

"Don't be afraid... Come to me."

At his words, I thought my heart would burst with joy. Trembling, I put my hand in his. He drew me to the couch and made me sit. He turned me with a tender gesture and slowly began to unhook the back of my gown. My bodice fell forward into my arms. Carefully, he removed the silk ribbons from my hair and loosed my combs. My hair tumbled down, pale and silken. He took it in his hands and kissed it. Then he undressed me.

When he was done, he said, "Turn to me chérie..."

Trembling under his gaze, I turned to him. His eyes were a gentle caress. "You are so beautiful," he whispered, "so very, very beautiful."

Our eyes met, tender and searching. The intimacy we shared in that moment seemed to surpass even what had gone before.

"Wife," he said softly, savoring the word on his tongue. "My little wife."

His words made me ache with both love and with sorrow. There was another he called wife. After this night—after the sweetness, the completeness of being joined to him—how could I bear to share him with her? My heart thudded fearfully. What if he should come to prefer *her* to me? How could I bear the anguish of it?

"What is it, sweet? Why do you tremble?"

I shook my head helplessly. I tried to smile, but the smile quivered.

"Tell me," he urged softly, "I would know, Danni."

I bowed my head, unwilling to answer. I would not go back on my word. Only an hour ago I'd been on my knees, swallowing my pride, telling him I would not object to her.

He sat up, took my face in his hands and lifted my gaze to his.

"Is it Starlight?"

Tears of sorrow and hurt pride welled up. I dashed them away.

"North, I'm sorry. I won't cry again, I promise."

Tenderly, he took me in his arms and drew me down on the couch. He held me close, stroking my hair, my cheek, as one might comfort a child.

"You're my wife, Danni," he whispered softly. "But don't ask me to measure what I feel for you against what I feel for Starlight. Be content to know that if I ever lost you, there would be such a hole torn in my life that it never could be mended."

His voice shook with passion as he spoke, and I could not doubt that he meant his words. Still, I ached, and I sensed the ache would not lessen but would increase as my love for North grew and deepened. I slipped my arm across his warm, comforting chest, and I held him to me as though to keep him from *her*.

"I . . . I am foolish, North. I have . . . too much pride . . . and I'm . . . afraid."

He lifted his head and looked at me.

"Afraid?"

"That you compare me to . . . to . . . her."

He kissed my forehead, then my temple, then my cheek.

"Does one compare the sky to the sea?" he said. "Or the earth to the wind?"

We said no more, and the questions hung in the air, unanswered and unlikely ever to be answered. Soon, the oil lamp burned itself out, and we slept and loved in each other's arms.

CHAPTER 18

A mockingbird woke me.

The bold bird perched in a magnolia tree just outside the cottage window. It greeted the dawn by rehearsing its clever repertoire of mimicry. First, the bird mocked the strident cry of the jay, then the mild cheep-cheep-cheep of the sparrow and last, it mimicked the chittering talk of the squirrels.

Through the window I could see rosy light in the east and a glimpse of spring ground fog hovering in the hollows. The fog would burn off with sunrise, I knew.

Sunrise.

And Jonathan was much like a bird, waking early, loud and ravenous. He would be screaming his head off by now, and Delia would be frantic, wondering where in the world I was.

I looked at North sleeping peacefully next to me. He was on his side, his back to me, his bare shoulder rising and falling with each breath.

I looked at him and felt a fierce happiness and contentment. This was my husband! North. Not Christian—never Christian. But North. North only.

241

Gently, I covered him with a robe and slipped from the couch. I fished around the floor for my clothing, pulling it on as I found it.

Suddenly, unexpectedly, I found myself captured by warm strong arms and pulled back onto the couch. North hugged me tightly as a bear, playfully growling at my neck and pretending to nip it. I yelped in mock distress.

"I don't want you to go," he said. "I like you close."

I laughed in sheer joy.

"You silly, let me go! I must feed Jonathan."

"No!" he said, petulant as a six year old.

I twisted around in his arms and kissed his rough, unshaven cheek.

"I mean it, North."

He laughed softly and let me go. He lay back with his arms under his head and watched me dress, watched with friendly interest but without lust. When my bodice needed doing-up, I sat on the edge of the couch and North laced it for me. It was a curiously touching moment, his fingers fumbling on my back. This is going on in bedchambers all over the world, I thought, where husbands and wives live in affectionate union. With a sense of wonder, it came to me: *This is the first day of our marriage.*

When North finished lacing me, he said, "I'm riding out to visit my horse farm today. Would you like to ride along?"

I turned in surprise. Was this invitation a portent of our relationship? Would we be companions in life as well as lovers? Friends?

I flushed in pleasure.

"Oh, North! Just the two of us?"

He raised one eyebrow and smiled faintly.

"On second thought, that might be boring," he said solemnly. "Let's take Aunt Sally and Mrs. Krause with us for company."

"North!"

With a chuckle he swung himself off the bed and began to dress.

"It's twenty miles over, twenty back. We'll stay overnight, if you think you can arrange things in the nursery?"

I wanted to throw my arms around him and shout for joy, but an odd shyness swept over me. I hardly knew how to behave as a wife.

"Mrs. Krause can find a wet nurse. She's offered before," I said. I couldn't keep the excitement out of my voice, and my words fairly danced.

North seemed pleased at my pleasure in the invitation. He gave me a disarming smile.

"The stable in an hour, then, Dianna?"

I turned to fly, but he caught me gently by the arm and pulled me back into his arms. He kissed me, then held my face in his hands and looked down into my eyes as though he were studying me.

"Good morning, wife," he said softly.

I melted.

"North . . . I love you . . . so terribly much."

He kissed me again, then sternly pushed me out the door, telling me to scat.

I flew back to my room, not even pausing to appreciate the cool beauty of the spring morning, with its coral sun mingling in pockets of ground fog, turning the world pink.

Delia, my new maid, Louisa, and Mrs. Krause were soon pressed into action, and I saw them exchange pleased, knowing looks.

I nursed Jonathan, then nibbled at a breakfast biscuit while I splashed quickly in a tub of warm water. As I dressed, I interviewed the wet nurse Mrs. Krause found for me. She was a happy, healthy black woman. I was satisfied.

I pulled on a white shirt and a riding habit of dove gray serge. While Louisa packed my valise, I brushed my hair, tying it at the nape of my neck with a ribbon. I pulled on a perky, gray velvet riding hat.

I ran to the nursery, kissed Jonathan several more times and flew down the hall, trailed by Louisa and my valise.

North's lips twitched in amusement as he took in my outfit, but he forebore commenting on it. He himself was dressed roughly in buckskin and riding boots. He looked like a frontiersman, or even a savage, rather than the prosperous Virginia businessman he was.

Two horses stood ready, the spirited chestnut for North and a more mild-mannered gray for me. A blanket roll was strapped to the back of each saddle.

North frowned at the valise as Louisa shyly handed it to him. With a sigh, he wrenched it open. He pulled out a gown— the dress I meant to wear for dinner that night—and tossed it at a very startled Louisa.

"North!"

"Dianna, the Pedersons, who run my horse farm, are simple folk. Mrs. Pederson probably owns a total of three dresses: the one she works in every day, a dress of India calico for the Sabbath, and a black silk which she saves for monumental occasions, such as funerals—including her own! Mrs. Pederson would find it incomprehensible that any woman should require *two* outfits for an overnight trip."

"Oh."

I felt suddenly ignorant and rather a snob, not knowing how simple folk lived.

He rummaged in the valise, yanked out a nightdress and robe which he also flung to Louisa.

"But, North—" I began in despair, then shut my mouth.

"You will sleep in your shift. And, pet, your bed will be a blanket roll on the floor in the common sleeping room."

I blinked.

He dug deeper and drew out a washcloth and towel, both of which suffered the same fate. Louisa tittered as she caught them.

"Now really! I must wash, North!"

His eyes teased, and even in the midst of this minor annoyance I gloried in the happiness I saw in him and felt in myself.

"You *shall* wash," he said, "but you must learn your manners, Dianna. In a border man's house, it is impolite to use anything but the one family towel."

He laughed as my mouth fell open, then snapped shut. I folded my arms in exasperation as he tossed item after item to

Louisa. To his credit, he did tuck three small items into his saddlebag before he flung away the empty valise.

"I will allow you your hairbrush, your tooth scrubber and the bar of lavender soap. But you are not to use the soap. Give it to Mrs. Pederson as a gift." He grinned. "Lavender soap in the country is as rare as a sweet-smelling woman!"

He looked down at me, his eyes full of amusement and challenge.

"Well? Do you still want to come?"

Tapping my fingers on my elbows, I stared at him. My mouth twitched. I could see the humor in the situation.

Coolly, I said, "I know your game, North. You want to discourage me so that I will stay behind, leaving you free to take Aunt Sally."

He burst into laughter, pulled me into his arms and kissed me soundly.

I pulled away. "Heavens, North, the servants."

"Heavens!" he mimicked. "They will spread rumors that we are in love!"

At his words, I felt as though my heart would explode with happiness. It was the closest he had ever come to admitting that he loved me. Oh, there had been the night of Jonathan's birth, but that didn't count. North had assumed I was dying.

We mounted our horses and started out, laughing like children in our mutual happiness. The servants and slaves stared after us, as though we were daft.

North's horse farm nestled in a green valley that was sheltered on all sides by low, forest-covered hills. As our horses picked their way down a trail into the valley, I could count at least a dozen buildings. Split-rail fencing zig-zagged as far as the eye could see, dividing the land into pasture and paddock. There was a huge racing ring and a field dotted with jumping hurdles.

The buildings were modest, constructed of rough wood, including a house that was set apart from the rest of the buildings. A large garden stretched behind the house, and behind the garden fruit trees blossomed. I could see a woman and children working the dark soil of the garden, and one youngster was swooping through the air on a wood and rope swing suspended from a huge oak tree.

Four Pederson hounds, their hackles stiff, came out barking at us. Our horses shied until two grinning Pederson boys came running and whacked good manners into the dogs.

Children and men appeared from every direction, and a tall, big-boned, fair-haired woman came running from the garden on bare feet. She had laughing blue eyes, and she was grinning as though Christmas had arrived.

"My God, Mr. Delveau, ye've done as y' promised! Ye've brung me a woman to natter with!"

As soon as I alighted, she grabbed me and gave me a bone-crushing hug.

"Y' don't know how starved I be for woman talk, Mrs. Delveau! Come in, come in! We'll have us a cup of tea and lace it good with rum, and we'll natter the afternoon away!"

As Mrs. Pederson dragged me off, North called teasingly, "Mrs. Pederson—shall I come, too?"

"Oh, you!" she said in friendly scorn, sweeping me along and leaving North with the grinning Ped Pederson who was a larger edition of his wife, same build, same hair, same smiling blue eyes.

By the end of the afternoon, I felt "nattered" to death. Mrs. Pederson talked non-stop, covering everything from her intimate relations with Mr. Pederson to problems with the vegetable marrows. Her chatter ranged from the hens that wouldn't lay to the amazing abilities and talents of her seven children. She demanded an account of my confinement, then gave me the same for each of her birthings.

Proudly, she showed me the snug two-room house. The main room had a stone fireplace along one wall, and the room contained a long oak table, rude benches, a large bedstead where four of the children slept, and two comfortable sitting chairs. The second room held a big bedstead where Mr. and Mrs. Pederson slept along with the three and four year olds, a handsome chest that had been Ped's bridal gift to her, a box bed for the baby and wall pegs from which hung the family's modest supply of clothing.

When I admired the bleached whiteness of the plank flooring

throughout the cabin, Mrs. Pederson beamed as though I'd paid her the ultimate compliment.

"Peddy, he put the floor in three years ago. The girls and me char it down regular with ashes and lime water."

She took me down through the trapdoor into the small root cellar under the main room. In the flickering light of a candle, jars of beets, peaches and berry preserves glowed like jewels. Mounds of cool sand were studded with last fall's carrots, turnips, rutabagas and onions. Mrs. Pederson considered the root cellar the best part of her house.

"If the savages gits troublous again, I'd tuck my young 'uns down here. Keep 'em safe as turnips!"

I shivered at her casual, unworried reference to Indian attacks.

She saw my shiver and grinned.

"Not to fright yourself, Mrs. Delveau. Them devils was drove over the mountains in '63. Ain't likely to show their hides *this* side of the border. Not since Washington and his men—they built forts along the whole of the Virginia border."

At last, as Mrs. Pederson and her daughters turned their attention to supper, I gained a few minutes to slip out and find North.

He was in the barns with Pederson and a trainer called Sven. I could see he was engrossed in horse talk, inspecting the animals, making recommendations. When I touched his elbow, he started, looking at me vaguely, as though he couldn't quite place me.

"Yes?" he said, his thoughts miles away.

"Your wife?" I prodded. "Remember? Dianna?"

He burst into laughter and casually draped an arm around my shoulders.

"Forgive me, chérie. Horses are my passion."

I looked up at him through narrowing eyes.

"And I? What am I?"

"You?" He laughed softly and kissed the top of my head. "You are only my wife."

He pulled me close, and we strolled along the stalls. But it wasn't more than thirty seconds before North's arm fell away. Another thirty seconds and I no longer existed.

247

With a resigned sigh, I trailed after the men, admiring the sleek, well-cared-for horses and listening to the excited talk of training, breeding, buying, selling.

As I trudged along through the crisp clean straw, I was drawn to a stall housing two exquisite dappled gray colts. Astonished, I stopped in mid-step.

"North! Colonel Washington's foals!"

North turned, his face registering, in turn, puzzlement, then understanding, then amusement. He strolled back to me as the men moved on. He plucked a piece of straw from my gown and studied it with a pleased, secretive smile. He looked at me.

"I *always* get what I want, Dianna."

"You're awful!"

"Yes," he agreed cheerfully.

"You won them that night at Mount Vernon?"

"Mmmmn."

"North, how could you! How could you concentrate on cards, knowing I was upstairs in your room!"

His dark eyes lit with teasing.

"I knew *you* would keep, sweet. But the foals wouldn't."

It was vexing, bewildering. Would I ever begin to understand this man? A year ago, at Brandley Manor, I'd considered myself the clever one, the one in control. But now? Who was wearing the bridle and who was controlling the reins?

"Damn you, North Delveau," I said with a laugh.

As Sven and Ped disappeared into a stall, North chuckled, drew me into his arms and set about erasing all doubt that he preferred horses to women. He gave me an unabashedly thrilling kiss, finishing the kiss by nipping softly at the corners of my mouth. I felt myself melt, shivering in his arms, sighing in contentment. He held me a moment longer.

"Damn the sleeping arrangements at Ped's house!" he said softly.

My deep sigh underscored his words.

Supper was a simple, hearty affair with all of the Pederson children ringing the table and scraping every last morsel from their wooden bowls. Each small Pederson, with the exception of the middle child Ephraim, was a blond, blue-eyed reproduction of his parents. Ephraim, though, had auburn hair and gray eyes that reminded me of Clarie.

Mrs. Pederson proudly told us Ephraim and his younger brother had gone to the marsh that morning and clubbed a dozen sorus for the evening meal. Ephraim squirmed and wiggled at the unexpected attention as North and I praised the taste of the wildfowl. Two tins of cornbread rounded out the meal, and we washed the food down with tin mugs of creamed coffee.

The Pedersons went to bed with the chickens and assumed all the world did the same. So, at about the time we would be sitting down to dinner at Twin Oaks, North and I were spreading our bedrolls in front of the dying fire. We'd vehemently refused the Pedersons' generous offer of the use of a bed. They were crestfallen and did not cheer up until we gladly accepted the use of a pillow.

North stripped and got into his bedroll as though he slept in one every night. He watched me, chuckling softly as I undressed while trying to avoid the curious stares of the four little Pedersons in the bedstead on the far side of the room.

To my dismay, the sight of my lacy shift afforded them great entertainment. They giggled wildly and dove under the covers to hide. With a sigh, I eased into my hard bed. The dying firelight flickered softly.

North gave me an amused but sympathetic smile, leaned over and kissed me lightly, a chaste, good-night-wife kiss.

The children found this funny. Giggles pealed from the bedstead. I turned my head to look at them, and four sets of bright eyes vanished under wildly tumbling blankets.

"I can think of four brats I'd gladly string up by the thumbs just now," North muttered good-naturedly, slipping his arm under my shoulders. This, too, proved hilarious to the young Pedersons.

We lay there awake, unable to sleep because of the early hour. I whispered, "Tell me. What does one do in bed with one's husband when one cannot be doing certain other things?"

North gave me an amused look.

"One talks.".

"What does one talk about?"

He chuckled softly.

"Oh, one could talk about how much one adores one's husband . . . one could talk about how intelligent and handsome one's husband is . . . one could—"

"Talk about what a braggart one's husband is?"

He tapped my lips with his finger.

"But one wouldn't," he objected.

"Why not?"

"Because, love, one's husband would up-end one and beat one's bottom."

I giggled softly, and four sets of curious eyes peered out from the bed.

We lay quietly and the children settled down.

I whispered, "I like the Pedersons, North."

"Um. Good, honest people. Before Ped came to work for me, the Pedersons lived on the wildest part of the frontier. On the forks of the Ohio."

I shivered. This farm was about as close as I cared to get to the frontier. I lay thinking about the Pedersons, about how sturdy and brave and practical they were.

I moved closer, whispering, "North, isn't it odd that little Ephraim has auburn hair and gray eyes while all of the other Pedersons are fair?"

North laughed softly.

"The sensible border man simply counts his blessings and looks the other way if one of his litter appears to be a stray. Women are rare on the frontier. A border man counts himself blessed if he finds a woman willing to share the hard, lonely life. He is a hundredfold blessed if he gets a wife like Mrs. Pederson—even-featured, a good cook and preserver of foods, a child bearer, able to sew, garden, tend stock, butcher meat. So let her have her Ephraim."

I looked up at him in surprise, revising both my thoughts on the dullness of Mrs. Pederson's life and my opinions of where North stood on moral issues.

"I had no idea you were so broad-minded."

He gave me an amused look.

"Sweet, I am *not* a border man. As a husband, you'll find me jealous, possessive, tyrannical. If you even look at another man, I will lock you in your room and only let you out on every third Sunday."

I burst into giggles at the picture he drew of himself, and the Pederson children bobbed up, tittered, then dove for cover.

North took the opportunity to caress my breasts. He was gentle, but I winced in sudden pain. I hadn't realized how full and uncomfortable I would become, not giving Jonathan his feedings. North realized the problem at once and took his hand away.

"We'll leave at sunrise," he said, the lightness and fun gone out of his voice. "You'll be at Twin Oaks by noon."

I lay quiet and sad-hearted, thinking about Jonathan, thinking about North. I felt torn between them. Jonathan would always be a thorn in North's side. Yet, I loved my little son. I loved North. Where would it all end?

"North?"

He turned his face to me. The dying firelight flickered on the gleaming whiteness of the tomahawk scar. I reached up and touched it with love.

"If you like, I could...get a permanent wet nurse....I could give up...feeding him. I could accompany you on all your travels..."

He raised up on one elbow, frowning, studying me.

"You'd do that for me?"

"Yes," I said without hesitation, though the thought of handing my son to another wrenched me.

After a long pause, he said, "No. I will not permit it. A mother and her child belong together."

I trailed my fingers along his jaw. It was smooth. He'd shaved at Ped's washstand.

"But there's something more. Aunt Sally told me that I'm not...I'm not likely to...get pregnant so long as I'm nursing..."

A look of pleased surprise lightened his face.

"And you want to be?"

I met his eyes steadily.

"I want to give you a child, North. I want to prove to you that I have grown up...that I have given you my woman's love."

He kissed me. It was a chaste kiss, but deeply stirring. When he finished, he drew back from me, and I stroked his cheek. The Pederson children giggled uproariously.

"I love you, Danni," he whispered passionately.

My heart lurched.

"But you still are wary of me. You still distrust me. I can feel it. If we had a child together . . . Oh, God, North, it hurts that you don't trust me."

His face darkened with quick anger.

"You must know it hurts me, too!" he whispered angrily. "To love someone and yet to be wary of her. I would rather be shot!"

We lay on our backs, silent except for our tense breathing. We stared up at the log beams forming the roof overhead, wanting to say more, yet not wanting to.

The Pederson children stared at us sleepily, then settled into their night's rest.

"We must talk about Jonathan, North. I want you to know how it happened."

"No! Goddamn it, no."

He rolled away, giving me his back.

I bit my lip in disappointment. Would the day ever come when I could make him listen? And if he did listen, would he believe?

Outside the cabin, the hounds began to bark and snarl. The uproar was followed quickly by the sound of riders. North was in his britches in an instant, musket in hand. Ped Pederson loped out of his bedroom in his long underwear.

Someone banged on the door.

"Open in the name of the king!"

"Redcoats!" Ped said with a sneer, laying aside his weapon. North put his musket away and slid back into his bedroll with a snort of contempt.

Ped opened the door a crack.

"Lef'tenant Stephen Renfrow. His Majesty's Royal Forces. You will quarter me and my men by request of His Majesty. I shall sleep in your cabin. My men will quarter themselves and their horses in your barns."

Ped muttered something under his breath, then stepped outside, shutting the door behind him.

"Can he do that?" I asked North.

"It's the king's privilege," he snapped.

Mrs. Pederson slipped across the cabin in her flannel chemise, her long fair hair plaited in one thick braid that hung down her back. Swiftly, she whisked the rag rug away from the root cellar trapdoor. She opened the trapdoor and carried down the kettle of leftover sorus stew, then the pan of cornbread, a ham, a slab of bacon and a crock of eggs. When she finished, she closed the trapdoor and slung the rug down over it. She rushed back to bed.

"What?" I asked North, bewildered by her actions.

He chuckled grimly.

"You'll see. We Virginians are hospitable, but *not* when the guests are rammed down our throats."

Ped returned.

"Nigh a dozen of the slimy things, Mr. Delveau. All rough and tattered like. 'Pears they been out in border country for weeks."

"Buying Indians, no doubt!" North said bitterly.

Ped agreed gloomily. "I'd cut their goddamn throats as they sleep, if I'd think I could git away with it."

I whispered, "I don't understand. Are Indians bought just as slaves are?"

Ped snorted at my ignorance.

North explained, "They are buying the services of the Indians—offering to pay a set price for each settler's scalp that is brought in."

I gasped in horror just as the door opened once more and the lieutenant strode in, demanding a candle be lit and food be brought. North pushed me down in my bedroll, and lay down himself as though he were half asleep.

Ped obediently lit the candle and called for his wife. Mrs. Pederson emerged, rubbing her eyes as though she'd just wakened.

"Food for the lef'tenant, woman!"

Mrs. Pederson's shoulders slumped in distress. In a voice I'd never heard her use before, she began to whine.

"Ped, there's naught but a bit of bread. The young 'uns, they et up everything at sup."

She stumbled to the rude food cupboard, flung it open and left it open so the lieutenant could observe the truth of her statement. She fished out a hunk of wheat bread. In the candle-light, I could see the crust was puckered with age.

The lieutenant took it and sniffed at it in disgust.

"It stinks of mold! You expect me to eat that?"

Mrs. Pederson, uncharacteristically, shrank back, whimpering and weeping.

"Never mind, never mind," the young man said gruffly. "Put some logs on the fire. I'm chilled to the bone."

Mrs. Pederson did as she was instructed, winking at me as she retired to her room. The officer grunted uninterestedly in our direction as he spread out his bedroll. Within minutes he was snoring loudly. I fumbled for North's hand, nervous at what he might do. He rolled toward me, pulling me against him and settling down for sleep.

"Don't worry sweet. I won't do any throat cutting," he whispered. "At least not tonight," he added.

Before daybreak, I hurriedly pulled on my clothes. By day-break, Mrs. Pederson was putting breakfast on the table. In no way did it resemble the generous meal of the night before. Breakfast was weak, boiled coffee and oat gruel without sweetener.

The lieutenant grumbled throughout his meager, tasteless meal while the Pederson children, obviously schooled in the protocol of entertaining redcoats, ate without complaint. Ephraim caught my eye and winked proudly. I winked back.

North broke the silence around the table.

"Lieutenant, I see you have been up into Shawnee country," he said coldly.

"No!"

The young man's denial came too quickly for belief, and I noted the startled look that passed over his face.

"We have been to the forks of the Ohio—and to Fort Pitt. We are doing fur trade business for the crown."

North jerked his head at the deerskin pouch the young man

wore on one shoulder. It was embroidered, decorated in an odd design.

North said, "A nice pouch. It's Shawnee. One can tell from the quill work."

The lieutenant grew pale, then reddened. He glanced at the pouch as though willing it to disappear.

"I purchased it off a trader. Whether it's Shawnee or not, I do not know."

North smiled. It was a smile cold enough to chill blood.

"I *do* know," he said. "It's Shawnee."

The Pedersons bade us a subdued but affectionate farewell, and we mounted our horses just as the lieutenant and his men mounted to ride off in the opposite direction. I looked back over my shoulder, watching the riders leave. One of the lieutenant's men had lagged behind. He was astride his horse, watching North and myself. I caught the flash of a yellowish eye and an oddly familiar grim mouth. But I could not place him. The man smiled to himself, then wheeled his horse and cantered off.

It was several miles before the disturbing face put itself alongside a name. I'd not seen that threatening smile nor thought of the name in many months.

I felt suddenly weak with foreboding.

"North?" I said with a shaky voice. "One of those men— with the lieutenant—it—it was the clerk I dismissed—Joseph Lasher!"

CHAPTER 19

"I want to be buried in the Sugar Islands. On Saint Croix. Next to Charlotte. Have I discussed this with you, son?"

I winced, aching for North. It was the third time that day that Andre had made the same request. His mind was failing.

North's shoulders slumped in despair. With effort, he straightened himself and went on filling the glasses with after-dinner port.

"Yes, Father. We discussed it," he said gently.

"And you promised?"

"I promised."

Andre relaxed visibly, his blue eyes shining brightly at North, then swinging to me.

"Why do you children stare at me so? Am I rambling like some foolish old man?"

"Of course not!" North and I objected in foolish chorus. We looked at each other, smiling sadly at our helplessness.

Andre chuckled softly, suddenly perceiving the situation with perfect clarity.

"I find old age a nuisance. One's brain slips and slides. One remembers vividly the details of an event forty years past, but one can't remember what happened only *ten* minutes past. Such a bore! Such a nuisance!"

I picked up the wine North poured and crossed the drawing room to Andre. I steadied his shaking hand until he managed to grip the goblet firmly. He gave me a smile, then speared North with an inquisitive look.

"I've forgotten," he admitted cheerfully. "Did you tell me about Charlotte's grave? In what condition you found it on Saint Croix?"

"Yes, Father, I told you."

Andre grinned, as though determined to make light of his failing condition.

"Dolt! Humor your sire," he scolded. "Tell me again."

All three of us burst into laughter at that, and North pulled his chair close to Andre. I perched on the arm of North's chair, my hand resting lightly on his shoulder. He glanced up at me and smiled. I warmed at the unspoken message. He was glad for my presence. I returned his smile, our eyes communing for a moment in shared sadness. We both loved Andre.

North gave his attention to Andre.

"You remember, Father, the grave is high on a hill over-looking the bay. Standing near her grave, one gazes down upon water more beautiful than turquoise. . . . It is the most beautiful spot on the island. The pink marble monument you had carved for Mother grows more beautiful with age, as sun and rain fall gently upon it. Her grave is surrounded by the gardenias you planted. When the flowers bloom, the hilltop smells as lovely as heaven itself."

Andre's eyes misted. He stared into space.

"It was her favorite flower," he murmured.

"Yes."

Andre's forehead wrinkled in sudden concern.

"No dogs maraud?" he demanded anxiously, sitting ramrod straight as though he would leap up and charge off to the Caribbean if there was the slightest danger to his beloved's resting place.

North answered with gentle patience.

"No dogs bother Mother. You'll remember the iron fence and gate we ordered years ago?"

Andre relaxed.

"Ah. The fence. I forgot."

He stared off as though he were seeing all that North described. Then, with effort, he jerked himself back to the present. He gave North a keen look.

"Have I ever told you how I met your mother?"

North took a sip of port.

"Yes, many..." I pressed his shoulder.

He leaned back, caught my hand, rubbed it on his cheek and smiled up at me.

"No, Father, you haven't."

"Ah, children, *there* is a story!"

Andre rid himself of his wineglass so as to have hands free for the telling.

"I was a hardened old bachelor when I met her. And she? A child of sixteen! I'd loved and lost—"

He beamed at me.

"*Your* mother, of course, Dianna. And I was determined that if I could not have my cousin Arabella for my wife, I would have no wife."

He sighed.

"A foolish cutting off of one's nose to spite one's face, but that is the way I behaved about it. The years went by. Lonely years. Oh, there were women, but none I wanted to make my wife.

"Then, one night at a ball in Paris, I arrived to hear some old biddies gossiping in the antechamber. Shocking, they said, a sixteen year old wearing a gown of scarlet. And the disgracefully low neckline! What could her parents be thinking of! The old cats hissed about the brazenness of the girl who snubbed all but the wealthiest suitors.

"I'd been planning to take myself straight to the gaming tables. Instead, I decided to have a look at this naughty child. I strolled into the ballroom, and there, surrounded by fawning young men, was the most enchanting creature I'd ever seen. In candlelight, her shoulders glowed like fresh fallen snow.

259

Her dark eyes flashed with gaiety and mischief. She was laughing, and the sound of her laughter rippled toward me like music.

"I was bewitched!"

Andre closed his eyes. I could see, from the movement of his lips and the smile that grew there, he was reliving the evening: the silken swish of Charlotte's gown, her white shoulders, the sound of her laughter. I could almost hear the echo of her voice myself.

As Andre dreamed, North drew my hand to his lips. He kissed it. Not sensuously, as he often did in the privacy of our bedchamber, but companionably. I'm glad you're here, his gentle caress told me.

Andre opened his eyes.

"Ah! I contrived an introduction, and by the time I gained admittance to her circle, I must have been frowning sternly—so intense was my determination to have her. Do you know what the enchanting creature said to me?"

Andre turned his bright eyes on me.

I laughed in delighted expectation, and Andre laughed too, remembering.

"The little minx said, 'Good evening, M'sieur Sobersides! Are you someone's grandfather?'

"I gave her a stern look.

"'I am *no* one's grandfather or even father, Mademoiselle,' I said angrily. 'But I *do* intend to become someone's husband, Mademoiselle. Yours!'

"The enchanting creature seemed stunned. She started, like a bird who is about to fly in fright. But then she laughed, her bewitching, musical laugh.

"'We shall see, M'sieur Sobersides!' she said, and went off to dance.

"I courted her for two years before she agreed to have me."

Andre's eyes misted over. A smile played upon his lips. Then he sighed.

"Ah. Possessing Charlotte as a wife was like possessing a handful of quicksilver. I was ever fearful she would slip through my fingers, and I would lose her."

A moment of sadness flickered in Andre's eyes, and then he brightened.

"What pleasure it was for me to give her everything she wanted: Paris gowns, jewels, houses, travels. But she, of course, gave me a treasure far greater than any I gave to her . . ."

He looked up at North.

"You, my son."

Andre suddenly closed his eyes. Telling the long story had cost him dearly. His lips seemed to go blue with fatigue.

He opened his eyes and smiled foggily up at me.

"I'm tired, Arabella," he murmured.

North and I flinched, gripping hands in fear.

Softly, I said, "I'll send for the carrying chair, Andre. North and the servants will help you up to bed."

His eyelids drooped as though weighted with lead. A gentle smile passed over his lips.

"Thank you, my darling," he whispered tiredly.

The ache in our hearts over Andre's worsening condition was not the only pain North and I shared as we felt our way into husband-wife companionship and intimacy.

There was Starlight.

Never before had I felt so intensely the reality of what the Indian woman meant to North. She was his wife—*wife*. And the cherished mother of his adored sons.

Starlight stood between us as we reached out for each other, reaching as inexperienced children reach for a beautiful flame. We warmed ourselves at that flame—warmed ourselves gloriously at times—but we suffered burns too. Without warning, caustic words would flare up between us, searing, burning, causing us to draw apart. And we would have to fumble our way into yet another beginning.

For my part, Starlight intruded as an unbearable presence during intimate moments. Often, when he came to bed after working late in his office, he would wake me gently by touching my hip just so, stroking the bare skin slowly and softly. Sensual with sleep, I would roll to him and lift my mouth to his, trembling in my eagerness to have him. He would kiss me, and then, unexpectedly, unwanted thoughts would come stealing in.

When he goes to her, does he begin in the same way? Does

he stroke her lovely brown skin until she shivers with wanting him, as I am?

Does he find her kisses sweeter? Is her body more precious to him because it has borne him children?

And yet, I dared not distress North with my private agony. I had given him my love unreservedly. I had sworn I would not speak of her. I couldn't revert to being "Dianna Brandley, the selfish child" and negate those promises.

I knew North went to Starlight at least twice each month, for these were the only overnight trips he made without explaining his absence. It was a tacit understanding between us. But I cried myself to sleep on those nights, and, in the morning, steeled myself *not* to heap censure upon him by either word or action when he returned.

I tried my best to be friendly and gay. North sensed what the effort cost me. I could see it in his eyes—the confused mingling of admiration and love, sadness and self-reproach.

Gradually, as I came to understand North better, I began to realize that he agonized over the situation far more than I. For all of his sophistication and French ways, he was, at bottom, as single-hearted as Andre. I could see his stress and tension build. I knew he could not go on in this mode forever. One day, he would realize that he must, for the sake of his own peace of mind, choose one of us and give up the other.

The thought of it terrified me. For truly I was beginning to know North Delveau. He would never give up his small sons. He would never put aside their mother. If it came to a choice between Starlight and myself, he would choose her. Loyalty would demand it.

Whenever North returned from her, his sense of self-reproach kept him from re-establishing our intimacy at once. For the following night or two, he would sleep in his office, no matter how harmonious our daytime meetings. I strove at lightheartedness, and I could see appreciation for my efforts in his eyes. But one evening, after one such return, I suddenly and unexpectedly burst into tears at the dinner table. I leaped up at once. I rushed from the room.

Behind me, I heard Andre's puzzled, "What is it? Is she ill,

North?" And then his delighted, "Well, well! Perhaps she's pregnant?"

North found me in the shadows in the garden. He drew me into his arms, holding me close, comforting.

"It is intolerable for you!" he said, anger swirling in his voice, anger without a target.

I brushed tears from my cheeks.

"For you also, my love . . ."

"Yes," he agreed in a whisper.

We fell silent, holding each other as though the holding could send the pain far, far away. But, of course it couldn't.

"It *tortures* me to hurt you, little rabbit." He pressed his lips to my throbbing temple. "You don't deserve to be hurt. When I see what joy you bring to my father's last days, I curse myself."

"No! Don't blame yourself, North. The hurt is of my own making. I trapped you into a marriage you didn't want. Now, if I burst into tears, it is only because I am weak and childish."

He gripped my shoulders, holding me at arm's length, studying my face in the moonlight.

"You're wrong, Danni. You're not weak. You are strong, far stronger than Starlight."

I shivered. I stared up at him, startled. It was the first time he'd spoken of Starlight in comparison with me, the first time he'd admitted that comparisons were forming in his mind.

I trembled at the portent.

If he were comparing, then perhaps he was approaching the day he would make his choice. If he found me the stronger, then was he saying I could manage in the world on my own? That Starlight and his sons must have his protection?

Anguish flooded through me. Was I to lose North just as I was discovering how truly I loved him?

In panic, I clutched at him, clung to him. I drew his face down to mine. We kissed, long slow kisses full of pain and longing.

When we finished, and stood breathless, looking at one another in the light of the rising moon, North put his arm around my shoulders and walked me to the door of the drawing room. There, he tilted up my chin and kissed me one last time. Then, without a word, he strode off into the garden shadows.

That night, and the next, he slept in his office.

In June came distressing news from the Virginia frontier.

A border man and his family had been massacred. The condition of the bodies pointed to the work of the Shawnee. A week later, the horrible incident repeated itself in another location on the frontier. Border men were incensed. Some of them retaliated by murdering an innocent hunting party of Delawares.

"The fools!" North raged, studying his maps and charts. "Those border men are playing into the hands of the British. Soon the whole frontier will be aflame again. And when war comes with England, there will not be an Indian in all of North America to side with us!"

When another attack took place about fifty miles west of North's horse farm, North sent instructions to Ped Pederson. He was to bring his family and the stock to the safety of Twin Oaks for the summer.

Ped sent the horses and anyone who wanted to leave, but he and his family and most of the men refused to budge. As ex-border men, they scoffed at running from savages. Besides, North had made Ped part owner in the enterprise. Ped refused to be driven off his own land.

I was lying in perfect contentment in North's arms. The July moon filled the bedchamber, cool mountain air blew in through the open balcony doors.

We had just finished making love. North had taken me with an ardor that had left me glowing and contented. I was falling ever deeper in love with him and had reached the point where even his casual, inviting grin over the breakfast table could render me weak with desire, anticipation. And at his touch, I could not help but melt.

For North's part, I knew he was equally pleased. Often, he told me so, letting me know in soft gentle words when my responses thrilled him.

He stirred. He ran his hand lightly over my body until he

found my hand, drew it to his lips and slowly kissed each finger.

"I love you so very much, chérie."

Startled at the sadness in his voice, I lifted my head, shivering suddenly. I couldn't see his face. What was he thinking? What sad thoughts were in his mind?

Alarmed, I rolled toward him. I rested my hand on his chest and tried to study his face in the dark.

"North, I can't live without you. You know I cannot. Please don't ever send me away—"

He stopped my words with a touch of his finger to my lips and drew me down against him.

"Shssh, little rabbit, shssh."

I lay against him, rubbing my cheek on his shoulder, feeling the strong comforting thump of his heart under my hand. We lay silent, sleep evading us both. I was painfully aware that he was only comforting me; he'd not denied he was thinking of sending me away.

Despair lay leaden in my heart. For all of our closeness, there were still untouchable areas between us, areas as large as oceans. There was Jonathan. Christian. Starlight and her sons. The only way to bridge those gaps was to talk about them. But the agony of trying to do so!

I took a deep breath. I steadied myself to make a small beginning.

"What are your sons' names?" I whispered, my voice shaking despite my efforts to be calm.

I felt North stiffen. Though he didn't move, at the same time I sensed he moved miles from me. I heard the breath catch in his throat. He expelled the breath slowly, as though acknowledging to himself that—yes—his sons must eventually be discussed. I felt the muscles of his body tighten.

"The firstborn is Jason," he said reluctantly. "Joel was born thirty minutes later."

I kissed his shoulder softly.

"You must be proud. They are beautiful babies. I saw them when she came to help the boy who was bitten by the snake."

He lay against me, tense.

"They are creeping now," he offered stiffly, "and they scuttle about, swift as chipmunks. I will not allow them to be strapped to a carrying board for the first two years of their lives, as is customary among Indians. My sons must be free to move at will."

I smiled sadly to myself, picturing two little imps. Scrambling off in all directions, driving a mother to distraction.

"Thank you for telling me, North."

He tilted my chin, then kissed me with strange, fierce tenderness.

"Always remember I love you, little rabbit!" he said, his voice swelling with anger.

I felt as though I might die. Intuitively, I knew the source of his anger. He was thinking of giving me up. I rubbed my cheek despairingly on his shoulder.

"I will remember, my darling, I will remember."

Lying in each other's arms, we eventually drifted into sad and troubled sleep.

While reading through the gazettes that Dr. Tibbs brought from Alexandria, I found an item that made my blood run cold.

A King's officer, Lieutenant Stephen Renfrow, was found murdered near the racing ring just outside Williamsburg. His throat had been cut. It was believed to be the work of riffraff who'd stolen the young officer's sword, rings and money. The article went on to demand that the governor provide better protection for the King's citizens in the capitol.

Shaking, I hurried to North's office with the paper. I gave him the article to read. He read it with disinterest and gave it back to me, his eyes cool, calm.

"But, North, it's that lieutenant—the one with the Shawnee pouch! The one you and Ped suspected of bribing the Shawnee to attack border people."

He showed no surprise. His expression did not change. He returned his attention to his ledgers.

"North," I demanded, "do you know who did this?"

"There *is* such a thing as frontier justice, Dianna," he said coldly.

266

Shuddering at the steely tone of his voice, I turned and fled from the office.

In early August, a packet of letters arrived from England. North smiled at my excitement as he handed me the letters that were mine.

"You pounce upon them like a cat pounces upon a mouse, my sweet," he teased.

I laughed excitedly and settled myself in a chair in North's office to read them. North went on with his ledger work, occasionally looking up to study me.

It was too soon to hear my family's reaction to Jonathan's birth, but still I hoped. However, these letters contained nothing of Jonathan. The news was mostly melancholy and sad.

Lady Olga had died of complications following the birth of her child, and Christian was beside himself with grief. He could hardly be consoled, my father reported, and tended to ramble on foolishly about "his dearest little sister, Dianna."

I held the letter to my bosom and stared off into space. Odd, how one's heart lurched slightly at news of an old love. I could hardly hold the letter steady in my hand as I read on.

Over the top of the letter, I saw North watching me, a strange, almost angry, expression on his face.

Clarie's letter was a surprise. She sounded so grown up. Her letter was full of Christian. She was devoting herself to his full recovery, visiting him every day and bullying him to come outside in the spring sunshine to play with the baby on a rug on the lawn. Dear Clarie! She told me confidently that she was certain Christian's spirits would mend by the end of summer.

Aunt Matilde's letter was full of housekeeping details. She was training one of Nan's sisters as upstairs maid. The chickens were not laying well and this she blamed on gypsies who'd traveled through the area. She was ordering new window hangings for the drawing rooms.

She made clear her displeasure at Nan marrying a colonial. She'd heard that all colonials of the lower class regularly beat their wives, and she begged me to look into the situation at once, rescuing Nan if the situation warranted.

I smiled to myself. Surely Sandy was the gentlest and kindest of men. If it ever came to blows in that marriage, I hadn't the slightest doubt which of them would come off worse.

The last letter made my heart jump. The letter was in Christian's hand. And the seal was broken as though the letter had been read.

I turned to North in puzzlement.

"North—this letter to me has been opened!"

He met my eyes.

"Yes," he said coolly. "I opened it."

I could hardly believe my ears.

"You *admit* you read it?" I found it astounding that he would do such a thing.

"Yes," he said nonchalantly, turning back to his ledgers.

"How dare you, North! It belongs to me!"

I was so angry, I shook. Jumping to my feet, I paced back and forth, stabbing him with my eyes.

"The letter belongs to you. But *you* belong to me. So, of course, I read it."

I whirled at him.

"You don't trust me—even yet!"

He did not deny it.

I scooped up my letters and rushed to the door. North was on his feet in an instant, and as I yanked the door open, he slammed it shut with his hand.

"You will read his letter here."

I glared up at him through tears of anger, humiliation. How could he treat me so? I loved him, and he loved me.

"You will read it here," he repeated.

"No."

He snatched the letter from my hand and the others spilled to the floor.

"Then I will read it and you will listen."

"No!"

I lunged for the door. North caught me by the shoulders and pushed me roughly into a chair. I buried my face in my hands. How could North do this to me? How could the man I love humiliate me so?

Coldly and with sarcasm, he read Christian's letter aloud.

My dearest Danni,
I have been in a black pit since the death of Lady Olga.
My only light is the memory of your sweet self. The brief
meetings we enjoyed before your departure come back to
cheer me—no, to save my very life. I mean to leave for
Virginia as soon as I am able. Will I still find you are my
dearest little sister, Danni?
    Your Christian

When North finished, he flung the letter into my lap. Silence
spread like a pall between us.

At last I whispered, "North, he was mad with grief. He
would not have written so if he were in charge of his faculties."

North snorted.

"The stupid oaf is in charge of his faculties for the first time
in his life! He means to have you!"

He drew himself up and gave me a chilling look.

"Tell me, Dianna, will he succeed?"

I stared up at him in disbelief. How could he ask such a
question after all the nights we'd lain in each other's arms?

My lips quivered. My voice was a whisper.

"You insult me, North, and you insult yourself. I am your
wife in body, mind and soul. Your wife in every way. *No* one
can destroy our marriage. Only *you* can do that with your dark
suspicions."

I watched emotions play upon his face. He wavered, hesitating, then swung away from me and slammed out of the
door, striding toward the stables. He was gone the rest of the
day. He returned just before dinner.

Freshly bathed, barbered and looking so roughly elegant in
a dark suit and shirt of cream, he seated me at table as usual.
But his hands lingered on the back of my chair, and with a
heavy heart, I looked up, questioning.

He stooped, shyly kissing my mouth. His lips were warm
and lingering.

I shivered in surprise.

"Forgive me, Danni?"

I felt a rush of happiness. It was the first time, ever, that North had admitted he was wrong.

Eagerly, I offered my mouth to be kissed again.

"Gladly, my love," I whispered.

His mouth moved on mine—gently, but with the promise of later delights.

Across the table, Andre beamed at us.

He quipped, "I have heard there are such oddities as good marriages without kisses. Rather like good dinners without wines, do you not agree? Nourishing, I'm sure. But terribly boring."

Summer was kind to Andre. The warm sun heated his bones and improved his blood circulation. By the end of August he was robust enough to sit out-of-doors watching Jonathan learn to crawl on a rug by his feet. The two, one so old and the other so young, spent many happy hours together under Delia's watchful eye.

Early in September, we were gathered in the drawing room for our usual evening port and conversation. For Andre's sake, a fire burned in the grate. The firelight played upon his fur lap robe, painting his face with bright spots and shadowy hollows.

"It is very dark in here, children," he remarked suddenly.

North and I looked at each other uneasily. There was plenty of light—the fire and several candles.

Andre swung his bright blue eyes to me.

I felt a prickle of fear spread up the back of my neck. Gooseflesh washed over my arms. His voice sounded strange with a faraway quality to it.

I set my glass down with a thump, and hurried to him, kneeling, taking his frail hand.

"Papa Andre? Are you all right?"

"Father!"

North crossed the room in a rush.

Andre looked up at North and smiled. Then he turned to me.

"My dear Arabella, would you . . ."

His voice faded. An instant of perfect peace lit his face. Then he sighed and fell forward into my arms.

Five days later, when the last of the funeral guests had left, Andre's sealed coffin was carefully crated and loaded on a wagon. It was covered with tarpaulin against the rain that was coming down steadily. Behind the wagon, a coach and horses waited.

A cold drizzle fell without respite. The day was as dismal as the task facing North. The air smelled of leaf mold and wood smoke, a harsh contrast to the gardenia-scented resting place that awaited Andre in the Sugar Islands.

I pulled a cardinal cloak around my shoulders and hurried out into the rain for one last farewell. North and I'd had no more than scattered moments of privacy since Andre's death. Between acting as host to funeral guests and tending to pressing business affairs that Andre's death brought to a head, North had no time. At night, he slept exhausted for a few hours in his office.

North was checking the wagon. He wore a long black cloak against the rain, but no hat. His face was white and taut. He looked weary. I touched his arm, and he turned to me, tiredly took me into his arms and kissed me, oblivious to the drizzle and to servants who stood gawking.

"Good-bye, Danni."

I winced at the lifeless quality in his voice.

I drew his head down and pressed my own warm lips to his cold mouth.

"I shall be here waiting for you, North." At his frown, my heart skipped a beat. "If you want me to be," I added hastily, hardly knowing what our relationship was to be now that Andre was dead. He scowled, and I clutched the cardinal round me, shivering. But then, he reached out and touched my face.

"If you were *not* here when I returned," he said softly, "I would turn the world upside-down searching for you."

A servant rushed up and pressed a hat into his hand. North looked at me a moment longer, then boarded the coach.

With a lurch, the small, sad procession of coach and wagons left Twin Oaks, spattering mud and stones in its wake.

I stood watching him go, turning his last words over and over in my mind as the rain fell, soaking coldly into my hair.

CHAPTER 20

It was as though the very heavens themselves joined us in mourning Andre. Rain fell cold and steadily for many days. A northwest wind off the mountains nipped the rain into particles of ice. Sleet battered the windows and balcony doors of my room—Charlotte's room—and when I slipped out for a walk to escape the oppressiveness of my own spirits, sleet lashed at my face with a vengeance.

I missed them sorely, Andre and North. It seemed unbearable to know that one would come back and the other wouldn't.

Matching the weather, Twin Oaks sank into a gloom. Servants dragged themselves about, cheerless, wearing long faces. None of us on the plantation—from mistress to lowliest kitchen slave—had realized that the heart of the place was a frail small man in whose veins flowed indomitable cheerfulness and optimism.

Mrs. Krause bustled about in her crisp and efficient manner, a tense determined smile pinned to her lips as she strove to return Twin Oaks to a state of normalcy. But her eyes were red and swollen. I suspected she wept when she was alone.

Even Nan and Sandy, who'd come to console us, were subdued and quiet.

Only Jonathan remained unaffected by Andre's passing. He was a happy baby. He consoled Twin Oaks. But it startled me to see him growing to look more and more like the man who sired him. His dark eyes were Sir Gordon's. They flashed silver fire when, in an infant's rage, Jonathan let the world know that some plaything had evaded his grip and had skittered maddeningly beyond his reach. His nose was losing its roundness and taking on an imperial look, like Sir Gordon's. Odd, I thought, how much Jonathan resembled North, too.

Evenings were cruel. I missed Andre and I missed North. After one attempt at dinner alone in a dining room so full of memories, I gave it up and ordered a tray in my room. I spent my evenings there, too, reading Charlotte's journals in the erratically flaring light of the oil lamp.

I'd scanned her journals earlier, in a cursory way. Now I read them slowly and with increasing interest. Who *was* this woman who inspired such adoration in husband and son?

Her earlier journals revealed an artless and flighty girl, entranced with parties, people and pretty gowns. An odd, two-year lapse in the journal left blank much of the time spent at Brandley Manor. She'd made no mention of North's birth. She began again at North's first birthday, and the journal took on a different, deliberate tone. It was as though Charlotte now wrote, not for herself, but for an audience.

It was this strange tone of deliberateness that drew me to reading between the lines, causing me to muse about all she left unsaid. Reading her diaries from start to finish was like watching the metamorphosis of a charmingly self-centered girl into a careful, calculating woman. I shivered as I closed the final diary. Somehow, I'd preferred the selfish charming girl to the socially smooth Charlotte of later years.

My days were taken up with work in North's office, his work and mine. North had left a stack of instructions for me, covering everything from management of the estate in France to the smallest business of the Pederson's horse farm.

On top of the stack were instructions concerning Starlight.

North listed supplies to be sent to her. My heart caught at one entry.

Needles and thread.

Surely a man who remembered, in the midst of his sorrow, so mundane a thing as needles and thread, was a man in love with that woman.

Needles and thread.

I swallowed, trying to make the lump go down in my throat. I was resolved to be stoic about Starlight. He had loved her long before he met me, and I knew my husband was a man of principles, passionately loyal. And yet, he was also one of those men who could not long tolerate a divided heart. With sudden searing pain, I knew that he would return to Twin Oaks with his decision made. Would he choose me? Or would he choose Starlight and his little sons? I hardly dared think of it.

In the first week of October, just as the hills burst into a blaze of color, we received news that portions of the Virginia Militia had been called out to fortify garrisons along the frontier. Bands of Shawnee were striking at random, murdering and scalping isolated settlers. Their itinerary was impossible to predict. Sometimes they struck well within the frontier before vanishing.

Border men who had been settled upon the frontier by the Ohio Land Company were demanding the protection that had been guaranteed them by the Company. Stockholders in the Company—North and Colonel Washington included—were dunned for funds to underwrite the militia. Gladly, I sent authorization for five hundred pounds sterling to Williamsburg. I knew North would be beside himself, knowing that the very people he'd helped to settle along the forks of the Ohio were being massacred.

That same week, terror struck close to home.

The Pedersons had been massacred. When I heard the horrifying news, I burst into tears of rage and helplessness. I wept for the Pedersons, and I wept, too, for North. When North found out, he would blame himself for not bodily dragging the Pedersons off the farm.

The Shawnee had slipped across the frontier despite patrols

from the garrisons. They seemed to have made straight for the pleasant little valley. The attack had come swiftly, with only the Pederson hounds sounding a belated alarm. My informant, a neighbor of the Pedersons, relayed the tale tersely. But his few words held horror enough.

At the first sign of trouble, Mrs. Pederson had kissed her girls and the baby and put them into the root cellar. She made Ephraim, her dark-haired favorite, go down also to take charge. Then she and her other sons bravely shouldered muskets.

When it was over, the three boys lay murdered, scalped in the mud of the stable yard, only a few feet from Ped's body and those of his stable men. Mrs. Pederson was found along the trail toward the border. The clothes had been torn from her body. She'd been tomahawked to death.

At once, I sent Sandy and a party of men to get the Pederson children. They returned on a day filled with golden falling leaves and bright sunshine—an utter contrast to the bedraggled, woebegone youngsters the men carried on their saddles.

It was almost the end of October. Day after day, the heavens continued blue and fair. The sun beamed benevolently upon us, and leaves glowed in bronze, russet, and saffron. It was as though Nature intended to grant one last blessing before she sent winter. What had the Fairfields called this soft and balmy weather? Indian Summer?

I was working in North's office. Outside, I could hear the Pederson children playing in the grove of chestnut trees. Probably Ephraim, dear serious Ephraim, was earnestly gathering chestnuts while the others romped. I could hear Delia and Nan quarreling loudly about which of them would have the pleasure of giving Jonathan his bath. I caught Jonathan's mischievous squeal, and I pictured him evading the women's grasp and scuttling off, fast as hands and knees could carry him. An independent baby, he tended to scream in rage when anyone dared interfere with his freedom by picking him up.

I could hear Sandy, crashing about in the fallen leaves, pretending to be a bear, roaring and chasing the delightedly shrieking Pederson girls. There was the sharp clap of hands. That would be Mrs. Krause. Mrs. Krause believed in schedules, and it was noon. At noon the children must march themselves to Aunt Sally's kitchen for lunch.

I smiled to myself and, for the hundredth time that day, thought of North. What would he say to finding his tranquil Twin Oaks turned into a circus? I could almost picture his expression: the astonishment spreading across his handsome face, the tomahawk scar dipping toward me as he scowled, and then, his dark eyes beginning to twinkle with humor.

He would say, "Little rabbit, tell me you are not serious. Tell me you do not actually expect *me* to live among this menagerie."

I laughed aloud. Oh, how I missed him! If only he would come this minute, I would throw myself into his arms and tell him, a hundred times over, no—a thousand—*I love you, North! I love you, I love you, I love you . . .*

Suddenly, a piercing scream tore through my reverie. I froze, not wanting to recognize the voice. Again, the terrible scream. Not the familiar little shriek of baby rage, but a scream of excruciating pain.

For an interminable moment, I froze, unable to move or breathe. With effort, I wrenched myself up from the table, moving on watery legs. Out of the office, through the gardens. Ignoring brick paths, I pushed through the bramble hedges, heading for the sound of my child.

Jonathan? Jonathan?

As I flew through the chestnut grove and up to the clustered group, Delia screamed hysterically. The Pederson children cowered to one side. Sandy, Nan and Mrs. Krause knelt over my tiny, writhing baby. Nan was sobbing and moaning. A knife blade flashed in Sandy's hand.

"No!" I screamed, throwing myself at Sandy.

"It be a snake," Sandy snapped. "I got to."

I cried out, clutching for Jonathan.

"Hold her," Sandy ordered Nan.

Nan grabbed me. I fought her, but she was too strong.

"Danni, he got to! He got to!"

I tried to pull free.

"Don't hurt him!" I screamed at Sandy. "Don't!"

But Sandy bent over the baby.

"Oh, God—God!" I buried my face in Nan's bosom as Sandy set to work. There was one tiny, terrible scream and then Jonathan's cry grew fainter.

"Oh, Danni, he was crawlin'," Nan moaned. "They was a pile of leaves, ever so small a pile, and—and—" She broke off, sobbing as she hugged me close.

Sandy finished. His face dripped sweat. Mrs. Krause ripped strips of bandaging from her underskirts and tied them tightly around the tiny arm.

I wrenched myself from Nan.

"Let me do it."

Jonathan was no longer writhing. He lay very still. His eyes were closed, his face was white. I kept touching the small bleeding arm, pressing bandaging to the wound as though to press life back into him.

"He'll be all right? Won't he? Won't he?"

Sandy pulled me away from the baby. He took me by the shoulders and shook me gently but firmly.

"M'am, he needs help. There ain't a minute to waste. Give me leave to take 'im to Starlight."

I looked at him numbly. I was beyond decisions, my mind focusing solely on Jonathan's white face. I only knew I could not let him out of my sight.

Mrs. Krause took command. She ordered the horses, Nan's and my cloak, more bandage strips and blankets.

We set off at once. In the numbness of shock, I refused to let Sandy take Jonathan from me. So Sandy attached a lead rope to my mare and led me. Nan followed, silent with fear.

The journey must have taken two hours on trails choked with scrub pine. But I saw nothing as we traveled; my eyes were on Jonathan. He was beginning to grow hot. Very hot. I could feel hysteria building in me as convulsive twitches began in his little body.

I jerked upright at the sound of yapping dogs. Indian children appeared on the path, then vanished as Sandy called urgently to them in their own tongue. A moment later, Starlight, clad in a faded work gown of India calico, came running to us. She brushed past Sandy's horse, her eyes wide with alarm.

She reached for Jonathan. I hesitated a moment, then lowered him into her arms. Our eyes met, and in that instant we were not rivals, but two mothers.

Starlight's intense gaze left my face and fell to Jonathan. She touched his hot brow gently, then turned and strode away with him down the path. As she went, her soft but authoritative commands darted out to the Indians who congregated, gawking in curiosity.

I slid off my mare. Blindly, I stumbled after her. I was vaguely aware of a clearing, a fire pit in the center of the clearing and several cabins among the trees at the edge of the clearing. Women and children made way for Starlight as she hurried through the camp.

I followed her into a rough cabin that was carpeted with bearskins. Inside, a boy was building up the fire in the fireplace. A young girl rushed in with buckets of water, and an old woman squatted on the floor, frantically stirring a medicinal-smelling paste in a bowl. Starlight spoke to her. The woman nodded and crumbled more dried herbs into the paste.

As I stood there, helpless and numb, Starlight worked with Jonathan. She gave orders in a low calm voice. A board was brought forth and covered with a sheepskin. Gently, Starlight lowered him onto it, strapped him down and then cut away his clothing. At her bidding, a young girl began dipping cloths in cold water, placing them upon Jonathan's hot head and hot convulsing body.

Nan pushed past me.

"Judas! I kin at least help git the fever down."

Starlight looked up at Nan as though assessing Nan's worth. She nodded, and Nan took over the girl's task.

Starlight went to a wall shelf and came back with knives. Snagging a burning stick to the edge of the fire, she propped the knife blades on it. The flames licked at the steel.

"Oh, no!" I cried out. "No more!"

Starlight gave Sandy a calm, commanding look.

"Take mother out," she told him softly.

Sandy's strong hands closed on my shoulders, and I sensed his determination. He would obey Starlight, not me. I took one more look at Jonathan. He lay so still, so white, and then Sandy guided me out into the blinding sunlight.

I wanted to weep. I wanted to stumble off into the brush and vomit. I began to crumble.

Sandy took my elbow firmly.

"M'am, you must be strong," he warned sternly. "If you cry and carry on afore Starlight's people, you shame North."

I stared dumbly around the clearing. Out of respect and good manners, the dozen or so women and children went on about their business. They seemed not to be watching me. But of course, they were.

A tiny, pitiful scream came from Starlight's cabin, and I trembled violently. I swayed. Sandy's arm went around my waist.

"Sit down," he ordered. "M'am, try to think of somethin' else."

I sank gratefully to the hard-packed earth, kneeling there stiff and tense, my mind and my heart in the cabin. Sandy sat close, occasionally patting my shoulder in his awkward attempt to console.

Valiantly, he tried to distract me. He gestured across the clearing to where a pretty, brown-skinned girl of about thirteen tended two frisky toddlers. She was rolling colorful round gourds for them, and they would scamper after the gourds, retrieving them with chortles of victory. They would bat at the girl with the gourds, and she would pretend to be frightened and flee from them. Giggling in delight, they chased after her on sturdy, chubby legs.

"That be Little Doe. Starlight's sister," Sandy said. "And them young 'uns—" He bit his lip. His face flamed. Turtle-like, he ducked his chin in his collar.

I looked at the babies with new interest. They were as alike as peas in a pod. They wore shirts of fringed buckskin and nothing else.

"They're North's," I finished for Sandy.

The day was darkening, and a damp cold fog was beginning to creep over the camp when Starlight finally emerged from her cabin. My heart pounded in fear as she strode to us. I jumped up, and Sandy rose too, slipping his arm around my waist. The few seconds it took her to cross the clearing seemed like years.

Then she stood before me. She smiled tiredly.

"North's son live."

My chest heaved violently as I strove to stop the sobs of relief.

"Come," she said. "Feed baby now."

I flew past her and into the warmth of the cabin. Jonathan was still lying on the sheepskin-covered board. Nan was still treating his fever.

She gave me a weary, trembling smile.

"He not be out of the woods, yet, Danni. But he be better. She says we mustn't move him. Moving kin pump the poison to his heart."

Nan's knees cracked as she tiredly hove herself to her feet. She patted my shoulder, then lumbered out of the cabin to find Sandy.

I knelt and cooed softly to Jonathan. His eyes were closed, but he knew my voice. He turned his head and smacked his lips hungrily.

Not caring who might be in the room, I opened my shirt, lay down next to him and helped him nurse. He sucked rapaciously for a few seconds, then fell asleep.

Starlight dropped to her knees across from me. Gently she changed the paste dressing on the wicked-looking wound. As she worked on his little arm, Jonathan whimpered, then nuzzled my breast, seeking the nipple. He sucked for a bit, then again fell asleep.

"Sign good," Starlight whispered. "If baby want eat, baby want live."

I reached across Jonathan and put my hand on hers.

"Two times you have given me my baby," I whispered, my voice shaking with gratitude. "Once at his birth, and now again. What can I give to you?"

She pulled her hand away quickly, as though she couldn't bear for me to touch her. She appeared not to have heard. Or, if she heard, she seemed not to understand. She went on tending Jonathan. The minutes passed. Then, suddenly, she raised her head, and with her two hands she brushed back her long black hair.

Her dark eyes were clear, honest and free of guile.

"Go, cross Great Pond," she said softly. "Give back to me my husband."

CHAPTER 21

That night and the next day Jonathan hung onto life by a thread. As I knelt over him tending him with Starlight, I lost all sense of reality, all sense of time.

His fever would soar. His eyes would roll, his body convulsing. Then his fever would subside. I dared not take my eyes from him, and yet, it was agony to watch his struggle.

My head pounded with pain as I saw what it cost him to draw and expel each tiny lungful of air. When his breathing grew labored or when he drew breaths so shallow that he seemed not to be breathing at all, cold terror seized me. How long could his heart endure such punishment?

When Starlight had to take a knife to reopen the wound, I thought I would go mad listening to his screams. But when the poison spurted out of the newly opened wound, I wept in relief. I bound his arm and gave him my breast for comfort. His fever dropped, and the ghastly color left his face. He slept.

"Danni, you got to rest. You be ready to drop," Nan scolded. She put her arms around me. She tried to lead me away, but I shrugged her off, unwilling to take my eyes from Jonathan.

The room was blurring, almost whirling. I was not aware of Sandy squatting beside me until he touched my arm.

"M'am, I be taking you back to Twin Oaks."

I looked up at him. I blinked, not comprehending.

Sandy's face was red with embarrassment, but his jaw jutted out in determination.

"M'am, I know my duty to North. He'd kill me if I let you stay here two nights. It ain't safe for a white woman, even if all the men be off on a huntin' trip."

I rubbed my eyes. I couldn't focus on his face. Things seemed to be floating. Then he was lifting me gently to my feet. I pulled away.

"No. No! Jonathan—"

"Git her cloak, Nan. We're leaving."

I struggled weakly as Sandy picked me up and carried me out to the waiting horses. "No! No!"

Sandy put me on his horse, then climbed up behind. I fought him, but he was too big and strong. Behind us, on her horse, Nan admonished Sandy to be careful with me. At last, exhausted and at the end of my tether, I fell asleep, my face bobbing against his rough jerkin.

I was delirious with fever for days, only clawing my way up to consciousness to ask about Jonathan. Assured by Nan that he was recovering, I would sink back into delirium. At last the day came when I felt better, and Nan put into my hands a letter from North.

I touched the parchment lovingly, knowing that North's hands had touched it, too. Oh, North! With trembling fingers, I broke the red wax seal. My first letter from my husband. I longed, with all my heart, for his written words to be words of love. But it was not to be. I swallowed my disappointment as I read.

Dianna,

    I have returned safely from the Sugar Islands. Business detains me in Williamsburg. I expect to reach Twin Oaks before November 1.

    Last night, little rabbit, I dined at the governor's palace in the company of the governor and his aide, Major Ham-

*ilton. Mrs. Hamilton—our charming Abby Fairfield—asked
me to send you her very warmest regards.*

*I do so, then, smiling as I pen this, imagining the quick
angry lift of your pretty chin as you receive Abby's regards.
Do I only imagine fire in your eyes?*

*Dianna, the voyage afforded me time to ponder my prob-
lems. I have reached the most difficult and painful decision
of my life. It would be unfair—no, cowardly—to write you
of that decision. I must tell you face-to-face.*

North

My hands shook. What did he mean? Dear God, was he
going to give me up?

My heart seemed to shrivel and crack open. Jonathan was
forgotten. Dry-mouthed, I read the letter again and again,
plumbing each word for hidden meaning.

He'd teased me. That meant affection. A man doesn't bother
to tease a woman unless he cares for her. And yet, missing
from the letter was the conventional salutation and farewell that
every wife had the right to expect:

"My dearest wife, Dianna."

"Your devoted husband, North."

The tone of the letter was frighteningly melancholy. It was
almost as if North had, in his own mind, already parted from
me. It was as though he thought of me as some fond memory
from the past.

Did he intend to send me back to my father? Would I live
out my life in England, retaining the respected Delveau name
but never again to set eyes on the man who had given it to
me? Never to feel his arms around me, never to hear his voice
murmur my name?

I couldn't bear it! And North couldn't bear it. Suddenly,
I felt more ill than I had ever been during the fever.

I clutched at straws of hope. He meant to send Starlight
away! He would send her and her sons across the border and
south to the Cherokee Nation. "Oh, yes?" I asked myself bitterly, "and then?" My harder, pragmatic self answered. "And
then the day will come when North will look at me and brood:
This is the woman who cost me my sons."

I lay back upon the pillow, sick at heart. Could North send his own sons away and not feel rancor for my son, as Jonathan grew to manhood bearing the Delveau name?

There was *no* solution. Dear God, none.

I tried to write North, telling him all that had happened, but I was too weak and shaky. The ink pooled and ran. My penmanship was an illegible scrawl.

It was Mrs. Krause who finally composed the brief note telling about Jonathan's accident. On the bottom of it, I penned in shaky script, "North, I need you. Danni."

Mrs. Krause sent a servant to Alexandria to post the letter to Williamsburg. With luck, North would be at my side in three or four days.

Two days later, I was in the saddle following Sandy on the clay path that meandered along the creek to the Indian camp. I urged Sandy to ride faster, but he would not. Stubbornly, he obeyed Dr. Tibbs who said I was not to exert myself.

Sunlight sifted through the trees, turning my mare's tawny head to a lustrous dark gold. The sun did its work on my spirits as well, and I felt my heart lighten. I counted my blessings. My son was recovered. I would bring him home. One or two days more, and North would be home.

The morose brooding I'd done during my illness vanished as I lifted my face to sky and sunshine. I refused to think that North might send me away. Parted from me, he could entertain such thoughts; but when the two of us were together, he was as powerless as myself. A chance brushing of hands and all the resolutions in the world could not stop North from reaching for me.

As for myself, I resolved to swallow my pride. Let him try to send me away. I would not go. I intended to throw myself into his arms, soften that dark scowl with warm kisses, until all resistance melted. Send me away? He couldn't.

"Almost there, M'am."

Sandy shifted in his saddle and looked back at me, grinning.

I felt a surge of excitement, eagerness.

I returned his smile.

"Sandy, forget Dr. Tibbs. Let's go faster!"

He laughed, but then, suddenly, his laughter died. He looked up at the sky, and I followed his gaze. Overhead, a dozen large carrion birds circled lazily.

Sandy stiffened. He reined in his horse, slowly drawing his musket from the saddle sheath.

"Sandy?"

He motioned me to silence. For a long while, we held our horses in. I strained to hear what Sandy seemed to be hearing, but there was only the squeak of leather against horse and the occasional impatient thump of my mare's hoof on the hard-packed clay.

"Listen, M'am," Sandy whispered.

"But I don't—"

"That be the trouble, M'am. The dogs. We should be hearing dogs by now."

His words chilled me. I'd forgotten the tumult of barking and snarling that had ushered us into the camp just a few days before. If the dogs were silent . . . if something was wrong . . .

"Jonathan!"

I lashed the crop across my mare's flank. She sprang forward, but as my horse lurched past Sandy, he lunged out and caught the rein. He brought the horse up short.

"M'am, you must do as I say! Stay here. If you hear me shoot the musket, ride for Twin Oaks."

"But what—"

Sandy urged his horse down the trail. He turned in the saddle, his face grim.

"You *are* to obey me, M'am."

I nodded, my heart pounding. At the jog in the trail, Sandy disappeared from sight. The wait seemed interminable. And now that Sandy had drawn my attention to it, the silence was frightening. Sandy was right. Dogs should be barking. Alerted by the dogs, children should be scampering up the trail, laughing and calling out.

My thudding pulse ticked off the seconds. The seconds dragged into minutes, and I could wait no longer. I tied my mare's rein to a bush. In panic, I flew down the path on foot. I had not gone many steps before I came to a dog lying dead.

287

A jagged wound gaped from its throat. Its eyes were open and glazed, its tongue lolling out.

I shuddered and hurried past. Three more dogs lay along the path and then the crumpled body of a child, his head crushed.

"Oh, God!" I cried out, gagging at the sight. "Sandy? Sandy?"

He caught me just as I burst into the clearing. He half-carried me, half-dragged me back down the path. I fought him, begged, beseeched him to let me go.

"M'am, you not be settin' foot in the village! M'am—the things there—you not be fit to see! M'am, stop! M'am—M'am—"

I sank my teeth into his arm, and he howled in surprised pain. For an instant, he let go and I flew down the path and into the clearing. I could not believe the carnage that presented itself. Bodies lay everywhere. Scarlet pools of blood glistened in the bright sunshine. The air reeked with the smell of death, and at my feet, a faceless body still jerked in terrible death spasms. I stared dumbly.

"M'am—M'am! Come back!"

I fled from Sandy's voice, running to the cabin where Jonathan must be, leaping over the bodies, my skirt trailing through blood. In the doorway of the cabin a woman lay staring up, unblinking, into the sun. Stunned, I dropped to my knees. I touched her face.

"Starlight? Oh, God!"

Sandy wrenched me to my feet, dragging me from the cabin.

"My baby!" I shrieked. "I *will* see my baby!"

I clawed at him insanely, and unable to do anything else, he slapped me hard. I broke down, collapsing against him and sobbing.

"My baby, my baby . . ."

"I'll bring him to you," he said gently.

I waited, my body shaking violently.

When Sandy emerged from the cabin, his lumbering steps were slow, hesitant. I could see he'd hastily wrapped Jonathan in a blanket. Reluctantly, he placed the small unmoving bundle in my arms, and I went numb. I stared, unbelieving.

"Why?" I whispered. "God, why?"

"Shawnee, M'am." Sandy's voice was heavy with sorrow. "Shawnee butchers don't need no reason—"

His arm was heavy on my shoulders as he led me away. Gently, Sandy tried to take Jonathan, but I pulled back. I *had* to hold him. My arms would be empty soon enough.

My senses in shock, my disbelieving heart was full of Jonathan during the endless ride home. I couldn't cry. I couldn't think.

It wasn't until we came in view of Twin Oaks that North's sons pushed into my mind. I knew, without asking. They were dead.

We buried Jonathan in the hilltop cemetery on Twin Oaks. Plantation activity ceased. No work was done, no noise made. It was a solemn and mute procession that trailed the tiny wooden box up the hill.

When it was over, everyone except Mrs. Krause and Nan drifted away. They hovered, unwilling to leave as I stood mesmerized by the small grave.

I turned to them dully. "Please. I must be alone. Just a little while—"

They were reluctant to go. Mrs. Krause kissed my cheek. She took off her black shawl and wrapped it around my shoulders to ward off the chill wind that had begun to blow from the mountains, whipping our skirts. She left. Nan, tears streaming down her plump cheeks, hugged me and sobbed aloud on my shoulders. Then she, too, stumbled off.

I stood staring at the grave, unable to think. The wind rustled the few remaining leaves that clung to the oaks and maples surrounding the small cematary. A few russet leaves tumbled down, resting for a moment upon the mound of fresh-turned earth, and then skittered off with the wind.

How long I stood there, withdrawing into myself, I do not know. I heard nothing. Saw nothing. Felt nothing. I was not aware of anyone near me until a voice broke the silence.

"Danni?" the voice said softly. "Sweetheart?"

The voice seemed part of a dream. I turned slowly, as though emerging from deep sleep. I stared.

For a moment, he seemed a mirage, standing tall and dark, his long black travel cloak whipping in the wind. I was afraid to move, afraid to make a sound, afraid that if I reached for him he would vanish like some cruel mirage.

"Danni?" I swayed as he moved toward me. "My poor little rabbit!"

I choked with relief as his arms went around me, crushing me to him, and I began to sob. I sobbed hysterically.

"Danni— Chérie—I'm here—don't—don't—"

I sobbed my heart out while he held me in his warm strong arms, comforting me. He stroked my face, raked his fingers gently through my hair. His mouth was warm and passionately comforting on my forehead, my temple.

When I'd drained myself, we stood in the lowing wind, silently clinging to each other.

"God, Danni, I *am* sorry," he whispered. "I came as soon as I received Mrs. Krause's letter. I resented him, it's true, but for an innocent to be bitten by a snake. And then to arrive and find him dead of it—"

I pulled away, startled. I searched his face. He didn't know! I choked.

"Sandy— I sent Sandy to find you, North, to tell you—"

"I haven't seen Sandy or anyone."

I felt faint. My knees buckled. I swayed against North. He caught me and picked me up, striding swiftly down the hill toward the house. I pressed my face against him, agony welling. I! I would have to be the one to tell him!

He carried me into the house and up to my bedchamber, ignoring the subdued greetings of the servants.

"Get some brandy," he yelled at Mrs. Krause.

In my room, he ordered Nan to move the settee close to the fire and then leave. Nan did as she was told, and North deposited me gently on the settee. He made me sip brandy, but I pushed it away and took his face in my hands. With a puzzled look, he dropped to one knee and half-knelt before me.

"Danni?"

"North—oh, my dearest, my love," I whispered, running my fingers over his face in a helpless attempt to prepare him. I cringed at the pain I must give. "I have to tell you—I must tell you—Jonathan—he didn't die of snakebite. He was with Starlight—the Shawnee—raided the camp—"

His head jerked back. All of the color drained from his face. Tiny beads of sweat formed on his brow. His mouth tightened.

"What are you saying?"

I choked back a sob.

"She's—dead," I whispered. "My love, they are all—"

He reached out, gripping my shoulders, as though he needed to hang on to something. His fingers bit into my flesh. I gasped in pain, but North was oblivious. He stared at me, his dark eyes frozen to mine. I watched helplessly as comprehension came. The muscles of his face contorted, his breath came in harsh rasps.

He demanded, "Starlight! She is—she—"

I winced in anguish, suddenly seeing two images of Starlight. Starlight, beautiful and alive; Starlight, the way I had last seen her. I tore my eyes from North. I couldn't bear to see his shock, his torture.

He shook me roughly.

"My sons?"

"They spared no one," I cried out, helpless to spare him.

He lurched to his feet. He staggered from the room like a wild and drunken man. My heart cried out to follow him, to comfort him as he had comforted me. But I knew he was not ready for comfort. First he must descend to the pit, to the raw and tormented place where comfort cannot go. He must grieve alone.

I paced my room, weighed down with my grief and North's. Twice in the afternoon, I went through the misty rain that was beginning to fall and tried North's office door. It was bolted.

"North?" I called softly. "Darling?"

There was no answer.

Later, when Sandy returned, I sent him to North. To my relief, North let Sandy in. Sandy stayed closeted with him.

When night fell, I refused Nan's offer to help me to bed. Instead, fully dressed, I curled on the settee. North might call for me, might need me. I tried to stay awake, but my death watch with Jonathan had taken its toll. Fitful sleep came. The muted chimes of the clock woke me hourly. Still, North did not come.

It was almost dawn when I roused to the soft whooshing thump of logs being added to the fire. I opened my eyes just as North tucked a blanket around me.

I reached for him with trembling hands, and he knelt beside me. I was shocked at his altered appearance. He'd aged years in only a few hours.

His hand went fumblingly to my face. He touched me as though he had never seen me before.

"Danni?" he said, his voice choked and husky. "Danni—I might have lost you, too—"

He buried his face in my bosom, and I held my husband as violent spasms wracked him. He sobbed uncontrollably, huge sobs of heartbreak and loss. His tears were hot on my breasts. I stroked his dark head, petting him, trying to console.

"Darling—" I whispered. "Oh, North, love—love—"

My sorrow lightened as I experienced a new, sad joy. Never had I felt so close to North. Never had he so trusted me, never had he so revealed himself.

I tried to comfort him with soft murmurings, but when his outburst was done, he was half-crazed, his eyes glazed with grief. I drew his hot face to the cool flesh of my bosom. Softly, then with a primitive urgency born of shock and unspeakable sorrow, his mouth sought my breasts.

I cradled his head, whispering words of love, content to be all things to him—mother, wife, lover. At last, he raised his head and looked into my eyes. I flinched, unable to bear the pain I saw. His hot mouth sought mine.

In bed, we made love with the hesitant gentleness born of sorrow. Each touch was a gift, each caress a healing. Each stroke of mouth or hand was balm for our grief, and at our throbbing moment of climax, all sense of separateness melted away. We were one.

Exhausted, North fell asleep. I held him in my arms. Although he slept deeply, his sleep was not deep enough to erase his shock. Every few minutes his body would jerk in spasm. I held him close, stroking his face to calm him. Once he thrashed wildly, crying out for Starlight. Gently, I kissed his lips, and he became calm. He slept.

I guarded his sleep. When the sky began to lighten in the east, my own leaden eyelids finally slid shut.

Much later, I awoke with a jolt. I opened my eyes and beheld a savage bending over me. I cried out in terror, the scene in the Indian village spearing me. Then North's face came into focus. He was bending over me, and he was clad in his buckskins. He stifled my outcry with a gentle kiss.

"I'm sorry," he said, his voice tense and taut. "It was thoughtless of me. I didn't mean to frighten you, Danni. I only wanted to kiss you good-bye."

"Good-bye?" I sat bolt upright, tugging the coverlets. "Not good-bye?" I cried out in alarm. "But where are you going? Why are you dressed in those clothes?"

Panic swirled. He *couldn't* be leaving me. Not now. Not when I needed him. But I searched his face and found it hard and determined. Fury blazed in the eyes where, last night, there had been only hurt and grief. This was not the man who'd wept on my bosom like a child.

He kissed me once more, roughly raking his fingers through my hair. I reached for him, eager to be in his arms. He pushed me back roughly.

"Don't look at me like that, Danni! You know what I must do. Starlight was my wife. Her death must be avenged."

Cold fear clutched at my stomach.

"I'm afraid, North. You won't go alone, will you? Surely the plantation men can—"

"Sandy and I will cross the border to the Cherokee. Starlight's father and brothers will provide men."

He touched my cheek for a moment, his fingertips lingering on my skin as though he were loath to pull his hand away. Then, suddenly, he wheeled and strode into his own room. I grabbed a robe, shrugged into it and followed him. Mute and helpless, I stood watching his grim preparations.

From a cupboard he took weapons that made my blood turn to ice: a tomahawk that looked razor-sharp, muskets, and then, a long, peculiarly shaped knife—the kind border men call a scalping knife.

When I gasped, he turned on me angrily.

"Go back to your room, Dianna!"

I backed away, but didn't leave him. He did not insist, but swiftly went on with preparations. When he strapped snowshoes to the tight blanket roll, I couldn't help but ask fearfully, "When—when will you be back, North?"

He scowled.

"When I'm finished, damn it!"

He slung his medicine pouch across one shoulder, then turned and considered me, the angry lines of his face softening.

"Come here, sweet."

I flew into his arms, and he held me so tightly, I couldn't breathe. We stood clutching one another, not daring to voice what was in our hearts.

At last, he whispered, "I want you to go to Alexandria for your safety, Danni."

I slumped against him.

"North, I can't."

"You must."

"I can't leave him, I can't. He's so little and so alone in the cemetery. I must visit his grave—"

He looked down at me, studying my face. He took my chin in his hand and kissed me with a gentleness that made me want to weep.

"He's dead, Danni. I cannot do what I must do unless I know you are safely away from Twin Oaks. Help me, sweet. Promise you will go to Alexandria at once."

Tears welled up. Reluctantly, I nodded.

He kissed the tip of my nose, then my wet lashes.

"Little rabbit," he murmured softly. He fondled my cheek one last time. When my eyes finally cleared of tears, North was gone.

CHAPTER 22

With funereal slowness, the days dragged into weeks. I grieved for Jonathan, and I was ill with worry over North as winter settled upon Virginia. The temperature plummeted. The winds howled from the northwest. Mountain passes to the west were reported blocked with snow.

In Alexandria, I kept to my bedchamber. I hadn't the heart to face the many callers who came, hoping to console me about Jonathan.

When Alexandria received a December blanketing of snow, I rejoiced. No callers would come. I would have no need to send down yet another lame excuse.

But I was wrong. A caller did come. Agatha Fairfield, her nose pinched pink by the cold, swooped into my bedchamber without so much as a by-your-leave.

"Dianna, you are to get up off that bed, get dressed and begin living again," she said firmly as I stared up at her in astonishment.

She shook her head, every inch of her motherly, corseted figure registering disapproval.

"I've come to scold you, my dear," she said. "You are grieving for your baby—well, that is proper. But you neglect our North, and you *woefully* neglect our North's business affairs."

I sat up, blinking at her. The attack stung. I would not have expected such words from this kind woman.

Stubbornly, I glared at her.

"North is gone, Mrs. Fairfield."

She snorted, tossed her bonnet to a chair and shed her cloak. She turned to me.

"Tush! At the moment, yes. But when he returns? What will he find?" She eyed me critically. "A wife who has ignored his business concerns. A wife who is gaunt, sallow-faced and ill-kempt."

I gasped.

"Come, Dianna, look in the glass," she pressed. "See if it isn't true."

Cut to the quick, I lunged off the bed and stumbled to the French looking glass. For the first time since Jonathan died, I studied myself in the mirror. My own image shocked me. Gaunt? Why, I was thin as a rail! My hair was dull and lifeless. The only prettiness left to me was my eyes. Framed in a too-white face, they were huge and the blue-violet color of bruised cornflowers. I turned away, aghast.

"I—I—didn't—notice—"

Mrs. Fairfield folded me into a motherly embrace and kissed me soundly.

"I had to be cruel, Dianna. For your good and for North's." She cocked her head to one side. She surveyed me with determination but with compassion, too. "Dianna, I am giving a Christmas party next week and I *insist* you come."

I quailed. The thought of facing all those sympathetic people! Their murmurs of condolence, reminding me of what I'd lost. And then their questions about North's absence . . .

"I can't, Mrs. Fairfield. Don't ask me to. Not just yet. Please—later—"

"You can. You must. I shall feel terribly slighted, Dianna, if you don't come. Order a new gown for my party. Wear white if you wish to come in mourning, but not black. Black is *not* your color. North would not enjoy finding you dressed like a drab when he returns!"

"When...he...returns..." I echoed, feeling the first surge of hope I'd felt in weeks. Unexpectedly, I found myself bursting into tears.

"Will he return, Mrs. Fairfield? *Will* he?"

She hugged me. Her corseted plumpness comforted me.

"Of course he will! You must have faith in him, Dianna. North is as at home in the wilderness as the canniest savage."

She drew back and searched my face, her eyes full of concern.

"Dianna, I do not know what went on in that Indian village, but I suspect that Starlight—yes, dear, do not look at me in surprise—I know of Starlight. You must remember I've been like a second mother to North for many years." She paused, patting my cheek. "I suspect Starlight is dead.... Am I right, dear?"

I swallowed.

"North's sons, too."

"Dear God in heaven!"

She fumbled to find the chair behind her and sat down heavily.

"Our poor, poor North!"

"Yes."

We fell silent.

"Dianna, dear," she began hesitantly, "is part of your grieving because you do not know if you can be to North all that Starlight was to him?"

She was so correct that her words stabbed. I turned away quickly and stared out the window at Captain's Row. Snow was collecting on the cobbles and sifting into the crevices. Soon, the road would be smooth and white. Children hauling sleds were already gathering, preparing to sail down the steep road and onto the wharf.

"Dianna, you are right to think he loved her," Mrs. Fairfield went on. "He did. And passionately so. But that was the passion of his youth. North is a mature man, now. As such, he needs a woman who can be all things to him—his passionate love, his trusted confidant and his amiable companion. He needs a

297

woman who can understand his world and share it with him. This, Starlight could have never done."

She smiled sadly and shook her head.

"But *you* can," she said. "Indeed, child, you already do. North loves you. Loves you as he never could have loved her!"

Agatha Fairfield's visit jolted me back to reality. I gritted my teeth and forced myself to return to a disciplined routine. The next morning, when I appeared downstairs for breakfast, the servants were thrown into a tizzy. Their smiles of relief welcomed me back.

I sent for the dressmaker. I sent for Mr. Downey, who'd been pressing to see me for weeks about my father's business. I also sent to Twin Oaks for necessary ledgers and papers relevant to North's affairs. I sent for his overseer.

I achieved at least an outward show of normalcy. At holiday parties I hid my downheartedness and strove to be pleasant, even gay. But each time I returned home from an outing, I did so with a pounding heart. Had North returned in my absence? Would I find him in the drawing room with his pipe and brandy? Each time, as I rushed into the house, I was met with disappointment that carried me close to tears.

December bore into January. January became February. Fear became my constant companion. Was North all right? Or did he lie ill or wounded, calling for me in his delirium?

"They're dead!" Nan burst out one day, wailing hysterically. "I know they be dead! They be froze to death or tomahawked! My Sandy—he be dead!"

I shook her roughly.

"Stop it, Nan. I forbid you to say such things. They are alive and well. They must be!"

But when the end of February drew near and, outside, along the brick walk in the garden the crocus began to send up hopeful green shoots, my own hope began to die. I went through my daily routine automatically, tending to business. Yet every beat of my heart thudded. "Dead? Dead? Dead?"

One afternoon, Mrs. Fairfield, young Susan and Caroline sat in my drawing room. I was pouring tea for them while Caroline, her plain face pink with pleasure, showed us the tiny cap she was crocheting for the baby she expected. Suddenly, the drawing room door banged open, crashing against the wall. With a start of irritation, I turned in my seat to give the offending servant a frown. But standing in the doorway was a tall, heavily bearded stranger. He was dressed untidily in dirty, torn clothes.

My heart stopped in mid-beat.

Silence thundered through the room. Then Susan Fairfield laughed.

"Why, it's North!" she whooped. "North, how funny and dirty you look!"

I set the teapot down with a crash, my hands shaking. Paralyzed, I could only sit there, staring up at him. I couldn't find my voice.

"Danni!" he said, laughing. He opened his arms to me. For an instant, I couldn't move. Then I went catapulting into the waiting arms, nearly knocking him down. He staggered back, chuckling, and the sound of his voice was music in my ears.

"North! Dear—tell me it's you. I was so afraid. Tell me I'm not dreaming—oh, North—"

He stopped my babble with a bushy kiss. We kissed with exhilarated abandon, then drew back and touched each other with the peculiar shyness that comes of not daring to believe one's dream has come true. His dark eyes reflected my own excitement and joy.

"Sweetheart," he whispered.

I flung myself against him, holding him, knowing I never wanted to let go.

"Oh, North!"

I could hear Nan's shrieks of delight in the back of the house, and pictured her radiance as she greeted Sandy. North hugged me again, so enthusiastically that my feet left the floor. Laughter and tears of joy bubbled out of me. North was filthy; shaggy and smelly as a bear but totally and completely wonderful!

Above my head, North addressed the tea guests I'd forgotten.

"Excuse me, Agatha," he said with good humor, "but I am taking your hostess upstairs.

299

"You're coming with me," he said, laughing and picking me up in his arms and carrying me unashamedly up the stairs to our bedchamber without even a backward glance at my guests.

"North—oh, North," I breathed.

Agatha Fairfield's good-natured voice trailed drily after us.

"Susan, run fetch the cloaks," she said. "I do believe tea time at the Delveaus' is over."

"North, please. Tell me what . . . happened," I began fearfully several evenings later in the drawing room. I had brought a glass of port to him and, on impulse, knelt beside his chair, resting my chin on his knee.

"Dearest? North? Please?" I coaxed softly. "I *must* know what happened out there in the wilderness. I must!"

He lowered the sheaf of papers he was reading. His hand, still weathered and frontier-rough, groped under my chin. He lifted my face gently, until my eyes met his implacable gaze.

"No, Danni," he said with finality.

"But—"

"Enough, Dianna. Justice has been done. That is all you need to know."

I groaned in despair and once again rested my cheek upon his leg. He stroked my hair. It was the first time I'd dared ask. From the first moment, I'd read in his eyes that the subject was closed to me. North had erected a wall around whatever had happened.

And my poor darling! His sojourn had left him jumpy as a cat. He started over ordinary household sounds, and when a servant girl padded noiselessly up behind him, he'd almost struck her as he whirled around. The girl had fled to the kitchen, weeping.

Nights, North slept poorly. Often, he rose to pace the house. It was as though he had to peel the savagery from himself layer-by-layer. While baths, barbering and fine clothes had instantly repaired his physical state, I was at a loss to know how to help him repair ravages of mind and spirit. And my spirit, too, could not begin to mend until I knew what had become of my baby's murderers.

"Jonathan was mine, North," I said softly, stubbornly. "I deserve to know."

He said nothing. I looked up at him.

"I *have* to know, North."

He frowned and looked away.

"Danni, there are things—"

"It is my right to know. It was my revenge, also. I *will* know—even the worst."

His head swung round. His face darkened with anger.

"You don't know what you are saying, damn it!"

I seized his hand, drew it to my bosom and held it against my pounding heart.

"North, I was *in* the village. I saw! I saw my baby's torn body! I saw Starlight lying there in her own blood! I saw—"

He shut his eyes. His head jerked back as though I'd struck him. Several minutes passed. When he at last opened his eyes and searched my face, he drew me into his lap with shaking hands. He touched my cheek.

"We will speak of it this once," he said grimly. "After this evening you will never again broach the subject, Dianna. Never!" he added vehemently.

Fearfully, I settled into his arms, my cold forehead against his warm neck. His throat muscles were stiff and taut as he reluctantly began the story.

True to his word, he held nothing back. Not even revolting, inhuman things that could make me shrink from him.

North and Sandy had gone at once to Starlight's father and brothers. The Cherokee chief and his tribe had been outraged at the Shawnee viciousness. Parties of ten were sent to fan the wilderness. North, Sandy and two of Starlight's brothers and other men had taken the party that proceeded in the most likely direction—northwest to the forks of the Ohio and from there, northward into Shawnee country and the area of Fort Detroit.

Many weeks passed before they finally tracked down and surrounded the Shawnee party just south of Fort Detroit. They laid careful ambush, so as to take many prisoners. Four Shawnee had been slaughtered in the fighting, the remaining dozen captured. Four were tortured to death immediately, as was the custom of the Cherokee. The tortured men revealed that a white man had been in the party that raided Starlight's village. The white man was the intermediary, paid by the British to buy Shawnee raiding parties against the frontier. That white man had vanished, but the Indians described him. He had strange, pale yellow eyes.

I shuddered in North's arms.

"Joseph Lasher?" I whispered.

"I don't know, Danni," North answered honestly.

Heartsick, I curled into North's arms and he went on with the pathetic and horrible story.

The remaining prisoners, their faces painted black as a sign they were reserved for torture by Starlight's father, were dragged south toward Cherokee country. As they traveled through territory that was impassable and choked with mountain laurel, a series of blizzards struck. The mountain passes were snowed shut. They spent weeks in a mountain cave. Hunting was poor. Food grew short.

Starlight's brothers slow-tortured two more of the prisoners to death and then used them for food—a not uncommon custom among savages, North told me. Revolted by the Indians' eating of human flesh, North and Sandy had struck out for home as soon as possible. They had come by foot, traveling through Fort Pitt on the forks, and then Braddock's Trail down into Alexandria.

When North finished the terrible story, we held each other in silence, each of us brooding upon our separate unbearable thoughts. I wondered at my own part in what had happened to Jonathan. If the white man was Lasher, had he struck deliberately at the little encampment near Twin Oaks? And the Pederson attack? Had that been Lasher, too, coupling personal revenge with his missions for the crown?

The clock on the mantel ticked loudly in the silence. The blazing fire diminished to bright embers and then to gray ashes. At last, sorrowfully and without words, we made our way up to bed, hand-in-hand.

In the morning, North seemed a new man. The sun was barely risen when he wrenched away the goose-down comforter and slapped me playfully on my bottom.

I yelped in sleepy surprise and jerked upright.

North was standing by the bed. He was dressed and he was chuckling.

I rubbed my eyes.

"North—what?"

"Do you know, Mrs. Delveau," he said, "that we have been married almost two years, and yet I have never had the pleasure of dancing with you?"

My mouth fell open. I fumbled for a robe and stared up at him in confusion. Dear God, was the man going mad?

"You—you—want to dance—now?"

He burst into rich laughter.

"Not *now*, little rabbit. Tomorrow night. At the royal birthday ball in Williamsburg."

I gaped at him, not comprehending.

"Up, Dianna! Up at once," he commanded, laughing at my confusion. "Get ready. We leave in two hours."

Stunned by his sudden change in mood and only half-understanding what he was telling me, I scrambled out of bed to call my maid. But with a playful laugh, North caught me and flung me back into the featherbed. I struggled wildly under him, giggling as he tickled me and telling him he was surely gone mad.

He quieted my struggling with a passionate kiss. When I lay under him, quiet and no longer struggling, he scowled fiercely.

"Why are you lolling in bed, woman?" he demanded. "Up! Get ready to go!" Yet he held me down.

I giggled.

"North, you *are* insane. Let me up."

For answer, he merely chuckled and kissed me again, a light teasing kiss. Then his eyes darkened.

"Danni," he said softly, "when I awoke this morning, it occurred to me that I've given you no gaiety or fun in this marriage. I mean to repair that error. The Williamsburg season is at its height. I mean to take you to a ball every night, to the theater, to parties, to gaming houses. We'll go to the racecourse and watch our horses race. We'll go to dinner at the governor's palace. . . .

"You are to order a dozen new gowns from the finest dressmaker in the capital. And then I intend to shower you with jewels. What do you prefer, sweet? Diamonds? Pearls? India rubies?"

I burst into giggles.

"Madman! I prefer *you*. You are my jewel."

We laughed together in our happiness, and North lowered his mouth to mine. He gave me a kiss that made me tremble with joy. Then he drew back and smiled down at me. My heart lurched at the sweet sadness in that smile.

"Danni, I've not heard the sound of your laughter in many months. Not since Father—" He fell silent, then whispered, "Danni, I need your laughter. It is . . . healing balm . . . for me."

CHAPTER 23

Williamsburg was not what I expected.

First of all, North's house there surprised me. I knew he kept a house in the capital, but I assumed it would be a simple, efficient business dwelling like the one on Captain's Row in Alexandria. I was wrong. The Williamsburg house was a three-story, red brick mansion. The moment I stepped inside on North's arm and beheld the Italian marble foyer and the splendid Oriental wallpaper, I knew whose house it was.

"Is this Charlotte's house?" I asked him.

"Yes. Mother designed it."

He looked about him proudly, as though seeing it all for the first time.

"Mother liked amusement. She enjoyed giving parties. She found life at Twin Oaks tedious. Too rural," he added with fond laughter.

He gave me a curious look.

"She was not like you," he said in a musing way, as though the comparison were only now beginning to dawn on him. "And yet," he said with a laugh, "she was *very* much like you. Quick-witted. Opinionated. An unbridled tongue that can both delight a man and drive him to drink."

I tossed my head and gave him a salty, provocative look.

"You would prefer a woman who is easily managed?"

He laughed, helped me off with my cloak and tossed it to the waiting servant.

"In both horses and women, sweet," he whispered, "I admit I prefer a challenge."

My country upbringing had done nothing to prepare me for Williamsburg. The capital, and the idle rich Virginians who gathered to play there, astounded me.

Williamsburg seemed one enormous and ongoing party. In the summer to come, when heat would bring clouds of mosquitos and the dreaded swamp fever, the city would empty itself of revelers. But now, in late winter, the city teemed with activity, and the atmosphere was one of self-indulgence and decadence.

By night, the city was as brightly lighted as though the sun still shone. Torches blazed everywhere. Everywhere there was the sound of merriment as revelers made their way to their various amusements.

The rich gave large, lavish parties and balls. Hostesses vied with one another in entertaining with extravagance. Often, at balls, a fine-looking young Negro was raffled off as door prize.

Liaisons and conquests seemed the order of the day. Married women dallied openly with their lovers, disappearing with them into the hedged French gardens whenever the ballroom music stopped. Ladies, conversing prettily behind spread fans, did not even blush to share recipes for abortives.

By day, Virginia's wealthy gentlemen engaged themselves in all manner of gambling from horse racing and cards to the detestable cock fights and bear baiting. And by night, the gentlemen seemed to wager on the ladies.

When word came to me that Lord Carleton-Withers had wagered twenty guineas that he would sleep in *my* bed before the month was out, I could hardly control my rage.

I poured out my fury to North, confident he would share

my shock and anger. But North startled and disappointed me by bursting into amused, tolerant laughter.

"Haven't you wondered, little rabbit, why I am loath to leave your side?"

I could only stare up at him in bewilderment. He chuckled softly and ran his knuckles over my cheek.

It was true, I reflected, North *had* been attentive. Extremely so. He'd even insisted on accompanying me to the dressmaker, where he slouched in a chair, smoking, bored, half-asleep during interminable fittings. Twice, though, to my amusement and surprise, he'd rejected the cut of a gown. He'd taken the charcoal sketch and redrawn the line that displeased him.

He chuckled at my discomfiture.

"I congratulate Lord Carleton-Withers on his excellent taste in women," he said flatly. "And I congratulate myself, sweet."

His easy acceptance of the decadence in Williamsburg, his careless reaction to a situation I personally found mortifying, cut me to the quick. I blinked back the tears of anger beading on my lashes.

I snapped at him.

"Then you would not care if Lord Carleton-Withers won his despicable wager?"

I trembled suddenly, fearing his answer, and I wished I had not asked the question.

He gave me no answer. Laughing, he pulled me roughly into his arms as though I were a wanton. Stung by his response, I jerked away. But he trapped me. His laughter both infuriated and wounded me. I pushed him, but this only seemed to amuse him the more.

"You are cruel, North," I said. "And you are about . . . to . . . make me cry."

Surprise jolted across his features. His laughter ceased at once, but he did not release me from his hard embrace. Instead, he drew me even closer. I shivered as he kissed my forehead, my eyes, my temple, shivered, weakening and growing pliant in his arms.

"Danni, love, you are hurt because I laughed. Don't be, sweet. I can laugh because I trust you totally. Little rabbit . . . in these past harsh months . . . you . . ." His words trailed away.

Then he began again. "A man could not trust a woman more than I trust you at this moment."

He took my face in his hands. His eyes burned with an intensity I'd never before experienced, and I shivered in pleasure. My breath caught.

"You are my *wife*, Danni. You are everything the word *wife* means to me."

I cried out softly, understanding what he was telling me. He'd put Christian from his mind. He'd forgiven me Jonathan.

In passionate gratitude I whispered, "And *you* are the husband of my heart, North. I love you more than life itself. I should die a thousand deaths if ever I lost you—"

I shuddered. Where had that frightening, last thought come from? I had not known it was even in my mind.

I clutched him, clung to him.

"Oh, God, North—if I should ever lose you—"

"Impossible!"

But the dreadful feeling of foreboding lingered.

"Make love to me, North? Now? Assure me, with your body, that I belong to you."

He caught his breath sharply, then slowly brushed his lips over mine. His knowing hands gently lowered my bodice, and we began again those tender acts that blotted out everything else in existence.

When we finished, we lay in bed in each other's arms. I basked in a golden drowsiness, feeling content, safe and unfrightened. The shadow of foreboding was gone.

At last, North roused himself and kissed my bare shoulder in a languid, unhurried manner.

"We were to have lunched with the governor at the palace, sweet."

I raised my head. I looked at the clock. It was after two.

"Oh, the governor. I forgot," I said drowsily. I ran my fingers across his chest. His heartbeat was strong, even, comforting under my hand. "I would rather be in bed with you, North, than be at table with governors...or princes...or kings."

He caught my hand and kissed it, chuckling.

"What a liar you are, Danni," he said fondly.

I raised up on one elbow, my hair tumbling onto his chest. He reached for a lock of it and idly played with it.

"I'm *not* a liar."

"You *are*, sweet. No woman prefers bed with her husband to lunch with a king."

I kissed his forehead lightly.

"Oh, yes, she does, North. Especially if she wants—"

I stopped just in time. I bit back my words with a smile. North gave me a puzzled look and laughed expectantly.

"Yes? Wants what, little rabbit?"

I opened my mouth to tell him, then changed my mind with a low giggle. I got off the bed to go bathe and dress.

"What is it you want, Danni?" North demanded good-naturedly as he lay back, his head on his arms, watching me. "Tell me, sweet. You shall have it tomorrow."

I burst into laughter. Turning from his mystified gaze, I went into the dressing room and closed the door. How could North, an intelligent man, be so obtuse? Surely he must know what I wanted! Surely he must know I wanted to give him a child. . . .

The weeks in Williamsburg eased our grief. I was aware of a growing bond of trust being forged between us. Without that trust, I would have been the unhappiest wife in the capital. For my husband attracted women as a flame attracts moths. The ladies clamored to have North as dance partner at balls and vied to claim him as supper partner.

Though North was handsome and elegant, and a teasing and lively conversationalist, it was not this that drew the ladies. It was his sexuality, his air of savagery that lay just beneath his sophistication. His experiences in the wilderness, his years of living with the Indians had granted him an air of excitement that women found irresistible.

To my irritation, and to North's amusement, his dance partners were ever contriving to accidentally brush up against him with their bejeweled bosoms. Abby Fairfield Hamilton was a particular thorn in my side. She wanted North. There was no mistake about that. She set her cap for him the moment we arrived in Williamsburg.

Abby's pompous and seemingly blind husband, Major Hamilton, appeared unaware of his wife's wanton behavior. To double my irritation, Abby, with her ravishing chestnut hair, green eyes and splendid tall figure, was even more striking as a matron than she had been as an unmarried girl.

Yet, at all of the parties, no matter who North and I took as dance or supper partners, our trust sustained us. Across the ballroom, our eyes would meet and the look that passed between us—an acknowledgment of shared grief and love—closed out all others.

He was mine.

I was his.

That trust sustained me during the most difficult times of all, the times I knew North was remembering Starlight, grieving for her and for his sons.

Some nights, thinking me asleep, he rose from our bed. He would dress and go out on the balcony to smoke and to muse for hours on end. Most nights I pretended to sleep on, knowing he must work out his own grief even as I had come to terms with my own sorrow.

But one night, six weeks into our visit to Williamsburg, I drew on a white silk robe and stole out onto the balcony. The moon was full, its light shimmering on the marble statuary in the garden below. The air was fragrant with the scent of early lilacs.

Noiselessly, on bare feet, I approached North through the shadows. In the bright moonlight, every feature of his face shone clearly, and I was aghast at the raw pain I saw. So he was *not* healed of it. Not yet. . . .

He turned, suddenly sensing my presence, and my heart caught as I saw his unguarded eyes. They were luminous, filled to the brim with unshed tears.

"Oh, my love!" I whispered, flying into the arms he held open to me. "Oh, my dearest dear—you miss her! You miss her and your sons so very much!"

He held me close, not speaking. It was as though he didn't trust himself to words. For a long time, he rested his cheek against my head. At last, he spoke.

"Danni?" he said hoarsely. "Let's go home?"

Joy coursed through me. Until that moment, I hadn't realized how badly I, too, wanted to leave the false gaiety of Williamsburg, wanted to go home.

I touched his face.

"I can be ready to start for Twin Oaks in the morning."

"Twin Oaks?"

He drew up in surprise.

"I meant Alexandria, Danni. I can't ask it of you—to return to Twin Oaks. It could be too painful for you."

I stood on tiptoe and kissed his sad, unresponding mouth.

"Twin Oaks is your home, North. And mine, too. . . . Dear, let's go home . . . and be happy there?"

CHAPTER 24

Spring was bursting forth in every corner of Twin Oaks. The plantation throbbed with fresh hope and happiness.

Everywhere—from the cavernous barns where mares nuzzled tottering, velvet-nosed foals, to the hearth in Aunt Sally's kitchen where brash puppies padded in, howling at the smell of roasting meat and receiving for their efforts only a trouncing from Aunt Sally's broom—everywhere, Twin Oaks was full of new life, new creation, new beginnings.

There were two new babies on the plantation. Each pair of parents, indentured servants from Dorsetshire, beamed at North's pronouncement:

"A fine, sound child! My congratulations!"

The Pederson children had blossomed with spring, too. They'd lost their air of forlorn shyness. They, too, whooped about the plantation as though it were truly home.

Mrs. Krause, for the first time since Andre's death, had put away her black dresses. She wore less somber browns, and sometimes even pinned a sprig of azalea to her collar.

But the happiest person on Twin Oaks was its mistress.

Each passing day added to my certainty. I carried North's child. I was almost sure of it. But to spare North a disappointment if it turned out not to be true, I said nothing.

North himself seemed to suspect. I would catch him giving me an intent, curious look across the dinner table. When I smiled in return, his eyes would light up expectantly, as though he were waiting for me to tell him some welcome piece of news.

Once, as he paused in his furiously busy day—between seeing a favorite mare safely delivered of another promising racer and heading for the mill on urgent business of broken equipment—North caught me and pulled me into his arms. He gave me a chaste peck on the cheek.

"Sweet, is it possible," he began, looking deep into my eyes, hesitating. "Danni, do you think you could be— Could it be that—"

"What, North?"

I smiled up at him, amazed to see a flush steal along his jaw. I bit back my amusement. North might be nonconventional and unnervingly direct, but there were old-fashioned niceties that clung to him like a second skin: *A wife must announce her pregnancy to her husband, not vice versa.*

I gave him no help. I only lifted my brows in pretended puzzlement. His face fell.

"I thought—perhaps—you're—er, chilly, Danni. I could send for a shawl," he finished lamely.

But my happiness became boundless one afternoon as North and I sat working over ledgers in separate rooms of the office cottage.

William, the schoolmaster and stonecutter, had come to consult me about the stone for Jonathan's grave.

When I finished my brief directions, he looked at me as though he could not believe his ears. He tugged at one earlobe.

"That is *all* you want carved on the stone, M'am? Only name and dates?"

His voice was incredulous, even tinged with reproach.

"Yes," I said quickly. Then, hoping he would go at once, "Thank you, William!"

But he did not move. I looked away, saddened, as William ruminated on my words. I knew what he was thinking. Most gravestones, especially ones for children, were embellished with tender loving words. Jonathan's could not be. It would be an insult to North. Jonathan was dead; North, alive. I must consider my husband's feelings, even though the mother in me ached to bury Jonathan properly, lovingly. . . .

William shuffled his feet, mutely urging me to reconsider. I drew a sharp breath, then dismissed him crisply.

"That will be all. Thank you, William."

In the next room, a chair scraped against the floor, and North's low voice preceded him into the room.

"William!"

I looked up fearfully. Why did he interfere? Did he still hate my baby? Would he deny Jonathan even the smallest, simplest marker?

I watched him, my eyes growing round with fright and dread. He met my gaze steadily.

"Of course my wife and I want more, William. If Mrs. Delveau approves, I think this will do."

I watched him, breathless, as he came to my work table, took paper, dipped a quill into the ink pot, and wrote rapidly. He pushed the paper toward me.

I read it, tears rising.

Beloved Infant Son of North Delveau and His Wife, Dianna Brandley Delveau.

I couldn't speak. Unable even to look up at him, I could only nod my assent and push the paper to William. William grunted his approval and rambled on to me about whether the stone should be granite or basalt. North, sensing my emotions were about to break, lay his arm on the man's shoulder and casually led him out-of-doors, speaking of mundane plantation matters.

When the door banged shut behind them, I burst into wrenching sobs. I hadn't wept since Jonathan's death, and now I cradled my head in my arms and cried until the well was dry.

It was a thorough cleansing of mind, soul and spirit. Jonathan, and all that Jonathan meant to North's and my relationship, was dead. Dead and buried. North's generous gesture had signaled a new beginning.

The issue of the gravestone was too emotion-laden to be broached. However, that evening after dinner, as North poured my port in the drawing room, I stayed his hand. Impulsively, I drew his hand to my mouth and pressed upon it soft kisses of passionate gratitude.

"I *love* you," I whispered with savage force. "North, I love you!"

I looked up at him, but he avoided my eyes. He drew away, as though drawing away from the subject.

"If the lady loves me for pouring port," he teased gently, "then what might she not do if I served her wine from Champagne?"

I was blissfully happy that spring. And yet, I was frightened too. Shadows darkened that happiness. I was ill at ease, aware of undercurrents I could not see. I sensed Charlotte Delveau was at the heart of my fears, but I did not know why.

I was frightened, also, by my growing love for North. The enormity of it struck terror in me. My love for him seemed so deep, so tall, so wide that it could not be measured. He had become more necessary to me than air. My heart was in his hands. I had never been so vulnerable.

At the same time, I felt fiercely protective of him. I was determined that no one—nothing—should cause him more pain. Andre . . . Starlight . . . two adored and adorable sons . . . He must suffer nothing more, I vowed vehemently. I would give my life to prevent it.

But the darkest shadow on my happiness was caused by something that did *not* happen. North had never explained the meaning of his letter, the letter he'd sent to me just before Starlight's death. And I couldn't ask. The words burned in my heart and soul, branded there:

Dianna, the voyage afforded me time to think and ponder our problems. I have reached the most difficult and painful decision of my life. It would be unfair—no, cowardly—to write you of that decision. I must tell you face-to-face.

Had he decided for me? Or had he decided Andre's death freed him to bring Starlight into his home as wife and mistress of Twin Oaks?

I shuddered, praying never to know the answer.

As for our physical life together, we both seemed stunned and awed at our deepening intimacy. Acts which might be expected to grow commonplace between husband and wife took on new dimensions.

Perhaps the most surprising development, though, was North's deepening respect for me. Where earlier in our relationship he was dictatorial, voicing his demands, then barking an order and stomping off, quite certain that I could do nothing but obey, now he was different. Now he took time to argue and even fight with me.

One of our angriest fights concerned a party. There was to be a week-long celebration for our anniversary. North proposed it. There would be a major ball; July in the foothills was cool enough for dancing. And there would be hunts, riding, races, cards, lawn barbecues and picnic outings. The Washingtons would come. The Fairfields, of course, and dozens of others.

But when North matter-of-factly stated that Abby Fairfield Hamilton and her husband were to be invited, I exploded.

"I will *not* have Abby in this house, North! I will *not* have her here, flirting with you under my nose."

He laughed and brushed away my objections.

"She's to be invited. Abby is harmless."

"Harmless? No! She *wants* you, North."

"Don't be tiresome, Danni," he said testily, turning to his ledgers in dismissal. "If I'd wanted Abby, I'd have taken her years ago. Abby's offers are hardly new."

I gasped.

"So she *did* approach you in Williamsburg?"

North slammed the ledger shut, his eyes narrowing.

"Goddamn it, have I married a shrew? Abby Fairfield will be invited because I have the greatest respect and esteem for Agatha Fairfield! I will *not* hurt Agatha by cutting her daughter."

Stung that he should value Mrs. Fairfield's feelings over my own, I bit my lip, drew myself up and persisted.

"Still," I said softly, "I will *not* invite her."

North gave me a grim smile.

"Still," he mocked, "you *will*. What's more, Dianna, you will be a gracious hostess to Abby in every way. If she wishes to sit on my right at dinner, you will grant her that privilege. If she wishes me to take her riding, you will see us off with smiles and *not* with sour looks."

"I would rather die!"

His eyes flashed with anger. He rose to his feet and for a moment or two, I feared he would shake me. But he merely took a deep breath.

"If that is so, little rabbit," he teased, his voice retaining a small measure of coldness, "then you'd best send Mrs. Krause for rope, poison or knife. Abby *is* to be invited, sweet."

I was working on my father's papers one evening only two weeks before the party when the door of the office creaked open and Mrs. Krause's brisk footfalls sounded on the oak planking.

"Mrs. Delveau?"

I looked up and smiled.

"There is a gentleman to see you. He is waiting in the main drawing room. He refused to give his name, but only said you were friends at Brandley Manor."

I froze, rooted to the chair, my scalp tingling. I stared at her without answer.

She gave me a perplexed look and patiently repeated her message. The blood drained from my hands. My fingers stiffened and the quill I was holding dropped, spraying ink. I began to tremble.

In the next room, North's chair scraped harshly against the floor. His boots thudded, shaking the boards as he hurried to me.

"North—North?" I whispered foolishly.

He took in my stricken condition in a glance.

"Thank you, Mrs. Krause. My wife and I will be in shortly. See to the gentleman's comfort."

"North— Oh, God—Christian?"

North gave me a quick angry look. Whether his fury was for me or for Christian, I couldn't tell.

"I can't see him, North!"

"You *will* see him. I demand it."

"No! Please—" I reached for him with shaking hands, but he shoved me away and strode to the window.

"If you are my woman, you have nothing to fear in seeing Cartwright. Either you are mine or you are Cartwright's. Which is it, Danni?"

I was stunned at the coldness in his voice. It was as if in one moment, all the trust we had so carefully built over past months had crumbled and turned to dust.

I gave a little sob of utter despair.

"I'm yours, North—only yours—"

He smiled. It was not a pleased smile but a cold one, grim and doubting. Slowly, he extended his hand to me.

"Come," he ordered harshly. "We shall greet your lover together."

I had never observed a condemned convict taking those final and terrible steps to the gallows, but now I knew a portion of what the poor creature must suffer.

North was condemning me without trial. His iron grip on my wrist as he dragged me along told me so. He strode purposefully, his mind on the confrontation ahead. He seemed oblivious to my sobbing protestations of love for him, oblivious to bruising my wrist.

Inside the house, I was aware of my heels clicking over the polished parquet. But as for feet, I had none. I was numb.

At the entrance to the drawing room, North flung away my wrist. With an oath, he wrenched open the door. The door shuddered, its hinges humming. He stepped in ahead of me, and I held my breath, my heart knocking madly.

Oh, Christian, be kind! Be sensible. Don't destroy North's love for me!

In a foolish attempt to forestall the inevitable moment, I shut my eyes. My head began to swim.

Immediately, there came North's snort of surprise, then, to my unbelieving ears, his low, relieved laughter.

"Good evening, sir," he said calmly, striding into the room.

When I opened my eyes, it was to a tableau that would be carved into my brain forever. A small summer's evening fire flickered in the fireplace, its light playing upon Charlotte's portrait over the mantel. Flanking Charlotte on one side was North; on the other side, a man who, though shorter, older and less handsome, might be taken for North at a glance. They were greeting each other with a handshake. As they did so, the firelight leaped to their faces, illuminating almost identical profiles.

Above them, Charlotte smiled her soft secretive smile.

It was a cataclysmic moment, and I swayed as the awful knowledge came rumbling toward me like thunder. The drawing room door suddenly lurched up against me. My hand shot out to hold it back, to hold back everything.

"God, no!" I begged in a whisper. "No—please—not that!"

As the two finished shaking hands and turned to me, they seemed to lurch and twist grotesquely. From an incredibly far distance, I heard their cries of alarm, and then knew nothing more. My knees crumpled. Darkness erased the scene. Then, nothing.

I woke to the faint chiming of Charlotte's porcelain clock upon the mantel. The hour was two, and I'd been put to bed with a dose of laudanum. I was intensely awake, like a night creature that stalks or is stalked.

A three-quarter moon dominated the sky outside the balcony doors, its white light mercilessly stark. Thin, elongated clouds skimmed through the sky, creating the illusion that the moon, itself, was racing.

At my side, North's breathing came deep and regular. He lay on top of the silk comforter, fully dressed, as though he'd stayed with me, worrying.

Hesitant, fearful of waking him but unable to stop myself, I reached out and smoothed the dark tousled hair from his brow. My fingers trailed the dear familiar scar. I remembered the first time my fingers had explored it. I'd touched it just so—in awe and wonder—on that first night at Brandley Manor.

It came to me with a wrench that I, and I alone, was responsible for all the unhappiness he'd suffered since that night.

I had destroyed his and Starlight's marriage. No doubt they had planned to live at Twin Oaks as husband and wife after Andre's death. And *I* had killed her. For surely Joseph Lasher's Shawnee raid was designed for revenge. Surely he'd meant to strike terror in my life by raiding on North's property. And his sons...his precious sons...I caused that, too...

Sick to the very pit of my being, I dragged myself from bed, found robe and slippers, and stole out onto the balcony.

I steadied myself against the rail and tried to think. I *had* to prevent North from learning the truth, from learning what *I* now knew about his parentage. The truth would destroy him. He'd adored his pretty and capricious young mother; he'd worshipped Andre.

Helpless, I stared into the night. Transparent clouds threaded the sky, racing across the moon and throwing a harlequin of light and shadow upon the gardens. In winter, I could step out onto the balcony and see beyond the gardens and far off to the little hilltop cemetery where Jonathan slept. But now, with trees thick with foliage, I could not see the hill.

Jonathan.

Slowly, gradually, new thoughts formed. Perhaps Sir Gordon's sudden appearance was only social. Perhaps he did *not* know what I assumed him to know. Perhaps he didn't suspect he'd sired Jonathan!

Of course! I'd been foolish to faint. Foolish to give myself away. I whirled around in sudden hope. Through the glass doors, I could see that North slept on. I turned, padding quickly down the balcony stairs. I would confront Sir Gordon alone. I would draw him out, find out why he'd come.

I hurried through the darkness, along the brick walk. I would find another door, make my way to the guest wing.

But as I passed the garden doors to the drawing room, I saw the fire burning brightly on the grate. Near the fire, on the settee, a figure sat waiting. I caught my breath. Before the man, on a low table, there was a decanter and two crystal glasses. I shuddered as the meaning of the scene sank in. He'd *known* I would seek him out. Did it also mean he knew about Jonathan, about North?

I wanted to run. But I had to face him. I went in.

"I've been waiting for you, my dear."

His voice was as I remembered it. Acerbic. Mocking. Yet, under the acid tone, passion, obsession. It was a dangerous combination, and one I feared. Was the cat-and-mouse game about to begin again?

I trembled.

"You are a devil," I whispered. "Why have you come? Haven't you done me enough injury?"

He made no answer.

I watched him warily as he lifted the decanter and poured wine into the two goblets. The wine swirled in the glasses, settling. Firelight played in the depths of the liquid. He watched the wine settle, a sly smile on his lips as though he were designing his game.

I tensed.

He picked up the wine and strolled toward me, coming insultingly near. He held out a wineglass to me. When I made no move to take it, he chuckled softly and set it aside. Casually, his burning eyes on me, he sipped his wine, then turned the glass and put the place where his lips had been to my mouth. I averted my face in disgust.

He laughed softly.

"So the rosebud has become a rose; the child, a woman..."

"Yes, a woman!" I hissed. "A woman deeply in love with her husband!"

He laughed again.

"But I counted on that, my dear, Dianna. It is precisely for that reason that when you come to my bed, you will come willingly..."

His words were pellets of ice, dropping into my heart, freezing it.

"I—I—don't know what you're talking about."

He laughed.

"I think you do."

I looked away, fearing pounding.

In a swift, unexpected movement, he lifted my chin. He raked his hot, wet lips over mine. I jerked away in revulsion.

"Touch me again and I'll kill you!"

He laughed softly.

322

"Good," he said. "You have not lost your spirit. Nor your courage. I was afraid my . . . son . . . might have tamed you."

At the word "son" I reached out to the wall steadying myself.

"Son? You have no son!"

He smiled. Slowly, he strolled to the mantel and stood looking up at Charlotte. When he turned again, his dark eyes mocked.

"I must confess, Dianna, until that night of the dinner party, when you pointed out how much North and I resembled each other, I must confess—I had no idea that my amusement with Charlotte had spawned such interesting consequences."

"Stop!"

I clamped my hands to my ears in a foolish, futile gesture.

"I forbid you to say such things in this house. North worshipped his mother! He adored his father!"

He snorted derisively.

"Andre was a saint, yes. But a blind one. Charlotte?" He gave a short, harsh laugh. "A delightful, hot-blooded young woman. I admit I was the first of her lovers. But after me?" He arched one eyebrow.

"Stop! I beg of you! In the name of decency—if you have any feeling for your son at all—you will go—go at once! North and I are happy!"

His face flushed dark. "I have no interest in my son by Charlotte," he whispered passionately. "I want to see Jonathan, the son *you* have given me."

I cried out in anguish, wrenching my hands away as he reached for me. So he knew everything! Everything but that Jonathan was dead.

I bowed my head in despair.

"How?" I choked. "How did you know?"

"When your Aunt Matilde told me the date of Jonathan's birth, I suspected at once. I looked into the matter. I have my sources, a network of well-paid solicitors on both sides of the Atlantic. My informants report there was no honeymoon before the *Joanna* or aboard it. In fact, they report that you and North were most hostile. And at Twin Oaks, you slept apart."

I stared at him without answer, hating him, loathing him, wishing him dead.

"Indeed, my dear, I know even more," he went on cruelly. "I know North has an Indian woman and children."

With arrogant confidence, he took my shoulders in his hands. His hot mouth went to my neck, and I jerked away.

"Dianna, I *will* see my son, Jonathan!"

I whirled to face him. How dare he claim my son! Jonathan was nothing but an accident of passion to him. But to me he'd been everything! I'd carried him in my body, fed him, worried over him, loved him, and finally buried him. How dare he claim a share in that!

Fury filled me. If I'd had a knife, it would have gone into his heart up to the hilt. I shook with angry passion, longing to have my revenge—for myself, for Jonathan, for North. A cold ugly impulse came.

"You wish to see Jonathan?" I whispered. "Then you *shall* see him. Come. Come!"

I flung open the garden doors, and stalked out into the night. Sir Gordon followed, grabbing my arm.

"Dianna! What is this nonsense? What are you about?"

I shrugged away his hand in vengeful fury.

"If you wish to see Jonathan, come!" I hissed.

I plunged through the garden, my slippers tearing against the rough brick of the walks. The paths shone brightly in the stark white light of the moon, and I rushed forward—driven by fury, hurt, and the need for revenge. From the gardens, I stumbled through the thick stand of hickory trees where the Pederson children often played, then ran through the cold, wet meadow and up the hill to the little cemetary.

Wind had blown open the low picket gate. Without pause, my feet knowing the way, I ran to Jonathan's grave and fell to my knees, breathless.

Sir Gordon was only steps behind.

"Dianna! What is the meaning of this!"

A cloud passed over the moon just as he reached me. We were thrust into sudden darkness. Then, slowly, the moon cleared. A shaft of bright light once again caught Jonathan's newly carved stone.

Eager for my revenge, for North's revenge, I turned to watch Sir Gordon. He was staring at the stone. He took two drunken, pitching steps forward. Then, suddenly, he clawed at his face as though to claw away the words he had read.

"Aaaaagh!" he cried out. "My son!"

It was a primitive cry, a long and piercing wail. Its primeval force, its eerie echo of unbearable loss, made me clap my hands to my ears in horror. His cry came again, against his will, tearing out of the inmost part of him, bending his body in two. He pitched forward onto Jonathan's grave.

"My son! I want my son!"

For several minutes he gave way to violent grief. Then, gradually, the wracking of his body diminished. He seized control of himself.

"Tell me!"

I did so. I told him everything. He listened without so much as a flicker of emotion. It was as though he listened to a tale that did not concern him. When I was done, he stood, his voice ice.

"The white man—the one who eluded capture—this Joseph Lasher, he *will* be found. If necessary, I will pour my entire fortune into avenging my son's death."

My breath caught at the madness of his statement and revenge was suddenly ashes in my mouth. I pulled myself to my feet, new fear surging.

"No, I beg you, Gordon, let it be. North doesn't know you sired Jonathan. He thinks Christian. Go. Please, go. North and I are happy—"

He looked at me as though I were the one insane.

"My dear," he said softly, "must I remind you that you belong to me?"

I froze. For an eternity, no response would come.

"You are mad!" I whispered.

"Mad?" He laughed his low mocking laugh, and the laughter held no trace of the anguish of only minutes earlier. "Mad with the desire to have you, my love. You *will* be mine, Dianna. In time, you will bear me another son."

I gasped.

"I love North! I love him more than life itself!"

"Precisely. For that very reason, you willingly will be mine.

You will do anything to prevent him from learning the truth about Charlotte."

I stared at him in horror, beginning to understand. He reached for me, and as his hands caressed my pounding throat, I shuddered. I turned from him and ran. Ran wildly, stumbling, falling, picking myself up and lurching onward.

Ahead, the house was aglow with lights. Candles and oil lamps flared in the drawing room. The doors stood open to the garden. I could see North inside, pacing.

I staggered in and fell into his arms.

"Danni!"

He crushed me to him, holding me. Then, roughly, he drew back and shook me viciously.

"God damn it! I've been worried sick! Where have you been? Where is Sir Gordon?"

I couldn't answer. I could only shake my head, weeping, sobbing.

With a violent oath, he wrenched me close, pressing my head to his heart.

"What the hell is going on, Danni?"

I looked up at him through my tears.

"Oh, North, I love you," I sobbed. "Hold me!"

He did as I asked. We were clinging to each other, thus, when Sir Gordon entered. I heard his boots sound against the floor, felt North begin to tense. I closed my eyes. I bowed my head to his chest like an animal bowing its head to the slaughter. I knew what I must do. And oddly, I knew peace. There was one gift I could give my beloved—the unsullied memory of Andre and Charlotte. The gift would cost me my life. I must go with Sir Gordon.

"You will give me an explanation, sir," North demanded, his voice cold and formal with fury.

"Certainly."

Sir Gordon's voice was light, confident, even tinged with amusement. I shivered. North's arms tightened around me.

"The explanation is simple," he said. "Dianna and I went out to visit . . . our son's grave."

CHAPTER 25

There was deafening silence.

North jerked violently, as though he'd been hit with a club. For an instant, he was dead weight upon me. I clutched at him, my knees buckling. Then, with an agonized intake of breath, he straightened himself.

His arms tightened around me protectively. But as his muscles contracted, taut and tense, my heart plunged. The movement signaled a shift within him. Trust battled with distrust.

"You," he said hoarsely. "It was *you* who raped her. By God—"

To my ever growing horror, Sir Gordon burst into mocking laughter.

"Rape?" he said lightly. "My dear Comte d' Delveau! Dianna came to my bed willingly."

I cried out, an anguished cry of denial.

With an oath, North crushed me safely to him and held me against his pounding heart.

"By God, sir, you will pay for your lies!"

"Lies?" Sir Gordon returned coldly. "I think not." He made a flip gesture. "Ask her."

North held me close. He cradled my face in his shaking hand and my tears ran wet onto his fingers.

"Don't, darling," he said angrily, "don't let him make you cry."

"I love you," I whispered, choking. "I love—"

His mouth moved on mine, as though to tenderly stop the wrenching sobs. It was a sweet and lingering kiss, purer than light, pure as love.

It infuriated Sir Gordon.

"Ask Dianna," he said viciously. "Ask her if she laid with me willingly."

I cried out under his torture.

"Look at us!" I beseeched him. "See how much we love! Only a devil would seek to destroy that! Have you no pity?"

But his smoldering gaze went to North's arms. North was holding me tightly, intimately and without conscious thought. One arm clasped over my breasts. One hand was spread low on my belly as though, deep within himself, on the instinctive and unconscious level, he knew his child quickened there.

Sir Gordon exploded in jealous fury.

"Tell him!" he demanded of me. "Tell him you came to me willingly!"

I choked at his cruelty. I lifted my hand in supplication, but he gazed at me, unmoved. Obsession burned in his eyes. He strode to the mantel. Deliberately and with perfect clarity of meaning, he stared up at Charlotte's portrait.

My head dropped in despair. He was mad. He would destroy his own son to possess me. And if I denied his accusations? If I allowed him to tell North the truth about Charlotte? What would I have gained? I would become the instrument of North's destruction. I had already cost him Starlight and his sons. Would I kill his father and mother also?

Dianna Brandley, I mused sadly. The spoiled girl who, on a selfish whim to possess Christian, had entered North's life and smashed everything in it.

I gave one final sob, suddenly knowing what I must do.

I bowed my head.

"North . . . I . . . went to him . . . willingly."

He drew a sharp, rattling breath. With a rough, urgent movement, he turned me in his arms and looked at me.

"I don't—believe you."

"Oh, dearest—"

I couldn't bear his eyes. I touched his face and his lips went to my fingers.

Our tenderness stirred new fury in Sir Gordon.

"You wed a warm and eager slut, Delveau. *I* had her. *Cartwright* had her."

I gasped at Christian's name, and North trembled.

"Shut up!" he snapped. "By God, your life is measured in minutes. Get out of this house or be carried out of it."

North's eyes, angry and tortured, searched mine, pleading for denial, pleading for the explanation I could not give. Helpless to comfort him, I could only watch as the light slowly died in his eyes.

Sir Gordon sensed victory. He pressed.

"You will see how willing our beautiful Dianna can be," he taunted. "Dianna!" he ordered. "Come. Embrace me."

With a cry of anguish, I slumped against North's stiffening body. I looked up into his face and died a thousand deaths at the shock and disillusionment that came as he realized what I would do.

I tore my gaze from him. Quickly, I stumbled across the room and into Sir Gordon's arms.

"Danni! God damn it!"

With a shudder, I lifted my mouth and gave myself to Sir Gordon. His mouth, rapacious, wet and hot with passion, raked mine, tasting, possessing. I swayed under him. *God . . . oh, God . . . God . . .*

North roared in outrage. He was across the room in an instant, wrenching me from Sir Gordon. I reached up to cling to him, but the crack of his hand against my cheek came so suddenly, so unexpectedly, that I crumpled to the floor at his feet. Stunned, I buried my face in my hands, cowering.

"Chillburn? Cartwright? How many others? And how many more since you have become my wife?"

"North! No, dearest—"

I shut my eyes, cringing as his hand went up again.

Sir Gordon sprang across the room with a murderous cry.

"Hurt her, and you answer to me!"

North looked down at me, then at his hand. He studied his hand as though he could not believe what it had done. He turned, lurching drunkenly to the door, then stopped, steadying himself against the wall.

"Take her," he said passionately. "She sickens me. I could vomit at the sight of her."

"No!" I cried out, shrugging off Sir Gordon's hands.

I dragged myself to my feet, stumbling after North. He had crossed the foyer and was striding up the winding staircase. At the top of the stairs, servants, roused by the uproar, cringed uncertainly. Mrs. Krause had one foot on the step, about to descend. She was wearing a brown wrapper, her gray hair plaited into a long braid. Her face was white.

"North!" I cried, rushing up the stairs, clutching at his sleeve. With a vicious swing of his arm, he slapped me away. I fell into the banister, twisted, and stumbled down several stairs before I caught myself.

The servants cried out.

"Mr. North!" Mrs. Krause shouted.

She pushed past him and flew down the stairs to me, gathering me into her arms.

"Mr. North! What *can* you be thinking!"

His cold, controlled answer made me shake in her arms.

"If you value her life, get her out of this house. For the next time I see her—by God, I will kill her."

Mrs. Krause gasped. She held me tightly. The other servants fled in fear.

"North," I whispered tearfully, "I love you—"

He winced. A muscle in his cheek twitched. He looked at me coldly.

"When I returned from the Sugar Islands, I planned to send you away," he said. "Would to God that I had!"

My body jerked as though a sword had been run through it. I doubled in two. Mrs. Krause caught me as I sank to the stairs and huddled there, slaughtered. It was a mortal blow, a blow so stunning it carried me beyond tears and pain. I crouched there, my face upon the oak stair. I couldn't think. I couldn't feel. I only knew my life had ended. Nothing mattered. Nothing.

CHAPTER 26

The coral reef, brown and scummy-looking, lay only a few feet beneath the sea's surface. The water covering the reef was transparent, a contrast to the dark blue of the deep channel leading to the green island on the horizon.

Already, I could smell land.

Lost in my sad thoughts, I watched without interest as the reef slipped along beside the ship. In the transparent waters, an incredibly gentle and beautiful world unfolded. Schools of lemon-yellow angel fish hovered over the reef in a thick carpet. Stirred by the ship's slow and careful passage, the living carpet moved away.

A parrot fish of iridescent colors swam gracefully over the reef, its long red streamers trailing behind. A grouper, ugly and large as a dinghy, tugged its food from the reef, unaware or uncaring that a ship passed. A manta fish undulated past the grouper, looking like a piece of black silk settling in some underwater breeze.

"You will like Barbados, Dianna."

At the unexpected sound of his voice, my fingers tightened on the rail. I had not been aware of him drawing near.

I turned, meeting his eyes coldly, steadily.

He was first to drop his eyes and look away. In that, I found a kernel of satisfaction. Had the rosebud become the rose? The child a woman? Yes, I thought, and more. The heart had become a stone. The spirit, an empty hardened shell.

I turned and gazed out at the reef. He put his hands on my shoulders. He hesitated, then touched his lips to the nape of my neck. I neither flinched, nor shuddered. There was no response in me. Quickly, as though he touched dead flesh, he drew his hands away.

Several minutes went by.

"You will like my villa," he tried. "It is spacious and built on several levels. A terrace of marbled balconies leads down into the gardens. To have a gardenia for your hair, Dianna, you need only stroll out on your balcony and pluck it."

I said nothing. The deep waters of the channel curled by, eddying and sluicing against the ship's hull.

"You will have everything you want, Dianna... *Anything* you want," he coaxed passionately.

I turned, eyed him coldly.

"And you. What will you have?"

He laughed softly. His eyes darkened.

"There has been no privacy since leaving Twin Oaks, and you have been very ill, my sweet. But at my villa..."

I met his eyes without fear.

"At your villa, you *will* leave me untouched."

Only the slightest flicker of his eyelids revealed he was startled at the new authority, the new hardness in my manner.

He laughed uncertainly.

"My dear Dianna, I would have you willing. But if not..." His voice trailed away, and we both watched as an eel slithered over the reef, pursuing a quarry that idled, unaware of its danger.

"May I remind you, my dear, that you are in my power now?"

I looked at him, my lip curling.

"You are quite wrong, Sir Gordon," I said without expression. "It is you who are in my power. I intend to kill you."

He was silent, shocked. Then he laughed. But it was thin laughter.

"My dear Dianna, how absurd."

I gazed out at the reef.

"You think I am not brave enough to do it. You are right. For myself, I could not. But for North's child, be assured that I will do it. His child must come to no harm!"

Without thought, he seized my arm and spun me around to face him. I stared at him, and at the coldness in my face, his hand dropped from my wrist.

"A child?" he said hotly. "Does North know?"

I looked away. It was the one remaining pain that I could still feel. The final, terrible wrench. I was giving my beloved a child, and he would never know it. . . . I would never experience the joy of placing my son in his father's arms.

"It—it will be my grandchild," Sir Gordon said, his voice husky and bewildered.

I looked up at him in surprise. I narrowed my eyes, studying him through my lashes. So it moved him, did it? That knowledge was a weapon. I would tend it carefully, keeping it safe and sharpened for future use. . . .

"Not grandchild," I said, honing the weapon on his ego. "Grandson. North's child will be male."

I left him standing at the rail, his face a collage of emotions.

The days drifted down in a melancholy sameness. They fell, one upon the other, much like blossoms of the plumeria tree, each falling to the earth in its appointed time. In the sameness of the days upon the island, I found an inner island for my soul. There, alone and in the center of myself, I grieved.

I thought I had come to terms with my loss aboard ship. I was wrong. Somehow, as long as the ship had been moving, some childish and irrational part of myself said—*I am traveling to North.*

But when I stepped through the tall cool arches of the villa and my heels echoed hesitantly through the vast chambers, I paled. This was no moving ship, but reality. Here, in this house, I would deliver North's child. His first tiny cries would echo off these cold marble walls.

And the wound opened.

North. Oh, North!

He was a constant presence. I imagined his voice everywhere. His low rich laughter was in the rumbling surge of the sea as I walked miles upon sloping sandy beaches. His love-whispers came to me in the rustle and hiss of windblown cane fields as I walked the dirt roads of the island.

Any figure on the distant horizon could command my attention and set my heart pounding. . . . One evening as I dined with Sir Gordon on the balcony overlooking the bay, I saw a tall figure move up the beach toward the villa. My meal forgotten, I pushed back my chair and rushed to the marble balustrade to watch.

A huge, molten gold sun had just dipped into the sea, and the bright coral of the tropical sunset was shooting up the western sky, spreading and reflecting upon the island until everything was tinted a delicate pink. The figure approached slowly. As he came nearer, my racing heart slowed. I bowed my head in disappointment. It was only a Negro fisherman, his crab box and gear balanced upon his head. I closed my eyes, absorbing the pain that such moments always stirred anew.

Sir Gordon's footfalls sounded behind me, then stopped. His hands closed on my shoulders.

"He will not come, you know."

I stiffened.

"If you touch me—" I hissed, "if you harm North's child—"

With a furious growl he seized me.

"I take what I want, Dianna. You would be wise to remember that, my dear."

I shuddered in disgust, revulsion. With effort, I straightened myself and dragged my eyes up to his. I glared at him through my fear.

"Touch me again and—"

"Enough of your charming bravado! I do not enjoy being threatened, Dianna." He smiled, pulling me so close I could feel his breath hot on my cheek. I shrank. "You think me in your power?" he taunted. "No, my dear. You are in *my* power. You forget that at any time I can send a letter to North, revealing everything about his precious mother, and her cuckold of a husband!"

With a cry of outrage, I jerked loose of him. I speared him with a look of pure hate.

"You are a devil!" I whispered.

"A devil?"

He laughed softly, and wrenched me close.

"A devil would take you here and now, without concern for your condition. But I value you, my dear. And I value the child that so prettily swells your small belly. My blood, too, flows in his veins. So you may have your pregnancy and confinement. I won't touch you. When you are fully recovered . . ."

I went cold, the chill settling in my heart. I felt numb. Oh, North . . . my beloved . . . my own true husband . . .

Slowly and in a proprietary manner, he drew his lips across my throat, pausing at the pulse point and kissing my throat with fevered passion. He trembled, and then, with an abrupt movement, he released me and strode from the balcony.

"I have news of *him*, Dianna."

My heart lurched. I sat up, nerves quivering. It was October now. Gordon had come to my bedchamber in the middle of the night. In the flaring light of his candle, his face was grim.

"Is he well?" I asked fearfully. "He's all right, isn't he? Tell me? Please?"

He looked at me as though I were insane. A dark look passed over his features. His lips twitched.

"I do not speak of Delveau," he said coldly, spitting out North's name as though it were poison on his tongue. "I speak of Joseph Lasher. Jonathan's murderer. He was seen in Philadelphia."

I lay back on the pillow, my heart pounding, aching with disappointment. North—he was all I cared about. And to be taken to the height in expectation of news of North—then, dashed to the ground. . . .

My eyelashes beaded with tears.

"I don't care about Lasher," I whispered.

"He killed our *son*, Dianna," he said hotly. "He *must* be punished. He *will* be punished. I will see to it."

There was an undercurrent in his voice, a tinge of megalomania. I knew he was obsessed with hunting Lasher. I knew he'd hired agents. But did he mean to take his revenge by killing the man himself? I shivered at such madness. And suppose Lasher learned Gordon was hunting him. Might he not assume North was involved? Might he not go to Twin Oaks and lie in wait some night, seeking to harm North?

I sat up, my heart in my mouth.

"Gordon, I beg of you, let it be. Jonathan is dead. No amount of revenge will bring him back. No—"

He silenced me with a hot glare. He stood, then took my face in his hands. His obsidian eyes bored into mine. When he spoke, his voice was guttural with passion.

"I promise you, Dianna, I will lay the corpse at your feet."

I cried out at the madness of his statement.

"Gordon, don't do this," I begged. "Don't do anything that could bring harm to North. After this baby is born, I—I—I'll do—anything you ask. I swear it. Only don't—don't endanger North—"

He cut off my babbling with a curse. He wrenched me from the bed, his eyes wild.

"North, North, North!" he thundered, his hands going to my throat. "By God, I would choke the name out of you!"

"Gordon," I gasped weakly as his fingers tightened. "In the name of heaven—"

Slowly, the rage died in his eyes, and he looked at me in alarm and horror, as a man might gaze at a valued treasure he'd come close to smashing in a moment of uncontrolled anger. He held me in his arms, stroking my hair as I trembled, sick with despair and fear.

"You wish news of North?" he said, coldly.

I gave a desperate sob.

"Oh, yes, yes! Is he well? He *is* well, is he not?"

He picked me up in his arms and lifted me back into the bed, gently settling me upon the pillows, covered me with the silk sheet. Then he stood looking down at me.

"North is well," he said tersely. "He lives in Williamsburg. My agent reports that more nights than not, Delveau does not return to his own house to sleep. He consoles a young widow. A Mrs. Hamilton."

For a moment I thought I might suffocate. There was no air, and my lungs seemed paralyzed. I searched Gordon's face, my lips quivering.

"The widow? Is she Abby Hamilton?"

"That I do not know. My agent reports Major Hamilton was aide to the governor. Hamilton died of swamp fever in July."

Slowly and with careful desperation, my eyes traveled every inch of Sir Gordon's face. I plumbed it for guile, for lies, for facile untruths. I wanted him to be lying. Yet, as I searched the stern lines of his face, I could see he spoke the truth.

Stunned, I was beyond weeping.

I rolled away, curling up like an animal curling round its bleeding wound. Abby, with her dazzling green eyes and red hair. . . . Abby, white shouldered and beautiful, lying like some exotic flower in North's arms . . .

A low uncontrollable moan forced its way out. The sound of it incensed Sir Gordon.

"Delveau doesn't want you, Dianna!" he said coldly.

I whimpered, my body jerking. Cruelly, he went on. "He replaces you as easily as a man replaces a shirt he has chosen to discard."

"No!" I whispered, grinding my head into the satin pillow as though to grind out his words. "No! North loves me! I love him! If he goes to Abby, it is only because he is terribly hurt."

"So you would forgive Delveau anything!"

His roar was the roar of an injured lion. I lifted my head from the pillow and, shivering, looked into Sir Gordon's furious face.

"He is my husband," I whispered.

Sir Gordon laughed. It was a harsh ugly laugh. Its knowing quality sent arrows of fear through me. I felt the blood drain from my face.

"Is he still your husband?" he taunted. "Are you certain?"

"Wh—wh—" My lips were bloodless and stiff. I tried to

speak but could not. Helplessly, I could only watch as triumph flashed in Sir Gordon's eyes.

"My dear," he said softly, hesitating, then going on in obvious pleasure, "Delveau has...divorced you."

All through the long month of October I clung to my disbelief. Stubbornly, I held to my disbelief far into the month of November as the cane harvest began and the island people flowed gently into the fields, setting the green undulating cane terraces aglitter with light as the sun caught the swinging machetes.

Each dawn I arose telling myself that North would never do such a thing to me. He would not make me bear the disgrace of being publicly labeled an adultress. He would not! If not for my sake, then for Andre's. For the sake of Andre's memory.

I turned a stony face to the evidence Sir Gordon presented as the weeks went by. I read the reports of his agents in silence, with cold rejection. Though my hand shook as I examined a document of divorce, I coolly told Sir Gordon the document was a fraud. I refused to listen to his explanation that a rich man could circumvent the problem of there being no ecclesiastical court in the colonies to grant divorce.

I expected my denials to anger Sir Gordon. To my confusion, he was only amused. He behaved as though I were a very bright child whose intelligence piqued and charmed him. I was bewildered by his attitude. Fear nibbled at me. Would he be so blasé if it were not true? With a shudder, I cast the thought from my mind.

In my mental battle with Sir Gordon, my child both gave and drained me of strength. The child *was* North.

Already, my love for my unborn son surpassed all that I had felt for Jonathan. This was North's child. North's! For as long as I lived, he would be my tie to North. But my son drained me, too. He stole my sleep. He grew, and my body daily became more ungainly. My poise faded. I had difficulty thinking clearly. My emotions were loosed, and I wept easily. In the final weeks of my pregnancy I would burst into tears whenever the image of Abby lying in North's arms drifted into my mind.

Still, I pitted myself against Sir Gordon.

One evening as I stood on the balcony, lost in sadness and watching the sun close out yet another day, Sir Gordon joined me at the balustrade. Possessively, he covered my hand with his. I pulled away, wondering how much longer I would have the strength to pit myself against him. Only the day before, as I returned from a short stroll on the beach, he'd come down and carried me up the long series of bricked terraces. My protests had been water off a duck's back.

"I don't wish you to touch me," I whispered now, into the sunset.

I braced, preparing to receive his anger. But he only chuckled. It was the sort of chuckle one might use when one indulges a child's whim, knowing that in the end, the child will lose.

Wariness filled me.

"When you are my wife, Dianna—"

I wheeled around. Had I heard correctly? Did he truly think he could usurp North's place? My God!

"Wife? I would rather *die*. I would rather—"

"Lose your child?"

His words took my breath away. I reached behind me, fumbling to steady myself against the balustrade.

"Surely you don't threaten—"

He gave me a black look, his lips twisting in displeasure.

"Don't be ridiculous," he snapped. *"I* do not threaten the child. *Events* threaten."

I stared at him blankly, heart hammering. Events? I held my breath. Surely nothing, no one, could separate me from my baby! He was all I had left of North.

"North has remarried."

I froze.

He lifted the crystal wind protector from the table candle, bent down and lighted his cigar. When he resumed his arrogant stance, he exhaled a thin streak of blue smoke.

"I don't believe you," I whispered.

"Then believe the *Virginia Gazette*. A packet of them arrived today. They are on your dressing table. Read them."

With a cry, I turned, flew from the balcony and into the villa. Picking up my skirts, I rushed up the marble staircase.

I had no thought for my baby, for my condition. I thought only of North. As I flew on, a horrified housemaid pressed herself against the wall, letting me pass but calling out in alarm. Behind me, Sir Gordon bounded up the stairs, shouting commands for me to stop.

I burst into my bedchamber. The *Gazette* lay upon my table. I seized it and ran to the window to read by the dying light. Panic blinded me. I began to sob hysterically as I could not find the item I dreaded seeing. Then I found it. Shaking my head in disbelief, I read it again and again.

"Dianna, North is sure to learn of the baby sooner or later," he said. "He will take it from you."

I whimpered, too weak to make more than a token protest.

Without energy, I whispered, "North would never be so cruel."

"Granted," he said, bowing his head curtly. "But his wife? The Widow Hamilton had no children by her first marriage. She may be barren. If she is, you may be certain she and North will demand your child." He hesitated. "And as a divorced woman, my dear, you have no rights."

I was stunned. Gordon was right. Legally, North *could* take our baby. And if Abby insisted? Abby, with her sharp tongue and her vicious ways, raising *my* child? I winced, imagining the light dying in my child's face as Abby tongue-lashed him for some petty misstep.

"What shall I do?"

Gordon gave me a small, tense smile. Then he dipped his dark head toward mine and brushed my numb lips with his.

"Give your son the protection of being born in wedlock," he said. "Marry me, Dianna."

"What was Jonathan like at this age, Dianna?"

His question jolted me and my book slid from my lap, landing on the marble balcony floor with a soft thud.

I blinked up into the sun. Gordon had taken Charlotte Arabella from her cradle. He was strolling the balcony with her as she jumped and wriggled in his arms.

He chuckled as she stared straight into his eyes for a moment, spouting serious-sounding gibberish. Then she dove for his gold waistcoat button and tried to wrench it off. When it would not, she stared at the button, transfixed, her rosy mouth moist with concentration.

Gordon kissed the top of her dark curly head. He turned to me, his brow wrinkled in thought.

"Was he like Charlotte? Jonathan?"

I looked away in confusion. I wanted no part of a sentimental Sir Gordon. I preferred to see my enemy in sharp focus. Black against white. No shades of gray. It was strong in me, this urge to be cruel. To inflict every possible wound. An eye for an eye.

My lip curled. I wanted to snap, "All babies are alike." But I could not. I couldn't use Jonathan in that way. I had loved him too much.

I rose from my chair and went to the balustrade. Arms spread along the rail, I stood looking out over the bay. Shallow-bottomed boats sculled over the reef. In the boats, island men stood balancing nets and lances as they fished for eel.

"He was a handsome baby," I said, closing my eyes against the sun as pain came flooding back. Sometimes it seemed only yesterday and not two years ago that I rode into the Indian village with Sandy . . . and . . .

"He was strong. At five months, he sat up by himself. . . . He was early in creeping. . . . He was independent, I think. He didn't like to be held overly much. . . . And he had a temper. When something displeased him, he would dissolve into a fit of rage."

Gordon laughed proudly.

"Yes. My son would be like that."

I turned and met his eyes, a sullenness in my soul.

"He was *my* son, Gordon. You had no part in him except to do me violence. *I* carried him, *I* bore him, *I* cared for him. Not you!"

He flushed. His lip twisted.

I looked away. Lunch was being laid on a small table. The linen cloth flapped like a white flag in the breeze. On the cloth, silver sparkled in the sunlight, imitating the glint of light that flashed from the sea as the sun caught a rising swell. The nursemaid appeared in the doorway for Charlotte. Gordon beckoned, and the girl rushed forward.

"The infant's dress is wrinkled," Gordon snapped at the girl. "Change it. Don't let me find her in this condition again!"

The girl blanched, her arms tightening around the wiggling baby. Swiftly, she padded away on bare feet, darting frightened looks over her shoulder.

His anger discharged, he strolled to the balustrade. He covered my hand with his. With a shiver of distaste I pulled it away. I tensed, expecting his wrath.

But his voice, when he spoke, held no trace of it.

"Jonathan was the son of my loins. And yet, you loved him, Dianna. I thank you for that."

I looked up at him in astonishment. His words were humble, totally alien to his person. My eyes narrowed. I watched him warily. What treachery did he plan? What was he up to? I searched his eyes for the usual mockery, the half-amused proprietary look. Nowhere could I find it.

He bent and kissed my cool and unresponding lips. Then he drew back.

"I had hoped," he said in a husky voice, "that as we approached six months of marriage, you might offer your affections freely, Dianna."

I snorted in derision.

"Six months? Six-*hundred* months would make no difference. You take my body, but you cannot take my heart. My heart belongs to—"

Warning flashed in his eyes. I ignored it.

"To North!" I said defiantly.

His eyes went cold, a blue vein throbbing in his temple.

"I charge you not to say that name, Dianna, or—"

I gave a cry of frustration.

"North!" I cried out. "North, North!"

It was a foolhardy thing to do. I knew it at once. I lunged away from the balustrade, but he captured me roughly. I kicked and fought as he picked me up and carried me into the villa. Grimly, oblivious to the astounded servants and to my cries and struggles, he strode up the stairs and down the corridor to my bedchamber. He kicked the door open.

Inside, a silk sheet fluttered over the bed as the housemaid worked. She looked up, her eyes widening in fear. She rushed from the room, pulling the door shut behind her.

Without breaking stride, he flung me down on the bed. The bed shuddered wildly under me. With a cry of fear, I scrambled to my hands and knees as the bed rocked.

"Please, Gordon. I won't utter his name again—only don't—"

His face was hard. He stripped off his clothes. He went to my bureau and rifled the drawers. He came to the bed with a handful of silk scarves.

"What—what do you—" I stammered fearfully.

He seized my wrist, and with vicious movements tied a scarf around it.

"You need taming, my dear," he said coldly, seizing my other wrist as I struggled wildly, not knowing what he intended and fearing it. "You need to be taught a lesson."

When he finished with his degradations, he untied the scarves from the bedposts, and I curled up in a ball of weeping misery. Love with North had not prepared me for a man who used a woman as he wished. I felt whipped, beaten. I knew I could defy him no longer. I hadn't the heart for it. What his physical abuse had not accomplished on that first night he'd taken me, his mental torture had accomplished.

"Dianna?" he said softly.

I curled into my ball more tightly. I buried my face in the satin pillow.

He drew the satin sheet up over me, tucking it round me as a father might tuck in his child. He knelt by the bed and kissed my wet cheek.

Numb with shock, I could not even shiver in revulsion at his touch.

"I love you Dianna," he said. "I wish I had not—"

His apology hung in the air.

A bitter sob broke from me.

"You have won, Gordon," I whispered. "Dianna Brandley, your high-spirited Dianna, is dead. You have killed her."

He drew a sharp breath, then expelled it slowly.

"I pray not, my dear. I pray she is only tamed."

I made to roll away, but he caught me. He kissed my un-feeling lips. When I looked up at him, his eyes were victorious with ownership. My tears came anew.

"Wean your child, my dear, or give her a wet nurse," he ordered softly. "I mean to have a son from you."

In May I had an unexpected respite. Word came that Joseph Lasher may have been sighted in Vera Cruz. Gordon booked passage and left at once. His obsession to kill Lasher with his own hands grew larger as each day passed.

In Gordon's absence, I finally found the peace to write my family. As Gordon suggested, I told them North had sent me to the Caribbean for my health and that I was under the pro-tection of Sir Gordon Chillburn. They would suspect nothing. They were too upright and middle-class to imagine that Gordon might have darker designs upon me. By now, they would have received the sad news of Jonathan. They would think it right and proper of North to send me to the warm tropics where I might convalesce.

I reveled in Gordon's absence. For the first time, Barbados seemed truly beautiful to me. In loose island garb, I wandered the beaches. I wore my hair loose or tied back, not caring that the sun stripped it of its color, turning it to pale silvery ash. My skin took on a golden glow.

In my shift, I swam in the clear shallow waters of quiet lagoons. Hitching my skirts up, I waded into fishing waters with laughing manservants and I learned how to entice the crab into the net.

I played games with my daughter, rolling bright balls for her and then jumping up from the grass to chase them for her. Laughter, a stranger to my spirit for the past year, sprang up and bubbled over. Yet the laughter was not without its tug of poignancy. It brought memories of North and the happy, teasing times we had shared.

I did not want Gordon to return at all. And then, very suddenly, I wanted him more than I had ever wanted anyone's physical presence . . .

Smallpox broke out on the island.

It began with a single case.

A seaman from a British ship anchored in the bay collapsed over a mug of rum in a tavern in Bridgeport. Thinking him drunk, the innkeeper put him to bed. For three days the man sweated and shivered with fever and chills. On the fourth day, the first oozing pustules erupted on his face.

The inn was closed at once by the magistrate, and all of the hired help fled in panic. A week later, an alegirl who'd worked at the inn fainted with fever as she sat milking her father's cow.

The epidemic began in earnest.

Immediately, I sent to the port for the doctor. He sent word back that he could not risk coming to the villa unless we had a true emergency. He was treating smallpox victims and couldn't risk spreading exposure.

My blood chilled.

I forbade servants to go to town. I ordered signs posted on the roads and paths leading to Gordon's estate. All entry was forbidden. Cart men from the ships were forbidden to travel onto the estate to pick up orders of sugar from Gordon's warehouses. I refused to let villa servants visit their families. Or, if they went, I forbade them to come back.

Still, rumors from the port managed to filter through to us. The smallpox was spreading. People were taking to their beds daily. The strong survived. The weak died. The town's children were being decimated. And when any baby contracted the dread pestilence . . .

I shuddered and hugged my little daughter as I listened to the servant's report. . . .

Medical help was impossible to get in town. But if a family nailed a white rag to the door of the house, a doctor or Catholic sister-of-mercy might see the signal and stop as they went on their wearying rounds.

The smallpox flag was being flown above the port, a clear warning to ships to pass on by. All ships in the harbor had weighed anchor and fled. Barbados was isolated, abandoned to its fate.

Each day when I stepped out on a landward balcony and scanned the horizon toward town, I would see smoke rising.

347

Yet another house or building was declared pestilential and set to the torch.

I was terrified for Charlotte. My God, I thought, better that I should have lost her to North and Abby than this! Each day, the pestilence crept closer to the villa. I sensed it. I knew it. And I despaired.

I prayed fervently for Gordon's return. For the first time in my life, I blessed him and his mad obsession for me. I knew he would not desert me. If his ship sailed into the bay and turned away, seeing the smallpox flag, I knew Gordon would coerce the ship's crew into dropping anchor. I hadn't the slightest doubt that he would commandeer the ship. Or strangle the captain with his bare hands, if need be.

It came to me like a blow in the stomach that North and Gordon were alike in this way. Both had the courage of a lion. Both were shrewd and would not hesitate to be cruel if the life of a loved one were in danger.

When one of our scullery maids could not rise one morning because of fever, panic surged through the villa. Immediately, I ordered a sick ward set up. I ordered a large and airy warehouse to be cleared of the sacks of sugar that were stacked from floor to ceiling. For want of a better place to put it, I ordered it stored in the ballroom and drawing rooms.

I ordered the warehouse swept clean and matted with fresh rushes. Cots, pillows, sheets, blankets, toweling and endless water pots were carried in. I ordered the cooks to prepare huge vats of nourishing broth which might be stored and heated as needed for the sick. I found three servants who had had the pox, and I assigned them to the sick house, tripling their wages.

The poor little scullery maid was carried to the makeshift hospital. Two days later, another servant was carried out, and the nightmare intensified.

I was out of my mind with worry for Charlotte. I allowed no one to touch her. I cared for her myself, and a dozen times a day I thanked God that I had not yet given in to Gordon's demands that I wean her or obtain a wet nurse. I fed her fresh fruit that I gathered from the trees, and I cooked her gruel in the fireplace. At night, I kept her in my bed.

Each day was grinding agony. When would Gordon come? When?

Then, one morning as I stood on the balcony, looking beyond the rolling green fields of cane and toward the port town, I saw a horseman galloping along the road from the village. When he galloped past the warning signs without pausing, I knew it was he.

With a cry of joy, I ran down the balcony stairs, dashed over the marble porticoes, under the arches and flew down the road. I ran like a demented woman, my arms flailing wildly. My feet pummeled the dirt road, sending up clouds of red dust.

Gordon brought his horse up short. He leaped to the ground. I cried out and threw myself toward his arms, but he stopped me with a shout.

"Don't! Don't come near, Dianna! I borrowed this horse from an innkeeper who looked ill. I may have been exposed."

Breathless, I gasped, "Oh, Gordon! I knew—I knew you'd come. I knew—"

He cut me short with an imperious gesture.

"I'll harness the horses to the coach. Have your servants pack you at once. There isn't a moment to spare. I've promised a fortune to the captain to tarry out in the bay. But if he sees many more pesthouses go up in flames, he may panic and sail out. Go, Dianna," he ordered. "Hurry!"

"Oh, Gordon," I whispered, reaching out to him in my overwhelming relief, then letting my hands fall limp to my sides.

His eyes moved over me. He smiled. A tired and gentle smile.

"My dear," he murmured softly.

For a moment, my emotions swirled in wild and confusing circles. Then, with a sob, I tore my eyes from him and flew back to the villa.

Within minutes, the coach was lurching down the dirt road that cut through the cane fields. The cane, neglected and untended in the weeks since the pestilence struck, whispered and hissed of dryness as the wind blew through it.

As we rode, we tied kerchiefs over mouth and nose so that we might not breathe the infected air of the port. I kept Charlotte swathed inside my cloak. She wailed her anger and discomfort as we jogged along.

The main road of the port was deserted except for dogs lolling in the center of the road, rousing themselves to move for our horses only at the last possible moment. The town smelled of smoldering wood ash. In the foundations of burnt buildings, wisps of smoke still rose. It was a ghastly sight.

Only a trickle of people flowed through the silent town, and those who did moved slowly and wore white kerchiefs over their faces.

Gordon urged the team on smartly, sending the dogs yapping and scuttling. As we passed the open door of an inn, I could see people stretched out on pallets upon the floor. Their moans echoed over the sound of hooves and carriage wheels.

Gordon drove the team to the water's edge, then pulled them to a stop. A small rowing boat waited there, its tie-rope held by a young man. The young man sprang to heave the trunks into the boat. Then he turned to hand me in.

"Fool!" Gordon thundered. "Don't touch her! You may carry the pox!"

The lad cowered.

"Get in by yourself, Dianna," he ordered.

I brushed past the boy, waded into the ankle-deep water and set Charlotte into the boat. I climbed in hurriedly. Gordon boarded, threw the brightening boy a gold coin and took up the oars.

Our trunks had barely banged onto the deck of the ship before the ship nosed about and headed out through the channel and into the fresh clean winds of the Atlantic.

As I watched the island recede, the gravity of my situation on the disease-ravaged island hit me. My knees turned to water. Charlotte might have died! Or her delicate prettiness might have been scarred for life!

As Barbados slowly sank into the sea, I grew weak with utter relief, utter weariness. Tears of draining tension welled up. Clutching my daughter, I slumped against the forecastle and sobbed. Charlotte, alarmed at my bizarre behavior, wailed her distress.

Gordon stood at a distance, helpless, watching.

When I regained control, I jiggled the baby, patting her, calming her fears. Soon, her tears sputtered to a stop.

I wiped the wetness from my face, kissed the baby's cheek to comfort her.

"Gordon?" I whispered. "Where does the ship head?"

He strode to the rail. He took a deep breath and stood looking out at the building swells. For a moment, I thought he hadn't heard. Then, abruptly, he turned. His face wore an odd, pained expression.

"I could not wait for the ideal ship, my dear." He hesitated, laughing in self-mockery as though the fates had played a trick on him. "This ship drops anchor . . . in . . . Yorktown."

I stared at him, my heart suddenly beating in rhythmless jerks.

"But—that's Williamsburg," I whispered.

"Yes."

CHAPTER 27

"It's settled then, Dianna."

He drew on his black waistcoat, buttoned it with quick angry twists of his fingers.

"I will go to Philadelphia at once and deal with Lasher. You will go to Nan. You will stay with her until I come for you. We shall sail for Europe on the first decent ship that presents itself in Yorktown."

I was standing at the window, only half-listening. I pulled the curtain aside and watched as a horseman clattered past the inn.

My nerves were stretched thin. I couldn't let one rider pass by without rushing to the window. And yet, if the passing horseman *should* be North, what did I presume to do about it?

Surely nothing, I mused, my spirit sinking.

He sent you away, Danni. From the first, he did not choose you. At the last, he did not choose you. He chose Starlight. Now, he chooses Abby.

Aching with unhappiness, I watched the rider trot by. The hooves of his mount whipped puffs of dust into the air.

But if it *had* been North this time?

I would have had to stand here, I thought, and watch him pass by, helpless as he tore my heart from its mooring and dragged it after him in the dusty street.

"You're not listening, my dear."

Gordon's voice was smooth with annoyance.

I turned with a start.

"What?"

His black brow twitched in irritation.

"What?" he mocked.

His eyes flashed. "Perhaps, my dear Dianna, you would prefer to remain in Yorktown during my absence? You could amuse yourself by standing at the window all day, day after day, waiting for Delveau to chance by."

I flushed. I dropped the curtain as though it were a stinging nettle.

"Don't be cruel, Gordon," I whispered.

He picked up a folded black travel cloak and slung it over his arm, then he crossed the room slowly, studying me.

Frowning, he reached out and cupped my face in his hands. His eyes moved over every inch of my face as though he were memorizing my every feature. Then he spoke.

"I love you," he said softly. "I will kill this cur who has robbed us of our son. Joseph Lasher *shall* pay, my dear. He shall pay a thousand times over. For every slash of the knife he gave Jonathan, I will—"

I trembled violently.

"Please, Gordon, forget Lasher," I begged. "I want to leave Virginia at once. It is torture for me here, Gordon. I only want to take Charlotte Arabella and go far, far away."

His answer was a soft kiss.

"In due time, Dianna. In due time."

Aroused, he began to kiss me, and my eyelids flickered shut in defense. I stood stiff and unmoving as his lips sought the response I refused to give. My coldness ordinarily incensed him. This time, it did not.

I opened my eyes in surprise.

He laughed softly.

"Farewell, little rosebud," he said. "Take care."

Again, he studied me as though preserving each of my features into his memory. His gentle leave-taking jolted me. It was out of character. No threats. No orders. Only quiet words.

He looked at me a moment longer, then swung away, collected his valise and weapons case, strode to the door and wrenched it open.

"Gordon!" I blurted out without thought. "Take care."

For a moment we looked at each other in confusion.

"I love North!" I said quickly, as though to find my footing in the emotional morass in which I found myself.

"Yes," he said drily.

My cardinal cloak hung on a peg next to the door. He reached out, drew it to his mouth and kissed it. Then, he was gone.

Nan and Sandy were overjoyed to receive me on their little farm. They were flabbergasted to discover the baby. As soon as they recovered from the shock of Charlotte Arabella, they set about making an enormous fuss over her.

They bombarded me with questions that I would not answer. I told them only what was necessary for them to know. North had divorced me. He'd remarried. He would take Charlotte from me if he found out about her.

"Judas! I knowed him for a devil the first I laid eyes on him!" Nan exploded loyally. "I seen him twicet this year when he rid by on the way to Williamsburg. When I asks him for news of you, Danni, he just scowls. He says, 'Nan, all you need to know is Danni's in the Caribbean and she's well.'"

Nan gulped for air. She went on, wild-eyed.

"Well, I says, 'you *got* to tell me more 'n that.' And *he* says, 'Sandy, goddamn it, muzzle your woman!'"

While Nan raved on my behalf, Sandy stubbornly took North's side. He insisted North would never divorce me, let alone remarry. He was furious over the suggestion that North would take my baby from me. He sputtered and stammered in a defense of North that made me want to throw my arms around Sandy and kiss him. So *he* loved North, too! In the argument that ensued, my heart flowed to Sandy even though Nan was the one on my side.

When I told them about the document of divorce and the marriage report in the *Virginia Gazette*, the argument ended. They fell into a pathetic silence. Neither of them could read.

Lying in the snug clean bed in the loft that ran above half of the lower floor of the small house, I could hear their furtive whisperings.

"Damn, Nan! North, he wouldn't never do such things. I know 'im. Know 'im like a brother."

"Humph! Well, he done 'em. An' if that's what your brothers be like, then I kin live without 'em."

There was a moment of silence. I reached out and patted Charlotte. She was sleeping in the cradle Sandy had made for Nan in the early days of their marriage, when they'd naively assumed that every year would bring a child.

They stirred restlessly upon their country mattress, filling the night with the rustle of grinding straw.

"Damn, Nan. North should know about his daughter. It ain't right, a man not knowing," Sandy whispered.

"Judas! You tell 'im, and that's the last you'll ever see of me! Danni, she already lost Jonathan. You want she should lose *this* baby, too?"

Sandy sighed.

"Aw, Nan. You don't know North like I know 'im."

"That's right!" she hissed. "An' I don't want to know him, neither!"

There was another long silence.

"Honey?" Sandy whispered. "Do I got to go to sleep without my kiss?"

There was a soft cooing sound and then a great deal of rustling of straw. I rolled away, covering my head with the pillow. Let them be happy, I thought, as I drifted into sleep. At least let Nan and Sandy be happy.

As the days and then weeks went by, Charlotte and I settled into the family. I refused to be treated as a guest. To Nan's amusement, I helped her with her work. In old gowns of India calico, I scrubbed the pine floor with ashes and lime water. I helped her tend the animals and weed the large vegetable garden behind the house. I helped with the cooking and the drying and preserving of beans for winter.

In late afternoons we sat out on the veranda that wrapped around the small house. We played with the baby, and cut and pieced a winter quilt Nan was making from old shirts and gowns.

At night, Sandy sat with us on the veranda, a refreshing breeze blowing from the hills, setting the tobacco leaves gently flapping in the fields. Fireflies were everywhere, bejeweling the soft Virginia nights. The thick sparkle of fireflies brought tears to my eyes, and I was glad for the dark shadows of the veranda.

Their diamond like flashing reminded me of that fateful night in the rose garden at Brandley Manor. I wondered if North ever looked at fireflies and remembered.

Four weeks into my visit, I confided to Nan that I was married to Sir Gordon and would sail to Europe with him as soon as he finished his business in Philadelphia.

She was tight-lipped with shock. Several times, she began to speak, then shut her mouth. She eyed me with disapproval, shook her head and went on peeling green apples for the pie. Slowly, the lines of her face softened.

"It's caught between two devils, you be," she said sympathetically. "North and Sir Gordon. Two cut of the same cloth."

Her perception jolted me. Quickly, I changed the subject. She was nowhere near suspecting the truth, but I couldn't risk letting her even approach it.

"Who's that, d'ye suppose?"

I lifted my dripping hands out of the laundry tub and squinted into the sunlight. It was a fine sunny day. Nan and I had dragged tubs out into the sunshine. We'd carried water from the well. When the sun had heated the water, we'd stripped the house of everything washable and begun our scrubbing. As we worked, Charlotte Arabella napped in her cradle in the shade on the veranda.

"Who's that?" Nan said again, nodding at the approaching horseman.

My heart began to bang even before my eyes focused against the bright sun. Somehow I sensed it. I knew.

I tried to answer Nan, but my mouth was cotton. I turned and fled into the house. I steadied myself against a chair.

Nan burst in behind me.

"Judas, Danni!"

I clutched at her with shaking hands.

"Nan, you mustn't let him know I'm here. I'll hide. I'll run out the back door and through the garden and into the woods. But the baby—" I stopped, panting and gasping. "I can't take the baby. She might cry. If he sees her, tell him—tell him—she belongs to a neighbor—"

I shook my head, unable to think.

"Oh, God," I gasped, "Nan, help me—help me—"

Her eyes widened in fear. She stared at me, as paralyzed as myself. Then she shook herself. She gave me a quick hug.

"Hide," she ordered. "I'll send him packin', or die trying! He'll not get the baby! He ain't hurting you no more, Danni!"

She stomped out, slamming the door.

I stood there alone, frozen. Something rose in my chest. I tried to swallow the hysterical sobs, but they burst through. On wobbly knees, I staggered to the wall where Nan and Sandy's winter cloaks hung on pegs. I pressed my face into the scratchy wool, struggling to calm myself.

North. Oh, North . . .

Shaking, I leaned against the wall for support.

Run, Danni. The back door. The garden. The pasture. The woods. Run. Never come back. Run!

But I couldn't. More than air or water or food, I needed to hear his voice, glimpse his face. Then, only then, could I flee.

The wild thing inside my ribs thrashed to get out. As if to hold my heart in my body, I crossed my arms on my chest.

At last I heard it. The voice dearest in the world to me. Low and male, stirring memories that made me want to weep.

"Good afternoon, Nan."

Her mind on the task she'd set for herself, Nan ignored amenities.

"Sandy, he be in the far field. If you ride right out, you kin catch 'im."

"I'll rest first."

My fingers kneaded the wool cloaks as his boots echoed on the porch.

"Have you anything to drink, Nan?"

Nan was unprepared for the question. She stammered unintelligibly.

"Cold water from the well will do," he said.

I heard Nan go crashing off the porch toward the well. I edged toward the window. My hand shook as I drew back the curtain a fraction of an inch.

I looked at him, melting. Physically, he was as I remembered—tall, handsome and savage. But he was changed. It was as if all life had gone out of him. There was a quietness about him that wrenched the heart. His eyes were flat, somber. In unguarded repose as he waited for Nan, the corners of his mouth sagged. It was as though he had tasted of life and found it sour.

It came to me like a thunderclap. North was unhappy! Irrational anger flared up in me. How dare Abby marry him and *not* make him happy! Oh, I wanted to kill her! More, I yearned to run to him and smooth the unhappiness from his brow.

When Nan returned with the large dipper of water, North drank it thirstily and thanked her. He stood leaning against the porch rail. He seemed weary, and I sensed it was not merely weariness born of the day's journey. My heart flowed out to him.

"You ain't stayin' the night?" Nan asked, her opinion plain in the tone of her voice.

North swung his head toward her in surprise. A wry half-grin took his face for an instant.

"Apparently not."

Nan heaved a big sigh of relief.

"About supper," she began, marching in a single-minded track to her goal. "You'll get you a good one at the King's Arms in Williamsburg."

North's lips twitched in amusement.

"Apparently I'm not staying for supper either."

He moved to leave, and I bit my knuckles to keep from crying out to him. Just then, Charlotte stirred in her cradle. She pulled herself up, her face moist and rosy from sleep. She blinked, trying to locate the deep voice. When she saw North, she began to jabber excitedly. I caught my breath, knowing she took him for Gordon.

North nodded at the cradle.

"When did this happen, Nan?"

Nan froze, unable to answer him a word.

North moved to the cradle and looked down at the baby with a shrug of annoyance.

"Why didn't Sandy send word? I would have expected to be named godfather."

"I—I—I—he—he—" Nan stuttered. Then, in a burst of inspiration, she brightened. "Sandy, he didn't send word because it's not a boy, sir. It's only a girl."

North gave her a furious look.

"Then Sandy's a goddamn fool!"

Charlotte raised her tiny hands to North. She beamed at him, spouting gibberish, confident he would take her from the cradle.

He shook his head no. Then, something in her sweet expression seemed to tug at him. He reached down and lifted her up. With all the confidence of a duchess, she settled into his arms, admiring him extravagantly with coos and chortles.

My heart caught. I shut my eyes as though to imprint the scene in my brain forever. North, *holding our child.* . . . When I touched my face, I was startled to find it wet. I hadn't been aware of tears streaming as I watched them.

Charlotte wiggled in his arms, grabbing at the tomahawk scar, fascinated by it, trying to pluck it off, and North laughed. But there was a sadness in the laugh.

Abruptly he said, "My congratulations, Nan." He moved to put the baby back into the cradle. "What's her name?" he asked without interest.

Nan grinned proudly.

"Charlotte Arabel—"

She broke off in sudden horror, and I swayed, faint with dizziness.

"Charlotte?" he snapped.

The baby jumped, terrified at the loud sound of her own name. She began to wail.

For a moment, I thought he would drop her. His lips went white. Then he cradled her close, patting her. His lips were in her hair, and as her wails died away I could hear his soft stunned whispers.

"Hush, love. Papa's here, Papa's here."

Nan was hysterical.

"Oh, sir, I didn't mean—"

"Where's Danni?" he demanded. "Goddamn it, Nan, no more games! Where is she!"

A sob caught in my throat. Terrified, I turned and ran blindly through the house and out the back door. I lurched through the garden, my flying feet uprooting the vegetables Nan and I had so carefully tended. Stumbling along, I crashed through Nan's rows of blue phlox and brown-eyed Susans.

At the far end of the garden, I wrenched open the pasture gate where the cow waited patiently for afternoon milking. Pushing past the animal, I ran on, stumbling, half-falling in my frenzy to escape him. Nan's black-faced sheep scattered. When I reached the far fence, I scrambled over it, sobbing as a wood splinter drove deep into the palm of my hand. My long loose hair caught on a thorn bush. I wrenched it free and ran on.

"Danni!"

As I ran, my feet pounding the ground, I looked back toward the house. North's white shirt flashed in the sunlight as he bounded across the garden.

"Oh, God," I prayed, sobbing. "Oh, God, don't let him catch me. Don't let him touch me. Oh, God, let me die. If he touches me and then goes away again, I can't bear it. I *won't* bear it. Oh, God!"

I clawed my way into the woods, lurching against the rough bark of elms and pushing my way through the brush. I fled on, into the stand of tall pine trees. I sobbed helplessly as my heels sank into the thick carpet of pine needles. Knives stabbed at my lungs. I could go no farther.

Defeated, panting, I sank to my knees and bowed my head to my thighs. I clamped my hands to my ears, as though to erase the thud of his footsteps. Within moments he was among the pines.

"Danni, my God!"

I buried my face in my hands, rocking back and forth, moaning in pain.

"North, don't!" I sobbed, gasping for air. "Don't touch me. Don't speak to me. If you have any pity at all, only go!" I choked on my sobs. "Take Charlotte from me, if you must. But, go! Go! Oh, God, North, don't torture me. Go!"

He dropped to his knees. Ignoring my pleas, he gathered me into his arms. I fought him until he gently pressed my head to his pounding heart. Then, feeling that strong familiar heartbeat, I could but cling to him, weeping.

He stroked my head, kissing my hot brow.

"Weep, darling," he whispered. "And weep, too, for a fool who valued pride above love."

Clinging to him, warm and safe in his strong arms, I could do nothing but weep for an eternity. When I'd wept my last, I raised my face to him.

"North?" I begged, trembling. "Let me live near you? I only ask to see you now and then, touch you like this. I would ask nothing more. I swear it."

His dark eyes filled with bewilderment.

"You ask little. But I would ask much. I ask your forgiveness, Danni. Come home. Be my wife."

"North, don't torment me! Don't make sport of me," I begged. I tried to pull away. "You divorced me. You have another wife."

His head jerked back. His fingers bit into my arms.

"What the hell are you talking about?"

I gulped for air. We stared at each other blankly.

I whispered, "Gordon showed me the document of divorce, the notice of your marriage to Abby in the *Gazette.*"

We looked at each other, comprehension growing in both of us. Then I slumped against him, sick to my very soul as the enormity of Gordon's deception began to dawn on me. A trick! It had all been a trick!

"Oh, God, North. How could he have been so cruel!"

A deep shudder shook him. His body grew hard with anger.

"What else?" he demanded hoarsely.

I gave a little sob and told him, haltingly and in shame,

about the threat of he and Abby taking Charlotte. I told him about my marriage. With my head bowed to his chest, I whispered that Gordon had taken me whenever it pleased him to do so.

When I finished, I looked up at him in fear. His face! It was cold and savage. And never before had I seen that silver fire in North's eyes, burning like ice set aflame. His eyes were suddenly Gordon's.

"He is a dead man, Danni. I promise you that."

I cried out in anguish.

"No! Haven't we had enough of death and unhappiness? Haven't we had enough pain?" I slumped against his stiff body, hugging it, clenching it. "Oh, North," I whispered, "I feel so dirty, so used."

As I clung to him, the stiffness slowly left his body. His arms went around me, warm and protective. I lifted my face to his and I thrilled at the love I saw in his eyes.

"You are my wife," he whispered. "You are not dirty. You are clean and sweet and ever-new to me."

Then he kissed me. Kissed me tenderly, whispering healing words of love. He kissed me until the world spun away into blackness.

It was dusk before we strolled back to the house, our arms around each other. Nan and Sandy were sitting at supper. Worry faded from their faces the moment they saw us. They grinned.

Charlotte was ensconced on Nan's lap, eating mashed food. She chortled when she saw North. He laughed, went to her and picked her up. She crowed in delight and I couldn't help but run to them and throw my arms around them both.

"You *do* think she's pretty, North?"

He kissed her pink cheek.

"She's the image of my mother," he said proudly. "She could only be prettier if she looked exactly like you."

That night we slept in each other's arms in the loft, not caring if the whole world should hear the thrashing of the straw in the mattress beneath us.

We were boarding the coach in Williamsburg when the messenger arrived with word of Sir Gordon.

He'd sent for me. He wanted me. He'd been wounded in killing Joseph Lasher. Obsessed with getting to Williamsburg, he'd rented a coach and made his servants take him on. Just north of Williamsburg he'd collapsed as the wound's infection spread in his body. His servants had carried him to a surgeon's house. He was dying.

I listened white-faced. I couldn't imagine it—Gordon, who'd always seemed larger than life to me, Gordon—lying on a cot waiting for death. Waiting for me.

I gripped North's arm to steady myself. He looked at me grimly, then turned to the messenger.

"Tell him to get on with his dying and not bother us!"

I swayed against North. He looked at me sharply.

I searched his cold eyes.

"I must go to him, North," I whispered. "He's dying. When I was alone on Barbados with Charlotte, the smallpox came. He risked his life to rescue us. If he hadn't, your daughter . . ." My words trailed away.

A muscle in North's cheek twitched violently.

"Get in," he ordered.

The surgery smelled of chemicals and of putrefaction. North and I looked at each other in shock. There was no need to be told the nature of Gordon's problem. We could smell it. It was gangrene.

I resisted the impulse to gag as I tiptoed up the narrow, uneven stairway to the reeking sickroom. The country doctor preceded us. He had been working in his yard at an anvil as we arrived. He still wore his blacksmith's apron. As we climbed the dark stairs, he spoke softly.

"He is in unbelievable pain, M'am. Yet he refuses laudanum. He insists on being alert when he sees you." The man paused on the stairs, sucking in his breath. "The infection has spread in the lining of his abdomen. I can no longer touch him without causing him to scream."

I shuddered.

In the room, Gordon lay still and white upon the cot. His eyes were closed.

Hearing footsteps he mumbled, "Open the windows, you fool. I'll not have her smell this when she arrives."

My heart went out to him. I gripped North's arm.

The doctor said, "There, there, sir, the outdoor air cannot be good for you. I've *told* you that, sir."

"Goddamn you," Gordon murmured weakly, "open the window!"

Abruptly, North pushed past me. He strode to the first window and wrenched it open. He did the same to the other window while the doctor sputtered his protest.

Gordon's eyes flew open. He searched the room. When he found me, he smiled weakly. He brushed his hand in a pathetic circle as if to say, "Isn't it absurd, Dianna? *Me*, lying in a place like this?" The weak wave of his hand took in the cheap tattered curtains at the window, the crumbling plaster on the walls, the rude crockery on the table beside him.

"My dear," he whispered.

North strode up behind me and put his hands firmly on my shoulders.

"She is *not* your dear," he said without mercy. "She is my wife."

Gordon's eyes flickered in surprise as he struggled to focus on North's dark face. Then, he smiled wryly through his pain.

His eyes, so alive as the rest of him died, speared into North. He laughed weakly.

"It must amuse you to find me like this, my dear Comte d' Delveau."

"I take no pleasure in it," North said coldly. "You deprive me of the opportunity to kill you myself."

A mocking smile twisted Gordon's lips. He closed his eyes, and I tensed as he fought a spasm of violent pain. He turned ashen, sweat breaking on his brow. Then, as the spasm passed, he seized control of himself.

"Well said, my boy. A Chillburn male could not have said it better."

My heart leaped to my throat. Oh, no, was he going to tell North? Or had he left papers revealing everything?

I pulled away from North. I knelt at the bed.

"Gordon?" I asked tearfully.

He opened his eyes and gazed at me. He laughed softly though it cost him terrible pain.

"Don't worry, my dear," he said. "My parting gift to you is . . . silence."

A sob caught in my throat. I wanted to weep in relief, but I blinked back the tears as they welled up. Only one tear spilled over.

Gordon watched it roll down my cheek. With a shaking hand, he reached out and touched it.

He smiled his mocking smile.

"For me, Dianna?"

I looked at him.

"No." I shook my head truthfully. "You have been cruel. May God forgive you."

He laughed weakly.

"I ask no forgiveness. I would do it all again." He paused as a spasm cut through him. He clenched his teeth to hold back his screams. When the spasm passed, he said with force, "I love you, Dianna. You are mine. You will always be mine."

Behind me, North choked on his anger.

"God damn you!" he said.

I looked up at North and then back at Gordon. Unbidden, a tear slid down my cheek.

Wistfully, Gordon watched the tear.

"This one," he said, "I will claim for myself."

Suddenly, his body was wracked with violent wrenchings. He swung his head to North.

"Get her out of here!" he ordered. "Get her out!"

North grabbed me and dragged me to the door. I wrenched free.

"Gordon, I'll stay—"

"Get her out!" he screamed.

North flung me from the room. He dragged me down the stairs and out of the house and into the fresh air of the courtyard. There, he held me in his arms as I shook uncontrollably.

It was only minutes later that the doctor emerged, followed by his wife and another man. He came up to us.

"It's over," he said simply.

Stunned, I looked up into North's hard angry face. It *is*

over, I thought. My beloved is safe. Safe from knowledge that could make his life a living hell.

"Thank God!" I whispered.

North cradled me in his arms.

"I love you, Danni," he said. "You're mine. Mine forever."

We stood there, shocked and clinging to each other.

The man who had followed the doctor out of the house came up to us hesitantly.

"Mr. Delveau? I am Sir Gordon's solicitor. He bade me wait until—" He broke off respectfully, then went on. "Sir Gordon's last will and testament leaves—"

"My wife wants nothing from him!" North snapped.

The man looked at us in surprise.

"Not your wife, sir," he said. "All of Sir Gordon's properties and money go to Charlotte Arabella Delveau. To your daughter, sir."

EPILOGUE

"But when will Papa come? Will the *Joanna* sail without him? I don't *want* to go to England without Papa! I don't *want* to visit Grandfather and Aunt Matilde if Papa won't come!"

Charlotte clambered up into my lap and held my face in her hands, earnestly making her point. At four, she was a little beauty with a cloud of fluffy black curls and a tiny pink mouth that was forever pursed in curiosity, asking questions.

"Papa will come," I assured her. "He had business in Williamsburg, remember?" I kissed her cheek. "Mama won't *think* of letting the ship sail without Papa."

She giggled in relief. She treated me to one of her generous hugs.

There was a flurry of footsteps and a bumping of luggage in the passageway. A low amused voice boomed into the cabin.

"Voilà, ladies! Papa is here!"

North stooped and entered the cabin. My heart did a wild flipflop. Would I ever get over being silly about North? Seeing him, after even the briefest separation, made me feel like a bride on her wedding night.

Charlotte squealed. Sliding from my lap, she dashed across the cabin and threw herself into North's arms. Chuckling, he swung her up and kissed her. But all the while his eyes were on me.

"And Mama?" he teased, raising one eyebrow at me. "Will not Mama fling herself into my arms?"

Charlotte giggled.

"Mama's too big!" she crowed.

"Mama will greet you later, North," I promised with a laugh.

"I will hold you to that," he said, his dark eyes meeting mine in shared intimacy.

Then he laughed. He carried Charlotte to the cradle where two-year-old Julia was napping. With Charlotte still clinging to his neck like a monkey, he squatted and inspected the baby.

"Come here, Danni," he said, smiling down at the baby.

I went to him and knelt at the cradle. He nodded at our sleeping child.

"She looks a bit like my father, don't you think?" he whispered. "Her mouth. The way she holds her mouth."

For an instant, the old familiar fear came rushing back. With effort, I brushed it away. I looked up at him and kissed his cheek.

"Yes," I lied. "She does resemble Andre."

"She's beautiful!" he said passionately.

Charlotte put her hands on North's face. She tugged his gaze from the baby.

"I'm beautiful, too, Papa," she said earnestly.

North's amused eyes met mine. He coughed to cover his mirth. With the greatest seriousness, he answered her.

"Indeed you *are* beautiful," he said solemnly. "You are as beautiful as the woman you are named for—your Grandmother Charlotte Delveau. And you are just as good and sweet as she."

She leaned against him, purring.

"Now you can read me a story, Papa."

"No." He kissed her. "Later. This is Mama's time."

Her eyes began to swim in tears.

North hugged her.

"Charlotte," he coaxed, "run and find Ephraim. Ask him

to open my satchel. See what I've brought you from Williamsburg."

With a shriek of delight she was gone.

"Mama?" North teased, standing and opening his arms in invitation.

I melted into them. We kissed as we always did after a separation, hesitantly, slowly, savoring the newness and the wonder. Then he kissed me thoroughly, and the familiar jolting fire that lovers experience began for us. I shivered.

At last we drew back from each other, knowing that if we kissed one moment longer we must bolt the door and make love while, all around us, the chaos of embarkation rumbled.

We drew sharp breaths, then laughed, easing the sexual tension. We linked hands.

"Where are Nan and Sandy?" North said, taking us to safer ground.

"They're not coming. There's been a change in plans. Nan is with child at last. Sandy wants the child born in America."

"Well, well!"

I laughed.

"Well, well!" he said again.

I closed my eyes and looked up at him through a screen of lashes.

"You may as well know, North," I said. "There is to be another 'well, well' for us, too."

The familiar smile began slowly, spreading. He gave a pleased laugh and drew me into his arms.

"Forgive me, chérie," he said. "I stand here grinning like a proud dolt, and I do not ask the important question. Do *you* mind, love?"

"Mind? About the baby?"

"The getting of babies is all pleasure for the husband. But for the wife—" His forehead wrinkled in concern. "Some women, after two or three babies, bolt the bedchamber door. I would not blame you, Danni, if—"

I stopped him with my fingers to his lips. I slipped my hands around his neck.

"*Some* women," I said, "are not wickedly in love with their husbands."

"Ahhhh," he said, kissing me with such thoroughness that simultaneously our hands went out to push the cabin door shut.

Just then, a bell rang, followed by a long erratic whistle. An excited hubbub rose on deck. Cast-off was imminent.

With a reluctant "Ah, well," North led me out on the deck. Julia's nursemaid slid past us to tend her. On deck, the seamen were furiously busy. They scrambled about to the cries of the first mate. Off to one side, Ephraim stood watching. Charlotte rode pick-a-back on his shoulders. She clutched a new doll.

It was nearly sunset. In the west, the Virginia land mass flamed with the rays of the setting sun. In the opposite direction, the waters stretched dark and rolling, the sky a clear blue. Only one small patch of storm clouds marred the horizon.

The captain strolled up, touching his hat to me.

"Fair sailing, Mrs. Delveau! Though perhaps a bit of a squall from the north tonight."

His words were unremarkable. Yet they rang in my ears with all the clarity of church bells. Yes, I mused, there would always be a bit of a squall from the north. But would I have it any other way?

I smiled.

"I have been through countless squalls from the north, Captain."

He squinted in surprise. "Indeed, M'am?"

"Oh, yes! By now I am an expert in handling squalls from the north."

North looked at me sharply. His eyes danced with amusement. Then he frowned. He scowled at me so fiercely that the tomahawk scar seemed to move forward from his brow. The captain flinched.

"Wench!" North snapped. "I understand the Brandleys have a rose garden. Take me to the stable by way of the rose garden!"

I dropped my eyes demurely and curtsied. To the captain's befuddlement, I picked up my skirts, turned and led the way to our cabin. North's step echoed behind me, his low rich laughter curling round me like a caress.

Behind us, the captain stood scratching his head, muttering.

"Daft," he said. "Those people are daft!"

"A rich, stirring novel of the westward
thrust of America, and of a dynamic woman
who went West to tame the wilderness within her."
The Literary Guild

PASTORA

JOANNA BARNES

The passions of two generations, and the rich,
colorful history of 19th-century California, are
woven into this 768-page epic of adventure and
romance! It follows one strong and courageous
woman through tragedy and triumph, public scandal
and private struggle, as she strives to seize a golden
destiny for herself and those she loves!

"Blockbuster historical romance!"
Los Angeles Times

"Readers who like romantic sagas with historical
backgrounds will enjoy this."
Library Journal

AVON Paperback   56184 • $3.50

Available wherever paperbacks are sold, or directly from the
publisher. Include 50¢ per copy for postage and handling: allow
6-8 weeks for delivery. Avon Books, Mail Order Dept., 224 West
57th St., N.Y., N.Y. 10019.

Pastora 12-81

BESTSELLING ROMANCE
by Johanna Lindsey

GLORIOUS ANGEL 79202 $3.50

This powerful novel of a nation and a family divided by Civil War follows the passionate romance between a sharecropper's daughter and a plantation owner's son, that leads from Alabama to Boston, to the wilds of Texas.

PARADISE WILD 77651 $2.95

From high-bred Boston society to the wilder shores of Hawaii, Corinne Barrows and Jared Burkett find a love so violent that it must either destroy them—or give them completely to the wild abandon of tropical nights in paradise!

FIRES OF WINTER 79574 $2.95

Abducted from Ireland across an icy sea, the lovely and dauntless Lady Brenna vows vengeance on her captors. But the Viking leader Garrick claims her, and between them is forged a bond of desire.

A PIRATE'S LOVE 75960 $2.50

Caribbean breezes sweep a ship westward, carrying Bettina Verlaine to fulfill a promise her heart never made—marriage to a Count she has never seen. Then the pirate Tristan captures Bettina's ship and casts his spell over her heart.

CAPTIVE BRIDE 79566 $2.95

Recklessly following her brother from London to Cairo, beautiful Christina Wakefield is abducted by a stranger who carries her off to his hidden encampment, where she is made his prisoner. Soon she learns to want the desert sheik as he wants her—and to submit to a stormy and passionate love.

Available wherever paperbacks are sold, or directly from the publisher. Include 50¢ per copy for postage and handling: allow 6-8 weeks for delivery. Avon Books, Mail Order Dept., 224 West 57th St., N.Y., N.Y. 10019.

(Lindsey 1-82)